All I Ever Wanted

LAURA DEVINE

ISBN (paperback): 979-8-9930496-1-8
ISBN (ebook): 979-8-9930496-0-1

To the Big Three. Without you, there is no me.

"I want the fairytale."
– *Pretty Woman*

CHAPTER 1

Cassie

I'm used to playing perfect. It's a role I know well.

Perfect smile, perfect pose and the perfect camera angle to capture it all in a single, effortless moment. I've built an entire career on the fantasy of it all.

Reality, I know, is much worse.

My hair is structured in gel, my face caked in makeup, and as I dip back to pose, a sharp pain shoots up my spine from the rigid posture I've been forced to hold all afternoon while strapped into six-inch heels.

After booking various one-off jobs, this one seemed slightly more promising. *Power Beauty* has some brand recognition, even if the product was founded by Daria Carter, a wannabe beauty influencer whose only talent came from having rich parents.

"Can you give us some non-smiling photos?" The photographer instructs, his eyes drifting to my chest. I've already walked out of his grasp three separate times over the course of the afternoon when his hands lingered on parts of my body he had no business touching. "This teen beauty queen thing you're giving me, isn't working."

I suppress an eye roll at the sudden change of direction. When I arrived on set this morning, I had been given explicit instruction to appeal to the younger age group while the model next to me was selling to the late twenty's demographic. I have a feeling the photographer's change of direction has more to do with the fact that I didn't let him touch me longer than a few seconds, but I try to ignore it. It's not the first time I've dealt with wandering hands, or eyes, for that matter.

I force a smile. "Sure, no problem."

I step to the side at the same time a producer grabs my shoulders, angling me into a new position. One of the various interns powders my face, someone else tightens my ponytail. I wince when I feel the sharp tug in the middle of my scalp.

All afternoon I've been trying not to study the movements of the more experienced model next to me. I recognized Sasha Woodes immediately and quickly searched for some clue that would tell me why we would be working the same job with vastly different media experiences.

It's not like I don't have a lengthy book of business. I've been working for the past three years, but I seem to lack the basic puzzle piece that everyone in Hollywood seems to have, connections. I know no one. That is the main reason I have not been able to climb out of the hole I find myself in.

Growing up, I was entered into every beauty pageant my mother could find. At the time, modeling didn't seem that different. After all, I'd spent most of my formative years covered in makeup, dressed in high heels and adored by crowds. The more I paraded across the stages, the more I became captivated by this idea of being perfect. It became an art form, the precision, the attention to detail, I've held onto it with every job I book.

I moved to LA because I wanted to earn a name for myself known outside the confines of the Midwest. The people I grew up with tended to spend most their lives talking about their dreams that stretched beyond state lines, but no one ever left. It was all talk to fill time. I wanted more and I had the support system that convinced me I could achieve more.

Small town dreams don't mean anything unless you actually take the first step. So, when I turned twenty-one, I moved out, set my sights on Hollywood and I've been busting my ass ever since.

At times, I feel like I've done it all. I've done commercials covered in feathers. I've participated in countless catalog shoots with the same permanent smile, I worried my jaw muscles would atrophy. I've rode horses, been dangled from harnesses, posed on platforms and nothing has amounted to anything more than a paycheck to get me through another month of rent.

My life is the side of show business that no one ever talks about. The side that sucks.

"Alright, that's it! We got everything for the day."

My shoulders droop as I let out a sigh. I step off the mat, peeling my heels off, one at a time, cautiously approaching the producer at the bench. She's working through film with the photographer, critiquing our work.

"Daria? Hi! I just wanted to thank you again for the opportunity."

"Oh, hi." She barely looks at me. "Yeah, sure. It's so great that you were able to step in so last minute."

"What do you mean?"

"Sasha's counterpart had to drop out. She extended her booking in New York and couldn't make it," Daria says over her shoulder.

"Oh, well, thanks for the opportunity anyway. If you ever need..."

Daria's attention is captured by someone with a headpiece, leading her away before I can finish. I stand there, shoes in hand, a part of me wishing that I had spent the day in bed.

I don't necessarily admire Daria. I know that she got to where she is today thanks to a few endorsement checks from her parents, admired tech CEOs with plenty of free time and discretionary funds to back their daughter's latest hobby. I doubt she understands the concept of hard work, but she's there, and

I'm here with no network, no connections, and a severe doubt she even remembered my name.

When I reach the trailer, I collapse into the chair, letting out a heaping sigh of defeat before I begin yanking the bobby pins out of my hair, one by one. A cough comes behind me and I whip my head around to see Sasha shaking out her long, dark hair.

"Oh, sorry," I say, my cheeks turning red. "I thought I was alone."

"All good." She waves, making her way toward the trailer exit.

"Hey, you're Sasha, right?" I ask, sitting up straight. "Sasha Woodes?"

She looks over her shoulder, shrugging. "Yeah. That's me."

"I'm Cassie. Cassie Taylor. I just want to say, I think you're really talented. I've been following your work for a while."

"Thanks." She smiles.

I bite my lip. "I hate to ask, but do you have any pointers for me?"

Sasha's warm, brown eyes take me in. She pauses long enough that I start to wonder if I crossed a boundary. "You're in your head too much, I could tell looking at your reel. Try not to overthink and just react. It comes through more naturally."

"Okay, got it." I nod, appreciating any sort of feedback that doesn't involve losing pieces of clothing, something that had been suggested to me in the past by the more handsy producers.

"You have talent, though. I can see it. Keep it up, girl."

She is gone before I can ask for any sort of follow-up that would allow her to elaborate or even ask to exchange contact information. Like everything in my life lately, another opportunity feels like it just slipped through my fingers.

I carry my stuff to my car, collapse into the driver's seat, and prepare for the long drive home. I'm still not exactly sure what I had expected when I hit LA a few years ago, but looking at my life now, I would chalk it up as a failure. I know that many people struggle for years in the industry to even get a chance to make their big break, I'd just been naïve enough to think that the long struggle wouldn't apply to me. A part of me truly believed that I would be the exception.

I've thought about leaving, giving up and going home, but there really isn't anything I hate more than a cliché, and if I packed my bags and headed back to Indiana with nothing to show for it, I would feel like any other small-town nobody who chased a dream that became a fantasy. So, for that reason, I force myself to tough it out. It doesn't matter that I have to work a side job that is starting to look more and more like full-time employment, since modeling jobs don't come as frequently as I expected. I refuse to accept defeat.

I cut the engine as I pull into the parking lot of my apartment and check my messages for the hundredth time. I stare down at a blank screen, empty of alerts, and throw my phone back into my purse.

It's not just the fact that my photoshoot essentially had been a waste of a day, it's that, coupled with the fact that my nearly yearlong relationship ended a few weeks prior, without my knowledge or involvement. Apparently, ten months together doesn't warrant a face-to-face break up. No, I am the type of girlfriend who can be blown off by a simple text message.

NOAH
I think we should take a break.

The last message from my boyfriend, Noah.

Sorry, *ex*-boyfriend.

My messages to him stopped last week. They had all virtually gone unanswered anyway. He was in London, and I was apparently just a pitstop on his way to fame, something he made abundantly clear when he fled the country after dumping me over text.

I push away the feeling of abandonment and make my way up the stairs. As soon as I swing open the front door, I am greeted by my roommate and the warm smell of dinner.

When I landed in Los Angeles, I dreamed of late-night parties on rooftops, walking down designer runways, tangling up with the occasional B-list celebrity, if I was lucky. In all actuality, my nights generally consist of salty Thai takeout eaten straight from the carton, cuddling on the couch with my roommates, sharing the cheapest bottles of wine we can find. Bellies full and eyes sore from laughing, it's a different kind of luxury, one that I didn't expect to fall in love with.

I clock my roommate, Marina, in the kitchen, then swing my gaze to her boyfriend, Mark, positioned on the couch, and frown. I desperately wish that he was gone and my other roommate, Lucy, was here instead. Lucy loves a pity party. Marina tends to search for solutions to the problem, believing everything can be fixed through sheer willpower.

Still, when all else fails, at least I have this. At least I have them. Moving across the country was already a risk. Coupling it with a bunch of random strangers seemed like a nightmare, but I had been fortunate enough to be gifted the two greatest roommates in the world.

"Hey!" Marina greets me from the kitchen.

"Hey." I sigh, dropping my things at the door before collapsing onto a bar stool at the counter.

Marina's curly, dark hair is tied up on the top of her head. She scrunches her nose, peppered with freckles, as she studies me. "That bad, huh?"

Marina was my first friend this side of the Mississippi. As a California native, she opted for a career away from the camera, sticking to corporate America. I'm not sure how much of that had been her choice versus her parents' instruction, but nevertheless, she's on her way to being successful. She just finished law school and is working for a firm in Beverly Hills.

"The brand owner is literally eighteen years old. I couldn't have taken more than twenty actually good photos because they kept changing direction on me, and the scummy photographer couldn't keep his hands to himself."

"Dick." Marina frowns.

"Asshole," I agree.

I jump when my phone vibrates on the counter next to me, snatching it quickly, hoping to see my ex-boyfriend's name displayed across the screen. I frown when I realize it's just my alarm, reminding me that I have to start getting ready for my second job. I groan, catching Marina giving the side eye.

"What?" I ask.

"Nothing." She shrugs.

"I know what you're thinking."

"Okay." Marina smiles, resting a hand on her hip. "What am I thinking?"

"Never mind." I groan, realizing I've fallen into a trap of sorts.

"Noah's a loser, Cass. You need to forget about him."

"I have forgotten!"

"We both know that's a lie. I am one move away from blocking his number from your phone so that you don't check your messages every five minutes."

I frown, but don't really have a counter argument.

I never expected my relationship with Noah to be a long-lasting love affair. What I did expect was to be treated with respect when he decided to up and end it. I deserved some explanation, not this silence. Like everything else in our relationship, Noah ended things on his terms. I just need closure, so I can move on. At least, that's my going story.

"You need a good lay," Marina offers. I snort at her suggestion. "Why is that such a ridiculous idea?"

"I didn't say it was."

"I don't get what the big deal is. Have amazing sex and then forget about him the next day."

"Right, just like what happened between you and Mark, huh?" Marina's boyfriend of four years, sitting on the couch a few feet from us, doesn't even turn around.

"First, that is one *very* specific instance. And second, you've *always* been a relationship girl. It's not a bad thing, but Noah was a dick. You broke up. You should move on and then under." She shrugs.

I lean my elbow on the counter, resting my cheek in my hand. I never slept around, mostly because I ended up getting too attached and invested in a relationship with a guy who didn't want one. Enter Noah, or all my high school boyfriends, for that matter.

Noah had been a struggling musician far longer than I had been an aspiring model. He finally got his supposed big break a few weeks ago. He broke up with me and packed his bags to move to London to sign with a new label. I could never hate him for following his dreams. He just made it clear that *his* dreams were the only ones that mattered.

"I should head out," Mark announces, joining us at the counter.

"You told me you could stay for dinner," Marina pouts.

I use the opportunity to sneak to the couch, grabbing the remote. I am just about to flip the channel when the front door flies open. Our third roommate, Lucy, rushes inside, pushing Mark out of the way before barreling through to the living room.

"Turn it on! Turn it on!" Lucy commands, dropping her things on the floor before she jumps on the couch.

"What?" I ask.

"*EDaily*! I helped write the feature that's about to air in two minutes!" She rips the remote from my hand.

Lucy is an aspiring *EDaily* correspondent. Dedicating her life to pop-culture transgressions and gossip, she has been working at *EDaily* for the past three years. She spends most her days editing the daily pop fluff pieces for the six o'clock coverage after grabbing coffee for the other studio executives in her office.

She flips the channel, and we're immediately bombarded by shots of Hollywood actor, Jackson Ridge. Unconsciously, I lean forward on the couch.

"Hello and welcome to EDaily*! I'm your host Courtney Davis joined by Victor Denton, and we've got all the latest on our favorite Hollywood heartthrob, Jackson Ridge. Here's the dish."*

Lucy squeals, turning up the volume.

"Is Jackson Ridge headed for another box office blunder? Early reports initially slated Annihilation *as this summer's must-see blockbuster, but first reviews are not looking great for Hollywood's favorite leading man. We know that Jackson Ridge loves to make headlines, but in recent years, it's mostly for his work off camera, not behind it."*

"We all remember Ridge skipping the Red Carpet at Cannes last year, which hinted at a disagreement between Ridge and his production team. The photo of Ridge stumbling out of an after-party at Cannes in lieu of supporting his movie with his castmates was one of the most circulated images of the summer and sparked further conversation around his media management, including speculation that maybe the sun has set on Ridge's career."

A series of images from last summer hit the screen. The old photos are now being recirculated to fill airtime.

"Not to mention, Ridge's less-than-stellar film slate as of late. Our sources say Ridge is at a pivotal crossroads with his management, and his representation is sparking further conversation with studio heads as they look to answer the looming question—is Ridge worth the financial investment?"

"What do you think? Is this the end of Jackson Ridge's illustrious career or just a pit stop? Chime in on the comments and stay with us at EDaily for more on your favorite Hollywood heartthrob, Jackson Ridge!"

"So, what did you think?" Lucy's eyes are bright while she waits for my response.

"I can't actually believe that they're still covering Jackson Ridge on *EDaily*," Marina comments from the kitchen.

"What's so hard to believe?" Lucy counters, turning on Marina. "Did you know that Jackson accounts for 15% of clicks on the site? Just his content alone can back us for months! Besides, this is my piece! Can't you be a little supportive?"

"I am supportive!" Marina argues. "I'm just saying, maybe the guy deserves a break. The press isn't exactly very nice to him."

"He chose the spotlight. He can't just turn it off when he wants to. It's our job to cover it, and if that coverage could help me get promoted, then you should be happy for me!"

Marina counters again and I sigh, giving up on the conversation. Even though she argues against it, I know that Marina secretly adores Jackson Ridge, half the world does.

I can see the fascination. He has a face that authors could write soliloquies about, poets spinning sonnets. Tall, of course. Gorgeous, obviously. He has these cool green eyes and light-blond hair that he usually keeps short. Kissable lips, definitely kissable. He has the sort of mouth girls dream about, fantasize about being the one-in-a-million person to experience one of his kisses.

"Cassie!" Lucy yells from the side of the couch, and I begrudgingly avert my gaze from the perfection on the screen.

"What?"

"I asked what you thought about it."

"It was great, Luce, really." I turn back toward the TV, but the images of Jackson have been cut, so I push myself off the couch to get ready for my second job.

"You're siding with her?" Marina complains.

"It's entertaining." I shrug. "Besides, you can't tell me that he isn't nice to look at."

"I have a boyfriend." Marina sniffs.

"Mhmm." I eye her and make my way to my room to begin the process of getting ready for work.

I fall onto my bed with a heavy sigh. Nine hundred and eighty-four days ago, I moved into this apartment, and I am still no closer to success. What a shitty realization.

I swallow back the lump growing in my throat and close my eyes, wondering what my life would have been like if I'd never left Indiana. I'm sure by now I would have had some sort of college degree, even if it was from a community college. I might be working a nine-to-five desk job, but at least I would have some sort of job security, maybe a boyfriend who loved me or at least had the maturity to text me back.

But that life is over; I have no choice but to keep moving, determined that I am one move away from the rest of my life.

CHAPTER 2

Cassie

There are better, more traditional options for a part-time job in LA, but one of the quickest ways to make money comes from serving the rich and powerful. Within my first two months of living in California, I quickly realized that throwing the phrase "customer service" into the title of just about any job is simply a marketing technique that I had overlooked before applying. Waitressing at *Avenue* is not exactly easy money, but it's fast and it's a way that I can earn most, if not all, of my rent, without sacrificing a booking or a shoot during the middle of the day. So, for the past year and a half, I've spent most of my Thursday and Friday nights covering the floor of the club, pocketing the extra cash to save for a rainy day.

I am greeted the second I walk into the staff room with a series of waves and hellos. The entire work force is full of people waiting around for Los Angeles to recognize their full potential. Mia is a waitress, hustling on the side to save enough money to record her first demo. Adrianne is saving up money to afford grad school. Amy was cast as a guest star in a series a few weeks ago.

We're all cashing in, understanding that this work, the kind that no one enjoys, is part of the dream, and sometimes it's all we have to depend on to see us through.

"How'd the shoot go?" Amy asks eagerly, throwing her blonde, bouncy waves up into a ponytail.

"It was . . . horrible, honestly." I laugh, thinking about it. "And the last thing I want to do is be here. So, a really great day, all in all."

"Oh my god, me too," she agrees with a sigh, bounding over to my locker to commiserate. "It was the first table read, and I totally fucked it up. I sounded like I had a stutter. I am a stutterer, Cassie!" She grips my arm dramatically.

"Remind me again why we do this?" I ask.

"Because we really want it?"

"That's why."

She sighs, shutting her locker as she goes. "See you out there."

I tuck my hair behind my ears, smear gloss across my lips, and take one more look at myself in the tiny mirror on the door before turning to clock in.

On the floor, it's easy to tell who will bottom out their bank accounts and who won't. It's a useful trick because there really isn't any point wasting your time schmoozing up to the people who just want to *talk* about how much they spent last night versus actually paying for it. I've learned to spot these different groups before even approaching their tables. I can pick out the wannabe influencers posing with their product placements from the playboy millionaires who are looking to blow off some steam before visiting the strip club or casino. They will be drunk, but not drunk enough to stop drinking.

I'm a bottle girl, which means that my uniform is designed to encourage obscenely large tips. I have experience posing for photos in less material, but the lack of fabric leaves little to the imagination and, unfortunately for me, gives people the idea that they have the right to put their hands on me.

It's not every group, and I wouldn't go so far as to label every man a pig, but I can always spot the worst offenders, and I try my best to derail their advances and sleazy smiles. I sweet-talk them to bulk up their bar tab into the thousands, expecting at least a 20% tip from these assholes who believe that since you bring them their Grey Goose, they can put their hands on you underneath the dim backlit booths.

Every night I remind myself, only a few more months, if I'm lucky, only a few more weeks. Soon, I will be able to leave this behind, and when I leave, I will stop being a part-time nobody and become a full-time somebody, and then all of this will be worth it.

The floor is crowded, but not packed for a Thursday. It should make the repetitive walks between tables and the bar easier, at least. Most of the night, I parade back and forth, raising sparkling bottles in the air while people take videos they are sure to upload to their feed within five seconds to prove to the entire world that they have an interesting social life.

"Hey, sweetheart." Hands go to my waist, and I quickly maneuver out of their grasp, turning to the freckle-faced redhead with a sloppy smile. "One more drink, how 'bout it?"

"How about another bottle?" I step away, asking the rest of the table. If they're going to make me stay, they might as well pay for it.

"Grey Goose, add it to the tab!"

I tap it into my reader, stepping away when I feel hands on my hips, turning me around. It's the freckle-face again. Up close, he smells like stale liquor and old cologne.

"How much do we have to order to get you to stay?" he slurs in my ear.

"Nice try, but I don't do lap dances." I tap his hand condescendingly, and thankfully, this time, he lets me go.

I weave through the club floor. The bass's rhythmic beats vibrate through my feet with each step I take. I check the clock, two more hours to go. I have a few hundred dollars' worth of tips in my back pocket that will get me through the next round of rent.

"Break?" Amy asks, loading a full tray of drinks.

"Finally." I sigh, straightening my shoulders, feeling my joints crack when I rotate my neck.

I eagerly exit toward the staff room, taking a seat on the only slightly comfortable wooden bench and reach for my phone. I'm scrolling through my messages when my eyes catch on an email notification from a few hours ago. My eyes catch on the words "Contract Extension" in the subject line. I scan the blocks of text, trying to make sense of the message, but my eyes zero in on the annotated sentence at the top of the page from my agency.

We received the attached contract from your shoot today with Power Beauty. They want you back next week for a follow-up shoot with Sasha Woodes. They were impressed with the social media posts and want to center the print ads around the shoot as well. Estimated traffic of over 20 million impressions! We'll send you more details as we receive them.

I had shot social media proofs today. Although the brand had a decent number of followers, posting a sweep on social media wasn't exactly the type of work that could change your career, but *this?* A contract extension into print meant that my face could make it on paper, in magazines, on billboards, even. This was it.

I memorize the email, and even when I am forced to finish another round on the floor, it's nearly impossible to remove the stupid grin on my face. It barely fazes me when the freckle-faced redhead makes one more pass at me while I collect my much-deserved tip. I received my first contract extension, and it's attached to one of the most successful brands I have ever been a part of. Is this it? Is this the moment that I had been working towards?

I am rushing to close out, practically racing to my car when my shift finally ends, and immediately call Marina without even looking at the clock.

"Are you dying?" Marina answers the phone in a panic. "Why are you calling me? It's 2 in the morning!"

"No, I'm fine, better than fine!" I am practically bouncing.

"Did you finally succumb to the pressures of giving a guest a lap dance?" Marina asks sarcastically.

I shake my head, beaming. "I have the best fucking news!"

CHAPTER 3

Jackson

There are two reasons why I show up at Sash's shoot today. One, she's a close friend, my closest friend, and she told me once that if I want to keep my friends, I have to make an effort. So, this is me, making the effort. Two, she's working today, which means models.

It's pathetic to admit I need an ego boost right now. Most people in the world know my name, but sometimes the love and attention of the world isn't enough. It's too far away. It's not tangible, not something I can hold on to. I need something in front of me now, like a hit to the system, and models always do wonders for the ego. So, I made a detour to set, showing my face before dinner.

Sash and I haven't been in the same city in a while. She spent most of the spring bouncing back and forth between Paris and New York, while I had been predominantly in Vancouver, filming my next big flop project. I've already seen some of the reviews and heard the bad press. I know my latest movie is gonna tank, and there's nothing I can do about it.

I take a deep breath when I walk into the warehouse. There's something about being on set that centers me. People running around, ordering others about. Hair and makeup trailers filled with people and noise. It's a distraction from everything, I think that's why I like it so much.

I nod when I spot Sash exiting her trailer. Her head tilts slightly when she sees me.

"I thought we were meeting at dinner?" She wanders over, though something in her tone tells me she knew I would be here.

That's the thing with friends; they can read you. They understand your motives, can tell when you're lying. It's why I don't have very many.

"I thought you told me I should make an effort." I open my arms, tugging her into my chest.

"You're such a shit sometimes."

I shrug after letting her go and lean my forearms against the railing. "How are you?"

"Fine. Tired." She lets out a heavy breath.

"Rip-out-your-hair-extensions tired, or need-a-weekend-at-the-Ritz tired?"

"Hmm." She looks up at the ceiling for a second, thinking. "Ritz, probably, though still undecided."

"Consider it on me then."

I lift my gaze when I hear orders being announced just behind Sash, and my eyes narrow in on the photographer standing way too close to another girl on set. I can't see her face, but I can tell she's uncomfortable. I grip the railing, at the same time Sash checks over her shoulder.

Damon DeLuca. He's a known photographer in our industry, though less prolific lately, largely due to his over-involved, *hands-on* approach. It's most likely what led him to the back warehouse in Burbank, shooting some influencer-brand campaign when a few years ago he was at *Vogue*.

DeLuca has been trying to rehabilitate his tattered image these past few years, but by the looks of how close he is standing to the girl on set, I'd say he isn't trying very hard.

"I can't believe that asshole is still working," I mutter under my breath.

"I know." Sash sighs, and I snap my attention back to her.

"Did he—"

"No." Sasha cuts me off before I can jump to the worst conclusion. "I'm fine."

I force myself to relax. I know Sash can handle herself, but I hate that it's because she's had experience. Years of fielding inappropriate questions, pushing hands off when they drifted below her waistline, ignoring men on set who only stared at her chest. She knows how to say no, but that's just because she learned the hard way. I guess we both did.

I sense a crowd forming, people getting closer, crowding my limited personal space. A camera flash goes off, and Sash rolls her eyes.

It's been this way for a while, at least over the last ten years. I can't imagine a time when it will stop, not sure I ever want it to. People clamoring to get close to me, using my name as if it is a national monument. First and last, always. I haven't been called Jackson in a while, at least not outside my inner circle, which sadly consists of Sasha, her boyfriend, Leo, and my agent, Zana.

No one really ever approaches me until I'm announced as fair game and Sash knowingly gives them the green light.

"Daria?" She smirks, not breaking eye contact with me. "Have you met Jackson?"

"Funny," I mutter under my breath before someone approaches my side.

"Jackson Ridge?" An audible gasp sounds beside me, and I turn to see a girl with bleached blonde hair approach me.

Sash has already explained the brand to me. The industry is changing in every aspect of Hollywood. Influencers with the right amount of cash can start a brand overnight, and jumping on the bandwagon is the best way to ensure you don't get left behind. It's the type of job that garners a lot of publicity, but it's shitty work. We've all been there.

"Jackson," I introduce myself.

The introduction is all that is needed to open the floodgates. More camera flashes, lots of gushing. Sash raises her middle finger in the air when she walks away, and I suppress the urge to roll my eyes, knowing she did it on purpose.

I wonder if it bothers her. We don't really talk about it, the fact that people climb over her to get to me. We were in the same lane for a while. She took a detour somewhere in Santa Monica, and I plowed straight ahead, going nearly 100 on the 101, barreling straight toward Hollywood and all that it entails.

I loved it.

I *love* it, I remind myself again, and I hate that it's more of a reminder than it used to be.

I'm aging out. Sash and I both are. On the cusp of thirty, the windows are closing in the consideration of the public. The roles that we had been playing are drying up, parts going to the younger kids with more social media followers than they know what to do with. They burn bright and then burn out. I should know; I had been one of them.

If I want to stay relevant, I have to switch genres, move to something that will get me out of the box-office blunders and into something actually substantial. The problem is, my CV is littered with trash, literally, shit work that earned me big fat paychecks but no respect.

I know what people say about me. I've read the articles. I can sell headlines, but not tickets. To studios, I've become a walking liability. The reputation that booked me so many projects in my twenties is now preventing me from going forward. Another reason why studios don't make the time for me or force me into an audition to prove that I'm worth it. I have *nothing* to prove. My name is practically a brand.

It's why I am ignoring my agent, Zana, who keeps pushing

new opportunities on my plate that are getting worse and worse. I've told her the direction I want to move in, and she insists that it's a bad move. She'd rather I work shit projects than gamble on good ones. So, here we are.

I need a break, at least a few days off. Cool down, let loose.

Hence, *models*.

I'm in the midst of taking selfies when my eyes catch on Sash talking to someone across the warehouse. It's the girl from earlier, the one the photographer had been standing too close to. I hadn't seen her face before, but now I take her in.

Heart-shape face, light-brown hair, legs that look like they go on forever, but I guess they're supposed to when she's wearing a dress that short. She's thin, tall, obviously, in the way that all models are, but she doesn't fit on the set. It's not that she isn't beautiful; she is. She has the sort of beauty that makes sense for her to be here, but there is something innocent about her, naïve.

Something in her expression reminds me of Sash from all those years ago. We were signed at the same time, around the same age, and had been thrown in the lion's den, forced to figure out the politics and dynamics of the industry on our own. We had both been wide-eyed and unprepared. We fumbled and fucked our way through it, but at least we had each other.

Sash nods her head in my direction and suddenly, the girl's attention turns toward me. While they start walking, I wait for the recognition to hit. There are usually obvious signs. Eyes widening, mouth dropping, cheeks turning pink. None of those happen. She looks . . . confused, almost.

I'm still waiting for her to react, not letting go of her gaze until she walks straight into a production assistant. Sash extends her arms to try to catch her, but she regains her composure quickly, standing upright and profusely apologizing to someone who looks less than interested and more than a little irritated.

I laugh under my breath, covering my mouth with my fist. Her head snaps up at the sound of it, and now she is glaring at me. Her eyebrows pinch together, but her eyes don't leave my face, so mine don't leave hers.

People never look at me like this, which is why I'm half tempted to check behind me to see if someone else is stealing her focus. I've gotten surprise, fascination, lust, obviously, but not hate, not annoyance, and I can tell she is annoyed by the set of her eyes and the pout of her full mouth.

A loud clap breaks her focus, forcing her to look away. I let out a breath, dragging a hand through my hair, and lean against the railing. I hadn't felt that way in a long time, whatever *that* was. A challenge? A dare? I'd be game for either, but unfortunately, my phone rings, forcing me away from the beautiful stranger who captured my incredibly short attention span.

"What?" I grunt into the microphone.

"Tell me you're on your way," Zana, my agent for the past decade of my life, barks into the phone.

"I can't make it. I told you." I look up at the girl next to Sash, but she doesn't look my way again. "I have a meeting in Santa Barbara."

"You know I track your location, right?" At that, I roll my eyes. "Burbank is a long way from Santa Barbara."

"Tell me why you need me there, and I'll consider it."

"You need to be here because I'm telling you to be here."

"I have the weekend off. *You* gave me the weekend off."

"Jackson—"

I hang up.

The quick conversation is not unlike others I've had with my agent over the past six months. She's frustrated with my lack of interest in anything on my plate, and I'm frustrated because I can't seem to break out of the mold that I created for myself so long ago.

Lose-lose situation for us both right now.

I lean forward on the railing. Stragglers linger around me while everyone else seems to get back to work. I tolerate some interns who giggle when they ask for photos and then focus on the shoot.

When they call a break, I lift a finger, motioning Sash over. She tugs on her ponytail, grimacing as she approaches.

"What?" she asks, hand on her hip.

"Who is she?" I lift my chin toward the girl on the other side of the warehouse.

She didn't look at me again. Not once in the entire hour they had been shooting, even though I had been watching her. The doe-eyed expression vanished the second a camera was pointed in her face, snapping her into focus.

"Who?" Sash turns to follow my gaze and then lets out a breath. "Oh, Cassie something."

I rifle through the list of names in my head, waiting for it to sound even remotely familiar. It doesn't.

"You know her?"

Sash lets out a muffled groan. "You're *so* predictable."

"Am I?" I allow a smile. "Well, if I'm so predictable, then you already know what I'm going to ask."

She drops her chin, guessing correctly. "I'm not bringing her to dinner."

"Why not?"

She throws me a look. "She's younger than you."

I force myself to shrug, like it isn't some ridiculous stipulation I live my life by. That all the women I've slept with over the course of my life just happen to be older than me, not that I prefer it.

"Besides, she's new," Sash continues. "I don't want to throw her in with the sharks just yet."

My smile widens, and I tilt my head. "Am I a shark?"

Sash glares. "You know you are."

"Ask her anyway. See if she says yes." I say as my phone rings. Zana on the other line. "I've got to take this." I lean forward, kissing her once on the cheek. "You look great, Sash. See you later."

"Bye." She sighs and turns back toward set.

I don't see Cassie again. She remains in the trailer for the short break they are allowed, and I am pulled away again, having to attend to business that I don't even want to manage in the first place.

"Go," I answer my phone, exiting the warehouse.

CHAPTER 4

Cassie

The shoot takes all day. Jackson disappeared somewhere after our first break, further supporting my theory that he was just a figment of my imagination sent to the back warehouse on a Burbank lot with no other purpose than to try to sabotage my future career potential. I almost let him distract me, when I nearly tackled a production assistant to the ground. Embarrassing enough, but then he had to laugh. At *me*. It was humiliating.

After I picked myself up, profusely apologized to someone who didn't care, I collected a breath and tried my best to ignore the captivating gaze of Jackson Ridge.

He was beautiful. I don't think there is another word for it. Everyone flocked to him and a small part of me was annoyed that he still looked so perfect, even in person. When he wasn't looking, I kept stealing glances, trying to rationalize how someone I watched on my TV was standing a few yards away from me.

Despite the quite literal misstep approaching set, I had been good, my best even, though I wouldn't be able to see the actual proof for a few days.

I scale the steps to my apartment in a daze, taking slow, lethargic strides. A fresh pop beat playing over our speakers greets me when I walk through the door, and I remember how much I love having roommates.

"Hey, Cass!" Marina smiles, wine glass in hand. "How did it go?"

"It was . . . weird, but good," I say smiling while I collapse onto the barstool. "I haven't seen the prints yet, but I just have a feeling, you know?"

"I'm sensing a big-break moment!" Marina cheers.

Lucy sticks her head out the bathroom, the straightener steaming her thick blonde hair. "You really think this was it?" Marina throws a glare over her shoulder that sends Lucy backtracking. "I mean, that's great news!"

I roll my eyes, not really surprised by Lucy's response. I am sure it must get annoying having to constantly reassure me through every booking. Marina is, and always has been, a better cheerleader.

I lean my cheek against my fist, my mind wandering back to the shoot, compartmentalizing what might have actually occurred versus the fantasy I most likely concocted in my head.

One, Jackson Ridge on my set. Well, not *my* set, but the set that I was on. Probably, a dream. Two, Sasha inviting me out to dinner tonight in West Hollywood. Most likely an illusion, but possibly real? I sort of blacked out when she asked. It was phrased as a group get-together, and I think I said yes before she even finished the question. It was the networking opportunity I had been waiting for, so I didn't bother listening to the details outside of when and where.

"What is it?" Marina asks, reaching to turn down the music.

I let out a breath, sitting up. "You aren't going to believe who was on set today."

"Who?" Lucy's head appears from the bathroom again.

"Jackson Ridge."

Lucy and Marina both gasp simultaneously, as if they are trying to suck all the air out of the room. The moment of silence is followed by their screams and shrieks of disbelief. I cover my ears with my hands.

"Shut the fuck up," Lucy yells, running from the bathroom, bouncing up and down. "You're joking. Tell me you're joking!"

Marina pulls her hands up to her mouth, squealing. She actually squeals. "What was he doing there?"

"Yes, I'm serious, and I honestly have no idea. He was there with Sasha Woodes. I think they know each other?"

"Are they dating?" Marina asks looking to Lucy.

"No! *But* they used to model together, before he booked *Sunset City.*" Lucy references one of the most popular teen dramas that came out in junior high. It was like *The O.C.* meets *One Tree Hill*, but way more sex. "They go like way back, look!"

Lucy sticks her phone in my face. I take in the much younger images of Jackson and Sasha. It would make sense why they seemed so close if they've known each other for over a decade. Suddenly, the phone is ripped away.

"What was he like?" Lucy asks. "Can I use a quote? That would definitely get me promoted. Cassie, you have to be friends with him!" Lucy clutches my arm in a death grip.

"Okay, ow." I pull my arm away from her, frowning.

"What happened? Tell me everything." Lucy demands.

"Nothing happened, he just showed up, out of the blue. I had no idea he would be there, and everyone was just crowding him. Eventually we moved on, and he just stayed and . . . watched."

"He watched you?" Lucy's jaw drops. "Oh my God, did you talk to him?"

"No, not like that. I mean, he was there for Sasha."

"Goddammit, Cass, I wish I knew! I would have sent you a million and one questions to ask!" Lucy rolls her eyes.

"That's good though, right?" Marina encourages. "If he was on your set, and it went well, this could mean that you are starting to book bigger jobs!"

"Yeah, maybe," I agree, though it mostly feels like pure luck that he showed up today, a total accident that would never happen again.

"Marina and I are meeting up with Mark and his friends tonight. You should come! We can celebrate!" Lucy offers enthusiastically, though I have a feeling she would rather celebrate my celebrity encounter than the actual shoot.

"I would, but I have plans tonight. Headed out for drinks with some girls from the shoot."

"You better not be lying and spend the night drunk-calling Noah." Marina tosses me a glare over her shoulder.

"I promise I won't be."

"You better not." Marina eyes me as she grabs her purse from the counter. "We're celebrating this weekend, though. Wine and pizza!"

"Deal." I laugh.

"Jackson *fucking* Ridge." Lucy grins, shaking her head. "What are the chances?"

"I know." I sigh, leaning against the counter.

"Text us when you're back," Marina calls over her shoulder as she follows Lucy out of the apartment.

"I will!"

I glance at my phone as soon as the door shuts. I have exactly two hours to get ready and make it to West Hollywood without panicking.

I can do this.

~

I am running at least twenty minutes behind, thanks to the perennial headache of LA traffic, even at nine o'clock at night. Sasha sent me this address a few hours ago. I had to search the restaurant to find the right attire, and I nearly had a heart attack when I looked at the prices on the menu. I would be sticking with only drinks for the night, and I'll still probably have to pick up an extra shift to cover it.

"Hi, I think the party I'm with already checked in." I breathe out quickly, hoping that I haven't driven all the way across town for the entire evening to be a joke.

"Name?" The host asks without looking up.

"Woodes."

"Oh, of course." He looks up, smiling. Apparently, he could give me the time of day once I named-dropped a celebrity. "Right this way."

I take a deep breath, inhaling the calming scent of wood and jasmine as the host leads me toward the back, directing me to a crowded, green velvet half booth with a wide table.

"Hey, you made it!" Sasha stands, wrapping me in a quick hug. "Everyone, this is Cassie. We work together. Be nice. That means you, Oli." She glares dramatically at a man in the corner who feigns shock.

"I'm always nice," he whines, placing a hand over his chest dramatically.

"And you're always lying," Sasha counters with a sarcastic grin, which he reciprocates.

I take a spot on the end and immediately order their largest glass of wine that is still within my price range. Sugar water, essentially.

"So, Audrey, what's the latest with Lydia?" Sasha asks, resting her elbows on the table. I realize she is talking to the woman with bright-orange hair sitting next to me.

"Oh, she's long gone." Audrey waves her hand, lifting a martini to her purple-painted lips.

"What? Why? I liked her!" Oli whines.

"I did too, but she just couldn't deal with the distance. I mean, I had to be in New York with Aria working on the album for the past four months, and she wouldn't travel to come visit. If she can't make that work, how would it ever last between us?"

"Aria, as in Aria Ford?" I ask, shocked, picking up on the name of the latest emerging artist in the pop world. She won Best New Artist at the Grammys this past award season.

"She's my client," Audrey says, barely turning toward me before raising her glass to the rest of the table. "Single again."

"Cheers to that!" Oli smiles.

We all lift our glasses in unison, clinking them together. I swallow the crisp, cool wine before the attention is put on me.

"So, Cassie, right?" Oli asks from across the table. "I suppose if you worked with Sash, you must also be in the modeling industry?"

"Yes, or, at least, I'm trying to be." I fidget with the rings on my hand.

"She shot with me today. You know the new brand I was talking about?" Sasha interjects on my behalf.

"Congratulations!" Oli smiles warmly and then points to Sasha. "Though if you're working with this one, I would say the sun has set on your career."

"I said be *nice*." Sasha rolls her eyes dramatically.

While they continue bickering, I try to guess Sasha's age. I would guess late twenties, same as Jackson. She's been around long enough that I recognize her. I know the age comment was a joke, but I already feel my own countdown ticking rapidly. The fewer jobs I get, the faster I imagine myself aging out, even though I'm only twenty-four.

The conversation ebbs and flows, exchanging comments around the industry, different parties they've attended, which ones were the best and the worst. I'm not able to really contribute, but I am a little shocked by the tone of the conversation.

I wasn't sure what type of crowd I would encounter tonight, but outside of Sasha, they all seem overwhelmingly unhappy. I can tell in their tone, their posture, their words. They are living the types of lives that I'm chasing, and they seem almost bored with them. Their descriptions of fame seem so different than the version I've dreamed of.

Oli starts on another story, commanding the attention of the table. When he embellishes the interaction, I lift my gaze to Sasha and suppress a smile as she rolls her eyes.

I am reaching for my wine glass when I catch the start of a commotion across the restaurant floor. I hear the muted noises and see a few camera flashes before I turn, and when I do, I find Jackson Ridge striding toward our table.

Eyes locked on *me*.

CHAPTER 5

Jackson

I ignore the camera flashes to my right and focus on the table in front of me, eyes catching on the girl from the shoot this afternoon. Her cheeks turn pink, and she looks away, muttering something under her breath before reaching for the wine glass in front of her.

Sash scowls at me when I get closer. I'm already running late, something that I know annoys her, but my arrival earns the attention of everyone at the table. I do a quick scan. Most I know, a few I like, others I pretend to tolerate.

"Sorry I'm late," I offer, taking the chair beside Sash.

"You're always late." She tries to glare but dissolves when I kiss her cheek in apology.

"Not always." I raise a finger in the air as a waiter scrambles forward. I quickly order an old-fashioned and unbutton my jacket, turning to Sash. "Intros?"

"You missed them. They were about forty-five minutes ago," she mutters under her breath, but when I raise an eyebrow, she sighs, relenting. "Cassie!" Sash calls across the table. "Have you met Jackson?"

Cassie bites the inside of her cheek, looking between us quickly. She's wearing a black, strapless dress that brings out the brightness in her eyes, which I can now spot from the other side of the table, a unique color. Hazel, sort of gold, a little green, narrow and focused on me, which are my favorite type of eyes. She's even more striking up close. Her light brown hair flows in soft waves down her back, tucked behind her left ear.

She doesn't say anything, but I allow her to take me in, assess me the same way I had assessed her a moment ago. She's not glaring so much now. There's less emotion, like she is indifferent, in a way that I haven't seen before.

"Jackson." I nod in her direction, hoping she will reciprocate.

She crosses her legs, allowing a small, forced smile. "Hi."

She looks away quickly, turning to the person beside her. Sash lets out a low whistle while I lean further back in my chair.

"That was fun." Sash smiles, leaning toward me so that our conversation can't be heard from the rest of the table.

I lift my eyes to Cassie. Her body angled away from me, like she is purposefully forcing herself not to look.

"So." Sasha pushes her dark hair over her shoulder, giving me her full attention. "How are you?"

"Fine." I stick to my usual syllables.

"I know you're in town for the movie, but what about your little side project?"

I know she's referring to my attempt to get out of the rut that I'm currently stuck in. Switch career paths, transition into a different lane.

"Fucked." I drag a hand through my hair. "Zana thinks it's a bad move."

"Well, as always, Zana doesn't know what she's talking about." Sash looks at me, but I don't meet her eye. "You can do it without her, you know. You have enough connections to meet with a studio." I ignore her, so she digs in deeper. "You want to be serious about it, be serious. Show them that you are more than just some headline."

I tear my gaze away from Cassie, throwing Sash a look. "Audition, you mean?"

"Yeah."

"No." I shake my head.

I don't tell her the real reason I won't consider entertaining an audition with a new studio. I bury that truth down so deep, it will never see the light of day.

"If it's going to help the studio, just do it."

"I'm not showing up to audition. It's fucking embarrassing that they would even ask me to," I complain, rolling my neck.

A laugh echoes from the other side of the table. It's not a high-pitch giggle, but more of a cough under the breath, and my eyes immediately lift to Cassie sitting across from me, her hand over her mouth.

"Something funny?" I ask, lifting my chin.

She wants to listen to my conversation, fine. She can join it.

"Easy," Sash warns under her breath, reaching for her martini.

Cassie tenses for a moment, as if realizing her mistake. She looks back and forth between us. Her voice small when she speaks next. "I wasn't really listening."

"Come on, now's not the time to be shy."

I don't know what it is, my tone, posture, or the way I taunted her, but she leans forward, surprisingly taking the bait. The entire table has gone quiet, waiting for her response.

"I just think it's funny that you wouldn't consider going to an audition, you know, for a job," she says coolly. Her voice dripping in sarcasm.

"You don't think I'm qualified to book one on merit?"

"I don't know. I guess that's what the audition is for." She reaches for her wine glass, tossing the rest of it back.

I know I should back off, give her the benefit of the doubt, but I'm not used to other people challenging me, and the next words slip out before I can stop them.

"And I suppose modeling auditions are so much more complicated? Taking off your clothes to book a job, right?"

She stiffens, eyes going round, and I immediately regret the cheap shot. It's the same jab people have taunted me with time and again, so I know that it hurts. Before I can take it back, she leans forward.

"Believe it or not, I can book them with all my clothes on. Not sure you could say the same."

My eyes narrow. "You think you know me?"

"I think I know enough." She lifts her chin in the air.

"Really? Well, I know nothing about you," I say coolly. "In fact, I've never even heard of *you*."

Her cheeks burn bright red, and before she can think of a retort, Sash reaches forward to diffuse the sudden tension.

"All right, new topic!" Sash waves her hands as everyone goes back to whatever conversations they had been having on the side. "Shark," Sash mutters under her breath, kicking me under the table.

I try to meet Cassie's eye again, but she doesn't look my way for the rest of the dinner. All night, I keep glancing at her, but she doesn't turn, purposefully avoiding me. I hate how much it's bothering me, her lack of attention. This was supposed to be easy. In any other situation, she would be laughing at a bad joke, sitting in my lap, eating out of the palm of my hand.

"You staying?" Sash asks at the end of the night.

I turn toward her. "You leaving?"

"I'm due in New York tomorrow." She says and then frowns. "Don't think I've forgotten about your *clothes off* comment."

I already feel like shit for the low blow fired at Cassie. I hadn't even thought about the implication on Sash.

"You know I didn't mean that."

"Make it up to me by not doing something stupid, please." She kisses my cheek. "I'll be back next week for the Harper show. Maybe we can grab drinks? Just us?"

"Sure." I nod.

Sash stands, turning her attention to the rest of the table. "Hate to be the buzzkill, but I have an early flight tomorrow.

Cassie, thanks for coming! I'll text you." She waves at Cassie across the table and then leans over my shoulder, warning me under her breath before she leaves. "Behave."

Others seem to follow Sash's lead and start peeling off, one by one. I hesitate when Cassie lifts her phone, presumably to call a ride home. I don't know why, but I can't leave it. At least, not like this. Now, it's a problem left unsolved. A riddle that needs an answer. An itch that needs to be scratched.

I down the rest of my drink and then stand, rounding the table. Cassie doesn't look up, not until I slide in beside her, not until my arm rests along the back of the booth.

"Can I help you?" she asks, pulling back slightly.

"I didn't catch your name." I start easy.

"Sasha told you my name."

"Your full name."

She sighs, releasing the tension in her shoulders. "Cassie Taylor."

I take her in. Now that she is sitting close to me, I can smell the perfume on her neck. It's nothing fancy, but the scent hits me. It's soft, ivy and something floral. Her hazel eyes look even more vibrant up close. I let my gaze dip down to her chest, a movement she notes, and then I bite the inside of my cheek.

"Hi, Cassie Taylor," I say at the same time her eyes drift to my mouth. "So, what do you say? Call it a truce?"

She sits up straighter. "I didn't know we were at war."

I extend my hand to hers as a peace offering. She hesitates before resting her delicate hand in my embrace. Her skin is soft, smooth, and I notice that she holds on until I release her.

"So, why were you on the shoot today?" she asks.

"I'm back in town for press and stopped by to visit Sash. Haven't seen her in a while." I shrug.

"Press? For which movie?"

"*Annihilation.*" I frown, raising a finger in the air for another refill.

Cassie leans back, crossing her arms over her chest. "What? You hate it or something?"

I tense before shaking my head. "I didn't say that."

"You don't have to. I can tell."

"Really?" I move closer. "And you think you know me so well?"

"I think I can read people pretty well, yes." She lifts her chin.

I realize that we are now alone in the booth. I want to keep her talking because I don't want her to leave. I have nothing but a giant empty house to head back to, and I prefer not to sleep in it alone.

Shifting tactics, I lean closer. "Want to play a game?"

"A game?"

"Mhm." I smile. "Let's see who can read who the best."

She narrows her gaze, trying to find the motive in my plan, though I would guess she already knows. My arm rests along the back of the booth, and I lift a finger, running it lightly through the end of her hair. She glances sideways, cheeks turning pink.

"Come on," I taunt her with a grin. "Play with me."

The corner of her mouth twitches upward. "Fine. The stakes?"

"A drink for every wrong assumption."

"Easy." She tosses her hair over her shoulder.

Right on cue, fresh drinks are deposited in front of us. I lift my old-fashioned, tapping it against her wine glass, and size her up.

"All right, we'll start with an easy one." I rub my lips with two fingers. "You're not from California."

Her eyes narrow. "That's too easy."

I shrug, nodding towards her. "Drink."

She reaches for her freshly filled wine glass, takes a sip, and then assesses me again. "You're an only child."

My eye twitches, but I disguise it with a blink and reach for my glass. "Wrong," I answer, taking a large swig anyway.

"I thought only the loser drinks."

I ignore her and pick an easy topic next, a sure win. "You follow me on Instagram."

She smiles, and her happiness is so authentic, I almost miss her answer. "No."

I glare at her. "You're lying."

"Dead serious, but you can check my phone if you want." Her eyes brighten. "Drink."

I roll my shoulders and take another sip, hating how much my incorrect assumption rattled me. I have over a hundred million followers. Statistically, she should be one of them.

"My turn," she says, sitting taller. "You hate LA." I blink, and her smile widens. "I'm right?"

My hand tightens around the glass. This was supposed to be a game, one that ended with her agreeing to come home with me. My next assumption comes out more aggressive.

"You don't know what type of wine you're drinking." Her smile drops, but when she goes to reach for her glass, I add another. "And you can't afford it."

She rears back before firing again. "You use sex as a distraction."

I smile at the same time her eyes widen, realizing her mistake. She brought it up, which means she's thinking about it. Everyone thinks about it, when I give them enough attention.

I answer her by reaching for my glass, taking a large sip, and then lean forward, speaking softly against the shell of her ear.

"You haven't been laid in the past month." I pull away, noting the pink spread across her cheeks. "You're blushing."

"I'm not." She lets out a breath and then finishes the rest of her drink before turning to fully face me. Her elbow rests on the table. "You're unhappy."

The accusation hits me suddenly and I push it down, as far as it will go, burying it deep beneath the surface, because I can't handle the truth myself, let alone handed to me from a stranger.

I rest my hand on the top of her thigh, fingers moving slowly. I feel her lean into me when my lips gently graze her cheek.

"You're coming home with me," I whisper.

She shivers before peering up at me. She's still close, our lips nearly touching, when a camera flashes over my shoulder. She brushes her mouth against the corner of my jaw and when I start to lean in, her voice cuts through the silence.

"No."

I flinch just in time to see her pull away from me, wearing a satisfied smile. Her eyes fall over my face before nodding to my glass.

"Drink."

CHAPTER 6

Cassie

I wake up the next morning to a pillow smacking me in the face.

"What the hell!" I gasp and lift my hands to prevent another blow, blinking to find Lucy standing over me, Marina by her side.

"How could you not tell us?" Lucy's voice is entirely too sharp this early in the morning.

"What are you talking about?" I complain.

"You went to dinner with Jackson Ridge last night!" Lucy accuses.

I falter, looking up at my two best friends. "I . . . how do you know about that?"

"*This*." Lucy shoves her phone in my face.

I blink a few more times before my eyes zero in on the photo of Jackson and me, leaning close together, in an empty booth. The image is blurry, most likely captured from a phone inside the restaurant. My eyes drift to the caption.

Celebrity Sighting: Jackson Ridge and Mystery Brunette Step Out in West Hollywood.

I sit up straight, snatching the phone from her hands. "Where the hell did you get this?"

"It's everywhere. I woke up to alerts on my phone from *TMI*," Lucy explains.

"Did you know he was going to be at dinner?" Marina asks.

"Of course not." I roll my eyes, skimming the article. "Does it say my name?"

"Not that I could tell," Marina says.

"But that is so you. You can't lie," Lucy challenges.

For some reason, I didn't really believe photographic evidence of us together could actually exist. A part of me imagined that I made the encounter up in my head, that I would wake this morning, very much the pumpkin in this fairy tale.

The entire night had felt like some sort of chaotic fever dream that had me wondering if I had imagined the feeling of his fingers teasing the hem of my dress. My heart had been racing in my chest every time he looked at me. My body screaming at me to stay, my mind needing to prove a point, but the entire way home, all I could think about was saying yes. In another reality, I would have been in the back seat of the car with him, seconds away from being in his bed if he hadn't been such a massive self-assured dick.

In this very real reality, my pride got in the way.

Marina and Lucy hover over me, and I know that I won't get out of this without some sort of explanation.

"Okay yes, that's me," I say quietly.

I immediately plug my ears when Lucy and Marina shriek, nearly breaking the sound barrier.

"Cassie fucking Taylor!" Lucy squeals.

"Okay, calm down. It's not that big of a deal."

"Not a big deal?" Marina asks, eyes bulging.

"You have dinner together once, and you're already featured in a spread!" Lucy practically screams.

"A tabloid. No one reads those," I mutter, stepping out of bed in search of an extra-large cup of coffee and Advil.

They follow me into the kitchen, hovering behind. Lucy screams when her phone buzzes again.

"Oh my god. *EDaily* picked it up!" Lucy flips her phone in my face.

I blink, studying another photo, one that was obviously captured when I wasn't paying attention. It was snapped when I leaned in, teasing Jackson with the promise of a kiss before pulling away. Apparently leaving him in the booth wasn't worth a photo, but *this* was. I frown when I see the title of the article and shove the phone back into Lucy's hand.

JACKSON RIDGE'S LATEST CONQUEST IS A NO-NAME-NOBODY.

"I need caffeine," I mumble, massaging my temple.

"You aren't going to tell us anything?" Lucy asks.

"There really isn't a lot to say." I shrug, pouring coffee into the largest mug I can find. "He randomly showed up at dinner, and the photo was just taken at a bad time. Nothing happened."

Marina and Lucy exchange a glance.

"What?" I demand.

"I mean, it looks like you guys—"

"We didn't. I slept here last night. You woke me up with a pillow in my face!"

"But—" Lucy starts.

"But nothing. It was a random fluke. I highly doubt that I will ever see him again."

As soon as I set down my coffee, a horn startles the three of us at the counter. The short, sharp blast of it echoes through our apartment complex. Slowly, we all turn toward the window.

"You don't think . . ." Marina trails off while Lucy rushes across the kitchen, ripping back the curtains.

"Holy shit!" Lucy whirls around, her jaw nearly on the floor. "It's him. Jackson Ridge. He's outside!"

Marina races to the window beside Lucy while I work to collect a breath. Once I have enough air, I step cautiously toward the curtain to find Jackson standing in our parking lot, his hand resting against the steering wheel through the open window on the driver's side.

His head dips when he spots us standing at the window, and then he raises a finger when we lock eyes, motioning me to meet him.

My jaw tightens while my hands curl into fists.

"I'll be right back," I mutter between clenched teeth.

I race down the steps of my apartment, charging at him in the parking lot. I don't care that I am in my pajamas and my hair is a mess. I am so angry I can barely think straight. The car horn ringing through my ears, his hand still firmly pressed against the steering wheel.

"What are you *doing*?" I shout over the noise.

Jackson pulls his hand off the horn, crossing his arms over his chest while he smiles, like he is proud of himself for making such a spectacle in the parking lot of my apartment.

"Good morning," he greets me.

"Who the hell do you think you are?" I yell.

"Jackson Ridge," he answers with a grin. "We met last night, if you remember."

"Oh, I remember," I seethe.

"I'm glad I made such a lasting impression."

"Touché." I glare, and his smile widens, like he enjoyed me playing along. "What are you doing *here*?"

"I came to see you, obviously."

"*Obviously*?"

"Obviously. I'm going to grab breakfast. Come with me."

I nearly stumble. "Was my rejection last night too subtle for you? Would you like it in writing this time?"

"Funny." He rolls his eyes. "Look, I'm assuming you've seen the photos, and I just want to talk."

"Talk?" I ask, clarifying. "With me?"

"You probably have a lot of questions, and I'm pretty sure I'm the only one who can answer them. So, what will it be?"

I cross my arms over my chest, turning over my shoulder to look up at my apartment window. Marina and Lucy, who just had their faces practically shoved up against the glass, scatter the second I catch them staring.

The headlines flash through my head again. The fact that my face is plastered across socials overnight is enough to cause a headache, but I certainly never thought I'd be discussing my potential PR strategy with Jackson Ridge, in my parking lot, at nine in the morning.

I toss him a look. "Just to talk?"

His lips twitch. "Of course."

"Well, I can't go like this."

"Get changed then. I'll wait."

"Fine."

"Good." He smiles and climbs back into his BMW, pulling into a parking spot in the lot while I scale the steps in a daze.

The second I step through the door, Marina and Lucy swarm me.

"What the hell is he doing here?" Lucy attacks. "Did you plan to see him again?"

"How does he know where we live?" Marina follows.

"Okay, let me just think for a second."

Marina and Lucy exchange a glance and then both take a step back. I cover my face with my hands and force myself to inhale at least five breaths before I look up at Marina and Lucy standing in front of me in their pajamas.

"I have no idea how he knows where I live. No, I didn't know he was coming, and *no,* I never expected to see him again, especially considering how last night ended."

"What does that mean?" Marina jumps on the end of my sentence, eyes cautious.

"He was a jerk!" I yell, hands in the air.

"Well, what does he want now?" Lucy asks.

"He wants to take me out for breakfast."

"*Now*?" Marina asks, shocked.

"Yes, now."

"What are you waiting for? Go!" Lucy hauls me off the stool and starts shoving me toward my bedroom.

"What if I don't want to?" I grumble, but I don't have the energy to put up a fight. Lucy is too strong anyway.

"Unacceptable." Lucy shoves me to my mattress before rifling through my closet. "You have to go. At least to see what he wants."

"I know what he wants," I grumble. "He wants to get the last word in."

"Meaning?" Marina asks, concern lining her brow.

"Here! Wear this." Lucy throws an outfit at me from my closet.

"Lucy?" I ask, forcing her to pause. "What *exactly* does this mean for me?"

She finally stops, glancing between us. "Well, the press doesn't know who you are, yet. They just have your picture. But Jackson tends to be a hot topic, especially with a potential new girlfriend so people will be asking questions. Honestly, I would be surprised if they don't identify you before the end of the day."

I sigh, falling back on my mattress, hands covering my face. If someone had told me yesterday that I would be not only photographed with Jackson Ridge, but would also be fighting off dating rumors, with him waiting for me downstairs, I would have personally escorted them to the psych floor of a hospital.

"This is ridiculous. Nothing even happened!" I groan, removing my hands.

Another honk comes from outside, more muted this time through my bedroom.

"What are you gonna do?" Marina asks when I sit up.

I clench my jaw, grabbing the outfit that Lucy tossed at me and stand from my bed. "I'm going to tell him to go to hell."

CHAPTER 7

Jackson

I wake this morning with a consistent thrumming in my temple cause I don't sleep alone or sober in my own house. Can't do it. I've tried, and it doesn't work. It's too quiet, and I feel too small when I've spent my entire life trying to feel big.

I drag a hand over my face, noting the blonde still asleep on her stomach. I don't remember calling Bree, but I'm not really surprised I did. I usually call her when I don't have anyone else to distract me. She tends to show up, no questions asked.

An annoying rattle comes from the table beside me. I reach for it, smacking my phone off without looking at the caller. I am granted ten seconds of silence before it sounds again.

"What?" I answer, standing from the bed, tripping a bit, because I practically blew through half a bottle of whiskey before I buried myself in the woman in my bed. I throw on pants, stumbling to the bathroom.

"I gave you one rule," Sash berates me from the other line.

"I followed it," I say, squinting against the harsh light of the fluorescents before leaning against the counter.

I leave out the part that I didn't actually follow Sash's advice to leave Cassie alone, but it didn't matter. Cassie didn't come home with me anyway, despite my best efforts, which is fucking annoying. I can't remember the last time I hadn't gotten what I wanted.

"Really? So, you're telling me you and Cassie didn't sleep together? Cause that's what's all over the tabloids this morning."

"What are you talking about?"

"You're so grumbly when you're hungover. Check your phone."

I remove the phone from my ear, my home screen littered with messages. Top of the queue is from my publicist, an article pinned to the text.

SADIE

What's the story you want me to run with this time?

I click the link, ignoring all the notifications and fucking noise that blasts me every time I open the social media app. I don't use it outside publicity purposes, but it's my main account, which means all fan mail, DMs and hate messages funnel right through my profile, straight to me.

I blink once, then twice, and it's right there. Right in my fucking face.

I saw a camera flash out of the corner of my eye last night when the restaurant was practically empty, but I sort of forgot about it. I can't anymore, now that it's on the screen in front of me. A photo of Cassie leaning into me, her eyes on my mouth, my hand on her thigh, slipping up her dress, and her lips, only an inch or so away from mine.

Fuck . . . it does look like we slept together.

I zoom in on the photo, eyes drawn to Cassie's heart-shaped face and perfect-looking mouth that I wanted to kiss. Lips that I wanted to taste.

"Jackson!" Sash yells to get my attention.

I flip the phone back to my ear. "What?"

"I told you to leave her alone."

"Would you believe me if I told you nothing happened?"

"No," she replies too quickly. I let out a breath, dragging my hand across my face. "You want to be taken seriously? Start acting like it."

"My personal life has nothing to do with my professional life."

"You know better than anyone that it does. Clean up your shit. You're messy."

I drop my phone, gripping the bathroom sink, head down low, avoiding my reflection. I splash water on my face and then flip through one of the articles, reading every word I come across.

For once, the papers aren't calling into question my career choices or reputation. Everything published is one of intrigue or interest. I can't remember the last time I read something about myself that didn't resurface everything I've ever done wrong in my life.

Sash's right. I need something serious to be taken seriously.

I've done it before, used the premise of a relationship to boost whatever project I had been working on, and for the most part, it's worked. It's allowed for greater visibility of whatever I want to sell at the moment, puts my face in the papers. If one photo of Cassie and I together had this much circulation, how much credibility could a spread do?

I push off the counter, storming back into the bedroom. Bree, awake now, does nothing to cover herself.

She stretches lazily, smiling up at me. "Morning."

"Nic will drive you wherever you need to go."

My dismissal is obvious, but she doesn't pout or complain. She rises from the bed, still naked, taking her time to put her clothes back on. When she's dressed, she brushes a hand across my chest, stretching on her tiptoes to kiss my cheek before leaving the bedroom.

"Do something for me?" I call her back. Bree tilts her head, waiting. "Don't tell anyone you were with me last night."

"I never do." She smiles before slipping out the door.

The reason Bree is the woman I call when I can't be alone is because she's older. I never asked but assumed mid-thirties, maybe. She doesn't care about stuff like the trades and the fact that I only fuck her behind closed doors.

I quickly hop in the shower, rinsing everything away, letting the warm water soak my shoulders. I press my left hand up against the tile, drag my other hand through my hair.

Need something serious to be taken seriously.

When I step out of the shower, I shoot my publicist a response.

JACKSON

Working on it.

It's what led me to Cassie's apartment on the south side of Santa Monica this morning.

~

I lean against my car, fighting a grin when Cassie stomps down the steps. Her hair is tied up on the top of her head in a messy bun, not a drop of makeup, and I prefer this look, ten thousand to one, over her evening attire last night. I can actually see her.

She's angry, which is fine. Anger is an emotion I can handle. What I can't handle is her indifference. Don't know what to do with it. *This* I can work with.

I held my breath when I offered her the option to get in my car. For a split second, I thought she was going to spit in my face and walk away. Even though she said she would be back, I braced myself for the small possibility that I would never see her again. Maybe I could have lived with it, but when I see her descend the staircase, stomping toward the parking lot, the light lift in my chest tells me otherwise.

Cassie slips in beside me, arms crossed, and does her best to glare. I ignore that and instead focus on the freckles across the bridge of her nose that were hidden beneath makeup last night. Sash was right, she's young. I don't think I noticed before, but now, fresh-faced in my front seat, in broad daylight, I can tell. She can't be older than twenty-five.

"Ready?" I ask.

"Not really," she grumbles, and I smile, spinning the steering wheel with my palm. I pull out of the lot, tires screeching when I make the quick turn.

Cassie raises her arm, clinging to the frame of the car while I mess with the gear shift, trying to alternate the pedals. I've always been shit at operating manual, and I can't actually remember the last time I drove a car that required it, but the conversation I want to have needs to be held in private and in a very recognizable BMW.

"Drive much?" she quips.

I roll my eyes, concentrating on the gears again. "I hate stick."

"Then why drive it?"

"Because it's the best." I toss her a smile as we speed through a yellow light.

The car jerks again, and Cassie leans back, looking down at my feet. "Release slower and concentrate on your timing," she instructs.

I tap the clutch lightly and then try to gently pull my foot off while shifting, a little smoother this time.

"You know how to drive stick?" I ask.

"I used to drive a truck."

"Really?" I ask, smirking. Her face softens a bit before she turns to look out the window.

We drive north, through Santa Monica, while I monitor the activity in my rearview. Some cars start following as soon as we pass Sunset, just like I knew they would. I drove this car because it stands out, and on a Saturday morning, after a photo of me had been released, I knew they would be foaming at the mouth for an update. In fact, I'd been counting on it.

"What are you doing?" Cassie asks, lifting her eyes to the rearview. "Someone behind us?"

"Paps," I say and take a sharp turn as the black car that had been behind us gets caught at the light. I zip around the block.

"Does this happen often?"

"Being followed? Sometimes, but usually—"

"No, I mean, any woman photographed with you, people automatically assume you're sleeping with them?"

My grip tightens on the wheel but I don't say anything. I quickly pull into a parking space behind a restaurant on Sunset. I had nearly an hour to think about how I wanted to phrase the idea. Now, I wonder if it's all bullshit.

Cassie lets out an exaggerated sigh. "You said you wanted to talk. *Talk*."

I rub a hand over my forehead, two fingers squeezing my temple. "I had an idea, a proposal of sorts, that I wanted to run by you."

"I'm waiting."

"How much do you know about me?" I ask. "Not *think* you know, but actually know."

She swallows, nervous. I can tell that whatever courage she summoned last night might have been influenced by the number of drinks she consumed. Still, she collects a breath and holds my eye when she delivers the first of many blows.

"I know that people care more about your personal life than your actual career and the last time you made a movie, it sucked."

She stops, trying to gauge the temperature in the car. I clench my jaw but nod for her to continue.

"I know that women who get tangled up with you generally tend to get their fifteen minutes of fame before you dump them aside."

"And you know this?" I ask.

"Yes. My roommate works for *EDaily*."

Fuck.

I lean back, staring out the front windshield.

EDaily, not my favorite news outlet, but a popular one. Their feature broke the scandal that stormed the set of *Sunset City* nearly a decade ago. The truth disguised as a rumor, the one that I've been running from for as long as I can remember.

"What am I supposed to do about the headlines?" Cassie asks.

"Right." I allow a breath. "I have a proposal for you. One that I believe will benefit both our lives, personally and professionally."

"I'm listening," she says, straightening her shoulders.

"You're obviously new—"

"I've been in LA for three years," she interrupts me, irritated.

"I mean, you're new to *this*." I accentuate the last word. "It's hard, trust me. I've been there. Most of us have, and it's nearly impossible to make it on your own. You need me."

"You lost me." She clasps her hands together in her lap.

"Was your booking with Sash your largest modeling campaign?" I ask. She turns away, sulking, which is answer enough. "That's what I thought. I just think that we can make the best out of our situation. I can help you."

"Why?"

"Let's just say, I am invested in a mutually beneficial agreement." She looks at me out of the corner of her eye, but I keep going. "I'm stuck in a rut, career-wise. I am not getting attached to projects that have any potential, and the only studios that want me aren't worth the investment. The big-budget, special-effect bullshit movies they pawn off every few months."

"You know, this might not be a problem if you just showed up to your premieres on time," she mentions under her breath, and something about the comment reminds me of Sash.

I lean back, pretending that it doesn't bother me, what she thinks of me. Pretend like I don't care what anyone thinks of me when, in reality, I use public opinion like a drug, always needing another hit.

"I know it's only a matter of time before the press gets tired of me and the options available to me right now are unsustainable. I need a change, something different. I need something serious to be taken seriously," I repeat Sash's words from this morning out loud.

"Why does your private life dictate what options are available to you?"

"Because image is everything, and if you don't give *them* a story, they will run with whatever the fuck they want, whether it's true or not. You can play the game or let them play you, but either way, that's all it is. A game. And I prefer to be in the driver's seat."

"What are you asking me, exactly?" she asks quietly.

"It would be beneficial, for my personal life, to be seen in a serious relationship, just as it would be beneficial for your professional life to be seen with me."

Her mouth falls open slightly. "So, what? You want to *date* me?"

"Not technically, but for publicity purposes, yes."

"Isn't that just a self-fulfilling prophecy? I mean, you can get anyone you want. Stop fucking around and get an actual girlfriend."

I smile briefly, her eyes drawn to it. "I don't want one, not in the technical sense. I'm not around and don't have time for it." I lie easily and then purposefully deliver an actual truth. "But I like you, and I'm feeling charitable enough to invest some of my time to give you what you want."

"And you know what I want?"

"Fame, fortune. Isn't that what you've been waiting for since you stepped foot in LA? So, let's make it work. I will help you . . . and you will help me."

She's quiet. I can tell that she's mulling over the proposal, weighing the pros and cons.

We can both help each other.

I roll my shoulders when the familiar voice rings through my head. It wasn't hard to come up with this proposition with

Cassie, mostly because I've had experience with it. It's not an unfamiliar bargain; a similar sort of offer had been extended to me at one point in time. I stopped wondering what would have happened if I'd walked away a long time ago.

"So, you're using me?" she clarifies.

I frown, considering it. "I prefer to think of it as us using each other. I believe it's called quid pro quo."

"And what exactly would I get out of this?"

"My time, my resources, my attention." I tell her, ignoring the fact that I'm referring to myself as a product meant to be consumed for pleasure, and then shrug. "Me."

She blushes, looking away. I want her eyes back on me, so I reach out, catching a piece of hair that falls in front of her face. She stops breathing when I tuck the strand behind her ear, eyes wide when she meets mine.

"How would this work, exactly?" She asks softly.

"Well, I have an *Amora* commercial shoot next month. They're looking for a female opposite me. We could start there."

"*Amora*?" Her eyes widen, recognizing the international fragrance brand that I am the Global Ambassador for.

"Yes." I nod. "We take it day by day, but I need you to come to parties and dinners with me. I need the press to take our picture and I need them to think that we are dating."

She swallows, eyes narrow, searching my face for a question that she has yet to voice. I don't interrupt her silence, just wait her out, not breaking eye contact until she eventually shifts, clearing her throat.

"Okay." She says quietly.

I lean back. "Really?"

"Yes, but I have conditions." I wait for her to name her terms as she inhales a breath. "We can't sleep together."

My eyes tighten. "Why?"

"It doesn't matter why," she says. "That's my condition."

I pause before nodding and then reach forward, my thumb

sweeping her chin, brushing her bottom lip while she stops breathing. I smile, pleased that she doesn't seem to be unaffected by me touching her, understanding that there are other private reasons to prevent her from engaging with me, intimately, at least.

"Okay." I agree, but when she starts to pull away, my words stop her. "But, I am going to have to kiss you."

"Have to?" She swallows, looking nervous.

"To make it look real." I clarify

Her eyes narrow as she leans back. "Fine."

"And hold your hand." I smirk.

"Now that's crossing the line," she mumbles. It was a half-attempt at a joke, but I laugh anyways, catching her face softening at the sound of it.

"So, we're doing this. You're in?" I ask, needing her to say the words for me to accept it.

"If my conditions are followed, then yes."

"Good." I nod, turning the car off. "Ready?"

"For what?"

"I'm taking you to breakfast."

"Are you sure this is a good idea?" she asks, hesitantly.

"Not really." I grin, unlocking the doors.

I step out of the car, Cassie following as I lead her towards the sidewalk. I reach for her hand just as we round the corner to the restaurant.

Once we turn, we are swarmed.

CHAPTER 8

Cassie

I scale the steps to my apartment in a daze. When I reach the top landing, I peer over my shoulder, watching Jackson's black BMW slip out of my parking lot. I reach for the doorknob, hesitantly, pushing it open carefully.

I let out a sigh of relief to find the apartment empty. I drop my bag on the floor, kick off my shoes and collapse on the couch in the living room, grateful for some quiet to sort through the chaos in my head. The terms of Jackson's proposal on loop as I carefully dissect each of the words he spoke.

He laid out a literal red carpet, minimal strings attached. He made it clear that it was my choice, but I had no reason to say no. I could have walked away, never to see him again. My name and face would fade, and I would go back to being virtually irrelevant. I hate to think that the press is the one missing piece of the equation on my journey to success, but I have never gotten, and probably would never get, as much exposure alone. With Jackson by my side, I could actually get the break I've been working towards for the past three years.

He was different than the arrogant, presumptuous asshole I met at dinner. I saw a piece of him that I have a feeling he doesn't let very many people see. He was still cocky, but it was a front, hiding this frenetic energy buried well below the surface and I wanted to know why. I wanted to know why I felt like I could trust him when I know I shouldn't.

I remember the color of his eyes, green and clear, light, in the morning sunshine. He barely touched me, brushed his fingers along my jaw, tucked a piece of hair behind my ear and I found myself leaning in without meaning to.

If he came closer, I would have let him kiss me, would have *wanted* him to kiss me and that's why I put the caveat on our fake-relationship. If this is going to be a mutually beneficial business arrangement, there is no need for my heart to be involved.

"Hey."

My eyes fly open, finding Marina at the foot of the couch.

"Hey." I sit up. "I thought you left."

She shrugs. "Heading out in a few, figured you needed a break."

"Thanks. Lucy gone?"

"She went out to lunch with her sister but said she'd be back before dinner and will be foaming at the mouth for an update."

"I bet." I sigh and tug my knees close to my chest, sinking back into the couch cushions.

"You wanna talk about it?" Marina asks cautiously. "Cool if you don't."

"Not yet," I say quietly.

"Okay." She nods. "I'll be back later. Love you."

"Love you," I tell her, waiting for the door to shut and lock behind her.

Once I am alone, I drag myself off the couch to my room. I shut the door behind me, change into sweatpants and crawl back into bed. I pull the thick comforter over my head, hoping that I didn't just make the most catastrophic decision of my career under the influence of Jackson Ridge.

CHAPTER 9

Jackson

It didn't really take long for the media to take the bait. Before the end of the weekend, Cassie's name was published, a few photos from her media roll had gone viral, and we were both moving toward the top of the news cycle.

My misstep last summer at Cannes and my upcoming box office flops are now buried under the pile of scoop the press dedicated to Cassie: old high school yearbook photos, pictures from social media, and a few prints from other projects she had worked on.

The Golden Girl is what they are calling her. All the news is positive for the time being, and I'll have my team monitor the press to make sure it stays that way.

I collapse at the bar stool at the kitchen counter, ignoring the swarm of chaos behind me. It's one of the rare times my house is full. It's stuffed with assistants, makeup artists, stylists. All the fucking noise. I can barely hear myself think, which is different than the times when I'm left here all by myself, too much time to hear myself think. I live my life in extremes, unfamiliar with the grey area. The normality of life is foreign to me.

Sadie, my publicist, is in a tizzy trying to keep up with the story, firing off questions about how we should frame Cassie and our narrative online. I tell her to run with what she thinks is best, but to perpetuate the storyline to confirm credibility.

I don't have many official meetings today. It's the calm before the storm. I'm wrapping the press tour for *Annihilation*, just waiting for the US premiere. Zana flutters around me, snapping updates in my ear, while Nic, my driver and bodyguard, observes, silently, from a corner.

I am propped and positioned while people take my measurements, fitting me for my next suit. My stylist fusses about colors and fabrics. People touch, yank, and pull at me in different directions until the late afternoon.

Only a few of my staff are left when I eventually walk away, needing their hands off me. My dismissal is obvious to everyone but one person.

"Where are you going?" Zana keeps up.

"We're done for the day, yeah?"

"Technically." She follows me into my room, not even blinking when I pull off my shirt. "You still owe me answers."

"All right, go." I order her to run through the list while I disappear into my closet.

"We're due in Santa Barbara in a few weeks for the meeting with Warner Studios. Ken Wallace will be there."

"I know," I say, stepping out.

"I also received a memo this morning from Silas Morland's office. Sounds like he is interested in setting up a meeting." Zana adds this piece of information under a controlled breath.

I know she only told me about this one behind closed doors because she doesn't want it to get out yet. Not until she had the narrative straight so she could control the story.

I've been wanting to work with Silas Morland for the better part of my career. Everyone wants to work with him, not everyone *gets* to work with him. He's the guy behind the studio with more Oscars than they know what to do with. Dodgy and problematic reputation aside, he prides himself on producing quality films.

War epics, moving dramas, nothing with CGI or anything that involves me with my shirt off, parading around set like a piece of meat.

I look up, watching Zana closely. "You say it like it's a bad thing."

"It could be. One wrong move and he can flush your entire career down the drain."

"Careful, Zana." I eye her with a smile. "I might actually start to think you care about me."

"It's my job to care." Her voice is devoid of emotion, and I roll my eyes, translating her message: *You go down, and I go down with you.*

"Book it for two," I say, shrugging into a clean shirt. "Cassie will come with me."

She does a horrible job of suppressing her dissatisfaction. "I should be there."

"It's not a business meeting, just dinner, and I can handle it."

Zana taps her phone against her hand. "How exactly do you imagine this playing out?"

I button up the front of my shirt, peering up at her. "Let me worry about that."

She stands there for a second longer and then starts toward the door, already occupied with something else on her phone.

"One more thing," I call her back before she slips out. "I need you to find the whereabouts of Cassie Taylor."

"I don't work for her."

"Yeah, but you work for me." I toss her a look, adjusting my shirtsleeves.

She gives me a tight smile and then is gone. A few moments later, I get a text message with the location of a studio and then an alert in my calendar for the meeting with Silas the following week.

I let out a forced breath, knowing I can't put off the conversation any longer. I dial the only other person, besides Zana, that I have on speed dial.

"What?" Sash answers on the first ring.

I smile, knowing she's cooled down a bit since we last spoke. If she hadn't, she would have let me go straight to voicemail.

"How are you?" I pick up my wallet and keys, heading toward the hall.

"Fine."

I know that she's just waiting for her entry point after dodging my calls since last weekend.

"Good," I say, nodding at Nic to pick up the bag at the stairs, then follow him out the door. "Listen—"

"Not that you don't already know this, but I just want to remind you that whatever it is you are doing with Cassie, it's a very bad idea."

I roll my eyes. "Noted."

The call transfers to speaker when I slip into my Mercedes. Sash continues to reiterate her point while I pull out of the gate. Nic follows in the SUV behind me.

"Like really, really bad."

"I thought you would be happy," I tell her. "You were the one who told me to get serious. I'm just following through."

"That's not what I meant, and you know it."

"Believe it or not, I didn't call you for a lecture."

"Why not? You could use one."

I let out a frustrated breath, getting to the point. "I'm coming to your show tonight."

"What? Since when?"

"Since now."

"Well, I don't want you there," she says defiantly.

I roll my eyes. "We really gonna fight about this?"

"Maybe we should." She presses and then sighs when I don't answer. "Is it even real?"

I panic at the mere assumption. *Real.* Nothing about me is real. What would I even know about a *real* relationship?

I sigh. "You already know the answer to that."

The silence drifts through the line while she makes me sit with the words. When she speaks next, it's in a small, quiet voice, like she's trying not to scare me off.

"I hate how much she fucked you up."

"Don't," I warn her, fingers tightening around the steering wheel at the reference of *her.* The one person I don't allow myself to think of, dwell on. Sash is the only person in my life who actually knows the truth, and still, she never brings it up, knowing it's a sore subject. "Don't go there."

Luckily, Sash keeps her mouth shut. "I'll make sure you're on the list tonight, but I'm still mad at you."

She hangs up before I can answer, and I realize I'm talking to myself when I eventually respond.

"I know." I say, letting out a deep breath when I let my head fall back against the rest.

Cassie is nothing like me.

I don't have to spend hours with her to know this. If she was like me, she would have gone home with me the first night we met. She wouldn't have hesitated when I offered her everything she ever wanted in my car last week, and she wouldn't have looked unsure about it.

We can't sleep together.

She put that caveat on the arrangement, but even without it, I would never force her to do anything she didn't want to do. That isn't what this is about. I asked why, not to convince her otherwise, but because *I* needed to know, because I was genuinely curious about her answer and wondered if it would have applied to me once upon a time.

The difference between Cassie and me is that I said yes and agreed to everything that it entailed. Ten years later, and I'm still living with the consequences. It follows me with every decision I make.

I suppress the memory and dial Cassie's number next.

"Hello?" She answers cautiously.

The sound of her voice isn't familiar to me, but it causes me to release my grip on the steering wheel, just a bit.

"Hey. It's Jackson."

"I was wondering when I was going to hear from you again." I hear people shouting behind her, voices firing last-minute directions from the shoot that I am en route to right now.

"I wanted to give you a few days to get things under control."

"Under control? Are you implying that I'm incapable of handling myself?"

I smile, merging lanes. "Not really, but I wanted to check anyway. How are you?"

"I'm okay. I've been . . . busy."

"Glad you're getting what you wanted," I say, relieved Cassie doesn't contradict it. "Don't want to keep you. If you remember, I mentioned a party last week."

She's quiet on the other line, but I know she's still there. I can hear the background noise just behind her.

When she finally answers, it comes out soft. "I remember."

"Good. I'll pick you up after your shoot."

"Tonight?" Her voice rises an octave.

"Yeah."

"I mean . . . I'm working now," she says, obviously flustered.

"I won't be there for another hour."

"Well, I have no idea how long it will be before we wrap, so I don't want to keep you waiting."

I suppress a smile. "Whenever you're ready."

"I don't . . . I mean, I don't have anything to wear."

"We'll take care of it. What's your size?"

She sighs after a moment. "Two."

"Shoe?"

"Eight."

"Got it."

She hesitates. A part of me panics, worried that she's going to call it off right then and there, without even giving it a chance, without giving *me* a chance.

"Cassie?"

She allows a breath and then answers. "Okay, I'll be ready."

"See you."

~~~

Cassie's wearing jean shorts, a sweatshirt and oversized sunglasses when I swing around to pick her up. She tugs the glasses down her face, glancing over her shoulder before slipping into my car.

"How did you know where I was?" she asks before I can greet her.

"I had my agent call yours. They worked out the details."

"Your agent knows my agent?"

"My agent knows everyone, which is why she is my agent," I say and then nod toward her. "What's with the glasses?"

"Oh." She reaches to pull them off, then holds them in her lap. "Nothing."

An ache of understanding hits my chest, and my eyes go soft. "If you're trying to hide, baseball hats usually work the best."

Cassie's head snaps up. She looks caught off guard for a moment before she nods, pushing her shoulders back. "Good to know."

I pull out of the parking lot, slipping into traffic. Luckily, we aren't far from the hotel. I fiddle with the radio, trying to find something to fill the silence when I notice Cassie's gaze. Her entire body faces me in the passenger seat. I peek over at her as I land on a generic pop station.

"What?" I ask.

"Nothing." She jerks back, like the sound of my voice had broken her out of whatever trance she had been trapped in. I toss her a look. "It's just, if anyone would have told me that I
~~~

would be in the car with *you* a week ago, I would have thought they were crazy."

"*You*?" I ask with a laugh. "Why does that sound like a bad thing?"

"I'm still deciding," she admits, fighting a smile.

"Keep me posted then," I offer. "What were you shooting today?"

"A catalog shoot. I had it booked a few weeks ago."

I raise an eyebrow, though I can already guess why she said it. She wants me to know that she can book her own projects. I know she can, that was never what this was about. She just deserves to book bigger ones. Cassie might have other jobs on her calendar, but I know the calls she most likely received this week were due to her name being printed next to mine. Not that she's the type of person to ever admit that.

"Speaking of, have you thought any more about the *Amora* shoot?" I ask.

She turns to look out the window. "No."

"Why? Seems like a no-brainer."

"A no-brainer for *you*. I don't want everyone to think that I got the part just because I'm sleeping with you."

My eyebrows tug together. "But we're *not* sleeping together."

"That's not the point, and you know it."

"Then what *is* the point? The best way to move up in any career is to network. Half of the jobs booked in Hollywood are because of nepotism or favors. I don't see how this would be any different."

"I know you don't," she grumbles under her breath. "That's the problem."

I exhale, crossing two lanes of traffic quickly. We are pulling up to another light when Cassie's phone lights up in the center console.

LUCY

MARINA SAID YOU BAILED ON MOVIE NIGHT! ARE YOU WITH JACKSON? IF YOU ARE, MAKE SURE YOU ASK HIM. . .

The message trails off and Cassie snatches the phone quickly.

"Sorry," she says, swiping the message away. "Just my nosy roommate."

"Is this the nosy roommate who works for *EDaily*?"

She fidgets in her seat. "Yes."

"You didn't tell her about—"

"Of course not!" Cassie exclaims, looking offended that I would even ask.

My shoulders relax. "Do you trust her?"

"I do," she says.

I look over to see her eyes set and I wonder what it would feel like to trust another person with the same force Cassie seems to trust her friends.

I cut into another lane of traffic, staying quiet for another minute or so. My fingers play with my bottom lip while I think about how her *EDaily* connection could work for or against my favor. I still don't have an answer when I turn to look at her.

"You can't tell her anything. My private life, any information I tell you, is completely off-limits. I can't have anything personal published other than what I want them to see. Do you understand?"

"I understand." She nods quickly.

I hold her gaze for another moment longer, and as soon as the light turns green, the car jolts forward, tires screeching while we cross another lane of traffic and pull into the circle drive of the hotel.

Cassie stumbles when she gets out of the car, eyes up, taking in the extravagant building in front of us. Her wide-eyed wonder is enough to squash the anxiety that bloomed a moment ago when she referenced her connection with *EDaily*.

She follows me while I lead her through the lobby. Once inside, I nod toward Nic when I spot him waiting for us.

"All good?" I ask.

"Good." He hands me the hotel key cards. A man of few words, something I appreciate.

"Cassie, this is Nic."

"Hi," she says timidly, arms behind her back. He offers a slight nod and follows us inside the elevator.

"My bodyguard," I explain while she eyes the looming figure behind us apprehensively.

When we reach the suite, there is a rack of clothing options waiting for us. Pleased with the setup, I turn, expecting Cassie to be right behind me, but she disappears onto the balcony.

I forget about the shock-and-awe factor of my life. I've become so numb to it over the past ten years I've been in the spotlight. The suite is nice, top floor, decorative, a little gaudy for my taste, but it works. Cassie enters like she just walked into a penthouse suite in Las Vegas.

She leans over the railing, taking in the courtyard below while the sheer curtains blow in the soft wind. I lean against the doorway, arms crossed over my chest and I realize it would be peaceful to view the world from her eyes. When she eventually turns, she is beaming, and it does something to my heart. Makes it race, I guess.

"Follow me," I say, motioning her back to the main room. Cassie trails behind, coming to an abrupt halt when she spots the rack of clothing. "You said you were a size two, right?"

She walks over in a daze. There are at least a dozen options, and although I assume she has seen racks like this before at photoshoots, her reaction tells me it's been nothing along the lines of these designers. She tentatively reaches out a hand, careful to brush her fingers over the fabric.

"*Jackson*." Her voice drops, and I fight a smile. "What is this?"

I take a seat in the chair across from her, crossing an ankle over my knee. "Options."

"I can't wear these."

"Why not?"

"Because I can't afford them."

I shrug. "But I can."

She does her best to glare. "You're an idiot if you bought all of these just to impress me."

"Come on, admit it, you're a little impressed," I tease.

A smile tugs on the corner of her mouth, but she turns around again so I can't see it.

"Try them on, all of them if you want. Whatever you want, it's yours."

She hesitates before picking a few outfits to try on before hauling the hangers over her shoulder, heading to the bathroom. As soon as she disappears, my phone buzzes, a message from Zana.

ZANA

Silas calling soon.

I stare down at the message a moment longer, and then my phone rings. I hate that my palms become sweaty, that I have to allow two deep breaths before I answer.

"This is Jackson."

"Jackson," he greets me in a low, booming voice. "Silas Morland, how are you?"

"Good, yeah."

I lean forward in the chair as Cassie steps out, wearing flare pants and a white top with feathers along the collar. She hesitates when she sees I'm on the phone, but I just nod. She turns in front of me, looking for my approval. I shake my head, too many feathers. Cassie smiles, obviously on the same page, and goes back to change.

On the phone, Silas starts boasting of his illustrious career that I already know about, everyone knows about, while I nod along. People like Silas are powerful but needy, and they always need their power to be understood and constantly reinforced.

He keeps talking while my attention falls to Cassie peeking around the corner again, this time in a bright-orange top and matching pantsuit. My mouth contorts into a grimace, and I stick my tongue out. Cassie laughs, not even bothering to step all the way out into the room.

"All that being said, I'm looking forward to our meeting next week," Silas brings the conversation back around. "We work with serious people. It's why I am reaching out now."

"I understand."

"I can't deny that I am fascinated to hear why you of all people are looking to leave behind the industry that made you your millions."

"Not leaving anything behind, just looking to pursue other options."

"Yes, well, we are interested to see if the Jackson Ridge stock can translate into our business, as long as it remains lucrative for us."

"Of course."

Cassie steps out, hands tied behind her back, and I am glad my conversation is wrapping so I can give her my full, undivided attention. I start at the ground, eyes working up her body. She's wearing tall boots, a short silver dress, and a black blazer. She looks nervous, waiting for my opinion, but I can tell that she likes it. So do I.

"I look forward to meeting you, officially," Silas says by way of goodbye.

I stand, walking toward Cassie. "Likewise. Talk soon." I pull the phone away, stopping just in front of her. "That one."

She peers up at me under her lashes, giving me a look that makes me want to find a way to get her into the California King behind us.

"Why are we staying in a hotel tonight?" she asks.

"So they can see us come back together." I tell her, pushing some hair over her shoulder. "I'll be staying across the hall. I left the key to your room on the table."

She pulls back, like she is just now remembering the caveat she put on our arrangement. "Okay. Good."

I duck down to find her eyes again, making sure she is still okay. "I'll meet you in the hallway, then? An hour?"

"Sure."

I linger for another moment in the suite, her answer not really convincing me. I don't think I hurt her, but I realize that I never want to ever come close.

CHAPTER 10

Cassie

It took me a few minutes to collect myself after Jackson left. He barely touched me, just looked at me with those cool green eyes, and he had my entire resolve crumbling. It wasn't until he told me that he would be staying in the room across the hall tonight that I remembered why I am even here. I remember why he dragged some unimportant, nonexistent woman to this hotel. He needs to *look* like he has a girlfriend to be taken seriously.

Outside of the mention of a party and the clothing options available to me to wear for the night, I have no idea what to expect, other than people will be there, watching us.

I tighten my hold on my clutch and turn the doorknob to my hotel room, bumping directly into a hard surface.

"Miss Taylor."

I look up, recognizing Jackson's bodyguard. "Oh, hi." I adjust my hair. "Sorry."

"My apologies." Nic steps backward to allow for some space between us.

I realize he had been standing guard outside *my* door, like I was the precious cargo. I straighten the hem of my dress and spot Jackson on the other side of the hallway, fighting a smile.

Before getting into the car with him this afternoon, I hadn't seen him in five days. I may have additionally stalked him on social media and accidentally watched all five seasons of his old teen soap opera, *Sunset City*, but we hadn't spoken until this afternoon.

I knew about *Sunset City*, the show that put him on the map, I just had never invested the time to sit down and watch all of it. It's one of Lucy's favorites. She has the full DVD set. So, this week, I binged all forty episodes, staying up until the early hours of the morning, watching on my laptop. I even shed a tear when his on-screen girlfriend passed away.

Jackson was young when the TV MA series premiered. So much younger than I thought. I know *Sunset City* was the start of his career, but Jackson couldn't have been older than seventeen when he first appeared on the show. He was also way more talented than I originally gave him credit for. Not that I will ever say *that* to his face. His ego is plenty big without my added compliments.

Jackson waits for me, leaning against the wall, and despite staring at him in his car the whole way here, the sight of him nearly takes my breath away. His face belongs on billboards that line the Boulevard. Tan skin, full lips, strong jaw. He's tall and lean, not super bulky, but sturdy, strong. I stare and can't find a single flaw. He looks like the type of perfect most people spend their entire career pretending to be.

I feel unstable, even from a distance. Being around him makes me feel like I just swallowed a gulp of champagne. Skin fizzling, head dizzy, bubbles *everywhere*.

He smiles, pressing his tongue to the inside of his cheek and nods towards me. "You clean up nice."

"Likewise." I follow him down the hall to the elevator. "You ever going to tell me where we're going tonight?"

"What would you say if I told you it's a surprise?"

"I would say it's been nice knowing you," I threaten, narrowing my eyes.

He tips his head back, laughing, and the sound of it makes my heart flutter. People could become addicted to the sound, and I have a feeling he doesn't laugh very often. "Fair enough. We have a car waiting for us downstairs, and then we are headed to a rooftop."

"And what will we be doing on said rooftop?" I ask, stepping into the elevator beside him.

He leans against the wall, hands in his pockets. "What are your thoughts on going to a runway? Sash's walking tonight."

"Really?" A genuine smile spreads across my face.

"Really."

I've never been to one before. My modeling history has strictly been commercial, but even I knew walking in a show would become necessary. I panic, realizing that we're going to a runway, in Hollywood, which means there will be opportunities to network. Tonight will be work-focused.

When we step out of the elevator, I have to rush in my boots to keep up with him through the lobby. A few people turn their heads, but luckily, it's mostly empty. He approaches the black SUV, holding the door open for me. I pause outside of it, arms crossed, refusing to get in.

"What?"

"I have a few more questions," I say.

"Fine." He sighs, rolling his neck. "Go."

"What designer?"

"Stella Harper."

"How many people?"

"Small, about three hundred, tops."

I swallow, anxiety creeping into my voice. "What if I fuck up?"

He drops his chin. "You won't actually be walking. You know that, right?"

"You know what I mean." I roll my eyes.

He shrugs. "You won't fuck up."

"How do you know?"

"Cause I've already seen you under pressure." His finger appears under my chin, lifting it slightly. "You'll be fine. Can we get in now?"

"Fine," I relent, climbing into the SUV.

Jackson's phone rings about five minutes into the drive, and it doesn't stop buzzing from there. He's on a call with his agent from what it sounds like, recapping whatever conversation happened in the hotel an hour ago. He doesn't really do much of the talking, just intermittently grunts his approval.

I stare down at my phone in my lap. The only messages I have are from Marina and Lucy demanding to know where I am. I sent them both a note that I wouldn't be home tonight, to which Lucy immediately responded, asking if I will be with Jackson, of which I have decided to ignore.

I try spotting recognizable landmarks when the car slows. Will people be waiting for us? Will they take our picture? I am obsessing over the possibilities while I twirl the rings on my fingers.

"Hey." Jackson's voice interrupts the silence, our eyes meeting across the back seat of the car. "You know I got you, right?"

There is something earnest about his tone, serious. The joking mood from this afternoon has evaporated, and he's looking at me like he wants me to trust him, needs me to.

"Why?" I blurt out the question.

"Why what?"

"Why me?" I ask. "Why would you waste your time?"

"I would never waste my time with anyone the least bit unexceptional."

I frown. "The only thing exceptional about me is that I am exceptionally average."

"I disagree."

"Every other modeling company begs to differ."

"Let's change their minds then, shall we?" He reaches out his hand, prompting me to take it, tempting me to trust him. I hesitate before placing my hand in his. "You said this was allowed, right?"

"Yes, this is allowed. But there are no cameras."

He smirks. "*Yet.*"

I follow his eyeline out the window, spotting the swarm of photographers waiting at the front doors. My heart starts racing when I lean forward, trying to contemplate how all these people could be here for me. Well, us, but *me*.

"Deep breath," Jackson instructs as the car rolls to a stop, eyes still on me. I force in a short, quick gasp of air and then squeeze his hand. "You can do this."

I nod, willing myself to believe it.

The second we step out of the car, we are swarmed. The camera flashes temporarily blind me as I bring my free hand up to cover my face, shielding my eyes. The rapid-fire of light and onslaught of noise is enough to cause a seizure. How the hell does he handle it?

I peek up at Jackson. His head is down while he leads us to the front doors. People are yelling, but I can't make out a coherent sentence or question being thrown in our direction. Just when I fear I might actually have a panic attack, Jackson's thumb swirls softly on the back of my hand. The small reassuring gesture is enough to force me out of my head and find time to breathe. He keeps me close to his side, using his body to shield me from the ravenous media.

I let out a heavy breath when the doors close. My ears are still ringing when I check over my shoulder to see them pressed against the glass, cameras still flashing.

"Keep walking." Jackson tugs me forward. I skip a few steps to keep up, following him into the elevator. "You good?"

I swallow but can't form the words yet, so I just nod. He studies me for a few more moments and must decide to accept my answer.

A breeze hits when the elevator doors break apart, and I stare out across the rooftop. Los Angeles sparkles just beyond us. The sunset fades over the ocean as night falls over the city. A low-fi beat flows through the speakers. It's soft enough that you can still hear bits of people's conversations spread out ahead of us, but loud enough to mask the content.

It's eerie, the effect that Jackson's presence has on a crowd. It's almost like a shift in the wind or a drop in temperature. Whatever it is, it's something you can *feel.* Eyes lift, bodies turn to find us, to find him. Slowly, one by one, conversations end, people attempt to subtly stare, their gazes locking in on their target, but Jackson doesn't seem to notice or care.

A few people are brave enough to greet him while we pass, but he just nods, brushing past them. His hand goes to the small of my back, guiding me to keep walking forward, only letting go when we reach the bar.

"Good evening, sir," the bartender greets us at the counter. "What can I get for you?"

"Whiskey neat and . . ." Jackson looks at me, raising an eyebrow.

"Prosecco." I order the classiest drink I can think of.

Jackson leans against the bar, looking out at the rooftop beyond us. People at least have the common decency not to stare when Jackson turns, but I can't tell if he notices that up until that moment, everyone had been looking.

The drinks are deposited quickly, and as soon as I grab mine, Jackson steps close to me. I look up at him, feeling lightheaded being so close to his body. He smells like expensive cologne, rich and powerful, and I instinctively lean in.

"Drink it fast," he says under his breath.

"Why?"

"It will make you less nervous."

I lift the narrow flute to my lips and take a long sip. The bubbles make my eyes burn, and I cough, clearing my throat. Jackson raises a finger to gesture for another, and by the time it's deposited in front of me, I have finished the first. My mouth is tart and I feel the sudden rush in my legs.

"Ready?" he asks, extending his hand for me to take.

I suck in another breath and nod before he leads me to a group gathered by the railing. Eyes lift before we get too close, and people start their greetings.

A woman with short gray hair and large, pink-rimmed glasses kisses Jackson on his cheek. "Jackson, always a pleasure."

"Diana, likewise." Jackson's arm wraps around my waist, pushing me forward. "This is Cassie Taylor. Cassie, Diana is the editor in chief at *Cosmopolitan.* Cassie is friends with Sasha. They recently worked a campaign together."

"What sort of work have you done? You know, we're always looking for new, emerging talent." The woman sips her cocktail.

"Oh, well mostly catalog shoots. I actually just wrapped a shoot for *Power Beauty* with Sasha."

"We recently partnered with *Power Beauty* for an advertising opportunity. Maybe we will be seeing each other more in the future."

"That would be great!" I beam just before Jackson snags my waist, pulling me away.

"Great to see you, as always," Jackson says goodbye and then leads me to another group to network with.

As we mingle, I feel as if I left the old Cassie behind and stepped into this newer, shinier version of myself that people like more. I kiss people's cheeks, shake hands, smile along as the people I meet boast of their powerful connections and impressive books of business. Just before we leave, I plug in a lead for myself, hoping that they will remember my name after the night ends.

Everyone seems to flock to Jackson, admirers, acquaintances, strangers. Every single person that he introduces me to has worked with him in some capacity. They seem content with my association not to ask further follow-ups. He is loved, that much is clear. Based on his reputation in the media, I realize, with surprise, he is also respected.

It's late when we are finally led to the runway. My hands are clammy when I take my seat, photographers point their cameras in our direction before the lights dim. I squirm again, turning away.

"All good?" Jackson asks. It's the first thing he has said directly to me since we ordered our drinks nearly an hour ago.

A part of me wants to tell him that I feel like a fake, a shadow superimposed onto someone else's life, stealing their moments and making them my own. I want to tell him how undeserving I feel to be here, but I don't because I'm not sure I have the right words to articulate it yet. So instead, I throw on a smile and nod.

Jackson places a hand on the top of my exposed thigh. His breath tickles my ear when he whispers, "You look beautiful tonight."

I pull back to study him. I'd been told I was beautiful my whole life, but somehow the praise coming from Jackson gives a new meaning to the word because Jackson's whole life is full of beautiful things.

A spotlight appears on the stage as an electric club beat reverberates through the floor. I lean forward when people appear on the runway, walking toward the edge of the pool.

There is something mesmerizing about the supposed perfection. Every angle thought out, every detail discussed, every pose precise and practiced. There's a degree of perfection attached to every bit of the show, which is what drew me in initially. When we model, we get to create our own stories, transporting us to new worlds, landscapes dictated by the designer. It's beautiful, and I'm captivated by the art being created in real time in front of me.

Sasha paces down the runway with a straight face in nearly four-inch heels, never faltering. Even as the song transitions and a new assortment of outfits emerge, I'm so entranced by the entire display that I forget where I am for a moment.

When the show ends, I follow Jackson to another group of powerful people who have the ability to change my life, but this time, I stay quiet, unable to shake the feeling that I am an imposter who doesn't belong.

Eventually, Sasha joins us. She tosses Jackson a scathing glare that I want to ask him about later and then pulls me in for a hug.

"Congratulations!" I greet her. "You were amazing."

"Thanks!" She smiles, spotting Jackson hanging in our peripheral, and then tugs me further away. "How are you? Everything okay?"

"Yeah." I shrug, trying to act normal. "Why?"

"When I left you at dinner last week, I would have thought the two of you were at war with each other."

"I don't know." I turn, noticing Jackson watching us, and then look back at Sasha. "We're just . . . hanging, I guess."

"Casual?" Sasha eyes me. I take another long sip of my drink to delay my response. "Well, no one knows the meaning of casual better than Jackson." Someone tugs Sasha's arm to pull her back to the group. She waves and turns back to me. "Thanks for coming. I'll stop by later, okay?"

"Sure, yeah," I say before she is pulled away.

I finish the rest of my drink, mulling over Sasha's comment which sounded more like a warning than encouragement. Jackson is still tied up in a conversation, so I use the free moment to get some air. I check my phone, spotting a new message from Lucy.

She sent me a picture from *EDaily*. Jackson and I sitting front row, captured just after he called me beautiful. We are both smiling, both seemingly in love. I stare at the picture, trying to find the line between fantasy and reality. I swallow when I realize it's harder to locate than I thought.

I pocket my phone and stare out at the city beyond me. I am so transfixed by the view that I nearly miss someone approaching. I tense in surprise when I feel a hand at the small of my back.

"You've been quiet."

Jackson appears over my shoulder. He leans backward against the railing, staring at me like I am vastly more interesting than the spectacular view of Los Angeles beyond the rooftop.

"Just taking it all in."

"You're not having fun?" he guesses. The soft tone of his voice causes me to meet his eye. His face is wary, waiting for my response.

"No, it's not that, it's . . ." I sigh, choosing my words carefully. "It's just . . . I sort of feel undeserving to be here. I feel like a fluke."

His eyebrows tug together at the same time his jaw tightens. Feeling like I owe him an explanation, I continue.

"It's not that I'm not grateful, I am. It just doesn't feel like this moment is mine? I don't even know if that makes sense." I look away, shaking my head and wishing that I'd just kept quiet.

"You deserve to be here," he says, capturing my attention again. "I saw your prints. I've seen your work. You have every right to be here. The only difference is you just aren't allowing yourself to believe it."

I pull back. "You've seen my work?"

"I did my research." He steps forward while I gaze up at him. "You think I do this all the time? Bring people with me for the sake of making connections? I don't. I see talent and potential, and I see all of that in you."

My face warms. In some ways, it's everything that I've been waiting my whole career to hear. My fears of not being good enough have always been there, but hearing the words from Jackson, I start to wonder why I even felt anxious at all.

His hand cups my jaw, tilting my face up to look at him. My eyes immediately fall to his mouth, to his lips, bottom heavy, in the most perfect way.

"I want to kiss you," he says quietly.

I lose my breath a bit when I look into his eyes. "Do people always do what you want?"

"Yes." He smiles quickly, the beauty of it distracts me, while his other arm slips around my waist. A certain hunger glimmers in his eyes when his hand coasts up my back to my neck, holding me there.

"Hmm." I let out a sigh, leaning further into his body. He stays still, like he is waiting for permission. "You can kiss me," I say, leaning forward on my tiptoes, lips grazing the shell of his ear. "But only because people are watching."

"I'll take what I can get," he says, softly.

His thumb brushes my bottom lip before our mouths meet. The kiss is gentle, more careful than what I had been expecting. His lips are soft, yet firm, and I can taste the whiskey on his breath. I am startled by the safety I had not expected to feel in his arms. The kiss isn't rushed. It feels planned, like Jackson Ridge had been made to kiss me. The way his lips meet mine in a soft caress has me begging for more. Instinctually, I lean in. I'm on my tip toes, pushing against his chest before I register a camera flash over our shoulder.

The spark of it snaps me out of whatever fantasy I'd been trapped in. I pull away, suddenly feeling like a prop, and step back from the ledge. I didn't realize how close I was until he touched me.

"Cassie." Jackson's eyes follow me.

I spin on my heel, rushing toward the bar. "I need a drink."

Unfortunately for me, everything after that drink is blank.

CHAPTER 11

Jackson

I am lying on my back when I wake, blinking to adjust to the morning light. I rub my eyes, lifting my head when the sheets rustle beside me.

"*Shit.*"

Cassie grabs my shirt off the floor before scampering into the bathroom. I wipe a hand across my face and piece together the night before.

From the moment we left the rooftop, Cassie had been drinking like a fish. Not sure why, but I figured it's not a habit because she handled her liquor poorly. We left the bar around 2 a.m., and I helped her up to her room before she asked me to stay.

My heart caught at the question and I wish I had a reason why. I've been asked before and never felt the need to, but something about the way she looked at me was different. She didn't want me to stay to use me, she just wanted me to stay. So, I did.

I lay there for a few more moments, rubbing my chest, thinking back to the kiss on the roof last night. I thought about it way longer than I should have. It was just a kiss, a fucking great kiss, but it's not like our clothes came off or anything. I've kissed more girls than I can count and for a reason that doesn't make sense, nothing's even come close to it.

It didn't feel rushed, it felt practiced, rehearsed, like I'd kissed her a million times before. Cassie pressed her chest into mine, melted into me and had me fantasizing about what she would let me do if she did trust me. The small sound she made when I touched her, tilted her face toward mine, until the camera flash spooked her.

I need to remember that she isn't numb to it like I am. I forget what it feels like to care about personal privacy, to ignore all the staring and pointing that makes me feel like a zoo animal. I forgot until she pulled away and then proceeded to get hammered, which tells me that it bothered her more than she would ever admit.

The faucet from the sink kicks on and I step out of bed, wandering toward the bathroom.

Cassie is brushing her teeth, glaring at her reflection, when I lean against the doorframe. She freezes when our eyes meet in the mirror, as if she's just now realizing that she is standing there, in my t-shirt and her underwear.

"How are you feeling?" My voice is deep, thick with sleep.

She bends towards the sink, spitting out the toothpaste, and then turns to me with her eyes closed. "How bad was I? On a scale of one to ten?"

I rub a hand over my face. "You know I have no frame of reference."

"A guess then."

"I don't know." I sigh. "A six."

"A *six*?" Her eyes bulge.

"Calm down. You were fine. Everyone at the after-party was hammered. I doubt anyone even noticed."

It's LA. No one really pays attention to anyone besides themselves anyway. Still, I'll have my team check to make sure that *if* someone did publish an unflattering photo, it would be scrubbed and substituted with another.

"Why did you stay with me?" she asks.

I smile briefly, looking up at her. "Because you asked me to."

Her cheeks darken and she looks down at the ground.

I hadn't planned on staying. The reason I got the room across the hall is so that I wouldn't have to sleep alone, something I hate doing, and there had been a girl at one of the parties who had been giving me these eyes that told me I could get exactly what I wanted.

I forgot about all of that when Cassie asked me to stay.

"Well, thank you," she murmurs back.

"I need a shower, and I'm sure you do too. So, unless you want to do that together as well—" Her head snaps up, and when she sees I'm teasing, she gives me an exaggerated eye roll. "That's what I thought. Do you want something to eat before we leave?"

"Sure."

"Good. I'll call up room service. Meet in my room in an hour?"

She nods, and I grab my things before exiting her room, replaying over the words I said to her last night while I carried her to bed. I don't know where they came from, but I know I meant them.

"It's okay. I got you."

~~~

Cassie steps out onto the balcony off my hotel room in the same jean shorts she had been wearing yesterday. She takes the chair across from me, tucking her feet under her. She seems relaxed, and I like the idea of what it might mean, like she is comfortable enough to be herself around me. Most people aren't.

I stare at her across the table, no real reason other than I want to look. Her light-brown hair flows over her shoulder, and I remember the rose scent of her perfume on the pillowcase when I opened my eyes.

I'm surprised she isn't wearing any makeup. It's not that she needs it. I'm just not used to seeing someone so fresh-faced. The
~~~

wind brushes her hair over her eyes, and she uses a hand to push it back, catching me watching her across the table. As soon as our eyes lock, I look down at my phone.

The photos of us last night had been posted from the angle that I had been hoping for. They were using the images from the rooftop. Us, front row at the show, kissing on the balcony, then leaving together, her hand in mine. I wonder how she feels about all the attention, she hasn't told me one way or another.

I filter through all the messages I missed yesterday, scanning for details to give me an indication of my schedule this week, when I notice Cassie still staring.

"Did you call the paps on us last night?" she asks.

I shrug. "Technically, my publicist did."

"Do you do that often?"

"I've done it before, but not often."

"Why?"

"It's easier to control the narrative when you're in the driver's seat. If I call the shots, I say what runs."

It's a philosophy I had been selling to myself for the past few years. It provides greater control, or at least the perception of it. When she frowns, I can tell she doesn't buy it.

"What was up with you and Sasha last night?" she asks.

I roll my eyes and answer vaguely. "A difference of opinion."

She waits, sighing when I don't give her anything else. "Is that all you're going to say?"

"It's all you need to know," I tell her.

She sits up straight. "I was thinking, we really don't know a lot about each other," she says. I raise my eyebrows, not hearing a question. "Don't you think people are going to start asking?"

"Unlikely."

"Shouldn't I know something about you other than whatever assumptions I can come up with?" I ignore her, looking down at my phone. "How about I name a rumor I've heard, and you tell me if it's true or not?"

I peer up at her and then pocket my phone, allowing the distinction. "All right. What have you got?"

She twists her lips, trying to come up with one of the thousands of different rumors people have published about me. I lean forward, sort of interested in which one she thinks of first.

"Do you have a third nipple?"

I tip my head back and laugh. The question catches me off guard, as does my laughter. I can't remember the last time I've done it without it sounding forced. She smiles, watching me, resting her chin in her hand while she waits for an answer.

"No, I don't," I say, still smiling when I reach for my drink. "Where did that rumor come from?"

"Bad paparazzi photo from Hawaii when we were filming *Sunset City*."

She smiles. "Did you really party with Leo in Ibiza?"

She pronounces it wrong, but I don't correct her. "Yes."

"Well!" She waves me on to continue. "How was it?"

"Technically, I think I'm still under NDA." I smile, recounting the memory. Don't remember much of it. I was wasted most of the trip. "It was epic. That's about all I can say."

"I bet." She leans back in her chair and fires off her next question far too casually. "Is it true that you slept with a producer to get a job?"

A jolt goes through my body, one I know she sees. I have to roll my shoulders to relax and force myself to look her directly in the eye when I eventually answer.

"Mm-hm."

She sits up straight, her mouth falling open slightly. I can tell that she had been hoping it was a rumor. Me too, actually.

"When?" she asks, trying to meet my eye again, but I glance toward the skyline of Los Angeles, squinting when I answer.

"It was a long time ago," I say quietly.

"Jackson, I—"

"I don't regret any of the decisions I made to get me where I am today," I say, cutting her off, warning her not to pry. I keep the memories of those years locked away in a box that I threw away the key to a long time ago. It would do no good resurfacing now.

"I read you grew up in California," she tries again.

I lean back in the chair and just stare at her, losing interest in this game as a dark rain cloud settles over my consciousness.

"You implied that you have siblings. What are they like?"

I make a noise under my breath and reach for my phone. I didn't come here to talk about my personal life. Don't have time for it, actually. When it becomes clear that I am not going to fill the silence, Cassie clears her throat.

"My dad died on a day like this," she says, looking off to the horizon. "He had been sick for a while, so it wasn't really a surprise. It was a sunny day, our last trip to the hospital, and it made me think that the weather would predict some sort of miracle that we had been expecting since his diagnosis, but I was wrong. He passed away just before we got there."

I sit forward. Despite growing up worlds apart, the story resonates with me in a way I wasn't prepared for.

I shake my head. "What happened?"

"Lung cancer. He was a smoker."

"Is it just you and your mom then?"

She nods. "Her family is from Indiana, so it was nice to have the support, but it's essentially just the two of us now."

I reach for my drink again but don't say anything else. I know she wants me to reciprocate, allow a moment of vulnerability like the one she showed me, but I can't. I wouldn't even know where to start, so I stay quiet.

Another moment later, she blows out a breath. "You know, if we are going to spend all this time together, I may need something besides Google to point to as my source of truth."

"You are aware you just told me your friend works for *EDaily*, right?"

"I also told you that anything you tell me will stay between us."

"You're essentially asking me to trust a stranger."

She smiles, tipping her head. "Imagine that."

I sigh, rolling my eyes and quickly spit out the Wikipedia facts she apparently needs from me. "I'm from Sacramento. I have two older brothers and a stepfather. That about sums me up."

"You're supposed to give me something I can't find on Google," she presses, but when I don't break, she sighs. "You're the youngest? Why am I not surprised?"

"That obvious?"

"I don't know," she says, leaning back in her chair. "I guess I would have to get to know you better before I make assumptions." My lips twitch into a half smile. That smile is immediately squashed when she asks a follow-up. "What about your mom?"

The questions shouldn't hurt, and yet I feel as if I just had the wind knocked out of me. "She died when I was sixteen."

"I'm sorry," she offers, but I avoid her gaze. "Your dad?"

"Not in the picture." I end the conversation just as the door swings open.

Trays and platters descend upon us while I sit back. Cassie's eyes widen at the abundance of food left for us on the table. I didn't know what she wanted, so I ordered one of everything on the menu.

I try to note what she likes and what she doesn't. She drinks her coffee with milk, but no sugar, and picks at her food until she sees me reach for something, as if that means its fair game. She tosses a few more questions my way, each harmless but edging toward the border.

"So, about *Amora*." I tap my thumb on the table to take control of the conversation again. "I have to let my people know."

She stabs a strawberry with her fork and pops it in her mouth as if to delay her response. "Describe this to me again. You know I've never done a commercial before. I could be shit at it."

"One, it's a men's cologne shoot, so sorry to break it to you, but it's mostly gonna be about me." I toss her a grin. She crumples napkin from her lap and lobs it at my face. I catch it easily. "Two, it will be shot here, in LA, and there's going to be a scene of you in a house and a pool. Twenty seconds of film time. And three, yes you can do it, and you won't be shit, because it's all mind over matter."

"That's your big argument? Mind over matter?"

"You seem to have missed points one and two."

"It's not that simple, and that's exactly my point."

"Okay fine, maybe it isn't." I sigh, trying to see her side of this. "Look, you gave me conditions for…" I trail off, noting the blush staining her cheeks when I reference whatever the fuck it is that we're doing. "Whatever. If you gave me conditions for this too, would that make you feel better?"

"Probably." She tilts her head to the side, biting the side of her lip, drawing my attention to her mouth. "I would consider it *if*!" She cuts me off before I can say anything else. "*If* I audition with everyone else. I don't just want to be given the part. I want it on record that I showed up for the audition and I want their honest feedback. You can't intervene. Deal?"

"Sure." I concede, extending my hand. She reaches for it, and I take her hand in mine, my thumb rubbing gently along the inside of her wrist before she pulls away.

I lean back in my chair, chewing on the end of my straw. Cassie holds my gaze for another moment before her eyes drop, blushing again. I know that there is something else she wants to ask me.

I bend my head down a bit to meet her eye. "What is it?"

"Nothing." She sighs, shaking her head before reaching for her coffee.

I know it's not fair of me to demand answers when I've been resisting every question she's thrown my way this morning, but very rarely have I not gotten what I wanted, and it bothers me more than I care to admit.

CHAPTER 12

Cassie

It's almost impossible to ignore Jackson the days following the runway. Every time I open social media, I am bombarded with pictures of the two of us together. I haven't actually heard from him outside of a few texts scheduling our next outing together with cameras, all initiated by his publicist. He's essentially gone radio silent on me, deferring to someone else to coordinate plans, yet he is still so unavoidable.

Jackson was right. I am oblivious when it comes to the media. Maybe it's because I know that there really isn't anything extraordinary about my life . . . other than the fact that Jackson Ridge now took up a large chunk of it. Luckily, for now, the comments online are mostly ones of curiosity. The outlets are desperate to discover who I am and what I am doing with Hollywood's most in-demand actor. Honestly, I've been asking myself the same questions.

I crash on my mattress and pull up the links that have been spammed to my account, courtesy of Lucy. She's been adamant about alerting me to potential stories, some coming from sites I've never even heard of.

JACKSON RIDGE AND CASSIE TAYLOR SIT FRONT ROW AT STELLA HARPER SHOW—CLICK FOR THE CUTE CANDID.

CASSIE TAYLOR'S SATURDAY GRUNGE LOOK AND HOW YOU CAN RECREATE IT.

THE GOLDEN GIRL: FROM HOMECOMING QUEEN TO HOLLYWOOD HOTTIE.

The last headline makes me cringe. I wonder if I need to go back over my social media posts over the years, removing old images that are more embarrassing than flattering. Somehow, someone had dug up a photo of me from Homecoming over six years ago.

I breeze past all the headlines that mention my name and instead browse a few with Jackson's, coming across a topic that stands out among the rest.

JACKSON RIDGE PLANS TO MEET WITH SILAS MORLAND, IN TALKS TO STAR IN WORLD WAR I EPIC.

I read through the article. It spends a lot of space covering Jackson's recent missteps. Box office bombings, his skipped Cannes premiere. It does end on a slightly more positive note, and I wonder if these conversations are somehow possible because of what we're doing. He said he needs something serious to be taken seriously. Maybe this is what he wanted.

I roll over on my bed, holding my phone against my chest and stare up at my ceiling, my mind wandering back to last weekend. I had been drunk when I passed out next to Jackson, but that didn't mean that I didn't feel everything as I drifted to sleep on his chest.

I felt safe with him, for a reason that didn't entirely make sense, but it hit me again that next morning. My head on his warm, sturdy chest, his arm wrapped around my waist, holding me there like I was something valuable to him.

I am still contemplating what it even means when my phone buzzes. I swipe into the message, reading Jackson's latest text, shocked that this one seems like it actually came from him.

JACKSON

You should post a photo of us from this week-end.

We haven't texted since Monday, when his publicist arranged a dinner for tonight. Outside of saying yes, the conversation had pretty much ended.

CASSIE

Why? There are enough photos of us.

JACKSON

Because there should be a photo of us posted by us. Not from the media.

I haven't posted anything that directly led to the assumption that he and I are dating. Even one post feels too permanent. Who knows how long our staged relationship will last. If I post the photo from the previous weekend, it will be cemented in time forever, and that scares the shit out of me.

CASSIE

Why don't you post then?

JACKSON

It will look better coming from you.

I clench my teeth. *Of course,* it will look better coming from me. It will also look desperate.

I swipe out of his message, scrolling through the photos in my camera roll. There are a few from the rooftop and the after-party. I swipe through a few options to find a suitable contender. I'm standing next to Jackson at the bar, looking up at him. I can't remember exactly what we had been arguing about, but it had been harmless. I can tell by his smile and my half-hearted glare. His arm around my waist, pulling me towards him.

Instead of posting a photo of us first, I decide to camouflage it in a photo dump with several other pictures from the weekend, placing the photo of Jackson and I last. If people do see my post, hopefully, they won't scroll through to find it.

I open my social media app. Even more alerts appear in the top portion of my screen, notifications of mentions and messages that I don't bother to read. I flip to my profile, staring at my follower count. I am close to 50,000 now. 50,000 strangers want to follow my life.

I caption the series *LA Weekends x.* My heart hammers in my chest when I submit, and as soon as it's live, I close out of the app.

CASSIE

Posted. Hope you're happy.

Jackson's response appears a few seconds later, and his rapid response time is sort of mind-boggling. I've seen his phone before. He has at least 100 notifications on his message app every time he opens it. I shouldn't be at the top of his response list.

JACKSON

Last photo? Really?

Another notification from Jackson hits my phone. He re-posted the image of us on his story. Any attempts at disguising our relationship are immediately squashed while I watch, in real time, as my likes multiply. I shut out of the app just before I reach the three-thousand-mark threshold, venturing out to the living room.

"Is it normal for celebrities to call the paparazzi on themselves?" I ask, collapsing onto the couch.

"Not if you are actually relevant." Lucy snorts and then lowers the screen of her laptop, peering over it. "Why?"

"Just curious. Jackson mentioned that he knows people who do." I can tell that Lucy has another follow-up question prepared, so I change the subject. "What should I wear to dinner in Beverly Hills?"

Lucy leans forward at the same time Marina reaches for the remote, turning down the volume on the TV.

"Going out in Beverly Hills on a Friday night? That's like paparazzi porn. You are totally getting photographed again tonight," Lucy says.

"This is like date three, right?" Marina asks.

"It's just dinner. We're casual." I say it, more as a reminder to myself at this point.

"He took you to a rooftop fashion show. That's not casual. That's spectacular," Lucy counters.

"I bet the sex is amazing." Marina sighs, resting her cheek in her hand.

"Loads better than Noah," Lucy adds, and I roll my eyes. "You don't have to answer that. I already know."

"You liar. You couldn't hear anything."

"Exactly." Lucy raises her eyebrows, and Marina coughs out a laugh.

I pick up a pillow and toss it at her, but she catches it easily.

"Come on, Cass. You have to give us some details." Lucy sets her laptop aside, letting me know that I have her full attention and that she will not let me out of the conversation until I give her something.

I sigh, leaning back against the couch, and decide to just

focus on the smaller details. I could give them part of the picture without lying, I think . . .

"Oh my god, oh my god!" Marina shrieks, looking at her phone. "*Hey Marina, it's Noah.*" Marina begins reading the message aloud, pausing to look up at me for dramatic effect. "*I'm not sure if Cassie changed her number, but I have been trying to get a hold of her for the past few days and haven't heard back. Can you have her give me a shout? Thx.*"

"What the fuck!" Lucy yells.

"He has most definitely seen you out with Jackson and wants you back!" Marina squeals in excitement.

"Has he texted you?" Lucy asks.

I shake my head. "Marina set up blockers on my phone last week."

"*Can you have her give me a shout?*" Lucy cackles, kicking her feet up and down.

"Revenge plan is 100 percent working." Marina high-fives Lucy.

"I'm dying," Lucy exclaims dramatically. "He is totally coming back for you after your latest *rebound.*"

"Jackson's not a rebound." I shake my head, cringing at the thought of Jackson being someone's rebound. He is someone's dream, nothing less.

"Really? Then what are you doing with him?" Lucy asks.

I know Lucy doesn't mean it *that* way, but I can't help but feel the insinuation. What the hell would Jackson Ridge be doing with someone like me? I think it too, all the time. Even with this ridiculously organized PR relationship, I still can't fathom why he chose me. It's probably what the rest of the world is thinking anyway.

"You know what, I don't know what we're doing, and I don't care." I clap my hands together. "I'm just going to enjoy it. Fuck Noah, and help me pick out a dress for tonight."

"I'm pretty sure you could wear a garbage bag over your head and it would appear on the cover of *Style Now*." Marina calls over her shoulder as she leads the way into my bedroom.

"Can you wear Crocs tonight? I've been waiting for them to make a comeback, and this could finally be their chance!" Lucy claps her hands together, skipping to keep up.

I roll my eyes, suppressing a smile before rifling through my closet, sorting through the limited options I have.

CHAPTER 13

Jackson

I'm already in a shit mood when I slide into the back seat of the dark SUV. Tonight's dinner with Silas has to be perfect or the future of my career might just get swept away with the tide. It's an emotion I've been struggling with for the better part of the decade. I have incessant anxiety, knowing that one wrong move, interview, film, and my entire career could be ruined. There is already a long line of no-name nobodies clawing their way to the top. I can't get left behind.

"Good day today, Mr. Ridge?" Nic asks when I am settled in the back seat. It's his usual way of greeting and the only words we generally exchange.

"Ask me three hours from now," I order in a cool voice.

I've networked before, but most of it had been casual interactions at parties. Business meetings, dinners, these are the sort of gatherings that can fast-track any decision. They also happen to be the thing that I hate doing the most.

I've spent the past decade creating a brand for myself. I've taught the tabloids what to expect, walked the carpet that Zana rolled out for me all those years ago. I accepted that version of my fate for that point in my life, but now, it's time for the public's perception of me to change.

I know I have a mountain ahead of me to climb and will probably spend the next five years untraining the media while I work to rewrite a new narrative, one that I actually want to be a part of. And that all starts now.

Tonight, I will be playing the role of a serious actor, one I've always felt unequipped to play.

I can't fuck it up.

The unrest clangs through my head, bouncing back and forth between my temples, creating a dull headache resting behind my eyes. I open the window a crack, allowing a bit of fresh air, and lean against the back seat.

My fingers tighten into a fist as I channel all my frustration into my hand. I can feel the tension cord up my arm. I repeat the motion while I close my eyes, allowing smooth, even breaths. Focusing it into something small, something controllable.

It's been my defense mechanism for the past ten years. The anger welling up inside me, threatening to break through, causes me more harm than good. My go-to outlets are usually a couple rounds at my gym, a stiff drink, or burying myself inside a stranger. None of those are options now. After a few minutes, I let my palm open, exhaling deeply. I stretch out my fingers and then shake my hand.

I know it's a bad idea, but I want something to distract myself, so I flip out my phone, checking the trades, scrolling, consuming all the shit people write about me, good and bad. I comb through all the garbage, and wish that I could stop. I hate how much it means to me. The anonymous words alter everything I do, what I think, how I feel. When they're up, I'm up, and when they're down, it's like I can't remember the color of the sky anymore. That's how far I can fall.

I wish it didn't mean anything to me, wish it didn't mean *everything* to me.

I flip my phone off, hating that I even looked in the first place. Instead, I focus on the studio team that will be at tonight's dinner. There was no direct business meeting per se, but everything I do and say will be evaluated under a microscope. I roll my shoulders if only to loosen the pressure when the car glides to a stop.

Nic pulls the door open for Cassie, and I notice two others standing on the stairs, bent over, trying to peer into the back seat.

"Hi!" Cassie smiles widely, sliding in beside me before Nic shuts the door.

I grip the door handle when I am hit with the subtle scent of her rose perfume. It's enough of a distraction, coupled with the dress that she is wearing. It's smooth and hugs her in all the right places. The light, velvet green brings out the warm color of her hazel eyes. Her thick brown hair flows over her shoulder in soft, styled waves.

She's stunning. It's hard to imagine how she could be so insignificant in the realm of Hollywood, and at the same time, I could have everything I wanted. The reminder hits me suddenly, burrowing deep in my chest. I cheated to get to where I am, that's why. And I've spent the last decade of my life trying to feel worthy of a job that only manifested through pure luck.

"Who are they?" I lift my head toward the girl with curly, dark hair and the short blonde, lingering on the staircase.

"Oh, those are my roommates, Marina and Lucy. They didn't believe that we were . . ." Cassie trails off, her cheeks turning pink. "You know."

I roll my eyes and go back to my phone.

We're both silent most of the drive to dinner. Cassie stares out the window, fidgeting with her hands. I can tell that something is bothering her, but I don't have the mental capacity right now to consider why or even ask.

"Who's coming to the dinner tonight?" Cassie finally breaks the silence as we near the restaurant.

"No one you know."

"Anyone I should be prepared to talk to—"

"No, this dinner is for me. Industry people," I answer quickly, pocketing my phone.

"Oh. Okay." Cassie mutters the next sentence under her breath. "Maybe they will be in a better mood."

I snap my head up. "What?"

She turns her shoulders to face me, head on. "You know, I had to trade shifts at work to be here tonight. If you just want to parade me around, give me a heads-up next time. Then at least I won't try so hard."

I blink, trying to identify what I had said to make her feel that way. "That's not what I want."

"Then why are you treating me like portable arm candy?"

The answer gets caught, and before I can say anything else, we round the corner into the parking lot, cameras already waiting for us. I suck in a short breath, clenching my fist before turning away. I know Cassie needs an answer, she is owed an answer, but I can't give it to her right now, so it will have to wait.

"Do you want me to pull into the back?" Nic asks.

"Front is fine," I answer.

The car comes to a stop, and when I reach for Cassie's hand, she hesitates. It's only for a second, but I see the indecision flash in her eyes, as if she is questioning whether she should not only get out of the car with me, but if she should be here at all. I incline my head slightly and after another moment of pause, she places her hand in mine. I rub my thumb along her smooth skin just before Nic opens the door.

As soon as we are out of the car, we're crowded again. I keep her next to me, using my body to shield her from anyone who gets too close. I keep tabs on her out of the corner of my eye, afraid there is going to be a breaking point, when Cassie will look up at me or this life that I threw her into and will decide that it's not worth it. That *I'm* not worth it. I look for signs every time we are together.

She lets out a sigh of relief once we're safely inside. The floor of the lobby is dark. The large dining room in front of us is decorated in rich blues and steely silvers. The tables are spaced out, allowing for privacy between parties, creating the illusion of intimacy.

"Mr. Ridge, thank you for dining with us tonight," the hostess greets us, batting her fake eyelashes dramatically. Cassie makes a sound in the back of her throat, and I can imagine her rolling her eyes, but I ignore them both, looking to the full table just beyond us, counting the number of studio executives that surround it. "Follow me."

I use the contact of Cassie's hand to center myself as we walk through the restaurant floor. She turns, taking in the people who don't have the common decency not to gape with their mouths hanging open as we pass.

I gently tug her forward. "Don't stare."

She frowns up at me. "*They* are staring at *me*."

"Relax." I lean down, lips brushing her ear. "They're staring at me."

I pull back, smiling when I find her glaring up at me, then squeeze her hand again as we approach the long table filled with at least ten people. Only two seats left at the end, directly across from one another.

"Jackson." Silas Morland stands, shaking my hand. "Glad you could make it."

He's surprisingly short for someone with such a looming presence in Hollywood, and when I pull my hand away, I feel an incredible urge to take a shower just to rinse the entire exchange off me.

"Appreciate the invite." I force a smile, noting Silas set his sights on Cassie. A predatory sort of smile spreads across his weathered face, and I feel the need to shield her from those eyes.

"Miss Taylor, I presume?" He extends his hand. "Silas Morland."

Cassie takes it gracefully, forcing a smile, though I doubt he can tell the difference. "It's nice to meet you."

"The pleasure is all mine." Silas lifts her hand to his mouth, placing a kiss on the back of it. I stiffen at the gesture and don't allow a breath until he lets go. As soon as he releases her hand, I swear she wipes it on the side of her dress. "Please, join us."

"Thank you." I nod, taking a seat beside him.

Introductions happen quickly, and drinks are ordered. I am grateful for the glass of whiskey in my hand to act as a sort of calming agent, so I am more prepared when Silas eventually turns to address me.

"The famous Jackson Ridge," he begins. My stomach flips when he says it, but I work to keep my face neutral. "It's hard to believe we've never officially met."

"I appreciate you taking the time. I know how busy you are."

"I always have time for potential. Zana mentioned that you were in the business of redefining your narrative." Silas smiles, but the gesture does nothing to placate the unease resting in my stomach.

"Did she?" I take a sip from my drink, noting that Cassie is listening. She looks down the table, but when she brushes her hair behind her ear, I know that she is hanging on every word. "And what exactly did Zana say?"

"She sung your praises, of course. That's what all good agents do."

I force a smile, waiting for the catch. "But?"

"But." Silas smiles again, brushing a hand across his jaw. "She reminded me of the gamble, financially. If we were to pursue a business relationship, there would have to be guardrails. You understand. Studios betting on risks need to be compensated."

Tit for tat, quid pro quo. What will the studio get out of betting on me? A pay cut, a smaller role, something to lessen their financial risk. That's all I am these days, a financial risk.

"Aren't you in a position to persuade them to see otherwise?" I ask, even though I shouldn't.

"Perhaps if we were speaking on better terms. Initial projections of *Annihilation* don't seem promising, or have I misread?"

It's a threat, to let me know they are watching. I crack my knuckles under the table and force another smile.

"It's still early."

"It *is* still early," he agrees with a grin that makes me feel uneasy. "Why don't we regroup at the end of the summer?"

"Of course." I nod. "I'll speak with Zana and circle back."

"Certainly." Silas looks across the table, turning his full attention on Cassie. "And you, Miss Taylor, any interest beyond photography? I trust you would find acting more compelling work, keeping your clothes on to make a living."

I tighten my fist under the table, but before I can step in, Cassie leans forward.

"You give me too much credit," she says with an artificial grin. "I prefer to leave the acting to the professionals."

Silas laughs under his breath, reaching for his drink when she looks away. "I like her," Silas says to me quietly, a statement that has me clenching the table.

Cassie doesn't acknowledge me the rest of the night, making conversation with a forced smile. I suffer through at least two more hours of small talk, listening to the rest of the table boast of their own self-worth while I pretend to pay attention. Cassie has been watching me out of the corner of my eye throughout the night, but the second I go to meet her gaze, she turns away, pretending she hadn't been looking in the first place.

When we stand to leave at the end of the night, I worry Cassie might walk out of the restaurant, leaving me behind now that she sees what I have to do to get the things that I want, but she surprises me, reaching for my hand as we leave. We step outside together, into the chaos of the cameras, before slipping into the SUV to take us both home.

I struggle to find the words in the back seat of the car, but I know I have to break the silence somehow. Cassie's eyes flutter as she looks out the window, and just before she lets them fully close, I clear my throat.

"Thank you," I say and her eyes fly open. "For coming tonight. I know I didn't give you a warning, and that wasn't fair. I just . . . I needed to go, and I hate going to those things alone." I loosen the buttons on the collar of my shirt, giving myself room to breathe.

She lifts a brow. "Is that your version of an apology?"

My lips twitch upward. "Yes."

"Well, I appreciate the attempt. And yes, you should have told me."

"I know." I sigh, dragging a hand through my hair.

Cassie turns to face me. "Those people we had dinner with tonight, are they friends of yours?"

My eye twitches briefly. "More like industry professionals."

"But, you spend a lot of time with people like them?"

"Yes." I narrow my eyes at her. "Why?"

"No reason." She shrugs, but I continue to look at her, needing an answer. Eventually, she releases a short breath. "I guess it sort of makes sense to me now, why you are the way that you are."

"Successful, famous, popular?" I try to alleviate the tension with a joke.

"It makes sense why you came looking for someone like me," she says quietly.

I swallow, letting the blow hit me. "You don't have to worry about me."

She frowns, head tilting. "Who else does?"

The question lingers in the quiet, and I obsess over the words. Not sure I've ever let anyone get close enough to wonder what might be on the other side of the picture-perfect life that I made for myself. I'd hate for anyone else to realize that it isn't enough.

I change the subject. "You didn't eat much."

She wrinkles her nose. "Caviar and escargot don't sound appetizing, ever."

"Did you even try it?"

"I don't need to. It's disgusting."

Sensing her imminent departure, I fire off a suggestion

before I can change my mind. "Are you still hungry? We can go somewhere."

"Are you serious?" she laughs. "They just dropped, what, a couple thousand dollars tonight, and you want to take me out for another dinner?"

"If you want, I would, yeah," I say, mostly because I don't want her to leave yet.

"You don't have to . . ."

"What do you want?"

Her cheeks turn pink. "I could go for a burger."

"*In-N-Out* over a Michelin-star?" I grin.

"Nothing beats an *In-N-Out* burger."

"You might be right," I say and lean toward the front seat. "First one you find, Nic."

There is something completely juvenile about ordering cheeseburgers and fries through a drive-thru window. I can't remember the last time I even ate fast food, but Cassie was right; it's better than the overpriced dinner ordered for the table. More comfortable as well, despite us both being in evening attire in the back seat of my car.

"The man we met with tonight, Silas?" Cassie asks, reaching for a fry. "Why do you want to work with him?"

"It's not just him. It's his team, his studio. He is a producer with connections. Connections I need if I want to be seen as something else, someone new."

"You have connections too. You have, what, a dozen movies on your résumé? Do you have to work with someone so . . . slimy?"

"It's not the same." I shake my head, frustrated. "You don't get it."

"Then help me to." Her eyes soften. "I'm entering an industry that I have no idea how to operate. I need to know what to do in these types of situations. How do you handle people like that?"

"Don't worry. It won't happen to you."

"Why not—"

"Because I won't let it," I snap, holding her eye.

She leans back, brow wrinkling, as if I just gave some piece of myself away that I hadn't realized. An answer to a question that she had been looking for. I let out a breath, preparing an apology when her fingers gently brush my wrist, flipping it over to hold my hand.

"You're a good guy, Jacks. I don't know why you pretend not to be."

Jacks.

I falter, staring at her. I can't remember the last time I heard my name without tacking Ridge on the end of it. I like the sound of it entirely too much.

"Jacks?" I ask.

She shrugs. "It's just a nickname. Would you prefer it if I called you Jackson Ridge all the time? All proper?"

"No, I wouldn't." I grin, shaking my head. "I like it."

"Good." She smiles, pleased with herself.

She lets go of my hand, reaching for another fry, and I hate the absence of her touch. My hand feels cold where it felt warm in her embrace a moment ago. We finish our burgers, stuffing our trash into the bags. It's nearly midnight when we pull into her parking lot.

"Well, this is me." She unbuckles her seatbelt after we come to a stop.

"Cassie?" I lean over the middle seat, calling her back just as she reaches for the door handle.

She turns to face me. "Yeah?"

There's just a whisper of a breath between us. Her lashes flutter, and I wonder what she is thinking. The way she looks at my mouth makes me wonder if she wants to kiss me. I want to kiss her, but I can't. I can't because she doesn't lean forward any further, and I won't take what she won't give.

"The first night we met, I made a cheap shot at your career. It was wrong, and I shouldn't have said it." I apologize, holding her eye.

"It's okay." She shrugs slowly. "I'm used to it."

"That doesn't make it right, and I am sorry," I say the words again, wondering if she recognizes that I rarely think them, let alone give them out willingly. "I don't think of you in that way, I hope you know."

"I know you don't." She smiles and then leans forward, kissing my cheek softly.

I completely freeze. The gesture is so tender and gentle and one I hadn't been expecting. I feel like a boy on the playground who just had his first kiss. My skin is warm where her lips had been, but before I can form a rational thought, she slips out of the car.

My eyes are glued to her figure. I watch as she scales the steps to her apartment, reaching for her keys. I don't look away until she disappears from view.

"Good night tonight, Mr. Ridge?" Nic asks from the front seat.

I snap my gaze back around, realizing that I had been caught staring. I look ahead in the rearview, noting the suppressed smile on my driver's face.

"Home, Nic."

CHAPTER 14

Cassie

The past week and a half passed in a blur. If I wasn't being poked and prodded on set, I was being harassed and taunted in the nightclub. Although my social media post had garnered a couple thousand additional followers and an insane amount of likes, now that I had begun associating myself with Jackson, it was hard to disassociate. And it was all anyone could talk about.

Whatever Jackson had promised me weeks ago seemed like a lie or something like it. The perks were there, I just hadn't thought about the consequences that came along with them. However, the main point of his agreement was being delivered as promised. I have work, even better, consistent work. My schedule is becoming so busy a part of me has even considered quitting the club, which has become . . . suffocating.

I am crowded every free moment, fending off questions and rumors, like the concept of privacy ceased to exist the moment Jackson held my hand. The people I had thought were my friends have been given an edge, and being around them has turned my supposed comfort to claustrophobia.

"What's he like?" My coworkers crowd me.

"I heard he's into three-ways," another chimes in.

"Is he like . . . big?" Amy's eyes widen with a slick smile.

I stuff my things into my locker, pushing past them to the floor.

"I'm running late." I pick up my tray while Amy trails behind me.

"Come on, Cass." Amy slides to my side, resting a hand on her hip. "You know you can tell me anything."

"I know I can," I lie. "There's just not a lot to say. I'll catch you later."

I shoulder past her to the floor. My tables don't seem to recognize me, but every step I take, I worry that eyes are following me. I catch Amy's glare over my shoulder, and my insides squirm when I realize that the people I had once called friends are now nothing more than windows to the press. Anything I have ever told them, I realize in encompassing dread, is now fair game.

It is nearly 1 a.m. when I clock out, and there isn't anything more exciting than going home to my warm bed. I pull my hair into a ponytail after I climb into my car and finally look at my phone. I have a message from Jackson from over an hour ago.

JACKSON

Ready for tomorrow? Want me to pick you up?

I ignore the text for now, blast the air conditioning, and pull out of the parking lot. I've been so busy between jobs for the past few weeks that I almost can't believe my *Amora* audition is tomorrow.

I opt for silence on the drive home, conversations from the club floor replaying in my head as I attempt to compartmentalize the short list of people I had considered close, now gone in the blink of an eye. The sudden invasion of privacy has me clutching the steering wheel with so much force, my knuckles go white. How does Jackson do this all the time? I can already feel myself losing grip, and it's only been a few weeks.

It's nothing compared to the years Jackson has had to battle through the trenches.

My eyelids are heavy when I pull into my parking lot. I round the corner and slam my foot on the brake when I realize there is a Mercedes occupying my reserved parking spot. A Mercedes that never parks in Seaside Apartments.

I throw the car in park and fling open the driver's side door. Anger and frustration surging through me with such force, I'm tempted to get back into my car and ram his Mercedes in the bumper.

"What the hell are you doing here? This is my parking spot!"

"I can see that." Jackson smirks, leaning against the side of his car. "You didn't text me back. I had a feeling you were bailing."

"I didn't text you back because I had to drive home from my six-hour shift after working another job this morning. I haven't showered in twenty-four hours, and I am exhausted, so I'm sorry that I didn't text you back within the designated time frame, but that doesn't mean you can just show up at my apartment at one in the morning!"

He tilts his head. "You're not bailing?"

"No." I roll my eyes because out of everything that I said, that is what he latches on to. He hesitates like he still doesn't want to leave. "Look, I'm really tired, so did you just drive halfway across town to ask about the audition tomorrow, which we could have covered over the phone, or are you coming inside?"

The left side of his mouth pulls up into a half-smile. "But you weren't answering your phone . . ." I narrow my eyes and he must know well enough to back off. "I'll park and meet you upstairs?"

I sigh dramatically before tossing him the keys, making my way around the car and up the stairs into my apartment.

Luckily, the lights are off, which means that Marina, and most likely Mark, are asleep in her room. Lucy is out of town, thank *god.* I can handle Marina, but I know that Lucy would have a heart attack if she spotted Jackson anywhere in this apartment.

Which reminds me, Jackson is about to step foot inside my home. I never even entertained the idea that he would be in our kitchen, let alone in my room.

I grab all the clothes on my bedroom floor and throw them in my closet, closing the doors behind me. I start tossing trinkets and small things that cluttered my desk into the drawers. I cringe at the sticky glow-in-the-dark stars on my ceiling, but nothing can be done about those now. I am a few seconds away from a minor panic attack when I hear the soft knock at the front door.

There are a few scenarios that I never had the creativity to even imagine. Opening the door to my tiny apartment on the south side of Santa Monica to see Jackson Ridge waiting for me is something my wildest daydreams wouldn't have even allowed me to entertain. Yet, here he is, leaning against the doorway, looking so perfect, it makes my heart ache.

I grab the front of his sweatshirt and yank him through the door, before anyone can see, towing him straight toward my bedroom, switching the lock behind us. He falls back on my bed, resting his arms behind his head, getting comfortable on my full-size mattress.

"Okay, here is what's going to happen, I'm going to shower and change out of these terrible clothes." At the mention of my uniform, his eyes travel down my body, taking in my crop top and army skirt. "Hey!" I snap my fingers, and he slowly brings his eyes back up to mine, a smirk proudly displayed on his full mouth. "Just . . . don't touch anything. I'll be right back."

I shut the bathroom door and immediately flip on the shower, eager to rinse the day away. I quickly wash my hair and scrub the grime on my arms and face with soap and water. I hop out, dry myself, and run a brush through my long hair.

Jackson is across my room, studying the framed photograph on top of my dresser, when I step out. I cross my arms over my chest when I see that stupid smile sneak its way up his face as he takes in my less-than-sexy pajama set that consists of lacy shorts and a white tank top.

"Shut up," I cut him off.

"I was just going to say I like your pajamas," he says, smothering a smile.

"Mm-hm, sure," I mutter sarcastically and lean up against my desk on the other side of the room.

Jackson grabs the picture from the dresser, pointing at it. "This you?"

I sigh. "Yes."

I never liked that photo of me as a teenager. I had bangs, braces, no sense of style, and it's right around the time I shot up nearly six inches overnight.

"You were adorable," Jackson teases, and I take the frame out of his hands, studying the picture taken nearly a decade ago. "Is that your dad?"

My eyes fall to my dad's arm around my shoulders. It was the picture he kept on his desk at work, gifted to me when he passed. That's the real reason why I kept it, proudly on display.

"Yeah," I say, resting the frame on the desk behind me.

Jackson nods, reaching for another photo on the dresser. An old Polaroid I forgot had even existed. "Who's this?"

"Okay, show-and-tell time is over." I stomp forward, snatching the image of Noah from Jackson's hand, tossing it in the trash.

Jackson raises an eyebrow, obviously looking for more information, but I change the subject.

"You gonna tell me why you're here?" I ask.

He sighs, crossing his arms over his chest. "I thought you might want some pointers for tomorrow."

"Pointers? Are you implying I can't handle myself?"

"Not at all. I just have this huge bias as to who I want them to cast with me, and I'm feeling charitable enough to give some tips."

"All right." I fight a smile. "Point away."

"Come in and introduce yourself right away. Let them know

that you are in control. That's what they are looking for. Ask questions about the brand, the vision. All the people in that room were a part of creating the storyboard. They want to talk about it."

I nod, cataloging all the recommendations, things that weren't even on my mind. I had been practicing, posing, imagining that's what most of the audition would be for anyway. Jackson's pointers are helpful not just for this audition, but for others down the line.

"Will you be there?" I ask.

"I'm the Brand Ambassador." He rolls his eyes as if the answer is obvious. "Yes, I'll be there."

"Will you be watching?" My voice shoots up an octave.

"Yes."

I tense, processing the angle that he just threw in that I wasn't expecting and stare over at him. "Are *you* nervous?"

"Not particularly." His eye twitches.

"Really?" I ask, not believing him.

He sighs. "It's the first campaign in the contract. I have two more to complete after this and . . ." He turns, giving me a view of his profile, his jaw tight. "I've just had a shitty track record recently. I can't blow this."

He cares. I don't know why that piece of information shocks me, but it does. The entire persona that he has portrayed to the media up to this point is that he doesn't care. He shows up late, skips out on premieres, appearing for red carpets with various girls on his arm, never the same more than once. It never occurred to me that Jackson would care, that he would relate to the nerves I feel before an audition or a shoot.

"Well." I clear my throat, offering him the piece of encouragement I would want to hear if I were in his position. "I believe in you."

His mouth tugs upward but it looks like it was forced, made with effort. For the first time tonight, I take him in. His shoulders are slumped, head low. Jackson looks tired, not just like he had a long day, but a rough month, year.

"Would it be okay if I stay tonight?" he asks.

His anxiety is still palpable, but maybe more sedated. My mind rushes over the question that I asked him last week after dinner. Who does he have to care about him? The fact that he showed up at my place in the middle of the night leads me to believe that he doesn't have anyone.

"Okay," I agree before pondering the implications.

Jackson nods, reaching to pull off his hoodie while I slide under the covers. Even though I had been on the verge of passing out on the way home, a new rush of energy shoots down my spine when Jackson, now shirtless, finally joins me. I reach for the light switch, flipping it off.

"You said you came from work?" Jackson asks quietly, and I roll over to face him. Although it's dark, I can still make out his features in the shadows. "Where do you work?"

"*Avenue*."

"A club?" he asks. "I didn't know you worked there too."

"I thought our personal lives were off-limits?"

"I didn't say that. I just implied mine was."

"Oh, great!" I say, laying on the sarcasm. "Glad we've established that you have double standards. How am I supposed to convince anyone that you're my '*boyfriend*'"—I make sure to add air quotes—"if you don't tell me anything about yourself?"

"You should have added 'exceptionally handsome' before the word *boyfriend*," he says with a smirk. "And don't use it in quotes. I don't want people to get the wrong idea."

I glare at him. I know that he is trying to get a rise out of me. He sighs after a moment, brushing the hair off my cheek.

"You know more than most," he admits softly.

My eyes flutter when he touches me. His rough fingertips trace the edge of my cheek before they disappear once again. I realize it is going to be very hard falling asleep beside Jackson, I'm too aware of his presence. So, I decide to keep him talking, trying to wear myself out. My mind goes back to my latest interactions at the club tonight. The people I had counted on as friends who have become insistent for information.

"Jackson?" I roll over on my side, looking up at him.

"Hm?"

"How do you separate the people in your life who actually care about you from the people who just want to use you?"

He answers with a heavy sigh. "I'm afraid I had to find out the hard way."

"What happened?"

"There was a story that got out. A private one that was better left buried."

"Someone sold it?"

"Mm-hm." He nods slowly, eyes far away.

"What was it?"

He looks at me, scanning my face like a visual lie-detector test, like he is asking himself whether he can trust me.

"Remember that rumor you asked me about? If I had ever slept with someone to get a job?"

I nod, keeping my eyes on him, even when he looks away. He sighs, turning over on his back, staring at the ceiling when he answers.

"I slept with a producer to get signed as a series regular on *Sunset City*. I'd been afraid I would lose out on the role, that they would write me off or decide not to renew my contract. I don't know how it got out, but it did, and I just sort of dealt with it."

I'm still processing his confession when he adds another blow.

"I can't really complain. It gave me everything I wanted." His voice sounds like a dead thing when he finishes, like he lost the conviction.

I don't believe it, but I can see how it would be tempting to buy the lie that everything you did was worth it to achieve your dream. I would guess his secret sits heavier with him than he will ever admit.

"How old were you?" I ask into the dark.

"Eighteen."

My stomach sinks. He had just been a kid. Who was there to look out for him? To protect him? I look up at him, wondering, in some fucked-up way, if he is using a part of this agreement to protect me since there had been no one there for him.

He glances over when he recognizes my silence. "Don't look at me like that." His voice is suddenly harsh.

"How am I looking at you?"

"Like you feel bad for me. Don't. In hindsight, the story is what put me on the map."

My eyebrows tug together. "But it hurt you."

He swallows, the only indication that he heard me. I roll over on my back, chest feeling tight, and look up at the ceiling.

It makes sense why Jackson doesn't see a problem with the dynamic that we are operating in. He's managed a similar landscape and survived. He probably can't imagine a scenario where anyone would feel any different.

"How did you move forward?" I ask. "When the story leaked?"

"I learned who I could and couldn't trust. I had to prioritize what was most important to me, and I didn't look back."

Like me, Jackson has built an entire career off playing perfect, but he doesn't understand the difference between perfection and reality. To me, there is nothing more freeing than stepping off set and back into my own life. I study Jackson and realize there is no distinction for him. He plays perfect all the time, terrified someone will uncover his secret, that he's human.

I forget to take another breath when he lifts his hand to my cheek. I know it's his way of changing the subject. For someone who thrives in the spotlight, he shrinks under this type of attention.

"You smell good." He sighs.

I let out a hum under my breath, my eyes feeling heavy. Instinctively, I move closer. His hand drops to my shoulder, coasting down my arm, leaving goosebumps trailing in its wake.

"Is this okay?" His question surprises me. Jackson seems like the type of person to take what he wants, when he wants it.

"Yes." I breathe softly.

I brace myself when his hand comes back up to the side of my face, cupping my cheek. When his thumb brushes my parted lips, I lose the ability to breathe for a moment. My eyes close, focusing on his fingers dancing across my skin, forcing myself not to entertain the concept of them exploring anywhere else on my body. A sudden, desperate heat travels from my neck to my belly. His hand brushes from my shoulder down my arm and then drops to my waist. My hips lift slightly, following his touch. It's harmless and soothing, and what concerns me the most is that I don't want the feeling to dissipate.

Too soon, his hand drops from my waist. I open my eyes to find him looking at me, an unreadable expression across his face. He swallows and then rolls over on his back. We both stay quiet, just the sound of our breathing in the dark.

"Why did you really come over?" I ask softly.

He's quiet, sorting through an answer before he speaks. "I didn't want to be alone tonight."

I look up at the cheap glow-in-the-dark shapes on my ceiling before I reach down, taking his hand in mine, lacing our fingers together.

"Anytime you need someone to talk to, I'm here. Okay?"

He squeezes my hand back. "Okay."

I turn my head at the same moment he does, our eyes locking, and then I move, curling up against him. His arm drapes over my waist, holding me there, and I fall into a deep sleep, for the second time, by his side.

CHAPTER 15

Cassie

I wake the next morning with Jackson still in my bed. A part of me imagined that I dreamed the whole thing up, but he's here, beside me, still asleep. I roll over, tucking my hands under my cheek, and look at him. He's lying on his back, his head tilted close to where mine once was on the pillow. He has one arm across his bare chest, his mouth parted slightly, breathing in and out.

He looks so handsome, even in sleep. I wonder how many times that face has gotten him out of trouble, made apologies seem miraculous, impossibilities seem believable. His tousled blond hair falls just over his forehead. My hand itches to push it off his face, run my fingers through it.

Last night cracked a small part of the riddle I had been trying to solve. I don't look at Jackson differently or with pity, like he accused me of. I just understand him a little better, why he does the things that he does, why he is the way that he is.

Dishes clatter in the kitchen, and Jackson stirs beside me. I move before he opens his eyes to find me ogling him, shivering when I emerge from the covers. After sleeping with wet hair from the night before, my hair falls in messy waves over my shoulders.

"Morning." Jackson's voice is thick with sleep. I turn over my shoulder to face him. He is leaning back on his elbow, dragging a hand over his face while my eyes catch on the look of his bare chest that I slept next to last night. "What time is it?"

I force myself to look away before I get caught staring. "Almost nine."

"Shit." He reaches for his phone, scrolling through the unread and unanswered messages. A frown forms the longer he stares.

"Bad news?"

"Not the best." He grabs his hoodie, throwing it on over his head. I admire the sight of his chest one last time before it disappears from view. "How'd you sleep?"

"Really well, actually."

"Me too." He says, looking right at me, and I have to remind myself to breathe. He's attractive in the light of day, but the way he looks when he wakes up is downright sinful. Hair messy, voice deep and then a lazy smile appears in the corner of his mouth. "Your hair is curly."

I blush, brushing the frizzy waves out of my face. "Oh, yeah. I usually try to tame it, but I didn't have the energy to do anything with it last night," I mumble, breaking eye contact, and throw my hair up into a clip. "Um, I have a spare toothbrush in the bathroom if you need it."

He nods, making his way to the tiny, shared bathroom I would have never sent him to if I knew Lucy was here. I can't imagine *that* wake-up call. Marina is here, most likely with, Mark, seeing as they rarely do anything without each other, but I can handle them.

I take a breath and run through the options of how I want to play this when Jackson steps back into my room, looking like a waking dream with his irresistibly messy hair.

"I hate to tell you, but my roommate is awake, so unfortunately, there is no avoiding the oncoming inquisition," I warn him.

"I guess I'm just going to have to meet her, then." He smirks, dragging a hand through his hair, and my belly does a little somersault when his sweatshirt rides up.

"I'm just warning you," I say.

Jackson smirks when he notices my eyeline. He steps forward, our chests nearly touching. "I think I can handle it."

Standing this close, I can smell the leftover cologne on him from the night before. My heart stutters thinking about his scent on my pillow where he slept. I remember his hand coasting up my leg. I turn away to prevent myself from leaning in and push my door open.

"Morning," I greet Marina as I make my way to the coffee pot, determined to act like Jackson Ridge didn't just step out of my bedroom behind me.

"Morning!" Marina sings from the couch next to Mark, not turning our way yet. "I didn't hear you come in last night. What time did you get back?"

"Around two," I say, moving through the kitchen.

"Really? I thought you weren't—" Marina doesn't finish her sentence because she turns, eyes landing on Jackson leaning against the counter. I watch her face break out into a mega-watt smile. "Oh my god!" She jumps up from the couch instantly, rushing into the kitchen.

"*Easy*," I warn her, wondering if it's possible for someone to have a heart attack while meeting a celebrity for the first time.

"Jackson Ridge! You're here? In our kitchen?"

"Hi." He laughs softly, seemingly unfazed by her enthusiasm as he extends his hand toward her. "Good to meet you."

"I'm Marina, Cassie's roommate!" Marina's eyes don't stray from Jackson's face. I look down at her hand, still clasped onto his, shaking it rapidly. "Cassie told me about you guys, but it's kind of like unbelievable! And here you are."

"Marina!" I call, snapping her out of whatever trance she was locked in. Jackson laughs as she finally drops his hand.

"I'm sorry. It's just…. it's really nice to meet you!" She beams, tying her arms behind her back. "I think you're really talented."

"Thank you." Jackson smiles.

The last sentence is what finally catches Mark's attention. He pushes himself off the couch, studying the stranger his girlfriend is crushing on in the kitchen.

"Hey, man, I'm Mark." The blank expression on Mark's face tells me that he has no idea who Jackson is. I stifle a laugh at his obvious lack of awareness.

"Jackson," he introduces himself, suppressing a smile.

"You're with Cassie?" Mark asks, looking between us.

"She's stuck with me," Jackson jokes before I can respond.

"What are you doing here?" Marina jumps in.

"Cassie texted me on her way home from work last night. You know . . ." Jackson's eyebrows raise, and Marina's mouth drops wide open at the insinuation.

I practically choke on my coffee.

"That is *not* what happened." I force the words out as I clear my throat. "He happened to show up at my apartment in the middle of the night. You know . . ." My eyes zero in on Jackson. "Like a stalker."

He shrugs. "It's not stalking if we're dating."

"*Dating*?" Marina squeals.

"Okay, Marina, can we have a minute?" I ask, facing her.

"Oh, um, yes. Of course. Come on, Mark." She grabs Mark's hand, dragging him back to her bedroom. "It was *really* nice to meet you, Jackson."

"Likewise." Jackson flashes another breathtaking smile, and I swear Marina melts.

Mark looks back and forth between Jackson and his girlfriend, who is shoving him into her bedroom. Just before the door closes, I hear Mark ask, "*Who was that?*"

"See, that's the reaction I usually get." Jackson points to Marina's door once it's closed. "That's the reaction I thought I would have gotten from you."

"Really? You would have liked me to worship the ground you walk on?"

"I'm not picky." He smirks, leaning forward. "You can worship me on your knees."

My stomach tightens at the innuendo, but I force myself to push him away, afraid of what I might do if he comes closer.

"That's not what I meant," I say with a frustrated sigh. "I haven't even told them that we're officially dating yet!"

"Why not?" The amusement and humor from a few moments ago have vanished.

"Something has to keep me tethered to reality," I mutter under my breath.

"Meaning?" His head tilts in confusion.

I pause, biting my lip, withholding that the reason I've kept our relationship a secret from my two best friends is because it's not real. Just because I have to play it up for the cameras doesn't mean that I want to drag Marina and Lucy into the mix. There are already too many variables, and I need something to keep me grounded. Otherwise, I'll get carried away in the fantasy. After last night, I already feel myself drifting.

"You know this isn't normal, right?" I gesture between us with my hand. "This isn't a real relationship."

His expression remains blank, like the obvious sentence I just uttered was spoken in another language, and it hits me, right there, standing in the kitchen, Jackson has never known anything different. I doubt he has any sort of frame of reference.

His phone buzzes from his pocket, breaking us apart. He frowns, looking down at the message before stuffing it in his back pocket.

"I have to head out, but I'll be back later to pick you up."

"For what?"

He stares at me. "For the shoot?"

"I'm not going there with you!" I nearly stutter at the improbability of his assumption.

"Why not?"

"Because I don't want people to know that we're together!"

He rolls his eyes. "They already know we're together."

“This was my condition, remember? I don’t want people thinking that I got the job just because I’m sleeping with you.” He goes to counter, but I cut him off. “I want to earn it fair and square. So, I hope for your sake that you have kept your mouth shut. Right?”

“Right.” He sighs, stepping toward the door.

“Okay, good. I’ll see you there.”

He turns before he leaves, a somber expression on his face.

“Thanks for letting me stay last night.” He squints. Before I can detect the emotion in his eyes, he turns, shutting the door behind him.

CHAPTER 16

Jackson

I sit forward when Cassie walks into the room. The sight of her walking through the door, head held high, is a breath of fresh air. I had been leaning back in my chair, watching tedious copycats' parade through the room all afternoon. Every single one of them looked toward me when they entered. I counted the pairs of plain brown, blue, and green eyes, how they widened in recognition when they saw me. Most smiled, a few waved. Cassie doesn't even turn.

I suppress a smile, licking my bottom lip, and rest my forearms on the table. She is wearing a white t-shirt and blue jeans. Her long, dark hair is brushed over one shoulder, falling in soft waves.

I forgot where I was when I woke up this morning. It's happened before, but generally only when I wake after a night of drinking. I had been sober when I fell asleep next to Cassie. I slept soundly, dreamed deeply. I can't remember the last time I had felt so . . . peaceful.

"Thank you for coming in today." Michael gestures her into the room.

Her eyes sweep the panel, but she purposefully doesn't look at me, even though I am watching her every move. I fidget in the seat briefly and realize that I want her eyes on me again. I always do.

"Thank you for having me." Cassie smiles, genuinely. "I'm Cassie Taylor, and I appreciate the opportunity."

"I'm Michael Wilcox. The rest of the panel are representatives from *Amora* and, the reason we are all here, Jackson Ridge." I nod, acting as if we are strangers, even if we did sleep in the same bed last night. I know this is how she wants it played. "I trust that you have reviewed the part."

"Yes," she says, clearing her throat. "But I do have a few questions."

The panel goes quiet, looking pleasantly surprised. I press a fist up against my mouth to suppress a smile.

"Please." Michael gestures for her to continue.

"I've reviewed the script, but I wanted to understand your full vision. What are you interested in creating?"

Danielle, the Chief Marketing Officer, leans forward, eyeing Cassie intently.

"We want the campaign to be reminiscent of Hollywood and all that it entails. Jackson Ridge is the epitome of the Hollywood lifestyle, and his counterpart needs to be seen as his equal. The goal for the campaign is, of course, to feature Jackson at the center of our latest cologne line, but we are also looking to expand into a new line of perfume. The woman that we cast would ideally be representative of both."

"You are looking to give an entire campaign to the person you cast?" Cassie asks with raised eyebrows.

"Ideally, yes."

She's immediately pissed. I can tell before she even looks at me. When she does eventually swing her gaze around, those hazel eyes find mine and harden. It's just a heartbeat of a moment, but I know I did the wrong thing keeping it from her.

I thought about telling her. Really, I did. I didn't purposefully keep it from her to throw her off or make her angry. I thought it would be for the best. I've seen her act under pressure. The first moment I stepped on her set, I could tell she wouldn't back away from a challenge, she would step up and face it. A part of me wondered what else she wouldn't shy away from. I think that's why I didn't tell her.

I'm used to testing people, trying to find their breaking point. It's not really conscious, but it's been a defense mechanism for so long, I don't know how to break it. Plus, I know that Cassie wouldn't have shown up, said yes to an audition, if she knew the potential. Some bullshit reasoning, like she doesn't deserve it. Working on getting through to her on that. Life is about opportunity, seized or not. You are defined by them. I know I am.

Cassie straightens her shoulders, pushes her hair back, a nervous tick I'm surprised I'm able to spot, and then smiles.

"Thank you. I appreciate the context. Where would you like me?"

"Step backward for me." Michael directs Cassie towards the center of the room, and then the photographer approaches her with a camera. "Take it away."

Cassie doesn't look at me as she tosses her hair over her shoulder, playing with it for a few different poses while the photographer captures the shots.

I find myself leaning forward, forearms on the table, trying to get closer to her. She opted for a natural look, minimum makeup, but applied to accentuate her best features. Her eyes are big, bright in the light of the afternoon, and she uses them to capture the lens easily, effortlessly.

She's beautiful, stunning. Her face belongs on billboards and magazines, yeah, but she is also the type of person people could fall in love with just by watching her smile, hearing her laugh. She is beautiful, inherently so, in who she is.

Objectively speaking, she is the best to have walked through the doors. It's obvious, and I know that the only reason she's been posing in back warehouses is because she hasn't gotten the opportunity to put her talent on display.

When the photographer finally lowers his camera, Cassie relaxes, letting out a breath, rolling her shoulders.

"Fantastic. Really great work." Michael nods toward Cassie. I lean forward to gauge the rest of the panelists' reactions, all seem impressed. "In terms of next steps, we will review the reel over the next few days and if we would like to move forward, we will reach out for a screen test with Mr. Ridge next week."

"Or we can do the screen test right now?" I offer, standing.

I don't wait for Michael or Danielle to agree, though they do, ecstatically. I hadn't offered before because I hadn't wanted to. I know that Cassie already booked the part without me, but this is what will seal the deal. Plus, I sort of want to be near her.

Cassie tenses when I approach, obviously caught off guard. I am a foot in front of her when I pull my t-shirt off over my head. I noticed her staring this morning, and I'm vain enough to want her eyes on me again. She swallows, taking a slight step back, and I note the pink stain on her cheeks.

"Where do you want me?" I ask her.

Apparently, the acknowledgement that she is in charge is all she needs to snap back into focus. She clears her throat and presses her hands against my chest, leading me back to a chair. I'm entirely too aware that she is touching me. People touch me all the time, but her hands feel different, warm, safe. She positions me to sit down and then stands behind me.

My eyes follow where she goes, not really meaning to, I just want to look at her. She wraps her arms around my neck, letting her fingers brush my cheek. At one point, she lifts my chin to look up at her face. I count the freckles on the bridge of her nose, try to name all the different colors in her eyes. She smiles slightly, but then it's all back to business after that.

For the last few frames, she leads me to stand and I forget for a moment that we are in a room of panelists. I forget that there are other people here, because I just want it to be the two of us.

Our eyes lock between the embrace, and the second our

chests touch, a rush of energy flows between our bodies. I place my hand on her neck, tilting her chin up with my thumb, our eyes holding. She smells like rose and ivy and I want to bury my face in her hair, kiss her neck. I can feel her heart racing like she also wants to be here, with me, our bodies pressing against each other just before—

"Well, I certainly think we've seen what you two are capable of!" Michael claps his hands together, and I turn toward the panel, all pleased with the display.

Cassie steps away from me quickly, like the sound is all she needed to hear to pull her back to reality. I throw my shirt back on while she stands a few feet away, awaiting further instructions.

"Great work, Ms. Taylor!" Michael addresses her. "I think we have all we need. Just know that we are looking to shoot next month, so you should hear back from someone on our team within the next couple of days."

"Thank you for the opportunity." She smiles.

I try to meet her eye again before she leaves, but she doesn't look at me again. Cassie drops her headshot and book on the table just before she slips out the door.

CHAPTER 17

Cassie

I've never sat at a bar by myself before, so I immediately feel self-conscious, but I need something to calm my nerves. I order a vodka soda and wait for the alcohol to hit.

Not only do I have the memory of Jackson in my head, throwing my heart into another erratic beat just thinking about our bodies being so close together just an hour ago, but I also now have the looming realization over my head that if I get the part, I would be featured as the lead in an international campaign.

I suck the bitter vodka down the straw . . . I won't get the part.

I know Jackson and I were acting. Rationally, I can make the distinction in my head, but I keep coming back to the feel of Jackson's chest against mine. The force of his body hovering over me. The look in his eyes when he stared at me. It made me dizzy to think about the possibilities, and despite what I want to tell myself, that the contract potential is the real reason I immediately located alcohol, it's not true.

I hadn't expected to actually be shooting with Jackson today, so when he stepped near me, I think I sort of blacked out for a moment. He took his shirt off, pulling it from the back over his head. His skin was warm, his chest sturdy, and when he moved closer, I swear his heart was racing just as fast as mine.

I know why women fall to their knees at his feet. I can imagine being one of those people who succumb to his wishes. There was an intangible power his eyes held over me, one I don't think I would ever be able to fully explain. I felt it, that day at the shoot, so many weeks ago, the first moment we locked eyes, and I felt it this afternoon.

I can't think clearly when I'm in his orbit, can't keep my hands to myself. I don't want to, but I have to. Because it's not real. *None* of this is real.

I finish my first drink when my phone rings. I frown when I see Jackson's name on the other line.

"What?" I answer quickly.

"Where are you?" Jackson asks urgently.

"I went out for a drink."

He pauses. "With who?"

"Myself."

"Okay. Where?"

"Some place called *The Tropics*."

"Great."

"Wait, Jackson—"

The line goes dead.

I sigh, ordering another vodka soda, needing a buffer before seeing him again. I am halfway through it when I feel a warm body saddle up beside me.

"Why didn't you wait?" Jackson asks.

I ignore his question, spinning on the stool, facing him square on. "Why didn't you tell me that the shoot had the potential to be extended?"

Jackson sighs, leaning against the counter. "Would you have agreed to it otherwise?"

"Of course not!"

"That's why." He points at me and then signals the bartender over for the check. "Why would you have said no?"

"Because . . ." I stutter, but words fail me. He waits, and I close my eyes, collecting my thoughts. "Because it doesn't feel fair."

"You auditioned with everyone else. That's as fair as it gets."

Jackson slides his card across the counter to close out before I can argue. I let out a breath and rest my elbow on the counter, my chin in my hand, trying to make him make sense.

"You confuse me," I admit out loud.

I swear he blushes before he changes the subject. "You been here long?"

"Two drinks worth," I say, lifting the vodka soda to my mouth, sucking the rest of it down.

Jackson smiles when I cringe from the bitter taste. His next question nearly causes me to fall off the stool.

"Come home with me?"

I swallow. At least this time he poses it as a question, not an assumption. I can sense some sort of . . . anxiousness in him that I can't place. I felt the same feeling last night when he asked to stay over.

"Why?" I ask honestly, thanks to the vodka I sucked dry.

He shrugs. "Because you want to."

I know my decision before I even make it. I remember the feeling of his body pressed up against me at the shoot. The skin-to-skin contact had stayed with me. I want more, more of him, and I know I shouldn't.

"Fine."

I toss Jackson my keys, and we make our way to my Camry. I cringe when I realize that he is going to drive my beat-up junker. I can't imagine someone like him in the driver's seat of this car. He belongs in Teslas and Mercedes, anything better than a 2008 leftover.

He climbs into the car, his knees almost resting on the steering wheel. He looks so big sitting in the driver's seat of my Camry. He adjusts the seat back to allow for more space and then reaches for the gear shift. My eyes fall to his hand, noting the tendons that run up his wrist to his forearm.

It's not my fault I'm objectifying his body, he was the one who appeared shirtless in front of me only a few hours ago. The memory of him walking toward me has been playing like a reel in my head and now I can't help but wonder what else I haven't seen.

"What?"

I tense when I realize I've been caught staring. A smile pulls in the corner of his mouth like he knew what I had been thinking.

"Just . . . be careful."

His hands hover over the steering wheel. "I haven't done anything yet."

"I know, just be careful," I say again.

"I promise."

He pulls the car into reverse, and we slide out of the parking spot. I inhale a deep breath and lean back in the seat, angling my head toward him.

"Why didn't you tell me?" I ask. "I mean, you came over last night to essentially prep me for the part, yet you left out the most important detail?"

"I didn't want you to overthink it. You act better under pressure; I've seen it. I thought I was doing you a favor."

"By lying to me?"

"I wasn't lying."

I glare, and he sighs, frustrated, dragging a hand through his deliciously messy hair.

"Okay, I can see how it might have looked like a lie. I'm sorry that I kept it from you, okay? Is that better?"

I don't answer. Instead, I cross my arms over my chest, staring out the windshield. Maybe he had a point. Maybe I would have overthought every step, every pose. *Maybe.* But I also know for a fact that I wouldn't have shown up at all if he had told me the truth, and I think *that* is the real reason he kept it a secret.

"Anything else you want to confess to while we're at it?" I ask, and it's Jackson's turn to glare. "Do I at least get to hear how the audition went?"

"They want you for the part, and before you object, I want you to know that I had nothing to do with their decision today."

I got the part. They want *me*. I don't have the capacity to consider how or why, but I got it. In a few weeks, I could be shooting a commercial that would define my career. It's such a wild concept, my brain has a hard time catching up with reality.

"So?" Jackson asks, looking over at me.

I realize that I had stopped paying attention to whatever else he said after he told me I booked the part.

"What?"

"Are you going to take it?" he asks.

The ridiculous nature of the question, coupled with the two vodka sodas I sucked dry, has me snorting a laugh under my breath.

"What was that?" He jerks his head in my direction, a look of sincere affection in his eyes.

"Nothing," I say, my cheeks heating.

"You snorted." His smile widens.

"I didn't."

"I heard you."

"You just caught me off guard," I say, trying to get back on track. "Besides, you seem to be implying that I actually have a choice in the matter."

"It is your choice. It will *always* be your choice," He adds, suddenly serious, tightening his grip on the steering wheel. I swallow, noting the sudden shift in temperature in the car. "I don't want you to do anything because of me."

"This was your idea," I remind him. "Do you *not* want me to do it?"

"Of course not." He sighs. "I just want to make sure you want it too. It's a big decision. Outside of the commercial, the contract extension will require a time commitment."

I know that, but his confirmation of the part that it will play in my career is enough to release another swarm of butterflies in my stomach.

"You looked beautiful, by the way," he says, softly. Our eyes meet across the front seat of the car. "You are beautiful."

"Eyes on the road," I mutter under my breath, trying not to smile.

He lets out a quiet laugh. "I thought models were supposed to enjoy compliments."

I look out the window, mulling over the news. Yes, I had agreed to the audition, but I had mostly agreed to it just to get Jackson off my back. I had been too worried about the actual process of the audition to spend any time wondering what it might be like to get the part. Now that I have it, I know the heavy weight of the decision I am making.

Up until this moment, I had booked dead-end jobs. My extended shoot with Daria last month was thought to be a once-in-a-lifetime opportunity a few weeks ago, back before I met Jackson.

I readjust in my seat to face him. "How did you decide?"

"You mean, how did I decide to take the part that led to my big break?" I nod silently and watch him exhale deeply. "It didn't feel like a choice." He says quietly, pausing, trapped in some far away memory before he shakes his head. "I wanted attention, I think that's what it all came down to. I said yes to everything that it entailed and decided not to spend my time worrying or wondering about what life would be like if I walked away."

The last light of the sunset fades behind the edge of the ocean, the darkness of the evening setting in as we start the long drive through the hills.

"But I didn't work as hard as you have," he adds quietly. "I was approached to model when I was sixteen. That job turned into commercials, which turned into a stint on *Sunset City* and then a full three-year contract on the show." A shadow appears over his eyes that I don't think he even notices, but I do. "Everything came together for me in under a year. I didn't have the capacity to question it. You worked for this, moved away from home and started over in a new city. You deserve a break more than I ever did."

I study the contours of his jaw, the lights from the street brighten his face before going dark again as we drive up the hill. Is that what this is about? It's a guilty conscience? Is that what led me to be in the passenger seat with Jackson, headed toward his Hollywood Hills home?

My eyelids feel heavy as we round the corner, pull through the gate and finally arrive in the circle drive of his home. He throws the car in park.

"Does that help answer your question?" he asks, facing me.

"It does."

"But you still have to think it over?"

I sigh. "I do."

"Fair enough."

I step out of the passenger's side and follow him to the house. Jackson flashes his key, pushing the front door, made entirely of black titanium, open. I follow him inside, staggering as I try to take in the entire space of his mansion, because I can't think of another name for it. The hallways are massive. Dark marble floors, white walls, everything crisp and cool. The foyer is vast, equipped with a sleek staircase and a long hallway. I peer into the room off the front when Jackson interrupts my inspection.

"My room," he says, fighting a smile. I swallow, nodding. "Do you want something to eat?"

"Oh, um, sure," I say, following him into the kitchen.

I slip out of my shoes and drop my purse on the bench by the front entrance. I feel the cool tile under my feet as I pad across the floor to his kitchen. Lights flicker on as we step inside, Jackson throws his keys on the counter.

The ceilings are tall throughout the entire house. A long, granite countertop separates the kitchen from the living room.

Every space, a shade of black, white or gray, barely a splash of color. I face the living room, which is bigger than my entire apartment. A modular, sleek couch faces an elevated TV with a fireplace underneath.

I spin, trying to take everything in and realize why something feels amiss. There is nothing on the walls or the counters, not even a blanket on the couch. Everything is propped or put away, leaving no signs that someone actually visits the space, let alone lives in it.

"How long have you lived here?" I ask.

"About five years."

His answer surprises me. The entire mansion feels vacant. To think he has lived here for half a decade doesn't seem plausible.

"And you live here, all by yourself?"

"Just me," he answers, walking toward the far side of the room. "This is the best part."

He pulls the black drapes open to reveal one of the most spectacular views I have ever seen. I take a step forward, dazed.

Los Angeles literally sparkles through the glass. I didn't realize how high up we were until I gazed out at the view beyond us. A pool lines the right of his property, but I look past it, pressing a hand to the window, wanting to touch the lights that dance on the horizon.

"It's . . . unbelievable," I say, nearly speechless

Jackson steps beside me, tugging the window, which is actually a door, open. The cool breeze coats my arms when I step outside on the concrete, making my way past the pool toward the railing that looks down at the city. The view makes me feel insignificant, tiny, in the grand scheme of things. I am in awe, terrified and inspired at the same time.

"I've never seen anything like this," I admit quietly.

Spare sirens hum below us. Car horns are just a distant whisper. The most potent sound is the thundering in my chest.

"I picked it for the view." Jackson slips an arm around my

waist, encompassing me in his warm embrace. I can't help but lean back farther into his chest, hoping that he's holding me just because he wants to. "It was more expensive. But it was worth it."

I wonder if I would ever be able to afford something like this. If my career trajectory would lead me to expensive condos and mansions on the better side of the 90210. Accepting the contract will make it easier. Easier, but not less complicated.

"Don't you get lonely out here?" I ask.

He shrugs a shoulder. "I'm rarely here, and when I am, I make sure that the house is full of . . . company." His hand slides up my shirt, resting on the lower part of my stomach.

I lean my head against the upper part of his arm, my gaze fixated on the lights sparkling below. "Just because you aren't alone, doesn't mean you aren't lonely."

I am so distracted by the view below that I almost miss his lack of response. I look back at him, his eyes on me. We meet briefly, and then he looks away.

"Maybe," he says softly. "Maybe it just makes it easier to forget."

I sink deeper into his arms. I know I should pull away from his hold, because there is no one watching, there is no part that I have to play, but his arms are warm and something about this embrace feels normal, for once. His thumb swirls slightly on the exposed skin on the side of my hip.

"I think I'm gonna say yes to *Amora*."

"Really?" He squeezes me tighter, and I can feel the thump of his heart in his chest.

I twist so that I can look up at him and smile. "Yes."

"I was hoping you would," he says softly and there is something so sincere in his expression, my heart squeezes in my chest.

I turn back to the view and breathe out quietly. "I know you were."

I just wish I understood why.

CHAPTER 18

Jackson

We order sushi for dinner. Cassie and I gather around the counter, sampling the rolls. She tells me about the first time she tried it, laughing freely as she recounts a disastrous incident with chopsticks. Apparently, a piece of fish went flying across the restaurant. She tells me the story with her hair up, feet tucked under her, while we sit at the counter.

It feels nice to live in this house, not just exist. It's been a while since the halls have been filled with laughter, with light. The times when I'm not here alone, the energy is chaotic, stressful. I'm surrounded by stylists, assistants, Zana barking in my ear all hours of the day. Then, when it goes silent, it's too quiet, like I can hear my thoughts screaming back at me. It's why I prefer to not spend any more time in this house by myself.

A few beers and a couple of rolls later, I find myself contemplating whether spending this much time together, away from the cameras, is really a good thing. Every time I'm around her, there is this invisible current that draws us toward each other. I felt it before and then again this afternoon, our bodies close, and I wonder what she would let me do if I only asked.

I look for opportunities to touch her, nothing blatant like grabbing her hand, but I'd brush her waist with my fingers or lean around her to grab something, tell myself that she's not leaning back into me when I do it, but I hope she is.

It's late when we finally clear dinner. I hang back in the kitchen while Cassie wanders into my bedroom. I pull out my phone to find what I had missed in the few hours I had been with Cassie. I have a few dozen texts, voicemails, most from Zana.

I pause when I come across an email from Hall Studios. The message came to my personal account, which means that Zana isn't involved. I skim the details, realizing they got in touch with me through Sash's boyfriend, Leo. He's worked with the studio and the recommendation to go directly through me instead of my agent is definitely from Sash, a comment mentioning her referral in the body of the message.

The email includes a meeting invite for a new film Hall Studios is financing independently. They had a breakout film at Sundance last year that I loved. I didn't realize they were openly casting their next project.

Deciding to continue to keep Zana out of this one, I shoot a reply with some open availability. It's just a meeting; it might not even go anywhere, and I want to brace myself for that very real possibility before involving anyone else.

I suppress a smile, hovering in the doorway to my bedroom, arms crossed over my chest, not saying a word. Cassie is lying on my mattress, eyes closed. Her dark hair spills across the white comforter, and I'm hit with the overwhelming feeling again, lingering in my chest.

I want her. I want to be close to her. I'm just afraid I don't know how.

"Comfortable?" I ask.

Her eyes flutter open, like she forgot she let them close. She leans forward, propping herself up on her elbows.

"I should head home."

I panic. I don't want her to go.

I know what I will do if she leaves, and I don't want to feel that way tonight. I've convinced myself that if she falls asleep next to me, it will chase away everything that keeps me up at night. She goes and I don't know how to block it all out.

"Why?"

"Because . . ." She trails off, and I know she is trying to come up with an excuse. "I don't have pajamas." I raise an eyebrow. "Or a toothbrush."

"I have both." I step forward, wrapping my hands around her ankles, tugging her towards the end of the mattress. The rashness of the gesture releases a giggle from her stomach, and I like the sound of it entirely too much. "I can make an argument as to why you might only need one, though."

She peers up at me, her eyes soft and trusting. I release her ankles, pressing my hands on the bed, on either side of her hips, and choose my next words carefully.

"I have a spare toothbrush in the bathroom, and I'll find you some pajamas. Just . . . stay."

She waits, processing the request, which sounds much more like a plea once I say it out loud. She eventually lets out a sigh, trying not to smile. "Which drawer?"

My shoulders relax, and I nod behind her.

"Top left."

She sits up, heading to the bathroom while I watch her go. The lights flicker when she steps on the tile, and then I go to my closet to change quickly.

She's brushing her teeth when I step back in to join her. She pauses, just briefly, when she sees me shirtless. I grab a toothbrush and stand beside her, our eyes locking in the mirror, and I can tell she is trying not to smile. Me too, actually. There is something so simple yet domestic about brushing my teeth next to someone. I don't think I've ever done it before.

I pretend to look away later and note her eyes drop in the mirror to take me in, tell myself I don't love her watching me, but it would be a lie. I leave her to finish getting ready for bed while I search my closet for something she can wear.

"Afraid that's all I have in the pajama department," I say, handing her the spare t-shirt when she comes back into the bedroom.

She studies it, shrugging. "This works."

I fall back on the bed, waiting for her to join me. I'm not sure if she does it on purpose, or if she forgets where she is, but Cassie steps out of her jeans in front of me, letting them fall to the floor. She reaches for her shirt when she pauses, eyes finding mine. I am propped up against the headboard, head tipped back, watching her.

Her eyes go wide again, like she just realized what she's doing. Her hands grip the hem of her t-shirt but don't move any further.

"Do you want me to look away?" I ask.

She takes her bottom lip between her teeth before asking. "Do *you* want to?"

I shrug. "Not really, but I will if you tell me to."

She swallows and then lifts the shirt over her head so that she is just in her bra. It's a light-pink one, lacy, nothing special, but it's now my favorite thing that she has ever worn. Her hands shake slightly before she reaches to unclasp it from behind, letting it fall to the floor.

Whatever confidence she might have summoned prior to taking off her clothes evaporates the moment the fabric falls to the ground. She doesn't cover herself, but she slips my old t-shirt on quickly. She is nearly swallowed by the size of it, and I change my mind just as suddenly. *This* is my favorite thing she's ever worn.

"Show's over," she announces, smiling and a little out of breath, when she skips over to the bed.

As soon as she slides under the covers, I slip an arm around her waist, pulling her towards me, needing her next to me.

"Can I touch you?" The words fall out of my mouth, out of habit.

She sucks in a short breath before saying the word I need to hear. "Yes."

I draw my hand up the shirt she is wearing, pressing my palm between her breasts, settling my hand against her heart.

My lips brush the shell of her ear. "I can feel your heart racing."

The words send her heart into another erratic beat, and I swear I feel her press her chest further into my hand. Her hair smells like her rose perfume, fresh but subtle. My hand drops, the edge of my thumb lightly brushes underneath her breast, and then I let it fall to her waist.

Her skin is soft, warm. I hear her breathing hitch when my fingers tease the elastic of her underwear. I brush my thumb beneath for a moment and then back up. I inhale a deep breath, sighing, when she nuzzles the pillow underneath her head, cocooning herself back into my embrace. We are both quiet, close to sleep, when the words slip out.

"I like having you around."

It's not that I regret them, I just didn't mean to say them out loud. I don't know where they came from.

Her comment from earlier today resurfaces while we fall asleep. She reminded me that what we have isn't real. It's not normal, and she's right. I'm not normal. I don't know what a normal relationship entails other than that I can't have one.

Why can't I date her? Maybe because I have no idea, no concept, of what to do in the confines of a relationship. Maybe because the only real experience turned all relationships sour for me. I accepted what I can get out of this life, money, fame, attention, but I can't do relationships. There are too many variables to consider, too many angles to factor in, and I know that if we were to go down that path, by the end of it, someone would end up bloodied and bruised.

I'd prefer to avoid that possibility entirely.

CHAPTER 19

Cassie

My eyes flicker open in the early morning light. I curl deeper under the covers, peering up at the clock on the bedside table. It's still early, barely past 7 a.m. I turn on my side, resisting the urge to press my face into the fabric and inhale deeply. I don't have to, anyway. It already smells like him. Sandalwood and cedar, and I wish that I had a bottle of it that I could use at any hour of the day.

I roll over on my back, lifting my arm to the now cold side of the bed where Jackson slept beside me last night. The words he admitted out loud last night are still ringing in my head. They twisted something in my chest, and the weight of them rested heavier with me than I expected.

"I like having you around."

I don't think he meant for me to hear them, but I dreamed of them last night, along with his hand slipping beneath my underwear, disappearing between my legs. I shove away the thought to prevent the need for a cold shower and run my hand through my hair before getting up to explore.

The longer I'm in the house, the more it feels like a museum. I search the other rooms for photographs of family or friends, artwork that represents some piece of his personality, but there isn't much. I turn when I hear muffled music coming from down the hall. I push open the door, stepping into a full gym. The lights are bright, and the music is loud. The gym is filled with all sorts of machines, bench presses, free weights.

I lean against the door frame as I watch Jackson work through a series of exercises until he finally lets up after several seconds. He breathes in deeply, resting his hands on the top of his head before scanning the room, his eyes catching on my figure standing in the doorway.

"Sorry!" I hold up my hands when I notice the trainer looking in my direction, indicating that I am interrupting.

"We're just about finished." Jackson breathes heavily, letting his arms drop to his sides. "There's coffee in the kitchen."

I nod in understanding, my gaze lingering on his chest before turning quickly, eager to escape the distraction. I'm on my way back to the kitchen when a bright light pouring into the hallway catches my attention. I push open a door, revealing an office, of sorts. The left side is a wall covered with various magazine prints of Jackson over the years. It's the first room I've seen that actually holds something of personal value.

I suppress a smile, coming across an early spread. Jackson can't be older than eighteen on the front of *Teen People*. I recognize the cover immediately. It was insanely popular at the time, and most of my friends in junior high pasted the photos in their lockers. Jackson posing on the beach in a white t-shirt, reaching to pull it off. His smile, so wide, it makes his eyes small. The headline reads: *Say Hello to* Sunset City *Star: Jackson Ridge.*

I stop in front of another cover, recognizing Sasha posing next to Jackson in a black-and-white photograph, his arm over her shoulder. They both look so young, definitely taken before Jackson made the headlines he does today. They are laughing, eyes bright, and I know why he keeps this photo proudly on display. It's a moment of pure adolescence, captured in time. Happiness and youth, frozen forever.

I step around the desk, nothing but a computer and a large calendar resting beside it. I am passing by, taking in the other covers, when I accidentally bump the keyboard, lighting up the screen. I don't mean to be snooping, but the temptation to learn more about the person whose bed I slept in last night overpowers me. I check the door before I lean closer.

A *Vanity Fair* article is pulled up on his desktop. A beautiful, older woman's picture featured beside it. Dark, jet-black hair and deep-blue eyes. My eyes skim the headline:

INSIDE VICTORIA BAXTER'S DYNASTY.

The name sounds familiar, but I can't tie it to anything substantial. I am in the midst of scanning the article when my eyes catch on a folder, the only folder, saved on his desktop, titled *VB*. My hand hovers over the mouse, itching to find out more. I quickly double-tap the icon to find dozens of articles saved, all labeled by date. I don't get a chance to read any of them because I hear the door shut from the end of the hall.

I close out of the folder and push around the desk, going back to the magazine covers on the wall. My heart still racing when Jackson steps into the room a few seconds later.

"Hey." He tilts his head to the side, like he wasn't expecting to find me here.

"Hi." I force my voice to sound breezy. "Sorry, I didn't mean to snoop."

"All good." Jackson shrugs, his eyes drifting to the desk quickly.

He steps behind me, so close that my head would rest against his chest if I leaned back. His arms could wrap around my waist like they had last night. I start to drift, but before I make contact, I remember who we are to each other and stand up straight.

"I had this one." I point to the *Teen People* magazine.

"It was my first cover," he says, proudly.

I look up at him. He is still insanely attractive, unfairly so, but his face has hardened over time. His jaw more defined, cheeks less rosy, eyes not as bright, somehow.

"You look so young."

"Yeah." His brow wrinkles. An emotion flashes in his eyes but quickly disappears. "Come on. Let's get out of here." He escorts me out of the room, and when he shuts the door behind us, I hear the switch of the lock. "You sleep well?"

"Yeah, I did," I reassure him, since it looks like he had been waiting for confirmation.

He nods quickly, pleased that I gave him the positive answer he was looking for, but he doesn't look at me. I get the odd sense of avoidance when he makes his way around the kitchen, grabbing things for breakfast. He starts talking, but I don't really register where the conversation is going, trying to gauge the sudden mood change this morning from the person I fell asleep with last night.

"I want you to come with me."

I sit up straighter on the barstool. "Sorry, I missed that part. Where are we going?"

"My premiere for *Annihilation*."

"A premiere? As in a red-carpet movie premiere?"

"That will be the one," he says dryly. "I will mostly be doing press, but for the premiere, I'd like to have you there. We haven't officially confirmed our relationship, so it would be good for publicity."

My shoulders sag at the clarification behind his words. The long glances from the night before, his hand slipping under my shirt, coasting up my stomach, are immediately erased. His businesslike proposal to attend his premiere reminds me again exactly why he wants me around. It's all for show. I let the reminder sit like a hard rock in my stomach.

"Yeah, of course," I mutter under my breath, feeling like a prop again.

"I can help you get a dress."

My heart catches at the insinuation, that I won't be able to afford one that would warrant a red-carpet appearance.

"I can get one. It's no problem."

"It's going to be expensive—"

"It will be fine. Honest."

I push away from the counter and walk back to his bedroom. I throw off his shirt, inhaling one last sniff of fabric before changing back into my own clothes. I reach for my purse in the hallway when Jackson rounds the corner.

"You leaving?"

He is either completely oblivious or doesn't care enough to consider how his words and actions seem to be sending two completely different messages.

"Yeah, I have to get back. I forgot Marina and I have plans for the day."

"Okay." He sighs, crossing his arms over his chest. "Thanks for staying last night."

"I'll see you later, then?" I ask, trying to be breezy.

Jackson pulls away but nods.

I spin on my heel, not wanting to dwell on last night's events any longer. The memories are already being displaced with a sense of unease blooming in my stomach. I step out into the bright LA sunshine, squinting into the harsh light. Eager to escape the unrelenting rays, I quicken my pace to the car and throw open the driver's side door. I jam the keys into the ignition and jerk the car into drive, leaving Jackson behind in my rearview.

CHAPTER 20

Jackson

Shame has a funny way of sneaking up on you. No matter how hard you try to suppress it, it seems to bubble to the surface when you aren't paying attention, spilling over when you swore you had the lid sealed.

It takes one article to turn my day on its fucking head.

I have a family, despite what the papers write. Estranged, I think that's what you would call it. I don't talk to them, and they don't usually talk to me.

At the time, I felt I needed to shed the person they knew to become successful, cut all ties to this previous version of myself to move forward, but in all honesty, I sort of hate what I've become. Now, we avoid each other because I don't know how to reconcile the two versions of myself. I always thought that since it was my choice to cut them out, it would make the decision easier. It does, sometimes.

Once my mom passed away, I thought my two older brothers would view my attempt to build a career the same way my father did. Like my obvious need for attention was so pathetically apparent, they would judge me for it.

My step-father tried. He tried to raise me after my brothers moved out. He tried to take care of me, he *tried* to love me, but he couldn't. It's not like I blame him for it. After my mom died, I was just a burden that he didn't want anymore, so I just removed myself from the equation.

I grew up fast because I had to. Back then, Sash and I were battling through the trenches. I quickly realized that I had a face that people loved. Producers fawned over me, gave me anything I wanted by following the simplest instructions. It became hard to say no. It still is, if I'm honest.

The older I got, the more I felt like a product, a commodity, something that could be used and consumed for mass entertainment. I ignored it, buried it deep down, because the job gave me the one thing I had been craving since I was a kid. It gave me attention and money, which gave me the freedom to do what I wanted.

And I think Victoria *knew* that.

I was her favorite on set, back when I first signed onto *Sunset City,* and she made it obvious. She gave me anything I wanted, catered to my every demand. At the time, it felt nice to be heard. I thought that I was understood. I didn't realize that everything she gave me came with strings attached. I went to pull away and realized that she already had her hooks in me. I couldn't say no, even if I wanted to.

I know all the choices I made got me where I am today, but I don't like to dwell on them. I don't need to. I survived, made it out, and learned to live with it.

But shame sneaks up on you, like right now, sitting alone in my office, staring at the article which hit my inbox this morning, boasting of Victoria Baxter's illustrious career.

I had sex before. Sleeping with Victoria at eighteen wasn't my first time, but it was definitely the most memorable. I remembered everything. What perfume she wore, how she undressed me, the words whispered in my ear. I felt like a dog performing tricks, preening under her approval. It makes me sick to think about it now, how I could have just let her get away with it.

We can both help each other. The words whispered in my ear as she laid me down on the bed.

It wasn't explicit, but when the meeting to discuss my future occurred in her bedroom, at The Plaza, behind a locked door, it became very obvious what I needed to do to move forward.

I keep reading the article on the screen. I don't want to, but I can't *stop*.

My eyes scan the page, scrolling through the paragraphs summarizing her lengthy career, shining accomplishments. It spans the past twenty years. She had been involved in projects before *Sunset City*, but that's what put her on the map. What put *me* on the map.

My jaw tightens while I stare down at the photograph accompanying the article. Her sharp blue eyes, such a contrast to her dark black hair, I remember the first time I saw them and thought they were beautiful. Now, I can't stomach the color.

Hollywood is smaller than it seems. I would run into her again. It's not like I've avoided her these past ten years. The last time I saw her was in Cannes, at my first panel, six hours before my premiere. We didn't talk, but she caught my eye from the crowd, and I hated what was looking back, like she had some ownership over me, responsible for me in a way that made me sick.

An overwhelming feeling of disgust washes over me, but I work to force it away. Before closing out of the article, I save it, label it by date, and drop it into the folder on my desktop.

I push away from my desk, locking the door behind me. I squeeze my eyes shut, press my thumb and finger to my temple, and try to forget. I've been trying every day for the last ten years, because everything that I hate about myself came from it.

Everything I hate about myself came from *her*.

CHAPTER 21

Cassie

Jackson has been both absent and inescapable in the week that we've been apart. When I wanted to ignore him, even for just a few hours, he'd appear on my TV or pop up on my social media. Without even meaning to, every spare thought seemed to be wrapped up in some version of him. Even the *Amora* contract, which is so dull and so dense it's making my eyes nearly bleed, is another reminder of the very important decision looming over my head. This contract has his fingerprints all over it.

I've been sitting here, on my mattress, for the past two hours, staring at my computer. My agent had highlighted the important contract stipulations and terms, which I had reviewed again this morning. I sigh, running my left hand through my tangled hair, and then finally check the electronic signature box before pressing submit.

I sit there for a moment, waiting for something extraordinary to happen, but nothing does. I imagined this decision to be more momentous. Balloons falling from my ceiling, confetti blasting out of a cannon, champagne bottles popping. Instead, I feel like I aced a test by stealing all the answers.

I roll over on my stomach and pick up my phone. It's been a few weeks since I've had enough downtime to check in. I toy with the idea back and forth, hesitating before putting my fingers to the keys. A few weeks ago, the thought that I could be Googled would have been hilarious.

I had been purposefully avoiding the tabloids, the tags on social media, and all the messages that have hit my phone from undisclosed numbers. I had been mostly successful, a fact that I was proud of. I know who I am. I don't need other people to tell me, but as I stare at the blank screen of the browser, I can't help but wonder. I bite my nail and click open a new tab, pausing before searching for Jackson's name coupled with "Cassie Taylor."

I am immediately bombarded with photos of myself and Jackson over the past few weeks. There are images of us from the runway in Beverly Hills, photographs from dinner. I scroll through each one, carefully studying my reactions in each of the sequences. In most of them, I am staring at the ground, holding onto Jackson's hand like I am holding on for dear life.

I pull up my personal account, clicking through to my profile. I had been relatively quiet on the app, outside of the photo dump I posted a few weeks back. I note the private message button light up with requests and notifications. I click on it, taking in the slew of unread messages. I open the first of many. In their long list of diatribes, I focus on the words that stand out the most.

SLUT.

WHORE.

My hands start to shake as I swipe line by line, reading each of the two hundred messages targeting me from anonymous people on the internet.

GOLD DIGGER.

Pieces of my self-esteem chip away with each message, but I scroll through them, unable to stop. It's one thing to post your opinion into the great abyss of the internet, but these are sent to my private account. These strangers don't even know me. How can they possibly have the nerve to send me direct messages attacking everything I thought I knew about myself? My looks, my personality, my entire character, it's all called into question by a panel of anonymous lobbyists, determined to burn me at the stake.

"Cassie, dinner!" Marina taps on my door, interrupting my spiral of depression.

I sit up, wiping my eyes with the sleeves of my sweatshirt. I know that it shouldn't matter to me, but the fact that this is on the internet terrifies me. I had been worried about being *temporarily* attached to Jackson. Now it seems like the connection between us, no matter how short, would be permanent. The articles written on the internet are posted in ink, supported by images that can't be scrubbed.

"Did you finally accept?" Marina asks when I step out of my bedroom.

"I did, yeah." I say, making a plate for myself that I have no interest in eating.

"Congratulations!" She smiles as I take the seat next to her, wishing I could reciprocate her enthusiasm. "So, how does it feel?"

"To be honest, it feels kind of anticlimactic."

"Maybe because it doesn't feel real yet?" Marina offers. "I mean, it's just a contract. I'm sure things will be put into perspective when you step on set."

I nod and look down at my plate full of pasta, moving the noodles with my fork, barely swallowing more than a few bites.

"I'm not sure I should tell you this or not, but Lucy mentioned that Noah is back from London. Apparently he posted on his Instagram this morning."

"Hmm." I raise my eyebrows, considering this piece of information.

Noah is still blocked on my phone, so I don't know if he

has even attempted to reach out outside of the text that he sent Marina a few weeks ago.

"I guess I just wanted to give you a heads-up. He might be around again."

"Lucky me," I mutter sarcastically under my breath, my eyes losing focus on the plate in front of me.

"Cassie Taylor."

I look up at Marina, but the sound of my name didn't come from her mouth. We both face the TV that had been playing in the background. Marina reaches for the remote to turn up the volume while Courtney Davis, host of *EDaily*, appears on the screen.

"Jackson Ridge is back in the spotlight this week, but don't worry, it's not the threat of his reputation that has his name in headlines. Jackson has been seen frequently with his up-and-coming girlfriend, Cassie Taylor, and things are looking serious."

"Check out the sweetest images of them at Stella Harper's *fashion show. I know I may be a sap, but come on, they are absolutely adorable."* Her cohost, Victor, comments while I watch, stunned into silence.

"Honestly, I love this for him. I mean, when was the last time we saw Jackson Ridge hand in hand with a potential new girlfriend while sober?" Courtney comments, and I tense.

"You know, I can't even remember." Victor takes over for Courtney. *"And the good news for Jackson seems to be piling in. Ridge has been rumored to have various projects in the pipeline. After meeting with Silas Morland last week, it seems like there may be a large project on the horizon. What do you think, Court? Will you be lining up to see Jackson in a World War I epic?"*

"Victor, you know me. I'm a simple girl with basic needs. As long as he has his shirt off, I'm buying a ticket."

"Looks like Ridge might be in the clear for now, but as we all know, good things with Jackson rarely ever last. Back to you, Gray."

I pull my legs closer to my chest at the foreboding ending of the coverage. Almost like clockwork, Lucy bursts through the front door.

"What the hell, Luce?" Marina stands. "Did you know about Cassie's feature?"

"What feature?" She drops her bag on the ground by the door.

"The one where they essentially insinuate Cassie is just Jackson's latest flavor of the month."

"How can you even ask me that?" Lucy asks, obviously offended.

"It's fine." I raise my hands in defense when I sense an argument coming, one I don't feel like being in the middle of.

"It's not fine." Marina presses. "How can you let them run this?"

"Right, like *I* have a say in what runs. I'm not even involved and besides . . ." Lucy trails off, looking my way.

"Besides what?" I ask, picking at her unfinished sentence.

Lucy's face turns a shade of pink. She crosses her arms over her chest, glancing between us. "I mean, Cassie, do you really think it's gonna last?"

"*Lucy Collins*!" Marina scolds.

"I'm gonna go to my room," I mutter.

"What?" Lucy asks. "I'm just saying what everyone is thinking."

I slam the door shut, but I can still hear the argument continue through the wall. I collapse on my bed at the same time my phone buzzes with a new message from Jackson.

JACKSON

Dinner tonight?

It's a harmless text, I know, but I'm mad, and I don't like how we last left things. I exhale and send a short reply.

CASSIE

Can't. Busy.

I toss my phone aside, not bothering to wait for an answer.

I lay my head back down on the pillow, arms crossed over my stomach, trying to plug the holes in me, but there are too many. The premiere for *Annihilation* is in two weeks which I'm supposed to be attending with Jackson. The following month, I am shooting the commercial. I have the next six weeks of my life booked out in front of me and a large, looming problem hanging over my head that I can't ignore.

Attempting to dissociate from reality for the night, I tuck myself under the covers, flipping on my favorite reality TV show, but even the drama-filled soap does nothing to distract me. I'm halfway through the episode when a knock sounds at my door, Marina poking her head inside.

"Hey." She smiles, tilting her head. "Can I come in?"

I nod, sitting up against the headboard, pulling my legs towards my chest. Marina crashes onto my mattress with a dramatic sigh.

"You ready to talk about whatever it is that's bothering you?" she asks.

"How do you know something is bothering me?"

Marina tosses me a look. "You're re-watching *Love Shack*. You only do that when you're stressed or hungover, and I know it's not the latter because Lucy drank all our wine last night."

I try to smile, but it feels forced. I reach for the remote, mute the TV, and inhale a shaky breath, summoning the courage to voice the words that have been sitting on top of my chest for the past few days.

"I just . . . I feel like I made a huge mistake. I'm in way over my head with Jackson. I don't know what we are supposed to be. He acts like he wants a relationship one minute, then he's distant the next. It's like I can never get a read on him. I got this job that I don't even know if I want anymore because it feels like a cop-out, like I cheated to get it, and the things that people are saying about me online—" My voice shakes. "I can't handle it. I don't know if I want to handle it."

"Oh, Cass." Marina moves closer, pulling me toward her chest. She hugs me for a few more seconds and then carefully lets go. I rub my eye again, wiping away the sentiment.

"I guess I just feel . . . sad, and I know that I shouldn't because my problems aren't big problems in the scheme of things but . . . what if this was all a waste? What if I worked to get where I am just to realize that I don't want it, any of it?"

Marina grabs my hands. "It's okay to be feeling all of these things. Don't discount them."

I nod, inhaling a deep breath, letting the air out through my nose.

"Okay, let's start with those fuckers online, shall we?" Marina raises her eyebrows. "Screw them. Do not spend any time reading any of it. I mean it, Cassie. It's trash, and it's untrue, and the more time that you spend obsessing over it, the more they win. We can set up blockers on your Instagram, disable comments, and hide accounts to prevent bullshit like that from even reaching you." Marina speaks calmly, and I already know that her reassurance is what I needed.

"Two, the job. I get it. You were hesitant to accept it even in the first place, but you did, and you should. Yes, people don't always get handed opportunities like this, *but*!" She lifts a finger as if to signify the importance of her statement. "It doesn't discount any of the work that you've done up to this point. Besides, without that work, you wouldn't even have gotten here. True?"

I shrug my shoulders. It's technically true. If I hadn't worked on the shoot with Daria and gotten re-booked, I wouldn't have met Sasha, who introduced me to Jackson, who got me the audition with *Amora*. Technically . . .

"It *is* true," Marina finishes for me. "And three." She sighs, glaring at me slightly. "Jackson Ridge. If he isn't making you happy, ditch him."

I bite my lip, considering it.

The problem is, Jackson does make me happy when he wants to, and Marina's suggestion to ditch Jackson has my heart sinking, a realization that surprises me. The whole point of our agreement was supposed to prevent me from feeling this way.

"I'm serious, Cass. If he isn't worth all of this, leave him. I know you are going to counter with the fact that he is a celebrity and the same rules don't apply, *blah, blah, blah*, but I don't really care. If you don't think all of this is worth it, dump him. I don't care if he is the best sex of your life . . ." She trails off, and I look up at her. I know she is waiting for me to confirm or deny. I kick her leg, and she smiles, shaking her head before letting it go. "Anyway, the point is, it's your decision. Did that cover everything?"

"You forgot about whether any of this is worth it. Did I just waste almost three years of my life digging myself into a hole that I can't climb out of? What if modeling is just a stupid talent that my mother convinced me to pursue at the age of thirteen, and I was dumb enough to chase it all the way out here?"

"Well, that one is easy." I wait for her to continue. "Do you still love it?"

Her question catches me off guard, but I already know my answer. I do love it. I love the precision that is required for each shoot. I love the challenge of becoming someone new. I love the opportunity to transform every time I step on set.

I just hate all the noise that surrounds it.

"I do," I mutter under my breath.

"Then the rest just kind of seems irrelevant to me. Nothing worth it is ever easy. You have to fight for it."

Marina's right. I made a decision, many decisions, that led me to LA. I made a decision with Jackson, and I'm not going to back out of it just for fear of what others might think of me. I worked hard to get here, and I don't want to give it up now.

"You make fair points," I relent, and she smiles, content with her quick and efficient diagnosis. "But just because you gave reasons for everything doesn't mean I can't still be depressed."

"That is very true, you are allowed approximately ten more

hours of grief, and then you must move on." She lifts her nose in the air, and I release a small laugh. "Now, are you going to unmute so I can watch this trash with you?"

"Obviously." I smile, lifting the blankets for her to slide in next to me. She situates herself against the pillows, and I flip the sound back on, letting my head fall to her shoulder.

Marina's right, something has to change.

CHAPTER 22

Jackson

I stare ahead at the table of people around me. Zana is doing most of the talking, so I just have to sit back and pretend to pay attention. Truthfully, I stopped listening the moment we started discussing *To Hell and Back*.

It's my next movie with the studio coming out this fall. Some rom-com, fluff project that I signed onto what feels like a lifetime ago because I wanted to star in their summer blockbuster, *Annihilation*. It was a mistake. The early projections are already estimating that *Annihilation*, which premieres in a week, will lose the studio money. *I* will lose them money. Without even really paying attention, I know that the entire point of today's meeting is to mitigate the financial risk for their other projects.

Me, essentially.

I hadn't been looking forward to the meetings today, any of them. I knew how they would go. The studio would complain about revenue, Zana would remind them of me, their asset, and they would haggle over strategies to boost engagement on a project that has no business grossing $100 million on opening weekend.

I sit back while everyone points fingers, trying to find someone else to blame. It's toxic, yet boring. I've heard a million and one of these, especially with studios getting more desperate.

The chatter around the table is entirely different than the Hall Studios meeting last week. I have successfully been able to keep Zana out of that conversation, for now. I figure it's only a matter of time before she gets wind of it, but for now, it feels good to have something that's just mine. I only met with the studio for a few minutes on a video call, but the entire tone of the team is different than anything else I've seen.

They seem collaborative versus the combativeness that I've come to know. It felt encouraging and even if it doesn't go anywhere, it gives me hope that other opportunities like that exist.

I lean back in my chair, clicking the pen on and off, staring at my phone. It lights up every few minutes with alerts and messages, but nothing substantial. Nothing from Cassie.

We haven't spoken in a few days. When I texted her last week, she bailed. It rattled me more than I would like to admit. It makes me anxious, not seeing her, but I'm too stubborn to tell her so.

"I appreciate the context, but I don't think you realize exactly what Jackson is capable of." I look up when I hear my name. Zana gestures toward me, while also pretending that I am not really here. "The fact that you're selling any tickets at all is because his face is on the motherfucking poster hanging on the side of your building."

I fight a smile. This is why Zana is my agent. She's a bulldog, doesn't take no for an answer, and very rarely does she not get her way. She gets the paycheck, at the expense of anyone else, at the expense of anything else.

"Of course." Ken, the studio executive, throws me a careful smile. "We're not negating that fact, but the movie itself wasn't supposed to be the gamble. It was supposed to be the profit that allows us to finance these passion projects your *client* seems so invested in."

"Get better writers then." Zana shrugs indifferently.

"Look, I don't think any of us sitting around this table doubts Mr. Ridge's . . . appeal." Ken says and I resist the urge to roll my eyes. "In fact, we believe that it's something worth leveraging."

"We're listening." Zana sits forward, speaking for both of us.

"*To Hell and Back*," he mentions the title of my upcoming stale romantic comedy. "It can't fail and we're here to make sure it doesn't. Heather is with our marketing department and has a few ideas to boost engagement." Ken gestures toward the blonde behind him.

I make a noise under my breath and look away, tuning it out. No one really acknowledges it. They already know what sort of shit deal it is. Press and publicity help sell the story. If you create enough stir, gossip, rumors, people will line up in the masses, not caring that they just paid twenty dollars to watch a shit movie. If people believe that my co-star and I are fucking, they will make the investment.

"Any objections?" he asks, eyebrows raised.

I glare at Zana, silently trying to communicate that I want her to tell them to fuck off, but she doesn't even look. She just taps her pen on the table, the rattle echoing for a few more seconds.

"None from our end," Zana eventually answers for me. "We all know Jackson will do whatever is needed to make this partnership successful."

The room goes quiet. All eyes swing to me. My hand tightens around the pen in my hand. I feel like I just swallowed a gallon of spoiled milk. Zana knew the exact implication she was making, and by the looks of everyone staring at me from across the table, they know it too.

I work to keep my face stoic, act bored, pretend that it doesn't bother me. Eventually, people look away and go back to whatever they had been pretending to do.

"Good." Ken nods. "Let's regroup in a few weeks."

"Excellent."

I glare at Zana until the meeting finally ends. Once we wrap, she stands, walking to the exit without even bothering to look at me, her eyes glued to her phone.

"Let's hope for more positive pre-sales, yeah?" She goads me once we are alone.

"It doesn't matter," I say, following her down the hall. "I'm not doing whatever they want to pitch."

"You'll do whatever they tell you to do if you want that paycheck. I think I made that clear."

"I'm not doing this shit again," I threaten under my breath.

"You don't really have a choice."

"Then get me something better," I order in a low voice.

She finally stops, turning to look up at me. Everything about her is harsh. Her eyes, her face, her tone. Sharp, defined. She'd scare the shit out of me if she wasn't my agent.

Her eyes narrow while she taps the phone in her hand. "I might have something. A bigger role, no pay cut. Opportunity, you might say."

"What is it?"

"Think of it as a mutually beneficial proposition." I tense, waiting for the hook. "Victoria Baxter is looking for a new lead—"

Pain.

I feel it everywhere, but it starts in my heart, trailing down my arms, seeping into my legs, making them heavy. I squeeze my eyes shut, like I can physically block it out.

"No," I say, brushing past Zana, storming toward the exit.

"You didn't even let me finish." She keeps up easily.

"And you don't need to," I call over my shoulder. "I'm not working with her, ever again."

"Might I remind you that she is the reason you are even standing here. Without her—"

"I said, *no*." I tower over her, using my size and temper to intimidate her to stand down and just fucking drop it before I implode from the inside out.

"Fine." Zana sighs, unfazed. "Let's hope you can still sell tickets with that stellar reputation of yours, Jackson Ridge." She pats my chest twice before walking away.

I close my eyes, clenching my hand into a fist before I step outside. I climb into the back seat of the car, ordering Nic to take me to the nearest bar as soon as I slam the door shut.

CHAPTER 23

Cassie

I grip the steering wheel, searching for tinted windows in the crowded parking lot, looking for people with cameras. I had specifically chosen a grocery store at least three miles from my apartment in hopes that it would be far away from wandering eyes. I think I'm safe, but I can't make myself move.

The *Amora* news broke this week, and since the press release made its rounds, I've been checking over my shoulder constantly. At first, I thought it was a ridiculous concept. I couldn't wrap my mind around why anyone would think any part of my life would be fascinating, especially one without Jackson by my side, but last weekend, a photo of me circulated from an anonymous post after I went out for a drink with Marina. I had been used to only expecting the press with Jackson, but I know that the post means I am now fair game.

I waited for this to feel normal, and then I wondered if it ever could. Jackson has been dealing with the press's fascination with him for the past decade, but he always looks so calm. Here I am, crumbling after only a few weeks.

I didn't hear back from Jackson after I cancelled dinner plans last week, and I haven't really tried to reach out. He made it clear that he only needs me around for events and appearances, which means that I am just waiting for the next appointment to be scheduled. I have a speech prepared in my head for the next time we see each other. I just need to be brave enough to use it.

I tug my baseball hat over my eyes and step out of the car. I roam the aisles quickly, sticking to the essentials, hoping that no one is directly staring, but I still can't help but feel the need to check over my shoulder every five minutes just to be sure. I let out a breath when I finally exit, groceries in hand.

I slam the trunk shut after unloading, eager to escape back to the safety of my apartment, when a familiar voice calls my name.

"Cassie?"

I already know who is behind me before I turn.

He let his hair grow long, sweeping across his forehead. Sunglasses cover his eyes, which is probably a good thing. Those honey-brown eyes got me into all sorts of trouble when we were together.

Noah.

I wasn't expecting to see him again . . . *ever*. The reminder that he ignored all my texts after he'd dumped me springs to the surface. He didn't even have the decency to reply to any of them, let alone pick up the phone and talk to me.

"What . . . what are you doing here?" I ask, scanning the parking lot.

"I need to talk to you."

I barely process his request. "Did you *follow* me?"

"I didn't realize you had a monopoly on the neighborhood Trader Joe's—"

"*Noah*," I cut him off.

He sighs. "I texted you."

I almost choke. "Really? Well, I wouldn't know. You've been blocked from my phone for a while now."

Noah's jaw hardens and he steps towards me, pulling his sunglasses off. Instinct tells me to keep my distance. He can talk his way out of anything, and I don't want him to believe for a second that he still holds that power over me.

"I just want to talk."

I cross my arms over my chest. "Well, I have nothing to say."

"I was in London, Cassie. I didn't see any of the messages until it was too late." His excuse is pathetic, as expected, he always had a problem accepting responsibility. Nothing was ever *his* fault.

"I really couldn't care less at this point."

I sense the increasing length of our conversation. There are many things left unsaid, but discussing the dynamics of our break up in a public parking lot isn't high on my priority list for the day, or ever, for that matter.

"Cassie, please, can we just talk about this?"

A flare of anger spirals through me at the accusation in his words. "Are you kidding? I don't want to talk to you anymore. I don't want to *see you*! It's too late."

"Guess I can't say I'm surprised, considering how fast you moved on."

My jaw nearly drops to the ground. "You broke up with *me*. You don't get to judge my choices after you left. You gave up that right when you dumped me."

"It wasn't like that—"

"We were together ten months, you broke up with me over text, then fled the country. Tell me then, what *was* it like?"

"You didn't give me a chance to explain!" he yells.

"I gave you more than a chance!"

"Cassie—"

"Just stay the hell away from me!"

I see the cameras before I can comprehend the location or direction of where they're coming from. I lift my hand in an attempt to block the onslaught of flashes, and then I lock eyes with Noah, walking away, still facing me when he shrugs.

I know why Noah showed up today. A public spectacle is exactly what he wanted.

I am frozen for just a handful of seconds before the paparazzi turn on me. I hold up my purse to cover my face as I fish my keys out. I feel like crying when I jump in, instantly mortified that people will see the car that I drive. I jam my key into the ignition, ignoring the ding from my lack of seatbelt, and punch out onto the main drive, merging quickly into traffic with cars chasing behind me. I am close to hyperventilating when I push the gas to take me through a yellow light, then jerk the car to the left, searching for an escape.

I manage to lose a few cars in the last intersection, but it does nothing to suppress my hysteria. They now have my license plate. If they follow me back to my apartment, they will know where I live. Without thinking, I jerk the car to the left, heading north.

My hands grip the steering wheel to prevent them from shaking. It takes a few minutes before I have enough control over the car to grab my phone from my purse. I dial Jackson's number, holding the phone on speaker as I scan the cars behind me. It's not until the second-to-last ring that I hear his voice on the receiver.

"Yeah?" His voice is rough, but I don't have the luxury of being offended.

"Hey, are you home?" I ask, voice shaking, while I check my rearview for cars merging lanes behind me.

"Why? What's wrong?"

"I just left and . . . I don't know how they found me. I got to my car, and they started following me—"

"Woah, woah. Who is following you?" he asks urgently.

"I don't know, people with cameras. He must have called them, and then they came at me, so I got into my car. They followed me onto the street but I don't want to go back to the apartment in case they're still behind me. I don't want them to know where I live and I—"

"Hey, it's okay. It will be okay," he reassures me and I can tell he's moving someplace quieter. "I can send you my address. I'll call ahead to the gate to let you in."

"Okay." I breathe, feeling his reassurance flow through me, enough to calm me down a bit.

"I'm in Santa Barbara right now. I don't think I'll be able to get back for a few hours."

"No, that's okay. I think I just need a place to sit for a while before I go home."

I take the next exit and although the adrenaline starts to fade, I still check my mirrors at the stoplight.

"Hey, Cass?" Jackson asks.

"Yeah?"

There is a pause on the other line, and I hold my breath waiting for him to fill the silence. The words that he eventually releases sound forced, like he meant to say something else but changed his mind.

"I'll be back as soon as I can."

"Okay."

Then the line goes dead.

~~~

By the time I bypass the gate and catch my breath, dozens of headlines are already circulating. My suspicions had been confirmed by almost every outlet. Noah called the press and then followed me to that parking lot. His name was now being published alongside mine.

CASSIE TAYLOR AND RUMORED EX, NOAH VAUGHN, REUNITE IN SANTA MONICA.

"We took a break when I went to London to record my debut album. I didn't think she would just move on so fast. I love her, you know. I always will."
~~~

I drop my phone in my purse before I can do anything rash, like unblock Noah and blast him through the phone. I know that silence is my best weapon. Anything I send to him will only fuel the narrative that he is trying to sell. The more I play into his games, the more I lose.

Jackson's house is dark in front of me. I can drive away and deal with everything tomorrow, or I can step inside and wait for Jackson to come home so that we can talk, really talk. I force myself to stick with the latter and push open the door to his empty mansion. My shoes echo on the cool tile when I step inside and stare into the empty house.

It's quiet. So quiet, it's like I can hear my thoughts echo through the hollow hallways. No wonder Jackson doesn't like staying here alone. I turn on every light switch I come across, if only to prevent the darkness in the house from gazing back at me.

I drop my things at the counter and then pull open the door to the fridge. I pour myself a large glass of wine and stand at the counter, staring out at the sparkling skyline. The lights and glow of the city beyond the glass seem less than spectacular now, almost foreboding. Everything looks beautiful when it sparkles, but now, I feel like I can see through it.

I don't want *this* version of the story. Nothing good will come of this. It will be a miracle if I come out of this with my reputation still intact.

It's not just Noah that I am angry with, I'm disappointed with myself. When did I become this person who allows other people to sell stories about myself? I let Jackson design a narrative for me to follow along with, and now I'm allowing Noah to paint a picture of my character for the entire world to see. Maybe I can't control Noah, maybe I never could, but I can control my life, and I can control my choices, starting with Jackson.

I finish the glass of wine and drag myself to the couch, falling against the cushions. I turn on the TV to prevent the silence from screaming back at me, and wait.

CHAPTER 24

Jackson

Cassie's asleep on the couch when I step into the living room, her dark hair spilled out on the gray cushions. After a fucking shit day, it's nice to walk through the front door knowing that there is someone else here, waiting for me, regardless of the circumstances.

As soon as I got the call, I scanned the media for the leak. It didn't take long to find the source. It was a setup from some wannabe singer, Noah Vaughn. It took me all of five seconds to piece together how they knew each other. She used to fuck him. I recognize him from the picture in her room. If I hadn't found it, it probably would have stayed there, tucked away for safekeeping. I don't know why, but the fact that she hid it from me makes me angrier than I care to admit. She should have told me.

I let out a controlled breath, crossing the room and take a seat beside her. I hesitate before my fingers brush her cheek, tucking some hair behind her ear. I hope that by touching her, it can calm a part of me down.

She fidgets, blinking a few times before opening her eyes, puffy and red.

"You've been crying," I say, working to dull the blade in my voice. She sits up, wiping her cheek, and shrugs with a heavy swallow. "How are you?"

"Sort of shitty," she says, flipping me to defense.

"What happened?"

"I don't know. I mean, he must have followed me. He had to have called the paparazzi, because they all swarmed the second he got there." She looks up at me, out of breath, eyes low.

She's hurt, I can tell, and still, I can't stop myself from asking. "He's your ex?"

"Yes." She winces.

"You still talk to him? See each other—"

"No." She cuts me off, shaking her head. "I haven't seen him in months. I haven't spoken to him since we met."

"Did you love him?" I ask quickly, even though I shouldn't.

She pulls back, clearly offended. "What does that matter?"

I shrug. "It's a simple question."

"So are mine, and you don't bother to answer any one of those."

I roll my eyes and stand, needing space to think. Cassie doesn't let me get too far, following behind as I make my way to the bar. I pour a healthy glass of whiskey and take a sip. It's not my first glass of the day. Not even my second. I am still searching for a numbing agent to linger in my chest, flood my veins. I've been searching for a solution since the meeting this afternoon.

"What is it?" Cassie asks, trying to meet my eye. "What's wrong?"

"What's *wrong*?" I ask, voice dripping in disdain. "Let's see, after a shit day, I come and find that you and your ex-fuck buddy made the front page. Every outlet is running the story, obliterating all the shit I've been trying to feed them instead." I allow a breath, trying to soften my tone. "If you just told me about him, I could have handled the situation. This would have never happened."

She rears back. "So, this is my fault?"

"It's not mine."

"Well, if that's how you feel, then maybe we should just take a break."

I come to a full stop, taking her in. Her face is set, eyes narrow. I can tell that she is trying to be angry with me, but when I see a glimmer of tears, I wonder if I took things too far.

"What do you mean?"

"I mean . . ." She inhales before the words fall out. "Everything is happening too fast, and I am in no state to handle it, whatever *it* even is. What if this isn't worth it? I see the posts online, hate messages from strangers. I am getting stalked. I'm nervous to leave my house. I'm supposed to handle all of this, just for a steady job? If that's the case, maybe I picked the wrong career."

I shake my head, trying to brush off the accusation she just tossed at me. What if this isn't worth it? I translate it in my mind: *What if I'm not worth it?*

"If this is about security—"

"It's not about that." She cuts me off with a sigh. "I just . . . I think we need to take a step back. I feel like I can't breathe. I need to breathe."

"How do you think I feel?" I raise my voice, and the migraine that I've been fighting all afternoon hits me with full force.

What the fuck does *she* have to complain about? It's a story, a shitty one, yeah, but it's nothing in the scheme of things. It's going to be old news in a day. The stories written about me follow me around for *life*.

"I can guess, and I don't know how you put up with it."

"Yeah, well, I don't have a choice!" I yell, hate that I am, but I can't stop.

"Yes, you do." She leans forward to reach for me, but I step back. I don't let her touch me, *can't* let her touch me.

"You don't get it," I say in a low breath.

"Then help me to," she pleads. "All I've ever asked is for you to be honest with me. Tell me. Why can't you talk to me? Why do we have to be like this?"

I lean forward, pressing both hands on the counter, my head

low. "There is a reason that I don't do relationships. I can't handle them, okay? It would ruin both of us."

"Why would you say that?"

"Because that's what I know." I glare over at her.

"Well, then why did you choose me for this arrangement? It's not like I was your only option."

"*Cassie* . . ." I exhale roughly as a warning.

I can't have this conversation now, won't do it, actually. The answer doesn't matter anyway. I can't tell her that when I'm around her, I feel like I can actually breathe, not when she isn't even on board with the idea anymore. If she doesn't even know if I'm worth it. I'm probably not, and that's a truth I've been running from for as long as I can remember. I don't plan to face it now.

"Can we not do this right now?" I practically beg her to stop.

"Why not?"

"Because I don't want to have this fucking conversation at one in the morning!" I slam the glass back down on the counter.

"Well, if that's how you feel, then I can't do this anymore."

"What's *this*?"

"This!" She gestures to the space between us with her hand. "This entire ridiculous arrangement. It's not like you are giving me any type of warning of what to expect, of what I am supposed to endure. When I tell you how I feel, you ignore me. When I ask for details, you walk away. I have to put up with all this bullshit without getting anything in return."

"*Nothing* in return?" I mock her, stepping forward, using my body to tower over her. "What more could you possibly want from me? I have given you *everything* that you could have asked for. Fame, jobs, status."

I know my cheap shot landed when I see her mouth fall open.

"So that's what you think of me?" she asks softly, tears filling her eyes, and I have to look away. I know I'm hurting her, but I don't know how to stop. "This was *your* idea! You were the one desperate enough to ask a stranger to be in this fake relationship!"

"And you were the one desperate enough to take me up on the offer!" I fire back. "What did you think was gonna happen? Did you think they were just going to love you overnight? No. You have to *earn* it."

"I don't want to earn it!"

"Then leave!" My voice echoes through the empty halls.

I pretend like the thought of Cassie leaving doesn't hurt me. Pretend like I can go on living just as I have and my life will be fine. I have to pretend because I don't want her to realize the sort of power she has over me. I don't want *anyone* to have any power over me. Not ever again.

"You don't like it? Get the fuck out!" I yell, pointing toward the door.

"You're an asshole!" she screams back.

"Believe it or not, I've been called worse," I say under my breath and start toward the bedroom, needing the conversation to be over.

Cassie follows, keeping up the pressure. "So, this is how you solve all your problems? By walking away?" I know she is baiting me. I can feel the spark nearing the end of the line. It's about to explode. "You're just going to completely dismiss our entire conversation?"

"I'm not dismissing it," I tell her over my shoulder.

"Not dismissing it, just avoiding it, then?"

"I'm not avoiding anything."

"You're avoiding everything!"

I turn, needing her to look at me, to hear me. "*This* is what I can't handle, okay?" I gesture in the space between us. "I can't handle *this*! I don't need you questioning every decision I make. I do what I want, when I want."

She shakes her head, stepping away from me slowly, like she just now sees me, truly sees me. A flimsy copycat of a person, a hollow shell.

"I wish I never met you," she says quietly, her voice wavering.

I roll my eyes. "I highly doubt that's true."

She delivers the final blow with tears in her eyes. "You're a coward."

I come to a full stop, channeling all the anger and frustration into my fists as they curl closed.

"Take it back," I order between clenched teeth.

"And you'll always be alone." Cassie turns, spinning on her heel before rushing out of the room.

"Fuck you!"

~~~

I down a drink, then another. Cassie stormed upstairs after our fight and I know it's only a matter of time before she leaves, after how I treated her. I'm leaning over the bar, hands pressed against the counter, head low, and I replay it all again.

I shouldn't have yelled, shouldn't have said what I said. I didn't mean it. I just . . . needed a way for Cassie to look away, to look at something other than myself.

Her words echo through my head.

What if it's not worth it?

"Fuck."

What if I'm not?

And then she threw the one truth back in my face that I've been running from for as long as I can remember.

I'm alone.

I'm alone, and all the fucking noise and distractions can't hide that simple fact.

I'm alone because I don't know how not to be.

I throw the door open to the patio, storming over to the ledge of the balcony and turn to glare at the house I bought for myself. The house that I hate. Cassie upstairs, alone, because I yelled at her for telling me how she really feels.

I've never asked. I just assumed I knew what she was thinking, how she was feeling, but she was always asking me. What I
~~~

think, how I feel, questions about my personal life that I don't want to talk about.

I know it's what normal people do. Normal people talk about their days, ask each other how they are feeling, but it's not something I do. I don't know how to even articulate what I'm feeling. Besides, why would anyone *care*? I bite my lip, shaking my head before I finish my drink.

If today hadn't been so completely shit, maybe I could have listened when Cassie told me how she was feeling. If Zana hadn't name-dropped the one fucking person I never want to think about again, maybe I could have let Cassie convince me that there might be another side to this life that I made for myself.

But I had a shit day, and Zana *did* say her name, and since then, all I've been trying to do is forget about it, about all of it. Reinforce the walls that Cassie is so desperate to tear down and just have her back off.

Fuck, am I like *her*? The one person whose name splits me in two. The name that has me self-destructing just hearing it? Are we the same? Using other people to get what we want, regardless of the consequences?

I drop my head. My grip tightens on the railing, and I try not to remember. I try, but the memories start flooding back. The way I felt when Victoria used me, the words she spoke that made me feel like a thing, not a person. Victoria chewed me up, spit me out, and threw away the pieces. Do I make Cassie feel the same way? Like she was trapped, following through with some obligation that she didn't even want anymore?

I didn't mean to hurt her. It's been a defense mechanism for so long that I don't think it was conscious. It was like I was on autopilot, watching myself in disgust but powerless to stop it.

I push off the railing, rushing inside. I scale the steps to the second floor and wait outside the closed door. I inhale a deep breath, lifting my fist to knock, but before I can make contact with the wood, it swings open. Cassie is standing on the other side. Her hair is thrown up into a ponytail, her eyes are red, and I know it's because of me.

"Hey," I test the waters.

"Hi." She wipes her cheek quickly. "I was just coming to find you."

I nod, swallowing. "Can I come in?"

She studies me for a moment, and then pushes the door open. I follow her inside, hovering at the edge of the bed when she climbs under the covers. She turns over her shoulder, and then nods, answering a question I didn't even ask.

I slip in beside her, wrapping my arms around her waist, tugging her back to my chest. As soon as I touch her, I immediately relax and let out a shaky breath.

I wonder for a moment that maybe this is it. Maybe we can't move forward. Maybe it's our last night together, and if it is, then I want to hold her so that when life becomes scripted and empty again, I'll remember what it felt like to fall asleep with her in my arms.

"I'm sorry," I admit into the dark.

She readjusts, burrowing herself deeper in my embrace. "Me too."

My shoulders relax. I didn't think I needed to hear the words until she actually spoke them. "I didn't mean what I said. I don't want you to go."

"I don't want to go either," she says, and I brace myself for the catch. "I just need you to talk to me, okay? I need you to tell me that things are going to be okay. I need you to try to relate to how I am feeling with all of this."

I know that in any other situation, they are easy requests, but to me, they seem almost impossible. I wish I was good at this, communicating, feeling. Wish it didn't feel so forced, wish it came natural, so I could be normal for once instead of this automated robot, programmed to distrust every single person I encounter.

I collect a breath and work to find the words she needs from me. "You asked me why I chose you." She doesn't say anything, but I can tell she is waiting. "I felt this need . . . to protect you. You're different from anyone I've ever met. You're authentic and real. I don't want to take that away from you. And the way you see me . . ." My arms tighten around her waist, like I am afraid she is going to slip away. "You don't see me the way anyone else does. You don't see me the way anyone else ever has. You make me forget."

"Forget what?"

"That I'm Jackson Ridge," I admit into the dark and collect another breath. "I don't want to lose you."

She tightens her hold on my arms but stays quiet.

I can feel it, right there, the lines that we drew in the sand have started to fade with the tide, and I realize I have no idea where we go from here. I just know that I don't want it to end.

I don't let myself fall asleep until I am sure that she's content. I close my eyes eventually, hoping to dream of a time and place where the two of us together make sense.

Because I know that if I wasn't so fucked up, we might be able to work.

CHAPTER 25

Cassie

I'm sitting in my car outside the restaurant, tapping my hands against the steering wheel, debating whether or not I should venture inside. When I got Sasha's text this morning, I couldn't imagine why she would want to meet me. I honestly hadn't expected to see her again without Jackson.

Curiosity. That's why I'm here.

Outside of Jackson's apology last week after our fight, we really haven't had a chance to discuss what happened. I'm going with him to the premiere this weekend, but I'm not really planning on it being the perfect place for us to talk either, even though I know there's still a lot that needs to be said.

JACKSON
Hair and makeup will be at the house Friday at 11 a.m. Let me know if you want me to pick you up.

I read Jackson's latest text before pocketing my phone. I look over my shoulder when I step out of my car, checking for any stolen glances. Luckily, the coast looks clear.

Sasha is sitting at a small table outside on the patio. Her hair is thrown up in a high ponytail and her dark skin practically glows in the afternoon sun. She raises a hand when she sees me, smiling widely.

"Thanks for meeting me on such short notice," she greets me with a quick hug.

"Of course," I say, taking the seat across from her.

"Can I get you two anything?" I hear the waiter's upbeat voice from my left.

"Two glasses of rosé, please," Sasha orders for both of us, handing him our menus.

I take a sip of water when my phone buzzes in my lap. I glance down at the latest text from Jackson.

JACKSON

Are you around later? On my way back and want to see you.

I swipe the message away, ignoring it for the time being.

"So, I bet you are wondering why I called," Sasha prompts as the waiter drops the two rosés on the table, moisture already collecting on the glass. Little drops of condensation drip down my fingers as I grab it. I take a sip, and the sweet, crisp liquid hits my tongue.

"I actually thought Jackson might be here."

She waves her hand. "I didn't think he was necessary."

"But you are here because of Jackson, right?" I guess.

"I am."

"I assumed he would be related. What's up?"

She leans forward, resting both her elbows on the table, and I brace myself for the worst.

"Jackson called me the other day. I know it's not my business, but I feel like you deserve some sort of explanation. I've known Jackson a long time, and I'd like to think I know him pretty well, despite what he keeps to himself. Once you spend time with him, he starts to make more sense, but I have a feeling, based on what he told me, you might not give him another chance."

I don't answer because, in all honesty, I haven't decided what to do. We both apologized for getting caught up in the heat of the moment, but it doesn't really change anything. Jackson can't give me what I want, and I can't do the same for him.

"I think it's important that you know he wasn't always like this," Sasha says.

I lean forward. "What was he like?"

"Different." She lets out a breath. "He didn't live his life with these made-up rules dictating what to say, how to act. He was kind, always, but he was . . . free. Free to be himself."

I swallow, knowing that the person I know now will always be different from the version that Sasha met nearly ten years ago. I reach for my wine glass, taking a healthy sip.

"I *know*, by the way." Sasha's words almost cause me to choke.

I cough, clearing my throat while I cover my mouth. "Excuse me?"

"He told me that you aren't dating, for real, at least." My cheeks immediately turn pink. "I didn't say that to make you feel bad, and please know that I wanted to kick him in the dick after he told me." She offers a smile to soften the blow, but it doesn't help. "I don't know why he does this."

"Has he done this before?" I ask, panic rolling through me.

"Yes, for the fact that he refuses to have a relationship with anyone. Anyone that he has been photographed with has just been a series of one-night stands or publicity stunts, never anything serious, not since . . . not for a while."

"*Why*?" I ask, thoroughly confused.

Sasha reaches for her wine, eyes heavier in a way. "Because someone hurt him a long time ago, and he thinks it doesn't matter."

I sit up straight. "You know?"

She doesn't have to say it out loud; she already gave me an

answer. Sasha knows that the rumor that follows Jackson around, that he slept with someone to boost his career, is based in truth.

"He believes that it was his choice," Sasha says. "That's why he thinks it doesn't matter."

"But you don't think it was?"

"No," she says clearly, meeting my eye. "Victoria was thirty-nine. He was barely eighteen. You tell me who was in control in that situation."

My heart breaks all over again, eyes filling with tears I try to force away. My mind flashes back to the article I stumbled across on Jackson's computer, the list of articles saved by date on his desktop, all related back to *her*.

I immediately hate her, and I don't know if I've ever truly hated anyone before.

"Do you know who leaked it?" I ask.

"I have a hunch." She swirls the wine in her glass, looking down at the table. "But no, it's never been confirmed."

"You knew them?" I ask, leaning forward. Sasha swallows another sip of wine. Her lack of answer is validation enough. "Does Jackson know?"

"No." She sighs. "He doesn't like to talk about it. He's made it clear it is do-not-enter territory. Given everything he's gone through, it's obvious why he keeps most things close. He doesn't let most people in, but I also know that he trusts you."

"*Me*?" I ask, dumbfounded. Yes, he has released small, minuscule details about his past, but only after I barged in with a wrecking ball. "Why?"

"Because you're staying. Because you haven't run and sold a story, sold any story, despite . . . everything."

I pull back. "Was he testing me?"

"I don't think he does it on purpose. I think he does it because he doesn't know any different. He's used to believing the worst in people."

I lean back in the chair, turning away for a moment. Jackson trusts me because I've kept quiet, because I stayed, yet here I am contemplating leaving him at the first sign of trouble.

All week I've been going over it again in my mind. I keep circling the idea that I need to get out now, while I still have my reputation intact. Each time I run through the scenario, I know the logical decision, but every time I arrive at the ultimatum, my chest compresses, because if I leave to protect myself, who will be left to protect him?

"It doesn't help the fact that he has decided to stay in a toxic environment that fucks with your head," Sasha says.

"Yeah, but so are you."

"Not really." Sasha frowns thoughtfully. "I mean, I was. Jackson and I both started in the industry at the same time. We had some modeling campaigns together, right around the time he was picked up as a guest star on *Sunset City.* It was flattering, at first, to be the center of attention, to have your name plastered on the covers of magazines, attending every party, every premiere, but . . . it was also suffocating. I stopped going to the events, piling up work, of course, but I didn't want to handle the publicity pieces. When I stepped back, Jackson leaned in. He became obsessed with it, with *all* of it. The events that weren't mandatory but certainly kept him in the public eye. I saw the cost that I would be forced to pay, and I said no. Jackson, on the other hand, was fine to make those sacrifices for the sake of his career."

My stomach bottoms out. "Sacrifices?"

"Everyone sacrifices something for their dream, right? Jackson has stopped counting them at this point. There are too many."

I swallow, bracing myself for impact while Sasha continues.

"He likes to set up these boundaries to prevent people from getting too close. He can't stand to be alone, but he doesn't know how not to be. He consistently sacrifices his well-being for attention, money. It's all he knows."

Alone. That word again.

I slump in my chair. Now I know the seriousness behind

the comment that I threw in his face the other night. He hurt me, and I threw it back because I wanted to hurt him, but I shouldn't have said it. I'm not that kind of person, and I don't want to be.

I feel for this person that Sasha describes. Alone by his own making, yet tormented by it. I'd hate to learn everything Jackson did to become successful. Everything that he left behind to move forward.

I tilt my wine in my glass on the table, wondering if I am going to be the next piece he discards when something better comes along, a new opportunity for fame or money. It's why he staged our relationship the way he did. An easy out when he needs it.

"Look, I don't know you that well, but I know him," Sasha says. "I'm not telling you these things to push you away. I'm telling you because I know that he won't, and if he doesn't, it will break the two of you apart. He doesn't want that. I know he doesn't. You're different than anyone he has been with, ever. I haven't seen him this happy in a long time."

"But it's not a relationship, Sasha. He specifically told me he doesn't want a relationship. How am I supposed to stay when he doesn't communicate with me?"

She sits back in her chair, thinking before she answers. "It's not that he doesn't want to communicate; it's that he doesn't know how. He's been programmed not to. Nearly everything he has ever told someone has ended up in the press."

An ache blooms in my chest. A feeling of longing passes through me, and I think of all the stories that have been published about him. How many had been released without his consent? How many had destroyed any semblance of privacy he felt?

"I know I am in no position to make demands," Sash says. "You can decide to get up and walk away from me, from him, from all of it, and *he* will let you go, but I know he will be worse for it. I'm asking you as his friend, because he's not able to. Give him time. Give him space if you need, but don't give up on him. At least not yet."

We close out a few moments later, hugging goodbye. Sasha's words linger long after we separate. I turn my phone off when I get in my car and drive in a daze, up and down the PCH.

CHAPTER 26

Cassie

"You're going to send us thousands of photos, right?" Lucy asks, leaning over the back of the couch.

We're back on speaking terms after Marina forced her to apologize for her comment last week. I was happy to put it behind us. Besides, I'm used to Lucy speaking without a filter. Most of the time, I love her for it.

"As much as I am allowed," I mention over my shoulder.

"I need to see the dress, in full glam, before you get there!" Marina chimes in, practically skipping down the hall.

"Of course." I laugh softly.

I grab my stilettos, throwing them into the bag I packed, along with a change of clothes for tomorrow. I don't know if I will spend the night, but going off our track record, the odds are high enough, even if we still have a lot of ground to cover.

"Eeep! My baby's first premiere!" Marina claps.

"I can't believe you are going to a premiere before me." Lucy frowns.

Outside of logistical planning and pick-ups, Jackson and I haven't exchanged more than a handful of texts. Sasha's words have been bouncing back and forth in my head since our meeting, but I need to see him, talk to him, tell him how I really feel and hope that this time, he can handle it.

"Well, wish me luck!" I exhale nervously.

"Luck!" They both shout enthusiastically.

Before I am even out the door, Lucy and Marina dart to the window. I have a feeling they will be sneaking a peek through the open blinds.

Jackson is waiting for me by his car. He leans forward when he sees me, reaching out for the bag and dress in my hands after I descend the steps.

"Here, let me take that." He offers, his fingers lingering on my hand for a moment before he pulls away.

I slip in the passenger seat and immediately sink into the soft but firm leather interior. The air is pumping heavily through the vents to combat the relentless LA heat, and I am engulfed with the intoxicating scent of his cologne. He joins me a moment later, sliding into the driver's side of the car before turning to look out the window.

"I think your friends are watching," he says, fighting a smile. I lean forward to find Lucy's and Marina's faces practically glued to the glass. "Who's the blonde?"

"Lucy." I sigh. "She's the one who works for *EDaily*."

"Hmm." Jackson raises his hand, waving. We both smile, watching Lucy nearly hyperventilate from the window before I lean back in the seat.

I look over at him, knowing that I can't avoid his gaze for very long. I'm afraid of what his sincerity might do to my already crumbling self-control. His green eyes watch me closely.

"I am sorry, Cassie. I hope you know that," he says earnestly, and the inflection in his voice allows me insight into his candor. "I wasn't thinking about you or how you would be feeling. It was selfish and wrong, and I wish I could take it back."

The implication behind his words from that night hit me like knives, carving me up from the inside out, not just because he used them purposefully to offend me, but because I had secretly known people would see us together and immediately assume the same thing.

The notion that I am using him to get ahead in my career, when it would have never even crossed my mind to begin with, hurt me. The thought that people would automatically assume the worst, nearly broke me. Maybe I could have survived knowing people spoke these words about me behind my back, but when Jackson gave power to the words, saying them to my face, he forced my deepest insecurities to become real.

"You hurt me." I tell him, holding his gaze.

"I know," he says, head dropping. "It's no excuse, but I had a shit day, and I wasn't prepared to handle anything you were throwing at me. I'm not used to people . . . challenging me or prying into how I live my life. I didn't mean what I said. I'm gonna try to be more honest with you. It's not something I am comfortable with, but I want to try."

For you.

He doesn't explicitly say the words, but they are implied. He's going to try for *me.*

"I'm choosing to believe you." I hold his eyes, letting the meaning of my words resonate. I tell him it's a choice, because it is. I want to let him know that I see him, the good and the bad, and I'm staying for the good. I am staying for *him.* "Don't make me regret it."

"I won't," he tells me, his face resolute.

I buckle my seat belt as he pulls out of my parking lot and onto the road. Silence drifts between us for the next few minutes and besides the lull from the radio, he doesn't say much. His fingers tug on his bottom lip, and I know he is spinning something over in his mind. He drops his hand when he catches me watching, and I decide to cut him some slack, breaking the ice.

"So, what am I getting into tonight?" I ask.

"A premiere. You ever been to one?"

"Oh yeah, I go to them all the time," I reply sarcastically.

His lips twitch into a smile when he shifts into gear while we merge lanes.

"It's mostly for the press and the fans, and us, I guess. Lots of cameras, interviews, photo ops," he says before launching into a thorough and detailed description of our schedule, almost everything down to the minute is pre-planned. He doesn't explicitly say it, but I can tell this is the part of his job that he loves.

His driveway is filled with cars when we pull through the gate. I grab my dress from the back seat while Jackson carries my bag into the house. I almost don't recognize the space now that it's crowded. There are team members, stylists, assistants, it's packed with people.

I tense when I notice a bleached blonde rush toward us. Her hair is pulled back into an extremely tight ponytail that whips behind her. She is wearing dark eyeshadow, and her lips are painted a deep maroon. Everything about her is intimidating.

"You're late."

She nearly pushes me out of the way to get to Jackson. I quickly step out of the way to avoid the near collision.

"Cassie, meet Zana, my agent. Zana, Cassie." Jackson gestures toward me, but Zana doesn't offer me an extra glance. Either she is uninterested, too busy, or both.

"Right, look, I need you in the other room for the press junket," Zana orders Jackson. "Other networks were promised interviews, so you are booked until we leave. I have everything set up. It's just missing you."

"Got it." Jackson barely gets the words out before she stomps away.

I glare at her. There is something inherently disingenuous about her, and within five seconds of meeting, I don't like her. I want to ask Jackson what he thinks, but he pulls me into another introduction.

"André?" Jackson calls past me, and I turn to see a much friendlier face. "Can you take Cassie's dress?"

I cling to the fabric in my hands, terrified of letting it out of my sight. I look up at Jackson, the fear apparently obvious. I spent a quarter of my signing bonus with *Amora* on this dress. It's the most expensive piece of clothing I have ever owned.

"Don't worry. André will take good care of it, won't you?"

"Of course I will." André stands in front of me, a hand on his hip as I relinquish my dress. "You're due in hair and makeup in ten."

I force a deep breath to steady myself. Jackson's hand rests against the side of my arm, calling me back to attention.

"You okay?" he asks, ducking to meet my eye.

"Yeah." I shake out my hands. "Just a lot to process."

His thumb sweeps across my jaw, and I have to remind myself to take a breath when I meet his green eyes.

"What about us?" he asks softly. "Are we okay?"

I swallow, collecting myself. "I—"

"Jackson." Zana interrupts us with a glare, disrupting whatever moment we had been trapped in. We both turn to face her. When Jackson hesitates, she pushes harder. "*Now.*"

"Yeah, I'm coming," Jackson responds and then turns back to me. "Go get ready." His fingers brush my chin. "I'll find you when it's time to leave, okay?"

I nod, inhaling a breath, watching him walk down the hall and into his office. Zana turns to glare at me before she slams the door shut.

~

I sit in complete rapture as André goes to work on my face at the same time someone fusses with my hair. I've been in countless hair and makeup chairs before, and this process isn't entirely different, except I know that this moment will no doubt change everything. Jackson and I are about to make our red-carpet debut as an official couple. We are about to confirm our relationship in front of a hundred cameras, and my life will inevitably change in a few short hours.

When André finally steps away, I lean forward, blinking. I barely recognize the regal reflection looking back at me. My hair is parted down the middle and flowing down in elegant waves. I have a deep smoky eye that makes my hazel eyes appear five shades brighter. I stand up and twirl slightly, studying my reflection from the side. I've been dressed up before, in crazy outfits and ridiculous makeup meant to disguise your true nature and match the brand, but I've never looked like this before.

"It's amazing. Thank you." I smile wildly.

"I barely did anything; you gave me a lot to work with." He smiles and then hands me my dress. "Time to change."

A horde of people follow me into Jackson's bedroom, tugging me into place. They help me out of my clothes and steady my arms to allow me to step into my dress. I feel like I'm on set right now. I've never had this many people around me. It's overwhelmingly claustrophobic.

I suck in as I step into the gold dress, feeling the cool, tight material against my legs. Once I'm zipped up, I move forward, needing their hands off me, and study my reflection in the mirror. The entire dress is covered in gold sequins. Although I don't have much in the way of curves, the dress accentuates my waist, pulling in to give me the look of an hourglass figure. People crowd me again, tending to my face, my gown, but I try to ignore them while I stare into the glass.

In all my years of modeling, I have never worn something that made me feel so . . .

"Beautiful."

I look past my own reflection in the mirror to find Jackson leaning against the wall by the door. His tie hangs around his neck, hands in his pockets.

"Leave us," he orders the rest of the room.

I watch as everyone disperses without another word, shutting the door as they go.

The tux Jackson is wearing hugs him close, and the dark color of the material makes his eyes a light green. His blond hair is perfectly messy, styled in a way that makes me want to drag my hands through it.

He stands across the room, tie around his neck, hands in his pockets, staring at me like I'm the most beautiful thing he has ever seen, which is odd because Jackson is surrounded by lots of pretty things.

"Thank you," I say and carry my heels over to the bed. "How are we doing on time?"

"About ten minutes before the cars will be here," he says, pushing off the wall, walking toward me.

I stand when I finish the last strap of my heel, running my hands along the sides of my dress. I keep my head down for as long as I can before I finally lift my chin to look at him. His green eyes hold mine, looking at me in a way that makes my whole body heat. The scent of his cologne is a rush to the head, and a part of me wants to bury my face against his neck, inhaling a healthy dose.

I startle when the door to his bedroom swings open. Zana steps inside without bothering to ask for permission.

"Jackson?"

"Give me a minute," he orders, without breaking eye contact with me.

Zana purses her lips before disappearing from the room. I don't move until the door latches.

"I'm going to have to kiss you tonight," Jackson says.

My heart is thundering in my chest and I force myself to swallow. "I know."

He steps closer. "I'm going to *want* to kiss you tonight," Jackson says, amending his statement. "Is that okay?"

I process the meaning behind his words. That he wants a kiss to be *real.*

"Okay," I breathe.

His thumb brushes my bottom lip and then he's kissing me. It's the first time we've kissed since the rooftop, but this kiss is entirely different. Jackson takes his time, pretending that the world isn't waiting for us, knocking on the other side of the door. There are no cameras or people watching, the reminder that it's just us, creates a rush to my head. The kiss is soft, like a whisper of a promise that has me leaning in, begging for more, and this time, when I step forward, he lets me. I sigh, opening my mouth wider to allow his tongue to taste me. My chest presses against his, my body wanting more.

A rushed knock sounds on the door and all too soon, it ends. He pulls away, our foreheads resting against each other's while we catch our breath. I steady my hands against his chest, using the space to re-focus because I had almost been tempted to step out of the dress that I had just been zipped into and let him have his way with me.

He clears his throat. "We should—"

"Yeah, we should." I nod, sucking in another short breath.

He takes a step back, looking down at the unfastened tie around his neck, struggling with the black piece of fabric.

"Here, let me help." I offer, grabbing the tie from his hands as I work the pattern I had memorized since I was a kid.

"How'd you learn?"

"My dad." I pull the tie from underneath and then adjust the collar, tightening it around his neck. "He had to wear one to work every day, so he taught me how to tie it. He said it would be a practical skill."

Jackson's eyes don't waver from my face while I work. My cheeks start to warm the longer he stares.

"There," I say, resting my hands on his chest when I've finished. He doesn't move, and so I don't either. When I finally pluck up the courage to look at him, his eyes churn with an emotion I can't place. "What?"

"Nothing." He smiles. "Ready?"

"Almost."

I grab my phone out of my clutch, remembering my promise to Marina and Lucy. I grab Jackson's hand, leading him to the floor-to-ceiling mirror and hold up my phone for a picture. His hands wrap around my waist when he stands behind me, resting his chin on my shoulder as I snap a photo.

He kisses the side of my cheek before we leave, and then we load into the back of the cars, chasing the road down to Hollywood.

CHAPTER 27

Jackson

She's nervous.

I can tell by how she fidgets with the rings on her fingers, pulling them on and off while we race toward Hollywood. Zana is firing last-minute notes, but I'm not really listening. My eyes on Cassie while she stares out the window.

I reach for her hand, holding it in mine the rest of the way, feeling her grip tighten the closer we get to the carpet.

"You, okay?" I ask as we pull to a stop.

"Yeah." She forces a smile, tightening her grip on my hand again. "Don't let me fall."

"Never," I promise.

The second we step outside, we are swarmed. I lift a hand to keep people from getting too close as Zana leads us through the crowd. Fans lean in from the bleachers, holding out phones, cameras, and pens with memorabilia to sign. To my right, there is the line of press, positioned at the top of a small staircase where they can get the best angles.

I lean down to Cassie's ear, whispering just before we step up to the interview platform. "Ready?"

Cassie nods once, resolute, and I kiss her temple before we scale the steps, where we are greeted by Courtney Davis, host of

EDaily. Bleached-blonde hair, eager eyes, and sharp cheekbones. I've grown accustomed to Courtney's aesthetic. She's blunt and always driven to get the dirtiest scoop, whatever the cost. I should know; I've been on the receiving end many times.

"Jackson Ridge, great to see you!" Courtney practically bounces as she greets us, and I know why. She's about to break the story every single outlet has been drooling over for the past six weeks.

"Good to see you, Courtney." I offer her a knowing smile.

"Would you like to introduce us to your date?" Courtney's eyes light up.

"Cassie Taylor." Cassie steps forward to introduce herself. I swing my gaze toward her in a moment of genuine surprise.

"Lovely to meet you." Courtney forces a smile before turning her attention back to me. "You two have certainly stirred up some commotion these past few weeks, anything you care to comment on?" She asks, practically shoving the microphone in my face.

"We are supposed to be talking about the movie," I remind her with a playful smile.

It's a weak attempt to change the subject, but I know she won't fall for it. This is the same song and dance I'm used to. Give them a little, make them beg for more, and then they will follow you wherever you go.

"You know me well." Courtney smirks. "You've been all around the world for *Annihilation,* with LA as your final stop on tour. How does it feel to close out this project?"

"Ready to celebrate."

"And what is this that I hear about you splitting with Warner Studios?"

"I have nothing but love for the studio, they have given me some great opportunities. I'm really proud of the work the cast and crew has done together to create something really special."

"Any truth to the rumors about your private meeting with Silas Morland? World War I epic is certainly a different genre than Armageddon." She raises her eyebrows.

I toss her a knowing smile. "I'm just happy to be here with my cast, celebrating this movie we made together last year for our fans."

"Well, your fans certainly seem to love it." Courtney extends her hand toward the crowd of people leaning over the barriers to get a closer view. "And, Cassie Taylor, I have a feeling we are going to be hearing a lot more from you. How do you feel about being the new leading lady for *Amora*?"

Cassie smiles, leaning into me slightly. "I'm so thrilled. It's honestly a dream come true. I can't wait to get started, and I'm so lucky that I get to have Jackson by my side through it all."

"Well, you two make an adorable couple. I can't wait to see what is next, from both of you!"

"Thank you." I nod, lifting a hand to wave toward the cameras before I move my other hand to the small of Cassie's back, leading her back down the steps.

"How did I do?" she asks under her breath. "Did I do okay?"

"You were perfect," I say softly against her hair, pulling away to see her smile up at me.

We spend the next forty-five minutes making our way down the line for the press. Cassie watches carefully while I take each question in stride. When the microphone is eventually pushed in front of her face, she crafts her answers to follow the same tone and rhythm I've been giving. She's a natural. Every moment farther down the carpet, she becomes more relaxed. I can tell in her posture, the loosening of her grip in my hand.

By the end, I know the red carpet accomplished the second part of tonight's goal. I needed the press to be interested in Cassie on her own. After the past few weeks of reports, attention tends to fall off unless the rumors are confirmed with a story, and I know our appearance will make headlines in record time.

Once we finish with the press line-up, we stop against the giant backdrop for the movie promotion.

I tug Cassie close to my side. "I'll be right back. You good?"

"Yeah." She nods, smiling.

Fans practically climb over each other trying to get as close to us as they are able. I sign every piece of memorabilia shoved in my face. I lean close when phones come up, demanding selfies. I spend more time with them than any other interviewer today, feeling like I owe them a debt of sorts, like without them, I wouldn't be here. I feel a similar sort of responsibility with the press, though it's more on the indentured servitude side of things, like I *have* to endure them to get all of this.

This is the part that makes everything I have to tolerate, worth it. The invasion of privacy, the lack of respect when it comes to personal lives or boundaries, somehow that seems to be easily forgotten when you're standing before a crowd of this size as they shout your name back at you.

I wave my hands in the air, earning another round of applause before I go to find Cassie again, watching me with a slight smile on the sidelines.

"Ready?" I ask, wrapping an arm around her waist.

"Ready."

Our last interaction with the press for the night positions us against the backdrop of the movie poster. Cassie is pressed up against my side when she allows her hem to drop, letting the train of her dress drape beside her.

Photographers crowd each other, pushing against the metal barrier. I tighten my grip around Cassie's waist, ignoring the different commands shouted at us. I look down at Cassie, noting the way her eyes dart around, not sure where to land over the yelling.

"Cassie, over here!"

"Cassie, care to comment on your relationship?"

"How long have you been dating Jackson?"

"Cassie Taylor!"

She stumbles briefly, leaning further into my side. I give her a gentle squeeze meant to steady her, and when I do, she smiles up at me.

It hits me again, when her eyes meet mine. She's here. She stayed, for me. We hold each other for another moment, just the two of us, before we turn back toward the cameras.

When I am sure that they've caught enough, I lean in, pressing my lips against Cassie's ear before I whisper. "Your turn."

Her eyes widen as I take a step away, my hand lingering on her waist until I am far enough away to let my hand drop. As soon as I am out of the picture, photographers flock toward Cassie, wanting to capture *her* photo.

She's a natural, walking down the red carpet, photographers following her every move. She turns, giving the cameras a view of her sparkling dress from every angle. I watch closely out of the corner of my eye, waiting for her to panic or flee, but she doesn't. She remains calm, eyes wide, smile bright when she poses for their photographs.

"How long am I supposed to tolerate this?" Zana asks under her breath while we hover by the entrance of the theatre.

I keep my gaze forward, not turning away from Cassie. "As long as I say."

"She's stealing your spotlight and you're just . . . letting her."

"It's not mine for her to steal."

"Don't fucking make me look bad," Zana warns under her breath before stalking away.

"Hey." Cassie approaches, and her eyes flick to Zana's retreating figure.

"Hey." I straighten my shoulders and slip my hand into hers. "Good?"

"Good." She nods, smiling.

It's dark when we step inside the lobby of the theater. We are the last few to enter before the doors shut. Before walking to our seats, I stop, pulling Cassie back.

"Thank you," I say.

"For what?"

I contemplate all the things to thank her for and start with the most important.

"For staying."

Cassie's face softens. She places a hand over my chest and leans forward to kiss me. This one didn't have a meaning or a signal behind it. She didn't kiss me in front of others or the cameras so that people could see. She kissed me because she wanted to.

When we pull away, gazing at each other, I wonder if she is thinking the same thing, wondering if we are finally on the same page. Lights flicker in the lobby, signaling the start of the movie.

"Come on." I say, reaching for her hand to lead her inside.

The theater is buzzing with energy while we take our seats. After the speeches, when the theater lights dim and the opening credits appear, Cassie leans her head against my shoulder and I wish that I could freeze this moment in time, indefinitely.

CHAPTER 28

Cassie

LUCY

Are you freaking kidding me with this dress??

I read the message from Lucy in our group chat. The after-party has turned into the after-after party, and we are approaching 1 a.m. I have stopped drinking wine, knowing it will only put me to sleep faster, and instead, I've been keeping up with the endless supply of images Marina and Lucy have been sending me.

It was a shock, honestly, the press' reaction to our debut on the red carpet. I had been planning to avoid social media entirely tonight, worried that the comments or sound bites from an interview would surface where I stuttered or stumbled, but everything that Lucy and Marina have been sending me has been wildly positive.

EDaily boasted of breaking the story, but every outlet has been posting photos of Jackson and I from the red carpet. I scroll through a few and pause when I reach the last image, enlarging it on the screen. In the photo, Jackson is looking at me, but my attention is on the cameras. My smile is wide, and his arm is around my waist like I remember, but it's not my expression that I look at. It's his.

When I wasn't looking, I didn't realize how he looked at *me*. His eyes don't stray from my face even when I turned toward the press. I take in his slight smile, and I remember his hold against my waist. He is looking at me the way I always imagined he would. He is looking at me like he—

"Callie, right?"

I turn over my shoulder to see a beautiful brunette leaning up against the bar beside me. Her eyes are dark, coupled with catlike eyeliner that make them look even more narrow. She is wearing burgundy, her lips painted an equally dark red.

"Cassie," I correct her with a cautious smile.

"Right." She rolls her eyes. "Sorry. I'm Jenn Hamilton."

I know who she is. I just spent an entire movie watching her by Jackson's side. The two of them lip-locking after they saved the world together.

"So, you're Jackson's date for the night?" she asks, taking a sip of her martini.

I've met women like Jenn before. I know how they operate. They search for insecurities to exploit, and I refuse to give her one. I keep a tight smile on my face and try not to flinch against her cool accusation.

"Girlfriend, actually." I lift my chin in the air.

"Of course." She gives me an unsettling smile. "It's so hard to keep up with him these days. When we first started filming, I just got used to all the girls that he would bring to set. I kind of lost track."

"Mm-hm." I nod while she orders another drink, and luckily, Jackson swoops in at the perfect time.

"Hey." He appears behind me, arms around my waist, pressing me tightly against his chest. Jenn's eyes narrow. "I see you've met Jenn?"

"I have," I answer, looking her right in the eye.

"Cassie is lovely, Jackson." Jenn smiles, too widely. It's so obviously fake and I wonder if Jackson notices.

"I know," he says smugly and then turns to me. "Ready to go?"

"Yeah." I smile, looking up at Jenn, who seems annoyed not to be getting her way.

We say our goodbyes, and I say a silent prayer that I never have to see her again when we step outside, climbing into the car waiting for us.

We're approaching the twelve-hour mark since the premiere started. I assume it's the adrenaline rush that comes with attending these types of events, but I don't know how Jackson has the stamina to do this over and over again. I look out at the sparkling lights below as we climb higher and higher up the Hills toward Jackson's mansion. My eyes grow heavier after each mile.

"So?" Jackson interrupts my train of thought, pulling me against his chest.

"So?" I clarify, and even in the dim lighting, I can tell he is rolling his eyes.

"What did you think?"

"That's a profound question." I sigh, and I feel him laugh underneath me. "My feet hurt, I've had entirely too much wine, and I'm exhausted but . . . in the best way possible. I really don't know how you do it."

"You get used to it," he says melancholically, a tone that makes me wonder if you ever can get used to a life like his. "You'll see what I mean soon enough."

I pull forward. "What do you mean?"

"Isn't this what you want? What you're working toward?"

I fall quiet in his arms. Is this what I wanted? It seems so different than what I had imagined.

Jackson's arms tighten around me, and it feels like he is holding me just because he wants to, just like how we kissed outside the theater. We had been alone, no signals, no cameras, and our lips met in the most natural way, in a way that just made sense. Something shifted then. I don't know what, but it was seismic, something that we could both *feel.*

"You looked beautiful tonight." His thumb swipes down my leg, up and down, in a motion that makes me dizzy. "Did I mention that?"

"A time or two," I say, smiling up at him.

When the car pulls into the driveway, I reluctantly pull away from his embrace. His hand is in mine while he leads me into the house.

"I can't wait to take these damn heels off," I say, stumbling against the doorframe once inside as I kick off one of my stilettos.

I peer up to find Jackson watching me. He leans back against the opposite side of the wall, loosening his tie, keeping his distance. He's looking at me like he wants to undress me. Looking at me in a way that makes me want him to undress me. I know that I can bend down to pull off the heel myself, but I don't want to. I want him to touch me, and by the look in his eyes, I'm guessing he wants to, as well.

"A little help?" I ask, my voice soft.

Jackson's eyes meet mine, a silent question before he pushes off the wall, stepping forward, careful at first. He kneels before me, green eyes peering up at me while his hand cups my calf. As soon as he makes contact, my head falls back, a soft sigh escapes between my lips. His thumb makes a slow, circular motion, sweeping back and forth.

"Is this okay?" he asks.

I nod, my mouth going dry at the sight of him on his knees before me.

"Out loud," he commands, and his fingers still while he waits.

"Yes," I breathe.

My head falls back against the wall while his hands coast up my leg, my eyes closing when his lips brush the inside of my knee. He trails light kisses higher up my thigh. I press my hands against his shoulders to keep balance while Jackson carefully pulls off my heel.

I open my eyes when his touch disappears, just as his mouth crashes against mine, his body pressing me back against the wall. I kiss him eagerly, wrapping my arms around him, not wanting to let go.

Jackson had been holding out on me. His mouth claims mine passionately, slipping his tongue inside while I gasp. I grip his biceps, steadying myself while his hand presses to the small of my back, holding me there. His other hand falls to the base of my neck, tangling in my hair. There's not enough oxygen, not enough air. I forget to breathe, consuming him instead.

"What about this?" He pulls away from my mouth briefly, his breath tickles my neck, causing me to sigh. "Is this okay?"

My body tightens, and I tip my head so his lips can find the sweet spot just above my pulse. I let out a soft moan when he finds it, and my hips lift against his, feeling the hardness there.

"Yes," I breathe, unable to say anything else.

He slips an arm around my waist, lifting me off my toes. I wrap my legs around him while he carries me into the bedroom. The strap of my dress falls down my shoulder when he lays me on the bed. The skin isn't exposed for too long before his mouth is on me, making his way closer to my breast. My heart hammering in my chest when his hands find the zipper on my dress, dragging it down.

The warmth of his body disappears momentarily when I slip out of the material. He pushes it to the floor but when I go to reach for his shirt, he captures my hands in his grasp, holding them away from him. He swallows, releasing me as I fall back on the bed and he unbuttons his shirt himself, casting it aside.

The pause only lasts for a moment and then he's kissing me again, his body over mine, sealing me to the mattress. I clasp my arms around his neck when his left arm sinks underneath me, lifting me easily, in one swift move, as he positions me higher up on the bed. His body is warm and heavy on top of mine and despite the temperature, a shiver rolls through me when he takes my breast in his mouth. A sharp intake of breath and the feeling stuns me, sending a heavy pulse right to my core.

He works his way down my body, and I twitch underneath his movements. My hands are tangled in his hair before he looks up at me, a smirk on his ridiculously handsome face before he buries himself between my legs.

I jerk suddenly at the feeling of his mouth on me as I squirm against him. My back arches off the bed but his hands hold me down, the pressure of his fingers against my hips and the movement of his mouth is almost too much. I'm floating, flying. I can feel myself pull tight, threatening to break, but it isn't until his tongue slides against the center of me that I cry out in release.

By the time I catch my breath, his mouth is back on mine. I almost whine when I feel his lips pull away, even for just a fraction of a second. I force my eyes open as I see the desperation looking back at me. He reaches his hand down, cupping me between my legs, rubbing against me as I arch my neck back into the pillow.

"More," I beg between breaths.

"Tell me what you want," he commands.

"You know what I want."

He shakes his head slightly, his breath tickling my skin before he places another kiss on my collarbone. "I need to hear you say it."

"I want you." I lift my hips.

"You sure?" he asks, breathing heavily.

"Don't make me beg."

He swallows, nodding. "Eyes up." He instructs. "I need to see you."

I nod, ready to comply. Jackson spreads my legs with his knee, kissing me hard when he slips inside me. My eyes squeeze from the pressure, and he stills for a few moments while I come to. It's only for a moment, while we adjust to each other, and then he's moving.

Jackson above me, our eyes locking and I realize I could fall apart right here. When Noah and I had sex, it was in dark rooms. There was always a playlist, something in the background to distract me, or him, or both, I don't know. He never talked to me. He never looked at me, just buried his face against the side of my neck and rolled over when he was done.

I wrap my legs around Jackson's waist, clinging to him, as he supports himself on his elbows. His movements are slow and torturous. The pressure is building inside me, pulling tight, but I don't want to give in. I don't want to let go just yet. I need him, more than I ever have before, because I know that what we have isn't built to last, but I'm desperate to cling to it for as long as I can. My back arches, and I turn my head to the side, feeling tight.

"Cassie," he breathes when I close my eyes.

I know if I look at him, stare into his green eyes, it will all be over. The fantasy that we've been creating will come crashing down, and we will return to reality, where there are rules and boundaries that I don't want to exist anymore.

"Look at me, Cassie."

I open my eyes when he says my name, looking right at him, and as soon as I do, I come apart underneath him suddenly.

"Jacks." I whimper and kick my head back, back arching, eyes closing. I feel his entire body shudder. He groans when he bucks one more time and then sighs deeply.

It takes several seconds before I come down from the high. Jackson's body falls against mine, and I love the weight of him on top of me. He stills for a moment before rolling off, tugging me to follow. Small kisses scale the side of my neck. His hands gently caress my hips, and I sigh, letting my eyes close while he pulls up a sheet, covering us both.

I turn on my side, one arm wrapped around his waist, clinging to him while we both catch our breath. We don't say anything for several minutes, processing the glass that we both just shattered, but I don't have it in me to care. Those are tomorrow's problems. All I can think about is Jackson beside me, my head on his chest. I trace my fingers lazily up and down his arm, following the curve of his bicep, down to the veins that wrap around his wrist.

His eyes are closed, head tipped back, and he looks beautiful, so handsome. I try to memorize every piece of him. His blond hair, how it felt between my fingers. The curve of his mouth. The fullness of his lips. My legs squeeze together when I remember how they felt between my legs.

"You okay?" he asks, reaching down to brush his thumb against my cheek.

I smile, nodding, but it's not until I say the word out loud that I feel his body relax under me. "Yeah."

His fingers tangle in my hair, brushing it off my forehead. "Ask me."

"Ask you what?"

"Anything you want," he clarifies, but I can feel him brace himself underneath me. "Ask me anything you want."

I pause, taking in his request. Of all the things that I've wanted to ask him, he is now offering himself up like an open book. I settle on the first question that comes to mind.

"Do you like being famous?"

I feel his lungs expand in his chest, and then he lets out a sigh, a deep one. He doesn't look at me when he answers. His eyes are far across the room. "Sometimes. There are aspects of it that I like, others that I tolerate."

"Which ones do you tolerate?"

"The ones that make me out to be a toy that people get to play with. People with hidden agendas. Two-faced social piranhas that make me second-guess . . . everything about myself. I hate that I never know who is genuine and who is using me." His arm tightens around my waist while I lean further into his side. "I think I'm a little numb to the things that make this life bearable. Fans, selfies, premieres, they seem normal, which is strange, because there used to be a time when I couldn't imagine getting used to any of it."

"Is that why you skipped your Cannes premiere?" I ask carefully.

Jackson tenses. I feel it in his body. I wait for him to move, breathe, speak. I wait for him to release.

"No, that wasn't the reason," he admits eventually, though it sounds forced, like he only told me because he offered himself up as an open book and didn't want to let me down.

"You don't have to tell me," I say.

"It's okay." He lets out another deep breath, but it sounds like he is trying to convince himself rather than me. "I, uh, I saw someone at the press conference before we took the carpet, someone that I didn't know was going to be there, and it fucked me up more than I thought it would."

"Who was it?"

"Victoria Baxter."

My blood runs cold at the sound of her name. I push up on my elbows, but Jackson doesn't look at me when he continues.

"She was the producer from *Sunset City*. The one I—"

The woman he slept with when he was eighteen because she dangled a job over his head as leverage.

"I don't know. I saw her and just kept thinking, what the fuck am I doing here? I felt like I wasn't good enough, for any of it. This job, my career, my *life*. I think about it every day, all the time, even when I don't mean to, this feeling of not being enough."

I swallow, hanging on his every word, but I don't say anything. I wait for him to finish, sensing that he needs to get everything out, maybe for the first time ever.

"I know what I have to do if I want to move on, change career paths, but I'm so fucking afraid that it won't be enough, you know? That I won't be enough. It scares the shit out of me."

I reach for his chin, gently coaxing him to look at me.

"You are talented, Jackson. No one can take that away from you. *She* can't take that away from you."

I didn't realize how angry his confession made me. That he thought, after all his success, he was just a fluke. I hate what happened to him, and I hate that he thinks it doesn't matter.

"Is that why you never ask me about acting? Because of what I told you?"

I pull back to read him. "What do you mean?"

"I mean, you just never bring it up. My career."

"Is that a bad thing?"

"No." He frowns. "It's just everyone else asks me, and you never seem to . . ."

The unspoken part of his sentence hangs in the air. You never seem to *care.* Is that what he thinks of me?

"I care," I assure him, and his shoulders relax slightly. "You have this other life that is amazing and incredible, but that's not the only part of you. I get to see the side that no one else does. To me, that part is far more interesting. There are more redeeming qualities about you other than your status and money."

He forces a smile, fingers playing with my hair. "Like what?"

He avoids my eye when he asks the question, letting me know my answer means more to him than he will ever admit out loud.

"I love your laugh," I say with a smile. "When I've caught you by surprise, you toss your head back, and it's such a genuine sound, I feel it down to my toes."

"Yeah?"

"Yeah."

He swallows. "What else?"

"You care about people. You want to protect them, even if it means sacrificing pieces of yourself to do so." He forces himself to look at me, his eyes dark and guarded. I keep going. "You take risks, big swings. You're brave and . . . you are talented. You have the talent most people dream of."

He nods weakly, like he doesn't really believe me but wants to. His thumb moves to brush my side in lazy strokes.

"I don't like . . . not being in control," he admits. "Probably started with things in my childhood and then . . . you know." He doesn't say her name, but I hold him tighter. "The first time the cameras followed me, I felt like some zoo animal, locked behind a cage, being rewarded for tricks, but it gave me attention, and it felt good to be wanted, so I controlled it. Changed things about myself to put me in the driver's seat. Told myself it didn't matter if it was my choice."

His choice.

The words sit heavy in the air between us, and then it clicks. *Everything* clicks into place.

I think back to all the times Jackson touched me. He asked for my permission, *always*, multiple times, confirming my consent, repeatedly. He wanted it to be *my* choice. My heart tightens in my chest when I realize the potential meaning behind it now. No one ever asked him. He felt like he never had a choice.

"Anyway." He sighs. "It doesn't matter anymore. I made my bed a long time ago. No one cares how I feel about it now."

Tears fill my eyes, but I swallow them back, holding him tighter. "I do."

He looks down at me in his arms. His fingers trace my chin, and I lift my head, trying to follow the movement.

"Get some sleep," he says quietly, ending the conversation.

"Will you be here in the morning?" I ask.

"I'm not going anywhere," he promises.

I sigh, curling up against his side, tucking my body against his, and hold tight. Just before I fall asleep, I glance up at Jackson, propped up against the headboard, playing with his bottom lip, lost in thought.

CHAPTER 29

Jackson

It's late morning when I finally wake. The sun peeks through the edges of the blinds even though the room remains dark. Cassie, still in my arms, pressed against my chest. I breathe in deeply, when another sound comes from the bedside table.

Right, my phone. That's what woke me.

I reach around to grab it, frowning when I register the caller on the other line. I answer anyway.

"What?" I ask.

"I have good news and bad news." Zana cuts right to the point. "Which would you like first?"

I sigh, dragging a hand over my face before I get up, leaving Cassie in my bed. I reach for a pair of sweatpants, slipping them on, and then step into the hallway, shutting the door behind me.

"Bad."

"*Annihilation* estimates a shockingly low opening weekend," Zana tells me.

"And the good?" I ask through clenched teeth.

"The good news is that we have a safety net."

My mind flashes to the conversation in Santa Barbara last week. The contingency plan presented to us by marketing. I close my eyes, already knowing what she is going to say next.

"*To Hell and Back* press starts in August. The studio needs to secure a profitable release, which means they want the couple, Jackson. The relationship pitch between you and Jenn for marketing."

"Not an option," I tell her, my thoughts drifting to Cassie asleep in my bed.

"This is the part where I strongly suggest you do."

"It's not my problem if they can't market their own movie. I agreed to filming, traveling for press, attending the premiere, that's it. I'm not selling *that* story anymore."

"If this movie fails, which it can, you will be done. It's not a coincidence anymore, not when your last three box-office attempts have barely grossed the $100 million mark. *Annihilation* has already reported the lowest opening weekend for June in a decade. No studio will touch you after that, including whatever passion projects you are holding on to. You will have become *too* much of a liability. This is your chance. Pitch the couple between you and Jenn, sell it, make them their millions, and then you can walk away to do whatever the fuck you want."

I clutch the phone in my hand, wishing that I had enough strength to crush it in my palm, scattering the pieces. It's the same cycle over and over again, and just when I think I can break out of it, I realize that I made my bed a long time ago.

I don't want to fucking do this anymore, but I don't see a way out. What's my other option? Fading into obscurity? My thoughts drift back to Cassie asleep in my bed. She was supposed to make this part go away.

"Just do it," Zana pushes again. "A year from now, you'll forget why you even hesitated."

I lean my head against the wall. "I'll think about it," I tell her. "I'll be out for the rest of the day."

"Jackson—"

I hang up before she can finish, turning my phone off, watching the screen fade to black. My hand clenches into a fist, and it takes several seconds and multiple deep breaths to allow the muscles to release.

I stayed up until the early hours of the morning, replaying every moment with Cassie in my head like some sort of montage, and I came to one shockingly simple conclusion.

Life is better with Cassie in it.

I never told anyone outside of Sash what happened with Victoria. Never saw a reason to. A part of me expected Cassie to look at me the way I look at myself when I think back on that memory, with disgust. She saw what I had to do to get the things I wanted, but she didn't run. She stayed, and I realized just before I fell asleep that I want it to work. It has to, because without Cassie, I see only a future I hate in front of me.

Back in my room, I take a seat on the edge of the mattress. Cassie has the white sheets pulled up over her chest, tightened against her body, still naked beneath.

I brush my hand through her hair, memorizing the softness of the strands between my fingers. She stirs, blinking a few times before looking up at me.

"Morning."

"Mm." She sighs sleepily.

"I have a proposition for you."

She rubs her eye with her hand. "What?"

"We both take the day off and head up the coast."

A wide smile spreads across her face, and it's like seeing the sun for the first time after a storm. "You have the day off?"

"Not technically, but I am taking the day off." I amend the offer. "No phones, no Nic. Just you and me, what do you think?"

She beams up at me. "Okay."

Her expression catches me off guard and I get lost in the color of her eyes. They are warm and soft all at once, and I feel better looking into them, imagining what she sees when she gazes up at me.

"Feel free to shower. I have to finish up a few things and then . . ." I lean forward, pausing just in front of her. "You have my full and undivided attention all day." I kiss her deeply and flashes of last night pop to the surface. I am half tempted to let her pull me back into bed, but I know that before we move forward, if at all, I need to know if we are on the same page.

There is no reason to rush it, yet.

~~~

The sun is shining on our day off with the forecast reporting limited smog, so I grab the keys to my Jeep. In the three years I've had it, I think I've only personally driven it twice. Cassie steps out of my bedroom wearing her favorite pair of jean shorts, making her tan legs look a mile long.

She shakes out her dark hair, still damp from the shower, and extends her hand. "No phones, right?"

"Right." I sigh, dropping my phone into her hand. A weight presses down on my shoulders just relinquishing this little bit of control, but I made her a promise. I want to prove to her, and myself, that I can keep it.

I lead her down the back steps to the garage at the base level. The lights flicker on when we step inside, and I turn to gauge her reaction. Her eyes widen when she studies the rows of cars. Mercedes, a BMW, a Jaguar, and on the far right at the end, the Jeep.

"Jesus," she stutters, spinning around to take them all in. "Isn't one enough? Why do you need a fleet?"

"I like having options." I smile, walking backward so I can keep my eyes on her. "Jeep okay?"

"No, this actually won't work at all," she replies sarcastically before hauling herself into the car while I climb into the driver's seat.

I reach across to the glove compartment, grabbing an extra pair of sunglasses. "Here."

She takes the oversized Aviators, placing them on her face. They immediately fall down the bridge of her nose before she
~~~

pushes them higher. "How do I look?" She poses, a hand under her chin.

"Adorable." I smile, pinching her nose, and then throw the car into reverse, sliding out of the garage and down the hill.

I feel almost naked without my phone. The nagging notion that I have forgotten something haunts me. I immediately start listing off all the possible things that could go wrong in a day, the things Zana might need me for. I stop myself before spiraling too far and look at Cassie. She has the window rolled down, feet on the dash, eyes closed, facing the sunshine. The reminder that she's here is enough to center me, force a breath, and remember what the entire point of today is.

"Tell me something," I say, weaving down the street. "Tell me something you've never told me before."

She looks caught off guard for a moment before she clears her throat. "Uh, well, I used to perform in pageants."

"Pageants?" I lift a brow.

"Yeah, you know, like Miss Teen Indiana," she explains, and my smile widens. "Don't make fun." She leans across the console to gently shove my arm.

"I'm not," I say, choking on a laugh. "I didn't think that was still a thing."

"Well, they are," she says, nose in the air.

"What made you get started?"

"My mom was in pageantry, so I suppose you can call it a family tradition. She said it was meant to build character, and it looked good on a résumé. She wanted me to use it as a stepping stone to get out."

"Get out of where?"

"My town, Indiana, all of the above?" She shrugs. "It was important to my mom that I leave. She didn't want me to have the same life she did. I know she loved my dad, loved her life, but I think she saw how small it was. She always wanted me to have more."

"Are you close? You and your mom?"

"Yeah, I mean, decently close. She doesn't visit me much and she never wants me to come home, but we catch up on the phone." She pauses, thinking. "I think she's afraid that if we stay too close, I'll want to leave, go back to the familiar. She wants me to have a better life, that's the main driver of our relationship now." She finishes, her voice softer in a way.

I change the subject. "And were you good at this pageantry?"

"Yes, I was really good." She smiles. "It may seem stupid, but I really liked it, for a time. That's what made me want to get into modeling. My talent was singing."

"I didn't know you could sing."

She nods. "The 90's love ballads were some of my mom's favorites. I think I have all of Celine's songs memorized. Luckily, all the money that I earned helped me move out here. Otherwise, I don't think I would have been able to afford it, we wouldn't have been able to afford it." She says and then changes the subject. "You should have seen some of my outfits. I had to wear a blue sequin dress with a matching boa one year in middle school."

"Any photos?"

"Yes, but there is no way that you will be seeing them." She shoves my arm again, and I laugh.

"So, where to?" I ask.

"I was thinking Malibu. I know a quiet spot along the beach we could go to?"

"Okay," I nod and reach for an aux cord. "Here. I want to know what you listen to."

"What do you listen to?" she asks, her eyes narrowing.

"I asked you first." I toss her a look while she hesitates. "Just play your favorite playlist. Come on. I'm curious." My lips twist into a smile. "You can tell a lot about a person through their playlists."

"I know you can, that's why I'm hesitating."

She holds my gaze as long as she can before giving up with

a dramatic sigh. She bites the side of her lip, scrolling through a few different options before she looks up.

"Ready?" she asks.

"Hit me."

I wait for the music to kick in the speakers, and when it does, I immediately toss my head back, laughing. "Country?"

Figures, the one genre I hate is her favorite.

"Have you even tried listening to country?"

"No," I say, nearly cringing.

"It's a mix playlist that happens to have some country on it, so suck it up."

"Will you sing, at least?" I look over at her.

"Not with you staring at me."

She reaches across the console, pushing my chin to look away. As soon as her hand drops, my gaze swings back around to her. She smiles, reaching for the dial to turn up the volume.

I lean my left arm up against the frame of the window, feeling the ocean air drift through the car. Cassie's hand is out the passenger side. Her hair flows around her shoulders, and every so often, I get a whiff of the subtle scent of her perfume. She looks at me, smiling wide. It's the happiest I think I have ever seen her, and the sight of it nearly knocks the wind out of me.

Hope.

I had been trying to come up with the word before falling asleep last night. I stayed awake for several hours, trying to identify the foreign feeling that settled deep in my body and only once I found a name for it did I finally close my eyes.

Hope. She gives me hope. That's what I see when I look at Cassie.

The defined edges of the box that I had built for myself have somehow blurred. They didn't make sense when she smiled. I can't remember the last time I felt such freedom. The idea that the life I had been living has been put on hold, at least for the next few hours, and I can just . . . be. *We* can just be.

I look at Cassie, and I see a life ahead of me, one completely different from the rat race I am used to. I see a life I want to live. It would be easy, peaceful, like a drive down the coast on a Sunday morning.

"And if the house just keeps on winning, I got a wild card up my sleeve."

I whip my head in Cassie's direction the second I hear her voice. It's beautiful, like everything else about her. Soft and full of life. I want to hear more of it, but she stops when she catches me staring.

"Don't stop," I coax her to continue. "Keep going."

"And if the whole wide world stops singing, and all the stars go dark, I'll keep a light on in my soul and keep a bluebird in my heart."

"That's a perfect sound," I say.

"What is?"

"Your voice."

She smiles widely when our eyes meet as we soar up the coast. For the first time in a long time, I feel free.

CHAPTER 30

Cassie

We spend the next hour in the car, traffic mostly scarce for an early afternoon. Jackson is the most talkative he's ever been with me. It's like a spout had been tapped the night before. Once he got what he needed to say off his chest, the floodgates are now open. He asks me questions, but also answers anything that I throw his way, covering everything from childhood to his favorite movies.

I reach for the dial when we exit, turning the music down as we approach a stop light.

"Hungry?" I ask. "I think I know a place."

"Yes," he answers before I can finish, and I laugh, directing him toward the spot Marina and I visited the first time I was here. The Cantina, I realize, is a giant hole-in-the-wall. Not that it bothers me, but I worry if it's not up to Jackson's standards.

"It's a little different from what I remember. We can go somewhere else?" I offer as he throws the car in park.

"No, let's try it."

At the stand, we order an assortment of tacos, guacamole, dips, and chips, with two Coronas to go.

"To go where?" Jackson asks, pulling his wallet from his back pocket.

"You'll see," I say, handing my credit card to the cashier first. He frowns to show his disapproval, but lets me pay.

"We're not eating in my car," he adds, suddenly serious, and I laugh at that. Apparently, feet on the dash are allowed, but *god forbid* a taco makes its way into the front seat.

We pack it up in a bag and drive to the lookout I had visited only once before. The light touches the tips of the waves as they crash against the rocks to the side of us. Small groups of people gather on the beach, their laughter filtering up the uneven rock face that we hike. We take the trail path around, the people below us run along the beach, and surfers wait in the tides for the perfect wave. It's only about a five minute trek off-trail to find the place I remember, tucked away from the main path with a perfect view of the beach and the crystal blue ocean stretching out in front of us.

Jackson studies the view as I take a seat on the ground. "How did you find this place?"

"A friend of mine grew up a few miles from here. We came here one of the first weekends after I moved. I haven't been back since."

"Are we eating here?" he asks.

"Sure, why not?" I say, looking up at him from the ground. I push the oversized sunglasses that keep sliding down my face up the bridge of my nose.

"In the dirt?" he clarifies, not moving.

"Come on. You've never had a picnic before?"

"No." He huffs out a breath like it's the most absurd thing he has ever seen, eating food outside on the ground.

"A little dirt won't kill you." I rest my hands on my legs, waiting for him to join me, which he finally does after exhaling heavily.

He leans up against the rock, setting our bags of food on the ground with mild distaste. I unwrap one of the tacos, holding it by the paper and take a bite. Luckily, it's just like I remembered. I watch and wait for Jackson to follow suit, and when he does, I smile.

"Shit, this is really good," he comments.

I lean back against the rock as we finish our lunch, cracking open the Coronas. I push the sunglasses off my face and into my tangled hair. The sun is strong enough that if I close my eyes, the buttery rays and the sound of the sea could coax me to sleep. I inhale the salty sea breeze and turn to Jackson, remembering our conversation from the night before.

"When did you know you wanted to be an actor?" I ask.

He shrugs. "It may sound lame, but probably season two of *Sunset City.* The show wasn't Emmy-worthy; I knew that. But people watched it, talked about it. I had been a guest star in the first season and initially, I didn't know if they were going to sign me back." He looks away, eyes squinting when he brushes past the secret he told me last night. "Anyway, I was booked as a regular for season two. I started making my own money, and it gave me the freedom to do what I wanted."

"What has been your favorite project?"

"God, that's hard to choose." He rubs the back of his neck and starts prattling off titles of the projects that he has worked on.

Most I had heard of. Some I hadn't. I make a mental note to stream those in the next few weeks. Somewhere between the stories on set, I find myself lying against his warm chest, his arm wrapped around my waist, keeping me close.

I listen to him explain the differences between action set pieces and CGI, the work that he had to do in front of the camera and behind the screen to achieve the right vocal sounds or body movements when the special effects were added. He talked about why he wanted to break out of action films and convert to more dramatic roles, maybe even an indie film. He voiced his concerns about breaking through that barrier, worried that no one will take him seriously after his past line of work. The hard set of his brow told me that he would. I have a feeling that once Jackson sets his mind to something, he can achieve it.

As he talks, I realize that I had been doing him a disservice not asking these types of questions before. It's not that I wasn't interested; I am. There were just so many other things I wanted to get to know about him first. Now that I do, his answers make more sense. He is proud of some of his work and wants to share it with someone.

When he finishes, we are both quiet. I close my eyes, leaning against his chest, feeling the subtle thump of his heart. I could drift away right here in his arms, but his voice interrupts our small piece of quiet.

"You seem different today. In a good way, in a happy way."

"I am happy," I clarify. "I just realized, this is the first time we've spent time together outside the house, without the cameras. It's nice. You're different without them."

He looks at me for a moment, eyes narrow, like he doesn't understand the difference between the person he plays when people are watching and the person he really is behind closed doors. He chews on his bottom lip, deep in thought.

"What is it?" I nudge his elbow with my own. "What are you thinking?"

Jackson's eyes lock on mine, pausing for a moment. "I'm trying to come up with a way that you and I can work," he says and then shakes his head. "I hate that I don't know how."

"Well, things usually work best if we start with honesty."

Jackson's eyes find mine again, the sun making them a bright turquoise. His hair is windblown and messy in the most perfect way. I remember my hands tangled up in it last night.

"You want honesty?" he asks.

My breath catches. "Yes."

"I have wanted to kiss you every day since the moment we met. I think of your laugh when I don't mean to. Wonder where you are when we aren't together. Dream of you when I know I'm not supposed to."

The words fall out quickly, and I try to catch each one. My stomach dips at his admission. It's the most honest thing he has said to me since we met.

"You're better than what I can give you." He exhales roughly. "I don't want to take anything away from you or force you into something you know nothing about. I don't . . . I don't want to be like *her*."

Victoria. The name that we both know, but he doesn't say.

I sit up straight, grabbing his chin, forcing him to look at me. "You're not her. It's not the same."

He pulls away, eyes dark. "You can't say that. You don't know."

"Have you ever forced me to do something I don't want to do?"

He turns away further. "No."

"Have you ever taken advantage of me when I was in a vulnerable position?" When he doesn't answer, I answer for him. "You haven't, *ever*."

"But I hurt you," he says, referencing our fight last week.

"I forgave you."

"Why?" he asks, eyes narrowing.

"Because I know you didn't mean it." I lay my hand against his chest. "You are a good person, Jacks. I believe that, and this is *my* choice. You aren't taking that away from me or forcing me to do anything I don't want."

"*Cassie,*" Jackson murmurs under his breath, shaking his head.

"What if I want you?" I ask, hating that it comes out as a plea when I reach for him. "The real you?"

He pulls his hand away from mine, suddenly. "And what if I have to leave the country for a film shoot for months at a time, and we aren't together like we are now? What happens when they write the article that *you* used *me* to boost your career when it was my idea to begin with? When the real world gets involved, it will fuck up your life. I don't want that for you."

"That's something you'll never be able to control. What we can control is how we feel, how we act. I care about you more than anything they can write about me."

Jackson's eyebrows tug together like it's a foreign concept, like he can't imagine relinquishing control and not caring what everyone thinks about him, how the world perceives him.

"You think you know what's best, but it's my decision too," I tell him, letting my hand fall to his arm, drawing circles on his tan, warm skin. "This feels worth it. You're worth it."

His head snaps up to look at me, eyes darting across my face, searching for some answer to a question that hasn't been asked, one that only he knows. After a few more seconds of silence, I go to turn away, but before I can, he leans forward, lips finding mine.

I gasp in surprise, my mouth opening slightly as his tongue slips inside. I clasp my arms around his neck, deepening the kiss. His lips are soft, yet firm and urgent against mine. I can feel his strong hands on my back, eager to close the space between us.

The tang of lime still on his breath and I can feel the need from him on his mouth, in his movements, as I echo my feelings back to him. He pulls away briefly, his mouth slides down my neck, kissing me just below my ear.

"That's how I feel." His voice is steady and sure, and then he pulls back to look at me. "I want this to work, but I don't want to lose you over something that I can't control. If it gets too much, you have to tell me."

My hand brushes against his jaw, up his cheek, and his eyes close for a moment, leaning further into my touch. "You have more control than you know."

He stills, letting the words sink in. The hesitation only appears for a flash of a second, and then he grabs my hand, pulling me up so that I am resting against his chest. I lean my head back on his shoulder as we watch the sun dip closer to the ocean. I can feel the finality of the moment press upon us even though neither of us makes the first move to leave.

"You know, when you first brought me here, I thought you used to come here with someone," Jackson says, eventually breaking the silence.

"I did." I look up at him. "I came here with Marina."

His hand slips up my shirt, resting against my stomach, and my back arches involuntarily. "Not that type of someone," he whispers in my ear.

"Oh." I sigh, facing forward again. "No, I never came here with Noah."

"Hmm." Jackson's voice indicates interest.

I frown, wishing that I hadn't let it slip. I rest my head against his strong, warm chest and let my eyes close briefly. I don't want to think about Noah while I am here with Jackson.

"You seem concerned about my exes when I feel like I should be more concerned about yours," I say.

"What do you mean?"

"You don't have any famous exes that I should be aware of? I know you dated a Mary-Kate or Ashley back in the day."

"All publicity stunts to sell whatever project I was promoting."

"What about Jenn Hamilton?"

"Jenn?" He snorts. "No, we never dated. Not even close."

"Never?" I turn back to look at him.

"Never even thought about it. Not my type. High maintenance, too much baggage." His ears turn red, and he avoids my eye when he speaks next. "I've really only ever been with women older than me."

"How much older?"

"Varying degrees." He shrugs, changing the topic before I can ask why. "And if *I* have to tolerate Jenn, you do too. She's in my next film, *To Hell and Back*."

"Another one?" I groan.

He laughs softly. "We start the press tour in August."

"I hope it's a horror movie," I grumble.

"It's a romantic comedy."

I groan even louder, but before I can move away from him, he is hovering over me, my back lying against the rock.

"What?" He smirks, looking down at me, and I go breathless. "Jealous?"

All I can think about is the weight of his body hovering over me and the innate want to feel the pressure on top of me again.

"Yes." I swallow.

His eyes soften, like he hadn't been expecting me to tell him the truth. "You have nothing to worry about," he offers, more seriously.

I push up on my elbows so that our faces are close, kissing him for no other purpose than I want to. He leans forward, deepening the kiss when his hand goes to the back of my head, fingers threading through my hair and I don't want it to end. I'll never want this to end.

It's late when we finally pick up our things to head home. Most of the families have cleared out with the sun dipping just below the horizon. We hike up the path toward the parking lot and I reach for his phone in my back pocket, pulling us out of whatever daydream we had spent the whole day creating. I knew that reality couldn't be avoided forever, but it was nice to Jackson all to myself for a few hours.

"Interested in hearing the damage?" I ask, lifting his phone in the air. It had been off all day, and I'm surprised that he didn't ask for it.

"Hit me."

"Jesus." I breathe as the messages hit. There must be more than 100 notifications. I swipe through the messages next: fifty messages and ten new voicemails.

"How bad?"

"Bad." I grimace, scrolling through the messages on his locked screen. "Your music for the ride back?"

"Thank god," he feigns appreciation, climbing into his car.

"Admit it, my playlist wasn't that bad." I shut the door to the passenger side, sinking into the soft, leather seats.

Jackson leans across the center of the Jeep, reaching for his phone without warning. His fingers linger on my thigh before he grabs his cell phone from my lap. His face, mere inches from mine, and I see a ghost of a smile on his lips as he leans in. My heart flutters, and I prepare myself for the kiss, letting my eyes shut briefly, before his voice interrupts the silence.

"Regardless, mine's better."

My eyes fly open as he kisses me once, quickly, and then pulls back smirking. He whips the car in reverse, the tires screeching as we pull onto the freeway, leading us home.

CHAPTER 31

Cassie

The following weeks pass in a blur. If I wasn't at a shoot, I was organizing the next job. On the rare occasions I found spare time, I was with Jackson. His house was becoming more of a second home, and I couldn't complain about the lack of separation. Although the press hadn't been forgiving . . . having Jackson by my side made it better, made everything better.

I feel like after years of treading water, I can finally just float. I am swimming in the deep end, and even with the threat of a current, I no longer feel like I am drowning.

When I filmed the *Amora* commercial, it didn't feel like I was living my own life. I felt like I was watching a different version of myself through the lens. The poses I performed, the movements I mirrored, felt like they belonged to someone else. And just when I felt like it was too much, when I was close to hyperventilating, I would search for Jackson, and he would be there, already looking at me. The slight nod of his head, the narrowing of his eyes, made me feel seen and understood. It was enough to allow a breath to clear my head and focus on putting one foot in front of the other.

Not many people can do that. Not many people can center you like that. Jackson could.

He threw a house party the night the commercial premiered.

It was one of the first times I saw the house populated with people, hundreds of guests splashed throughout the house. Jackson aired the commercial on the TV in the living room. His arms wrapped around my waist as I watched myself through the frames. I had a hard time rationalizing what I saw in front of me was now a part of my body of work. As the commercial faded to black, Jackson whispered in my ear.

"I told you, mind over matter."

I leaned back against him, loving the feel of his arms around me. I tilted my head up when he kissed the edge of my jaw. We barely made it to the end of the party before our clothes were off, opting for the pool over his California King.

While I had been hopeful for smooth sailing after the commercial, Jackson had been right. I was now officially *news*. There were cameras following me almost everywhere now, even without Jackson by my side. It was becoming more difficult to keep my small piece of anonymous life that I cherished, private.

Navigating my tiny sliver of fame was hard enough, but it seemed like as my relationship with Jackson seemed to stabilize, my foundation with Lucy started to falter. Marina had been distant the past few weeks, mostly due to her hectic work schedule, but I know for a fact that Lucy has been avoiding me. The nights when I wasn't with Jackson, I made an effort to be home in my apartment at least three nights a week, but Lucy barely found the time to be around or was consciously looking for excuses to leave.

I'm in my bedroom when I hear the front door open, then slam shut. I peek out to find Lucy huffing through the front door, dropping her things on the floor then stomping toward the fridge. I don't have to be close to her to tell when she is annoyed. Lucy isn't hard to read. Every emotion she feels is plastered across her face.

"Luce?" I ask, but I doubt that she can hear me through her headphones. Whatever she is blasting is loud enough that I can catch fragments of the beat from the other side of the room. "Lucy?"

She moves through the kitchen, jumping when she sees me in the living room.

"Sorry," she says, pulling her headphones off. "I didn't know you were home."

"What's wrong?" I ask.

She hesitates, eyeing me up and down. "Nothing." She grabs a dip from the fridge and chips from the cabinet.

"Lucy—"

"I got cut from the story." She turns with a glare.

"What do you mean?"

"Jackson coverage? *EDaily* took me off."

"What? Why—"

"They want me to report on your relationship, dig up secrets, find the dirt." Lucy says, cutting me off. "I said no, so they promoted someone else. I'm losing out on job opportunities because I am *such* a good friend."

Oh.

My arms slacken at my sides.

"I don't blame you, and I know it's not your fault." She sighs. "It just sucks, okay?"

She holds my gaze for a few more seconds, letting the message sink in, before she slams the door to her bedroom, leaving me alone in the living room.

She lost an opportunity at work because of me. Is that why she had been avoiding me? I bite the side of my lip, wondering if I could have done anything different, but I come up blank.

I don't want to have to choose between Lucy and Jackson, but I can't help but feel another crack slicing through the foundation of my life. I'm afraid how many I've already encountered so far.

I am in the midst of breaking down the potential fallout when my phone lights up on the couch. I frown, seeing an unrecognized number but pick it up and pull myself up from the couch.

"Hi, this is Cassie," I say, shutting my bedroom door behind me.

"Hi, Cassie. This is Noel Franklin. I'm an agent with Luxe Model Management. Do you have a second?"

My hand holding the phone up to my ear immediately starts shaking. Luxe is calling *me* on the phone.

"Y-yes, of course," I stutter briefly and start pacing around my room.

"We are calling about an inquiry into representation. We have been following your work since the *Amora* partnership, and we would love to discuss an opportunity to work together under contract moving forward. Is that something that you would be interested in pursuing?"

"Yes!" I can't help but gush into the speaker. "Absolutely!"

"That's great to hear. We are extremely excited about the possibility of having you under our management. Can you confirm your email address? I will have my assistant send over some paperwork, and then we can talk about setting up a meeting to finalize details and outline next steps."

I give her my personal information, trying to keep calm, my mind still racing. I had gone from insignificance to an agency-backed model in the span of a summer.

"We are looking to start rather quickly. With Paris Fashion Week starting next month, we'd love to use the shows as an opportunity to introduce you under management."

"That would be amazing!"

"Great. We'll be in touch. Looking forward to working together."

"Thank you so much." I force myself to finish the call in a somewhat orderly manner and then drop to the side of the bed, sitting on the floor, head falling into my hands.

I am about to get signed with a management company that has been famous for working with some of the top designer brands in the world. *World.* I had barely seen the United States, let alone left the country.

I press a hand to my temple to keep the room from spinning. My mind races at a million miles per minute, but before I can land on a single thought, I call the first person on my speed dial.

CHAPTER 32

Jackson

I wanted to be there for her. For the first time in a long time, I wanted to show up for someone.

I caught the first flight out of New York. I didn't care that I was due back this weekend. I could hear it in Cassie's voice when she called, that she needed me. And I liked that feeling of being needed.

Cassie sent me the location of a dive bar outside of Santa Monica. I can't remember the last time I stepped foot in one, if I'm honest. Neon signs, cheap beer, sticky floor. It reminds me of the life I missed out on in a way.

I sift through the crowds of people, ignoring anyone who gives me a second look before I get to the bar and peer across the sea of bodies to find her. I spot Cassie before she sees me, but the second I lay my eyes on her, she turns.

It's a strange feeling, the notion that you can tell someone is watching you, even without looking. When Cassie turns, it makes me feel like we are on the same wavelength, the same frequency. Her mouth widens into an even bigger smile when she sees me.

Cassie pushes through the bodies, rushing to where I am standing, crashing into my open arms without hesitation. It surprises me, the closeness in public. It's not that I don't want it; it's just that we haven't been like this out in the open. She must realize it too, because a second later, she pulls away.

She glances to the side, noticing people staring out of the corner of her eye, but I don't. I tune it all out, just focusing on her in front of me, and when she goes to step away from me, I grab her arm to prevent her from getting too far.

"Get over here," I tell her.

She beams up at me, and I know that my permission was all she needed. She jumps into my arms and I catch her, folding her against my chest as she wraps her legs around my waist.

I don't care that people are watching. I don't care that her friends are cheering. I just care about Cassie in my arms because it's been over a week since I've seen her in person, and it's been too long. She runs her hands through my hair. Fingers drifting down my neck, tugging on my ear slightly, and I want her hands everywhere.

"I missed you," I breathe when we pull apart.

She nods enthusiastically, reciprocating the sentiment. I set her down, bending to keep her eye and let out a laugh.

"How much have you had to drink?"

"The perfect amount!" She grins and then grabs my hand. "Come on. I want you to meet my friends."

I don't let go of her hand the whole night. She leads me from group to group, person to person. It's hard not to note the wide eyes and smiles when people recognize who I am, but it's different. No one stares at me outside of the first introduction. No one asks me for a photograph or cozies up to me, asking me to solicit the most scandalous Hollywood rumor. The hours go by, and I feel like I'm actually blending. They leave Cassie and I alone. I'm not worried about my photo being captured or my words being taken out of context. It's nice and I decide I could survive with this level of normality.

I meet Marina again, though a much drunker version. She

practically melts when I tug Cassie against my chest, moving her to sit on my lap.

"You have a third roommate?" I ask.

"Yeah, Lucy," Marina answers, throwing Cassie a look. "She's hanging with her sister tonight."

"She's mad at me," Cassie says, biting her lip.

I tighten my hold around her waist. "Why?"

Marina exchanges a glance, and then Cassie turns, kissing my cheek. "Give me a minute?"

"Sure." I nod, while Marina and Cassie step off to the side, whispering under their breath. I don't know what they are talking about, but when Cassie eventually wanders back, her eyes are heavier in a way.

"Everything okay?"

"Yeah." She forces a smile, leaning against my chest. "All good."

I don't buy it, but I can also tell that whatever is bothering her, she doesn't want to talk about it.

"Drinks on me?" I lift my wallet.

"No." She rolls her eyes. "Drinks on me. I don't know if you've heard, but I just booked my first agency."

"I've heard." I tip her chin up with my finger while she beams up at me.

Despite my insistence, Cassie refuses to let me buy anything and each time she slams the shot glass down on the table, she leans into me further. We're touching all night, her hand in mine or my hands on her waist.

The bar is dark, crowded, and hot. The air becomes stifling just after midnight when Cassie pulls off her jacket before leaning back into my chest. She's unsteady on her feet, so I tighten my hold around her waist, kiss the side of her neck, and whisper into her ear.

"If you keep taking your clothes off, we're never going to make it home."

She spins around to face me, cheeks flushed, hair wild, and she's beautiful. She's always beautiful, but I am reminded of it most when she's happy.

"Haven't you ever heard of the concept of self-control?" she asks, her hands slipping down my stomach, resting just above the button on my jeans.

I lift an eyebrow. "I've heard of it, just not a regular participant."

She sinks into me, and her smile widens before she spins, back against my chest again. I throw my arms over her shoulders, holding her there.

"I think we're gonna head out," Cassie announces to Marina.

"Already?" Marina asks, shoulders slumping.

"Jackson has to leave tomorrow," Cassie explains. "Is that okay?"

"Yeah, of course." Marina smiles and then looks at me, pointing. "Take care of my best friend."

"Always," I promise, meaning it.

"Congrats again, Cass!" Marina calls after us.

I already have my car waiting out front. Nic opens the door for us and as soon as it shuts, Cassie slides onto my lap, straddling my waist. She sighs when I trail kisses down her neck.

She stays there, pressed against my chest, until we pull into my driveway. I carry her through the door, then to my bedroom, where I lay her on the bed, my body hovering over hers.

"Did I tell you I missed you like crazy?" I ask between kisses.

"I missed you too, Jacks." My name sounds like a song coming off her lips.

She wraps her arms around my neck, pulling me closer to her, barely allowing an inch of separation. I slip an arm under her, sliding her up the bed, and then our clothes start coming off. First her shirt, then my pants. I practically groan when she digs her fingernails into my back.

"This wasn't supposed to happen."

"What?" she asks breathlessly.

"You weren't supposed to be right." My lips trail down to her collarbone.

"Right about what?"

"Right about us."

CHAPTER 33

Cassie

I wake to a pulse echoing through my temple. My mouth is dry, and I nearly gag when I come to, tasting the leftover tequila on my breath. I lift my head from the pillow and struggle to keep my eyes open. I squint into the light to find Jackson sitting on the side of the bed. The blinds are still drawn, probably to protect my head and the massive hangover pressing against it right now.

I blink, closing my left eye as his frame comes into focus, and I realize that he is already dressed. I vaguely wonder what time it is as I run a hand through my tangled hair.

"How are you feeling?" he asks.

"If I said like shit, would you judge me?" I ask, grimacing.

Jackson laughs softly. "Not at all. You deserved to celebrate."

I groan, regretting drinking so much the night before. Although I was celebrating what seemed like a major milestone in my career, the side-effects were never worth it.

"How bad was I?" I ask, running my hand over my forehead.

"Before or after you performed a striptease?" My eyes nearly fall out of their sockets as I try to recount the activities from the night before. Jackson leans in closer, smiling. "Don't worry." He kisses me quickly on the lips. "That part was just for me."

"Don't do that to me!" I slap at his arm, causing him to snicker.

"Why? Have you ever done such a thing in public? I'd like to think I'm the only one who has experienced one of those dances."

"Shut up." I groan and rest my arm over my eyes, blocking out any form of light.

"Here, take these."

I lift my arm, peeling my eyelids apart to see two pills in his hand. I grab them quickly and swallow them back.

"Aren't you supposed to be on a flight to New York?" I ask.

"I changed it. I wanted to be here when you woke up."

"You didn't have to do that," I say, blushing.

"I know," he replies smugly. "Come on. I ordered breakfast."

I push myself up from the soft sheets, trying to ignore the thunder in my temples. Jackson's oversized t-shirt that I wore to bed as pajamas falls just above my knees.

"You know, I should start bringing my own stuff over here so I don't have to keep wearing your t-shirt to bed," I call from the bathroom while I assess the damage. I blink into the bright fluorescents, grabbing a towel from the drawer to wash the remaining make-up off my face and then brush my teeth.

"I like you in my t-shirt," Jackson says, leaning against the doorframe. I smile, spitting the rest of the toothpaste into the sink and turn, pausing in front of him. "Or in nothing at all." His arm snakes around my waist, squeezing me gently. "Have I told you congratulations enough yet?"

"There is always room for another." I smile, wrapping my arms around his neck.

"Congrats, Cassie. Seriously," he says. "I'm proud of you."

Chills sprinkle along my arms, and my heart squeezes in my chest. He tilts my chin up toward him with his strong hand and kisses me gently before leading me into the kitchen.

I hop up on a barstool, taking in the various to-go boxes that line the counter, and I can smell the coffee waiting for me on the counter.

"You didn't have to do all of this," I say, reaching for the carafe of coffee. My hangover immediately quiets at the aspect of caffeine.

"You wouldn't let me buy you drinks last night. I had to do something."

"Men and their ever-fragile egos," I mumble under my breath before taking a sip of coffee. "How was New York?"

He scoops fruit into a cup and slides it over to me. "Good . . . and bad." He sighs.

"Tell me about the good."

"Hall Studios wants to meet when I'm back in New York."

"That's amazing!" I smile. "This is the one you really wanted, right?"

"It's on the path that I want to pursue. I would be able to take a break from the box-office bullshit. I wouldn't have to work with someone as sleazy as Silas Morland, and it would finally give me the chance for people to actually take me seriously." He stops, green eyes meeting mine. "I really want this one, Cass."

"I believe in you," I tell him, resting my hand against his cheek. He leans further into it before pulling away and kissing my palm. "And what about bad?"

"Warner has been on my ass since *Annihilation* bombed. They were expecting at least three hundred million globally. We barely beat budget, which can be chalked up as a failure."

"Hey, it's not a failure. Thousands of people saw your movie. That counts for something, right?" I ask, but Jackson ignores it.

"*To Hell and Back* traffic isn't looking great either. I just can't have another movie . . . flop." His jaw tenses. "The studio has taken precautions, but their tactics to increase screenings are—" He stops, turning away.

"What is it?"

"The studios want the pitch," he admits, sneaking a glance at my face. "They want the marketing pitch to help sell tickets. The pitch that Jenn and I are dating."

"That's ridiculous," I mutter, trying to ignore the sinking in my stomach. "You can sell plenty of tickets on your own."

He shakes his head. "Zana is pushing it."

"Can't you just say no?"

"I just wish I never even signed on." He lets out a big sigh, telling me the conversation is over, but I register that he didn't give me an answer. "Anyway, it doesn't matter." He pushes away from the counter. "I'll be done with it soon enough, and then I don't have to think about it again."

"An optimistic outlook," I reply sarcastically.

He smirks. "But outside of that, tell me about *your* offer," he says, and I launch into the details about the contract.

I had spoken to Sasha after the phone call, since she is also represented by Luxe, and we talked over a few of the details. The contract that they sent me was . . . hefty, to say the least, so it felt nice to be able to rely on someone who has experience sorting through it before.

"They're booking me on a trip to Paris next month," I say, my voice smaller. Jackson looks up at me, eyebrows raised. "Will you come with me? I've never been out of the country before."

"I'll make it work."

"Thank you." I tug on the sleeve of his sweatshirt.

"Wouldn't miss it." He steps around the counter, grabbing my waist and lifting me easily to the marble countertop.

"I like this," I say, brushing the stubble on his jaw.

He smiles, leaning further into my hand, and I love him like this. Happy, carefree. He seems so much younger when he smiles, when it reaches his eyes.

"Keep it?" he asks.

"Keep it."

And then he kisses me while I run my hands through his hair.

"I had fun last night," he says, his lips drifting to my neck.

"Me too." I sigh, head falling backward.

"I can't remember the last time I went to a dive bar," he comments. "Or went out and wasn't recognized."

"Mm-hm."

I had a better response than that, but I forget what it was when Jackson's hands disappear under my shirt, coasting up my stomach. I sigh when he tugs down my underwear, discarding it on the floor.

"You fell asleep last night before I could properly congratulate you," he says, eyes locking on mine as he bends down, pushing the t-shirt that I am wearing up my thighs. He grips my waist, tugging me closer to the edge of the counter.

"Really? What does that entail?"

"I thought I could show you . . ."

I squirm when his lips press against my hip. My hands rest on his shoulders, feeling the movement of his muscles beneath my fingertips.

"That would—"

I don't get to finish because his tongue slides against my stomach next, diving into my belly button, and I forget my own name, let alone what we had been talking about. My hips jerk suddenly. His hands grasp my waist to steady me, and I sigh against the pressure.

"Move in with me," he breathes so softly, I almost don't hear him.

I sit up, causing his lips to lift from my stomach. "What did you say?"

"I said, move in with me."

My eyes flash back and forth, trying to read him. After reluctantly agreeing to make things official, with much resistance, he wants me to drop everything and move in with him, after just a few months together?

He sighs. "I can practically hear you overthinking my proposition."

He takes advantage of my silence, pressing his lips against the exposed skin on my hip. I sigh, leaning back as his hands slide down my hips, gripping my thighs. I close my eyes as he works his mouth lower, lifting the hem of my shirt higher. I place both hands on the marble counter, steadying myself.

He is moving too fast, not with his mouth, but with his proposal. Normally, I would be jumping at this aspect of a relationship. I have never lived with a guy before, and it means a lot to me to think that we might be at this point in our relationship. The only problem is, we aren't there yet. He can easily change his mind, and we would be back to square one. Moving in together feels too . . . permanent. Even though I want that with Jackson, realistically, I know we aren't even close to that milestone.

"Wait," I say, opening my eyes. The words come out in some sort of strangled gasp as he lifts his mouth from my stomach.

"What?" He sighs, annoyed that his distraction isn't working.

He doesn't move his hands from my thighs, pressing me against the counter. His thumb swirls lightly on my stomach, and I force myself to get the words out fast so we can get back to...whatever he had in mind.

"You want me to move in? Like today? What happened to the guy who didn't want to be in a relationship?"

"He changed his mind." He shrugs.

I catch his chin before he bends down. I lift it gently, forcing him to look at me. "Changed your mind, just like that? Who's to say you won't change it again?"

"I won't." He smirks.

I roll my eyes as he presses his lips against my hip again. I go to argue but forget my point, concentrating on his mouth moving down my body.

What would I do with my stuff? I would have to tell Marina and Lucy. They would have to find a third roommate to take over my—*wait*! Am I actually considering this?

"What happened . . . to sharing a drawer first?" I can hear the throaty sound of my voice as I attempt to continue to have a rational conversation with his mouth between my legs.

He laughs softly against the inside of my thigh. The warmth of his breath makes me squirm. "I don't want to move that slow."

I let my head loll backward as he spreads my legs wider. His fingers press into my hips.

"I would have to park my car . . . next to your Mercedes. I don't . . . think it would fit."

I'm grasping at straws, but even as his mouth works me, I know that I am not ready for such a big step. It's a big deal for me, and I want it to happen at the right time. My head falls to the side as I grip the counter harder, trying to force myself to stay in this reality, despite his actions that make me want to leave it.

"Think of all the money you will save on gas."

"That's your main argument?" I sigh. "Saving the environment?"

"Not my only argument."

I gasp when his mouth moves to the center of me, between my legs, and I give up on any attempt to converse. My hips jerk, and I grab the top of his head. My fingers sift through his hair. I arch my hips, but he uses his left hand to hold me down, preventing me from seeking the friction I want.

"Jacks," I mumble out his name as he flicks his tongue again.

I tense, kicking my head back, wrapping my legs around him when release suddenly flashes through me, in pulsing waves. I lie on the counter, catching my breath when Jackson grabs my arm, pulling me upright. I throw my arms around his neck, burying my face against him while I stabilize. Eventually, my hold loosens, and I pull away. I run my hand through his hair and meet his green eyes.

"This is a major decision," I warn him. "What if you hate having me around all the time?"

"I could never hate anything about you," he says sincerely.

I bite the side of my lip. "Can I think about it?"

"If you need to." He shrugs, looking away, which tells me that my answer hurt him, in some small way.

I am about to explain when he grips my hips, pulling me off the counter. I wrap my legs around his waist, kissing him deeply.

"I have to leave for LAX in an hour," he says, breaking the kiss, breathing heavily. "Finish what we started?"

I nod, giggling when he squeezes my waist, carrying me into the bedroom.

CHAPTER 34

Jackson

It felt strange, walking into a meeting alone. I can't remember if there ever was a time when I didn't have representation with me, but I wanted this to be on my own, before I let the world into it.

The Hall Studios meeting was everything I wanted it to be. So vastly different from every other studio roundtable I'd been a part of. It was a conversation, not a mandate. Decisions were being discussed, collaborated on. I spoke to the writers, asked questions about the script.

I felt respected and realized it's been a long time since I'd felt that way.

"You have everything you need from me?" I ask before exiting the room.

"Everything." Chris Abbott, the producer, smiles.

He has a friendly face. Tall, dark hair, glasses. After an entire day of meetings, I was sold, about everything. He was someone I wanted to work with, someone I felt like I could trust.

"Nicole will be in touch with next steps to meet with the LA team. The audition and screen test are slated for the end of the month. After that, it's just paperwork."

I nod, jaw tightening. The anxiety that I had been trying to keep at bay all afternoon creeps back in. I would have to audition. A screen test to prove myself. What if I can't? What if I fail?

"Don't sweat it." He claps a hand on my shoulder. "You're a natural. You have nothing to worry about."

"Thanks." I reach out, shaking his hand before we depart.

It's been a while since I heard gentle words of reassurance. Zana generally resorted to intimidation when she wanted me to focus. It usually reinforced the negative. *Don't screw up or you will lose everything.* Those kinds of threats.

Has this been here for me the whole time? Why have I spent the past ten years climbing a ladder when I don't even want to reach the final destination?

I have about a dozen missed calls from Zana. She thinks I'm in New York for personal reasons. I didn't want to tell her about the potential opportunity, at least not yet. I know she's bound to find out eventually, but for now, it feels good to have something that is just mine.

I try Cassie's cell phone just a few hours before dinner. Of everyone in the world, I figure she would have the best perspective on all the noise in my head, but it goes right to voicemail.

I thought about taking the red eye home immediately after the meetings, but Sash is here for work, and she has been pestering me for a visit, in person. I'll admit, having a friend in the city makes the distance more bearable, but Cassie is better company.

I can't stop thinking about Cassie when things go quiet. She's on a loop in my head, replaying conversations, the sound of her laugh, all of it. All the time. I wonder if this is what it's usually like, how it feels to fall in love. I'd never allowed myself before, but after years of feeling like I am free-falling with no parachute, Cassie feels like a safety net, waiting to catch me before I hit the bottom.

Sash's eyes light up in surprise when I stand to greet her for dinner. A kiss on the cheek, always the same.

"You're early," she says when she slides into the booth next to me.

"Trying something different."

"I like it." She smiles widely

"You all right, mate?" Leo approaches, extending his hand toward me.

"Yeah, great," I say, shaking it and then turn to Sash, who is still staring at me. "What?"

She moves her head, tilting it, like she is trying to get a better look. "Something's different with you."

"Same old." I shrug, taking a seat.

"You're smiling." Sash pokes my side.

I roll my eyes. "I can't smile?"

Sash shrugs and orders drinks for the table.

Nobu is one of Sash's favorite restaurants. Mine too. We've been to one in nearly every city we've traveled to together, but New York is our favorite, more for sentimental reasons than anything. Sash is from Manhattan, and I know the second she retires, she will move back. It's just a matter of time at this point.

"So, what are you doing in New York?" she asks, popping a roll into her mouth.

"Business meetings."

"Mm-hm." She waves a hand to keep going. "More specific, please."

I had purposefully kept it vague to protect myself. Hall Studios isn't a done deal yet. I still have to audition and complete a screen test. I can still find a way to fuck it up. I know Sash will just keep pestering me if I don't give her something, so I provide the basics.

"I had a meeting with Hall Studios today. Subtle endorsement by the way." I eye Sash, referencing the email referral.

"You took the meeting?" She asks, sitting up straight.

"Only to get you off my back," I tease while she rolls her eyes.

"I've worked with them for a while now. It's a good company." Leo chimes in.

"Yeah, it seems like a good opportunity."

"But?" Sash easily catches on.

I throw her a look. "No buts, just nothing to report yet."

"You want it?" she asks.

"Yeah, of course I want it. I wouldn't be having this conversation with you if I didn't."

She smiles, resting her chin in her hand. "Happy looks good on you."

"Leo?" I turn away from Sash. "How you been?"

She eventually accepts the misdirection and falls back into the conversation.

Leo and Sash have been dating for the past five years, and every time I see them, I look for any indication of a proposal. I know if Leo had it his way, they would have been engaged and married within the first year they started dating, but throughout the years that they've been together, there is still no ring in sight. I know Sash is the reason that things are stagnant.

Not that it's a bad thing. They are in love, no one could ever doubt that, and a ring doesn't prove shit, but I worry that the reason Sash drags her feet when it comes to commitment has more to do with the things in her past that she has yet to address. I can't blame her for it. *Fuck*, I know I've got a decade or more of issues I still have to sort through, and I had the short end of the stick in that entire situation.

We're developmentally stunted, and we both know it.

"Will you be going to Paris with Cassie for Fashion Week?" Sash asks after dinner when Leo steps out to take a quick call.

I go to answer, but my eyes catch on my phone lighting up on the table. An alert I had set with Cassie's name attached to it fills the screen. I snatch it quickly, sliding the notification open, and flip to the article while the noise in the restaurant fades to static.

CASSIE TAYLOR RUMORED ESCORT? HERE'S THE TRUTH BEHIND THE LIES OF JACKSON RIDGE'S LATEST CONQUEST!

It's not just the title on the page that makes me sick; it's that the link is coupled with images of Cassie in her cocktail waitress uniform, most of which have been taken without her knowledge or even her fucking consent. At the bottom of the article, there is a photo of her at a table, some other guy's hands on her waist, her back to the camera.

My grip tightens while I sift through the trash. If people knew where she worked, they might understand, but they don't, which means they won't. They will assume and jump to the worst conclusions.

"What is it?" Sash asks.

"Be right back." I storm out of the booth and find a hall where my conversation can't be overheard. I call Cassie first, but her voicemail picks up before I get through the first ring.

"Cass, it's me." I wait, but the silence lingers. "Give me a call when you can."

I hang up, immediately sending a text to my publicist with a very explicit message. *Fix it.* She replies within seconds, already working damage control. I linger in the dark hall, running a hand over my face.

I think I'd been waiting for something like this to happen for a while. I knew it was inevitable, but I still feel like there should have been something I could have done to stop it. If Cassie hadn't been with *me*, this wouldn't have happened, and that hurts.

"Everything good?" Sasha asks with raised brows when I return.

I don't answer, just push my phone across the table. She frowns, scanning the article, making a noise under her breath before she slides it back.

"This stuff is such shit," she complains.

"I know it is," I say, because I do know. I know it well. Every single fucking thing published about me has the capacity to ruin my day or bring me to a new high, and I wish I wasn't so dependent on it. And I wish this wouldn't happen to Cassie just because she is associated with me.

"How is she?" Sash asks.

"Don't know. Went straight to voicemail."

I rub my forehead, trying to catalog all the good I've been able to do for her. I make a tally in my head, hoping that when we measure the scale, there will be an equal balance to convince her to stay, but the sinking sensation in my stomach hits when I realize this is just the tip of the iceberg. It's all downhill from here, and there is nothing I can do to stop it.

"Don't do that," Sash says, catching my spiral.

"What?" I roll my neck, trying to release the tension in my shoulders.

"Don't think that you're not worth it."

I let out a breath, pressing my forefinger and thumb to either side of my temple. "This is what I was afraid of."

"You always knew this was going to be a possibility, okay? Cassie is stronger than you think. Give her a chance to show you."

I stare at my phone lying on the table, screen still dark. I wouldn't blame Cassie if she doesn't want to talk to anyone, but especially me. It's my fault to begin with. The day my worst article was released, I didn't leave my apartment for an entire week.

At the end of the night, after we say our goodbyes, I wander the streets of the city, taking the long way back to my condo. I always loved New York. There was a level of anonymity that I could control here, unlike LA, where I always felt that people stared at me like kids pressed up against the glass at the zoo. There are always people around here, but it's private, in a way. It's easier to blend here, easier to pretend.

I am a few blocks from my condo on the park when my phone finally rings. I answer it quickly.

"Cassie?"

"Hey." I can immediately tell her voice is off, like she has been crying. I grip the phone tighter. "I, uh, thought you'd be asleep. I know it's late so I was just going to leave a voicemail."

"No, don't worry about it. I was up anyway. How are you?" I ask urgently.

"Could be worse . . . definitely could be better."

I can practically feel the distance between us, all two thousand-plus miles of it. I'm not there to comfort her or to distract her. I am here, on the other side of the country, with nothing to reassure her. Nothing that would mean anything, anyway.

"I tried to call you earlier," I say to soften the blow a bit, to show her I care about how she is feeling with all of this, unlike before. "I called as soon as I heard."

"I know. I just . . . didn't want to deal with it. Talking about it makes it seem more real."

"Don't pay any attention to it. It will be old news in a day."

"You're not mad?" she asks quietly.

"Why would I be mad?"

"Well. . . because, the article essentially implies I am sleeping with you because you're paying me."

"I don't care about any of that. It's all bullshit."

"It's sexist, that's what it is."

"I know it is."

I wish I could tell her it won't happen again, but I know that would hardly mean anything. It *will* happen again, and we both know it. As long as she is associated with me, something like this will happen again.

"Which one hurt more?" I ask, trying to differentiate between this article and the one published about her ex, needing to know where she draws the line.

"This one." Her voice wobbles. "The one with Noah was bullshit, I know that, but this feels worse. They have photos of me, photos I didn't even know people were taking and . . ." She sniffs. "I don't know, it makes me feel like my body is someone else's property that people are entitled to have an opinion about."

A small ember flickers in my chest, a flame that I thought had long been extinguished. Her words resonate with a dark part of me. I stay quiet, repeating the phrase again and again and again . . .

"I quit my job today."

Her voice pulls me back. I slow my pace when I see my building come into view and take a seat on the bench that lines the park.

"Because you wanted to or felt you needed to?" I ask.

"A little bit of both, I think. I don't really need the extra money anymore, though."

"Well, if you wanted to quit and now you can, that's a good thing. And if you felt you needed to . . ." I take a deep breath and try to sort out an answer. "I hope you didn't feel like you needed to. No one pays attention to tabloids anymore. Besides, you just had a write-up for signing with Luxe. That counts for something, right?"

"So, for every good article, I have to suffer through a bad one?"

"That's not what I'm saying." I sigh.

She's quiet for another moment. "What was your worst article?"

I flinch. "You know my worst article."

"That wasn't a rumor, though."

"It was a story, and it still hurt." My voice is laced with frustration, and I collect a breath to dull the blade. "It's still the worst thing that has ever been written about me."

"Why?" she asks, not a pressing question, but one of concern.

"Because I feel like my whole career is dictated by it, like I'm not good enough for the life I have."

It's quiet between us for a few more seconds before Cassie speaks again. Her voice wavers when she does.

"I'm sorry that happened to you."

I want to shrug, tell her it's not that big of a deal, that I learned to deal with it and that I don't think about it often, but all of that would be a lie. It does still hurt, and I do still think about it when things go quiet.

"Me too," I admit after a while.

"Is that a siren?" she asks, more urgently now. "Where are you?"

"Just outside my condo."

"Jackson!" She exclaims, the first color I've heard in her voice all night. "It's after midnight there!"

"It's New York."

"So? You can't just walk around in the middle of the night—"

"Why? Worried about me?"

"Yes."

She responds quickly, absolute in her answer, and I smile. I don't like that she is worrying now, but I think I like the idea of having someone close enough to worry about me.

"It's fine. Besides, I'm talking to you."

I say it like it holds more weight than I want to admit, holds more weight because just talking to Cassie isn't even just the highlight of my day, but my entire week.

"What did you do today?"

"Mostly meetings. Had dinner with Sash."

"How is she?"

"She's good, yeah."

"Is she your closest friend?"

I frown, shrugging. "I guess, yeah. She's my oldest friend."

"Well, she's a good one."

The observation settles deep in my chest, because I know it's true. Sash has been better to me than I deserve.

"You gonna be okay?" I ask softly, sort of afraid of her response.

After a while, she answers. "Yeah, I'll be okay. Are you back tomorrow?"

"I should land around six," I say. "Come over?"

"Yeah," she says and then a pause. "I wish you were here." She whispers the words into the phone.

"Me too," I tell her. "Try to get some sleep."

"Okay. Goodnight."

"Night."

I hang up, holding my phone in my lap, but I don't get up off the bench. I sit there, in the middle of the night, wishing that I was on the other side of the country, wondering what I would give up to make it there.

CHAPTER 35

Cassie

At this point, I'm considering tossing my phone into the garbage and never coming back for it. Once the article about my apparent side job went public, I can barely make it a week without another story being published. I sit in the driveway of Jackson's house, flipping through another article spammed to my phone, hating that this one is true.

CASSIE TAYLOR AND JACKSON RIDGE HOUSE HUNT IN BEVERLY HILLS.

After Jackson returned from New York last week, we went browsing for condos. I thought my disguise had been adequate, a baseball hat, sunglasses, an oversized sweatshirt. Jackson tried to blend in as well, but I guess there really is no escaping the scrutiny of the public.

I think the part that bothers me the most is that I didn't even notice. The grainy film on the front page of the article looks like it could have been taken by any random passerby who saw us. Somehow that betrayal hurt more, and I wonder how much money they were paid for our picture.

I throw my phone in my purse and push through the front door of Jackson's home. He gifted me a key last week, encouraging me to be here as much as possible. A compromise when I told him I wasn't ready to move in with him yet.

I kick off my shoes by the front door and set up my laptop on the counter. Although Jackson and I are not moving in together, I am looking for a place of my own. I have a steady income and jobs that allow me the opportunity to move out. All exciting things, except for the fact that I haven't told Marina and Lucy. They would now have to find out that I was potentially moving out before I even attempted to broach the subject.

Fucking paparazzi.

The garage door groans, signaling Jackson's return when my phone lights up, a text from Lucy. I slide open the message and see the link to the article about house hunting with her accompanying message.

LUCY

WTF?

I am about to type back a response urging her not to jump to conclusions when Jackson walks through the front door.

"Cass?"

"In the kitchen," I call, clicking my phone off, deciding to deal with it later. Jackson rounds the corner wearing black joggers and a white t-shirt with a Dodgers hat.

"Hey." He lifts the cap on his head before leaning down and kissing me. "How are you?"

He's been more attentive than usual lately. I'm guessing the subject of the article is the source of his concern. In a way, it's a bit of what he warned me about. Once the press gets involved in our lives, they would threaten to break us. I know that, but I can feel the effort from Jackson to prove that they can't break us if we don't let them.

"I'm okay."

It's a half truth, but I mostly say it so he doesn't worry.

It's not like I loved my job as a cocktail waitress, but it had been mine, and I worked there for nearly three years. Without it, I wouldn't have lasted six months in LA, and suddenly, it was gone. Another thing that was mine had simply vanished from my grasp. Another part of my reputation, destroyed.

Jackson weaves his fingers through my hair, clasping the base of my neck with his right hand, holding me there, almost as if he is trying to read between the lines of my vague answer.

"I'll be okay," I amend my earlier statement, and his shoulders relax. "How was your day?"

"Good," he says. "I had a follow-up meeting with Hall Studios about the part. Screen testing with the other lead is scheduled at the end of the month."

"Really?" My eyes light up, and he nods. "The trades haven't reported anything on that."

Jackson drops his chin, peering up at me. "I thought you didn't read the trades?"

"I'm in them now." I sigh. "I feel like I sort of have to."

"You don't," he says with a careful eye, like he believes I am one story away from bolting. "Does it feel like how you thought it would?"

I twist my lips. "Sometimes. Most days when I look in the mirror, I just stare at myself, trying to see what other people see. I feel like my appearance must have changed overnight, and I didn't notice or something. It's the only way I can rationalize all this attention. But nothing is different. I'm still me."

"That's good." Jackson sounds relieved, which leads me to believe it's been a long time since he saw his true self on the other side of the glass.

"Did you get more information on the schedule for the movie?" I ask.

"Yeah, I did." He sighs. "They are predicting a three-to-four-month shoot, with the majority of filming in London."

My heart squeezes at the location and duration of his

potential next project, but I ignore it. If this made him happy, I'm happy. I already promised myself a long time ago that I would never put someone through a situation like the one Noah put me through.

"It's a pay cut and a gamble. I've never done anything like this before." He chews on his lip and then raises his green eyes to meet mine. "If Zana knew, I know she would tell me it's a bad move, too much of a risk at this stage of my career."

"That's because she's more concerned about money than your well-being," I say with a sigh. His eyebrows pull together, like no one has told him that before. "What?"

"Nothing." He smiles, kissing me once on the lips, and then moves around the counter, pulling a beer from the fridge. "You been here long?"

"Just a few minutes before you," I say and go back to my laptop, skimming through the paragraphs of instructions on what to expect when getting documents expedited for my Paris trip next month. I sigh, lowering the screen when I sense Jackson's eyes on me from across the counter after he grabs a beer from the fridge. "I thought going to Paris would be fun. Right now, it's just stressful."

He smirks, pulling the bottle up to his lips. "That's because you've never been out of the country. And you don't have an assistant."

I roll my eyes. "I don't need an assistant."

He's mentioned the suggestion to me a few times before, but the entire concept seems ridiculous. I had just started booking consistent work, and I sure as hell don't want another percentage of my paycheck to be given away to someone who can do the same things that I can.

My phone buzzes again, another message from Lucy that makes me groan.

"What is it?"

"*TMI* posted a photo of us house-hunting." I grimace,

rubbing my temples. "I haven't had a chance to tell Marina and Lucy yet that I'm considering moving out."

"They'll understand."

"You don't know Lucy," I mutter under my breath. The wrath of Lucy when she feels she's been betrayed or abandoned is the stuff of nightmares. No one holds a grudge better than Lucy Collins. "Anyway, I'll deal with it tomorrow. Want me to make some dinner?" I ask, hopping off the stool.

Jackson doesn't answer, eyes caught on something else.

"Jackson?"

"Hmm?" He looks up.

"Want me to make some dinner?"

"Yeah." He nods, a smile reappearing, but he feels far away from me at the moment.

Whatever Jackson had been thinking, he keeps it to himself. Instead, while I make dinner, he distracts me with suggestions about our extended trip to France. I was going to have time off after the Paris circuit and Jackson was working to organize a break in his schedule as well so that we could travel together. Discussions about planning yacht trips and romantic dinners are far more exciting than thinking about the looming deadline and fast approaching timeline to get everything organized.

After we clear the dishes, Jackson refills my wine glass. The sun begins to set beyond the windows, tossing pinks and purples against the sky. A fitting country song hits the speaker, a slow beat echoes through the house, as Jackson pulls me into his arms. He spins me during the chorus then holds me close, rocking back and forth.

Despite being in his arms, his eyes are far away again, and I know that whatever caught him in a spiral before dinner is still there, spinning in his head.

"What is it?" I ask, resting my chin on his chest.

He peers down at me, pushing some hair behind my ear. "I was thinking about what it feels like to be normal. I like this aspect of it. I didn't think I would. It's the first time I've felt this . . . peaceful in a while." He says it like it's a foreign concept, an unknown feeling.

I hold my breath. "But?"

"I keep waiting for it to end," he says quietly. "I don't want it to."

"It doesn't have to," I say, and he holds me tighter. "I'm here."

"You're here," he says, taking a deep, steadying breath before pressing his forehead against mine. "And you'll stay?"

"I'll stay," I promise.

He holds me close while we sway back and forth, and it hangs there in the air between us. It's a whisper on my lips. I can hear it in the quiet, in the beating of his heart. I look up at Jackson, our eyes catch, holding each other, and although we don't say it out loud, I feel it in his arms. I close my eyes, resting my cheek against his chest and make a wish.

Don't let me go.

CHAPTER 36

Jackson

There are few circumstances that throw me off nowadays. I'm used to a schedule, a routine laid out for me that requires little to no thought. Zana has my calendar planned out almost to the minute, every week of every month in the year. Yes, there are obstacles thrown my way that I have to swerve, but I can usually handle them.

Usually.

It's a sunny afternoon, typical for August, but it was the first day in a while where I felt content. The oppressive heat of LA didn't bother me. I had been trying to stay off my phone more often, ignoring the headlines that had the capacity to dictate my every mood, and being with Cassie made it better.

Cassie makes everything better.

It's like after a shit day, I used to want to drown in distractions, now I just want to drown in her. I love listening to her talk about anything, about everything. I love what she says, her perspective, why she thinks the way she does, what she likes, doesn't like. I've been cataloging all of it. I've never done that before. I've never wanted to.

I'm on the studio lot. I've stepped in and out of meetings all afternoon while Zana worked to carefully fill my calendar for the next few months. My phone buzzed, so I was distracted when I heard my name called.

I haven't heard her voice in years but just the sound of it immediately brought me to a completely other time in my life. A time when I had no connections, no power, when I had no control.

I kept my distance at Cannes. One look from the press table and I left before she could reach me, before she could touch me. Now, I feel trapped, like someone just locked me in a room and threw away the key. I have nowhere to run. I have nowhere to hide.

Victoria Baxter walks towards me, wearing all black. Her dark hair is cut short, resting just above her shoulders, and she's wearing the sort of high heels that I always remember her wearing. I catalog all of these details before she even approaches me. I don't know why. It's like my mind is trying to process the person in front of me, but I can't accept it, not until she stops right in front of me, not until I am hit with her scent of perfume. I stop breathing through my nose. The night appears in flashbacks at just the smell of it. Her eyes are covered by dark, big sunglasses, which is good, because I can't stomach the color of them.

She looks the same. I think that's what fucks me up the most, that she would still look the same as she did back then, but I am a completely different person.

When you're eighteen, you feel older than you are. I was treated like an adult, so I acted like one. I think that was the rationalization. I felt old enough, but every single time I look back on photos or catch a glimpse of my younger self, I can't even see it. I was just a kid.

I feel hot and itchy, like I want to tear out of my skin just to get away from her, but my feet have stopped moving. I'm caught on her leash. I can't go until she releases me.

"I thought that was you." She smiles, or attempts to, her face barely moves.

She pulls me in for a hug, and I don't know what to do except allow it to happen. She doesn't stop touching me when she pulls away. Her hand rests on my elbow, and in some way, it feels like a brand singed to my skin, declaring ownership.

"How are you?"

"Fine." My voice sounds like sandpaper.

"It's been a while."

"Ten years," I answer for her.

"Time flies," she muses and then pulls the sunglasses off her face. I look at the ground. "Walk with me."

It's a statement, not a question, and I forget what I was doing, where I was even going, to say no. I can't actually make my mouth work, so I just nod, matching her pace, hands in my pockets, looking down at my feet.

"What's new with you?"

"Not much," I answer, rifling through the list of short phrases I can offer before I run out of things to say.

"Not much? Leading two blockbusters this summer alone. That's not nothing." I stay quiet. My heart hammering so loud, I wonder if she can actually hear it. "Zana tells me that you are looking for additional opportunities—"

That catches my attention.

"You talk with Zana?" I turn on her.

I immediately regret the decision when we come face-to-face. Her catlike eyes narrow, and I stare into the blue that I want to forget. It's a deep color that I remember looking black in the dark.

"Of course. We've stayed in touch over the years. I wish we could have as well," she says with a smile that makes me feel funny. "She mentioned that you are interested in expanding your scope. I do have some new projects on the horizon, if you're interested." Her hand brushes up and down my arm, starting from my shoulder down to my elbow. "It can be whatever you want it to be."

"No." I step away and shake my head, trying to clear the fog. "I mean, I have other projects. So, I don't—"

"Hall Studios? Quite ambitious."

I blink. How the *fuck* does she know about that? I haven't told anyone outside Cassie and Sash, the only people I trust in the world. If Victoria knows, it must mean. . .

"I told you, Zana and I have stayed in touch," she says, and I hate that the information shocks me. "The project is a bit of a gamble, no?"

Her tone pulls me back, the implication that she is not impressed, and I suddenly become aware that I still want to impress her, *need* to impress her. I don't want to ask, but I have to know what she is thinking, what she thinks of *me*.

I look at her sideways. "You don't think it's a good idea?"

She frowns, looking bored. "I don't think it's the right fit for you. You worked so hard to make a reputation for yourself. You should deliver what people want."

My stomach twists, like someone wound up a rag and tugged tight.

I always kept a pulse on what people said about me, thought about me. I just didn't realize that everything I had been doing to try to change the perception was a worthless attempt, until now.

I can't change. I can't be enough. I never was.

"Zana and I have been discussing your future, and there are some great options I can give you," Victoria says. "I'd love to work with you again. We made a good team."

My eyes flit up to hers because now, I want to read her. I take her in, her puffy lips, tight face, and then stare into her dark-blue eyes, but there is nothing there.

No embarrassment, no regret.

I see nothing looking back at me.

"Think about it." She smiles, leaning forward to kiss my cheek. I jolt at the contact that I don't want, that I've never wanted, but I can't move until she pulls away. "Stay in touch."

Then she's gone.

I stand there for a few more minutes, heart hammering in my chest, pulsing in my ears, and then turn, walking back toward the parking lot. Nic is waiting for me by the SUV. I must look bad, because Nic, who always remains stoic, steps forward, eyebrows tight, when he reaches to open the door for me.

I order him to take me to the only thing that can help this feeling go away.

"Home."

It's late when we pull through the gate. I breathe a sigh of relief when I see Cassie's car parked in the driveway. As soon as we roll to a stop, I throw the car door open, rushing inside.

"Jackson?" I follow the sound of her voice. "Hey!" Cassie greets me barefoot in the kitchen.

I watch her face fall slightly when she sees me, and I wonder what I must look like. I feel shaky, like my body doesn't really belong to me, like there is something wrong inside of *me*.

"Everything okay?" she asks cautiously.

I don't answer, *can't* answer. I cross the foyer, scooping her into my arms, and kiss her. She's tense at first, probably too shocked to do anything but kiss me back, which she does, eventually. Her shoulders relax, and she melts into me like she always does, throwing her arms around my neck while I carry her into my bedroom, kicking the door shut behind us.

I lay her down on the mattress, hovering over her. Her eyes are wide but wary, and I can't believe that she's here. I can't believe she's mine. For whatever reason, she *chose* me.

I pull off my shirt. "Say yes," I tell her, because I need to hear it. Because I *always* need to hear it.

"Yes," she breathes.

It happens fast. I'm in no mood to drag it out. Our clothes come off, and Cassie is naked in my arms only a few seconds before I slip between her legs. When she reaches for me, I grab her hands, holding them above her head, because as much as I hate to admit it, this is about me and what I need.

It doesn't take long before she's gasping for breath. Like instructed, she keeps her eyes on me the whole time. I need to look at her and remember that it's Cassie underneath me and no one else. I need to make sure that she hasn't changed her mind, that she still wants this, that she still wants *me*.

She whimpers when she's close, legs tightening around my waist, and I kiss her, hard, tongue in her mouth, my hands tight around her wrists. The pressure intensifies, my back straining while she arches further into me, and then she shatters, moaning my name when she does. I'm not far behind her, pushing through, dragging it out as long as I can.

When I pull out, I roll off her, lying on my back, and stare up at the ceiling. I rest my arm over my eyes when they start to warm, and a wave of disgust washes over me. I feel like crying, and I hate myself for it.

Cassie touches my arm, slowly pulling it away from my face. Our eyes meet for just a moment and then she reaches for my hand, tugging gently. I follow the movement, resting my head in her lap. Her hands fall into my hair, scraping her nails softly against my scalp and then my eyelids become incredibly heavy and eventually close.

CHAPTER 37

Cassie

Jackson has gone quiet, and I don't know why.

I know *something* is wrong. I could tell when he came into the house last week, scooped me up in his arms, and took me to bed. That night felt like a first of whatever *that* was. It was like an exercise, a routine. He was going through the motions without really even being there.

It wasn't until he rolled over that he seemed to come back from it all. I pulled him onto my lap and he fell asleep with his cheek on my stomach, arms wrapped around my waist. I stayed awake for hours, going through every possible scenario that could have wrecked him like that.

He was hurt. I saw it in his eyes, but I don't know *why*.

He's been spending more time in New York and the few days he is home, I try to be at the house when I can. I hope that eventually Jackson will walk in, sit me down, and tell me everything that has been going on, but it's been nearly two weeks, and I am just as in the dark now, as I was then.

When he is home, we sleep together almost every night, and when we do, he always asks for my consent, sometimes more than once. He looks at me the whole time, making it very easy to fall completely apart under his gaze. He holds me close when we eventually fall asleep, pressing me to his chest, so tight it's hard to breathe sometimes. He holds me like he loves me, so I stay, and I wait for this phase we have been living in to end so we can both float to the surface and breathe again.

I am sitting at the counter, flipping through the latest press packet for Paris, when I hear the front door open. I lean forward, waiting for Jackson to find me in the kitchen, but the door slams, and he goes straight to his bedroom.

I know he's been stressed about his screen test today with Hall Studios. It's the project that he actually likes, the one he is excited about. He told me this before he stopped talking to me, almost altogether, but I had the date in my head, hoping this might be the turning point that flips everything around so we can go back to the people we were before he went quiet.

I hold my breath, pushing off the counter, and follow him into his bedroom.

"How did it go?" I ask.

Jackson pulls his shirt off, stepping into his closet. I allow a short breath, releasing it when he reappears, stumbling as he tugs on a dark hoodie.

"Jacks?"

His head pulls up, as if he just realized that I was here. He stares at me for a bit. His eyes are dark and hazy, like he's far away from himself at the moment.

"How was the screen test?"

He frowns. "Didn't go."

I tense. "Why not?"

"Didn't see a point honestly," he says with a shrug, and I hear it, the slight slur in his words.

"No point?"

"Yeah." He holds my gaze a moment longer, and I see a sort of darkness there that I hadn't seen before.

I let out a breath, stepping toward him. I've given him space.

I've given him time. I've let him push me away for weeks, but I need answers. I need *something*.

"Jackson," I say, resting my hands on his chest. I can feel his heartbeat hammering away under his hoodie. "What happened?"

"Nothing." He shrugs. "I'm going to sign on for another movie, so it wouldn't work with my schedule anyway."

I pull back. "Why? You loved the script. You said it was the break you've been waiting for."

"Changed my mind." He steps back, away from me, so my hands fall off his chest. "Am I not allowed to do that?" he quips sarcastically, tilting his head.

"That's not what I meant." I roll my eyes. "I just meant that you were excited about the other project, the team that you would be working with, the script. You want to throw that all away?"

"Yeah." He looks at me, his face blank. "I do."

"Where is this coming from?" I ask, trying to keep up.

"The paycheck is considerably larger. There is more attention that I can get from a bigger studio. They can give me more."

"At what cost, though?" The words fall out, and I feel like I just got caught on a trip wire. I immediately know it was the wrong thing to say as I watch Jackson's eyes darken.

"You do realize that if I don't book anything substantial, I will lose all of this!" He gestures to the monstrosity that is his house. As if the only reason I am sticking around has to do with the size of his mansion and paycheck.

"You know that doesn't matter to me."

"So then, what's the problem? I'm happy about this. You should be too." His voice is flat.

"Jackson, I know that you think—"

"You don't know *anything*. Got it?" He nearly growls under his breath, holding my stare for a moment, letting the message sink in. A warning that I am treading in dangerous waters. "I'm having people over tonight." He brushes past me, reaching for his phone.

"What about our plans?" I ask, my eyes following him out of the room.

"Not tonight."

I stand there, trying to decide if I should leave or stay. I need to talk to him and hope that eventually he will choose me, so I stay and make my way out to the kitchen. I reach for my laptop, noticing movement outside on the patio. Jackson leans against the railing at the edge of his property, his head dipped. A glass of whiskey in one hand, cigarette in the other.

I linger for a moment, wondering if I should go outside and join him, but I don't want to fight, and I know that if I keep pushing, he will snap. I grab my laptop, taking the stairs up to the second floor before a party breaks out below me.

I am able to focus for about an hour before the steady thrum of house music filters upstairs. Another forty minutes later, I am massaging my temples and eventually give up. I pack up my things, ready to pass out behind a locked door when my phone pings, a message from Lucy linked with an article.

LUCY

Just a heads-up. Thought you should see this.

I swipe open the *EDaily* article and stare at the headline, willing it to make sense.

JACKSON RIDGE TO SIGN MULTI-FILM DEAL WITH VICTORIA BAXTER AT THE HELM.

I skip ahead, skimming the part of the article that summarizes Jackson's recent missteps before going to the heart of the piece.

"The soon-to-be collaboration marks the first time Ridge and Baxter will be working together since their match-up in 2014 for the hit soap opera, Sunset City. *Baxter is not immune to the rumor that stormed the set nearly a decade ago, one that alluded to a relationship*

with Ridge. Baxter continues to deny the story, mentioning that it most likely came from their close friendship. 'Over the past ten years, Jackson and I have kept in touch. We've been waiting for a project to work together again and are ecstatic that we found the right one.' More to come on this developing story."

He's signing with *her*? When and how did this even happen?

I take the stairs down quickly, not caring that there are nearly a hundred strangers on the first floor and I am in sweatpants. I push past the bodies, weaving through a few more crowds before I am on the patio. I lift myself on my tiptoes for a better view, and that's when I see Jackson leaning up against the railing, smoke blowing out his mouth.

I don't have to be close to know that he is teetering on the edge. I can see it in his slow, lethargic movements. I step around the pool deck and stop in front of him. It takes a few more seconds for him to recognize me, but when he does, his mouth pulls up into a sloppy smile.

"Hey, Cass," he mumbles my name.

I give him a quick smile before I turn to the people surrounding him. "Give us a sec?"

They nod, dispersing. Jackson leans back against the railing, a cigarette hanging out of his mouth. He grips the sides of my hips to pull me close.

"You still wanna *talk*?" he asks sarcastically.

I ignore the jab and grab the cigarette hanging loosely from his lips. "You know I hate this." I grimace, pinching it between my fingers before throwing it in the pool.

"It's a party." He rolls his eyes.

"It can kill you." I counter, but it doesn't register. I reach for his face, taking it between my hands and force him to look at me. His eyes wander, eventually meeting mine, but I can tell they are lost and unfocused. "Why didn't you tell me about the article?"

His voice is lifeless when he eventually answers. "What article?"

"You're working with her again? Victoria Bax—"

"Don't," he warns. His body tenses, eyes going dark.

"*Why*?" I nearly beg. "Why would you ever want to work with her? Why would you give up everything you've been working toward?"

Jackson's eyes churn with an emotion I can't place, but then he blinks, and the cool, stoic mask returns. When he looks away, I grab his chin, forcing him to listen.

"You don't need her."

His hands drift down my hips, resting behind me as he squeezes gently. His mouth carefully makes its way up to my neck, his nose lifts, tilting my head to the side. The scruff on his jaw tickles my skin, and it takes everything in me not to lean into the gesture.

"Hey, come on, save that for later." I grab his hands, lifting them back to my waist.

"Later sounds interesting," he murmurs, and I can hear the distance in his voice, the slowing of his speech, the slurring of his words. Nothing productive will be said now, so I pull him to stand.

"Come on. Let's get you to bed."

"Mmm, are you coming with me?" he murmurs against my neck.

"Sure." I step back, guiding him inside.

He wraps his arms around me from behind, using my body for balance, as I lead him back to the bedroom. As soon as I lock the door behind us, he presses me against the wall, his mouth on mine. I can taste the whiskey and smoke on his breath as I carefully pull away to breathe. Despite the urgency behind his kiss, I know how this will end. He will be passed out the second I lay him down.

"Come on," I say, holding his face away from mine. "Bed."

He groans, trying to roll his eyes. I pull back the covers before he stumbles to the edge of the bed and then bend down to untie his shoes, removing them one by one. I reach for his hoodie next, pulling it off as he falls back on the mattress.

He stares up at the ceiling while I climb up next to him, brushing his forehead with my fingers but he still won't look at me.

"Why won't you talk to me?" I plead softly.

His eyelashes flutter, fighting to stay open. His chest rises and falls in a slow rhythm before he whispers quietly. "Can't."

And then he's asleep.

The party crashes about an hour later. I don't go back to bed until everyone is gone and the doors are locked. When I eventually slide under the covers, Jackson stirs, wrapping his arms around my waist, holding me tight. His hand slips under my shirt, and he presses me back, flush against his chest and lets out a sigh, like he hadn't let himself completely drift under before I was safe against him.

I eventually force my eyes closed and hope that tomorrow we can go back to the people we used to be together.

But I wake the next morning in a cold bed.

Alone.

CHAPTER 38

Jackson

"You look like shit."

Zana greets me with a grimace when I slide in the back seat of the SUV. I touched down in New York this afternoon, fulfilling an obligation I committed to a long time ago.

"Yeah, well I feel like shit."

I tug the baseball cap down further and slip on a pair of sunglasses. My hangover pounds in my temples relentlessly. I don't remember much about last night, other than Cassie putting me to bed at some point after she begged me to talk to her.

She wanted answers. Answers that I couldn't give her.

Why didn't I show up for the Hall Studios screen test? Because I knew I was going to fail, and I can't fail if I don't go. I can't be judged if I don't give them the opportunity.

Victoria's words have been on a constant loop in my head since the day we met on the studio lot. I can't get rid of them, I've tried.

The proposal for the partnership is something I expected, at least after I realized Zana and Victoria had been organizing the deal behind my back. It made sense why I ran into her on the lot. It wasn't a coincidence; it was a well-coordinated plan. They had been operating me like a piece on a chess board, pushing me around, directing my every move behind the scenes, and I was too blind to see it. Worse, I was too *weak* to stop it.

I can't remember actually agreeing to the partnership. I know I must have given them some sort of verbal commitment for an article to be written about it, but I don't remember the details. These past two weeks have been an out-of-body experience. I've been grasping at tethers to bring me back, but I can't find myself. I don't even know what version is real anymore. The person I am with Cassie or the one they made me?

"You're booked all day." Zana rattles off my itinerary while I dry swallow a pill, or two, trying to numb my mind like the rest of my body. "There are a few meetings we need to attend to in the office, and then you are slated for press with Jenn."

She lowers her phone, looking over at me. She asks the next question on purpose, already knowing the answer.

"How did the meetings with Hall Studios go?"

I turn away, looking out the window. Gray clouds hang low over New York, casting a dark shadow over the city as we cross the bridge into Manhattan.

"Not a problem anymore."

"Would you believe me if I told you it's for the best?" Zana asks, not giving me the option of an answer. "Partnering with Victoria and her studio is the contract that you needed. Once you sign, you will have a decade of lucrative projects. You need this. No gambles, all guaranteed profit."

I rub my temple, squeezing my eyes shut. My life feels like it's been thrown into a fucking blender. Everything that I had planned had been thrown into disarray. I'm exhausted, so fucking tired, of trying and realizing that none of it matters. None of it is good enough. *I'm* not good enough.

"Fine." Zana lifts a hand in the air, relenting. "Have you thought anymore about Warner's proposal for the press between you and Jenn?"

Even though I spent all last night avoiding Cassie, refusing to talk to her, to tell her what's really been on my mind, I wish she was here with me. I wish her hand was between mine because if I had physical proof of her, of the mistake I was about to make, maybe it would make saying no easier.

But she's not here, and I'm not good, and I can't say no.

"You want my advice?" Zana asks, sighing.

I press my tongue to my bottom lip and shake my head. My heart races in my chest. I feel like crying again because I don't want to do this. I don't want to be this person that needs to do this. I just don't know how not to be.

Cassie is herself, always. She feels *real,* where most days I feel like a broken toy. A replica of something made to look authentic, but hollow on the inside. I am a *thing.* Something that people used to adore but then got bored with along the way and forgot to tell me. It's why I'm so desperate for it, for anything, because I was trained to need their love and attention. I don't know how to operate without it. I don't need a shot of it; I need to consume it in large doses, disregarding any and all side effects.

I feel it now, slipping through my fingers. The control that I like to keep on a short leash has too much slack. It's drifting away, and the only thing I can do to get it back is a snap, a sharp yank, so I'll tug.

I know what I can do to make them care. I know what I have to do to make them want me, and I *need* them to want me. So, if I couldn't be better, then I would give them what they asked for.

"Go in there, play the part, and get paid. Deal with everything else later," Zana says. I swallow, trying to force my mind into the state of numbness I feel in my body. "You can trust me."

I swing my gaze back to Zana sitting across from me. I'm not sure I really trust her, just have never had much of a choice. I feel like a puppet who's never managed to cut his own strings.

My body is numb, my brain hollow, when I eventually answer her.

"Okay."

I'm on autopilot all day, just going through the motions, so memorized at this point, I've become desensitized by them. I smile when they tell me to, pose when a camera is pointed in my face, and the second it drops, I drag myself to the next interview.

We're close to Times Square. At the office of some trashy pop site, being interviewed by some puffy-lipped, stiff-faced brunette. She has to be nearly forty, masquerading as a twenty-something-year-old.

"Jackson Ridge and Jenn Hamilton!" Her excitement is so annoyingly upbeat, I fight the urge to grimace. "The dream team."

"I love that!" Jenn laughs, resting her hand on my thigh.

I don't move away, even though I want to. I stare down at her sharp, dark-red fingernails, brushing my knee.

"So, you know how the game works. *Never have I ever.*"

"Of course!" Jenn smiles animatedly, nudging me subtly with her elbow.

I force a smile, remembering that I am supposed to be playing along. I'm not really paying attention. I just nod and pretend to look invested when the camera pans toward me. I'm acting, and right now, I'm giving the performance of my life.

When we wrap, I stand in a daze. I don't even know what I said, but I walk away feeling like I had just been punched in the gut. I have no choice but to ignore it when Zana leads me to the next interview, and on and on it goes.

I walk around in a fog for the entire day until I am loaded back into the SUV. I want to go home, drown it all out, but we pull up to a bar instead.

We enter from the back alley to prevent photographers from capturing the moment, but the second we are inside, people's phones raise, flashes follow us to the private section. I collapse on the couch as soon as we are separated from the masses.

I don't want to be here, but I have nowhere else to go. I'm stranded on the other side of the country with nothing else to keep me distracted. I take a swig of tequila straight from the bottle, a large gulp of it, and cringe.

Jenn has made everything unbearable, as if it isn't hard enough being plagued by my own subconscious; she's everywhere I look. I didn't realize how shrill her voice sounded until I dreamed of someone else's.

My eyes struggle to focus on my phone screen, pulled up with Cassie's number. I thought about calling her all day, but I haven't because I don't know what to say. I stare at my phone until it becomes blurry and then pocket it away.

"Everything okay?" Jenn's hand touches my arm, and even though I don't want it on me, I don't pull away.

"No," I answer, closing my eyes.

I take back another swallow of tequila, even though I feel sick. Stomach bottomed out, free falling off a cliff, sick.

"You want to get out of here?" she asks, her mouth close to my ear.

I try to tell her that I want to leave, just not with her, but it doesn't come out the way I planned because when I stand, she follows. My car is already waiting outside in the back alley. I stumble into the back seat and before I can tell her no, Jenn slides in next to me.

"Where to?" Nic eyes me from the rearview.

"Home," I say while Jenn cozies up next to my side.

I see Nic's disappointed gaze, and look away, eyes out the window. Jenn's hands resting on my stomach, but they keep wandering lower. We are almost to my condo when I grab her wrists, gripping them with one hand.

"Stop."

"What's the big deal?" she whines, trying to loosen my grip. "You were all over me today."

"That was for the press, and you know it." I shove her hands away.

She ignores the rejection, pressing her chest against my side. Her leg moves to fold over mine, but I shove it away, letting out a sigh of relief when we pull up to my building. When I exit the car, Jenn steps out right behind me.

"You're not coming with me." I turn to face her, backing her up against the car.

She reaches out, touching my face, and I try to lean away, but I am unbalanced, and I think she knows it. "I can make you feel better," she says quietly, her lips brushing against my ear again, and I feel like I'm going to be sick.

"Stop," I mumble, trying to sort through the fog in my head.

Jenn drops her hands from my face, but then they are on my chest, wandering down my stomach, resting on my belt buckle. I squeeze my eyes shut before flinging them open, and when I do, I reach for her hands, capturing them in my grip.

"I said no." I deliver the blow, looking her right in her eye, pushing her hands away from me. "Leave."

Jenn pouts, her fingers brush across my chest before she steps away, slipping back into the car. As soon as the door is shut, Nic speeds away, and I stand there, watching them disappear around the corner.

I pull out my phone before going inside, staring at Cassie's number, but instead of calling her, I call Sash. The line rings but before the voicemail clicks over, I hang up.

I eventually drag myself upstairs. Once the door is locked, I climb up on the mattress, lying face down, on my stomach. I press my face into the pillow, squeezing my eyes shut, and pass out.

~~~

I wake to rattling glass. A blurry figure appears in front of the bed, walking back and forth. I blink as the figure becomes clearer and sigh when I recognize Sash. She's walking around the room, picking up after me.

It has to be early afternoon, judging by the light flowing through the curtains. I can't remember getting home or what
~~~

time I crashed. All I can remember is the bottle of tequila I had in my hand most of the night.

"What are you doing here?" I ask, dragging a hand across my face.

"You called *me*. At 3 a.m. no less." She glares, but her eyes soften when she takes me in, like she feels bad for me. "You're lucky I'm in town. I haven't gotten a late-night phone call from you in a while. I figured it was more of an emergency."

"My head." I groan, face falling into my hands.

"Yeah, well, that's what happens when you attempt to drink away your problems." Sash picks up an empty bottle, throwing it in the trash beside the bed.

I tense at the loud, sudden noise and fall back on the bed, hands over my face, trying to sort through yesterday's events. All I have is the pit in my stomach knowing that something is wrong.

There is something wrong with *me*.

"What happened?" Sash asks, taking a seat on the edge of the mattress.

I had been in a fog most of yesterday, but I remember it in flashes. My forced smiles, laughs, Jenn touching me, and I didn't pull away. I didn't fucking do anything. I just let it happen. I double over, afraid I might actually be sick.

"I think I fucked up," I admit.

Sash's eyes go soft. "How bad?"

"Bad."

I scan the room for my phone, and when I see it on the side table, I lunge for it. The rapid movement causes a pulse to spear through my head, but I don't care. I pull it open, scanning for any headlines, any articles yet published, but there is nothing. *Yet.*

How long before photos start circulating of Jenn and me? When will sound bites from our interview start getting edited out of context? How long before Cassie's name gets dragged through the mud, again, because of *me*?

"What did you do?" Sash's voice pulls me back.

My stomach twists, and I rush out of bed, grabbing my wallet and keys. "I have to go."

"Where?" Sash stands, eyes following me as I rush about the room, collecting my things.

To California? To LA? To Cassie. I just hope that I'm not too late.

"Home," I tell her.

I head for the airport, ignoring whatever it is Zana had scheduled for me today. I keep my phone on when I board the plane from the tarmac, silencing all other calls, scanning the publications, looking for something, for anything that tells me how bad it is, that tells me what I've done. I make it all the way to LA without a whisper hitting my screen.

I am about to breathe a sigh of relief, but the second I am off the plane, my phone finally buzzes. I grab it, hoping to see a message from Cassie, but it's an alert.

One hits, then another, and another.

I stare down at the screen, trying to sort through all the articles hitting my phone. Nearly every media outlet reporting the same story.

What have I done?

CHAPTER 39

Cassie

My eyes zero in on a couple on the other side of the restaurant. His hand reaching for hers across the table. I don't really know what made my eyes catch. For a moment, it feels like I am intruding on a private conversation, but I can't look away from the subtle intimacy exchanged between the two strangers. They are both smiling at each other, not a care in the world. I wonder if that will ever be Jackson and me, content to be alone, together, oblivious to anyone and everyone around us. I rest my cheek in my hand and lean my elbow on the table. An ache of longing passes through me when I realize maybe Jackson and my future had been a pipe dream.

I haven't heard from him since he left for New York. I try not to let it bother me, make up excuses in my head for why my phone has been silent. He's working, he's busy, he doesn't care. I try not to focus on the latter, but it creeps closer the longer we are apart.

I tense when I see a flash over my shoulder. I turn to find the source, but I don't see any cameras raised on the restaurant floor, or anyone pressed against the window. I shake my head, wondering if I am starting to hallucinate.

"Cassie?"

"Hmm?" I jerk my head back toward Marina, sitting across from me.

She exchanges a look with Lucy before speaking. "I asked, how long Jackson is going to be in New York?"

"Oh, um, I think until Sunday," I say, taking a sip of my sparkling water.

I focus my attention back on our conversation. Marina and Lucy are both laughing at some inside joke that I managed to miss. I sit there, at the table, feeling very much like an outsider between my two best friends, which is strange, because there was once a time, not very long ago, when I felt like the glue holding us all together.

We are all different, inherently so. Lucy is a freight train with no emergency brake. Marina is a warm hug after a long day. I fall somewhere between them, but I never felt like any of us needed to fit into a specific box. We all just worked.

Now, as I look between them, I realize that I've become an outsider of sorts. Without my knowledge, I've bumped myself to the outside track, operating on the sidelines of their lives instead of being an active participant. I feel like a stranger, standing on the curb, pressing my face against the glass, trying to see inside.

I lean forward, forcing myself to re-engage in the conversation at the mention of Marina's brother, Alex. Even though I had zoned out of most of their conversation, the lines of concern on Marina's forehead tell me she's worried.

"What about Alex?" I ask.

Despite the Andrino's obscene fortune and exhaustive privilege, Alex hadn't been able to live up to his parents' expectations. He came out in high school and his parents' solution was to force him back into the closet. He moved away after graduation, but at the age of twenty-six, he has already been to rehab twice, both times failing to stick.

"He's fine, seriously." Marina sighs, looking down at the base of her wine glass. "If I start asking questions, I know it will get worse."

"Are your parents . . . helping at all?" I ask.

"Only if he pretends like he's not a gay, relapsing alcoholic." Marina forces a harsh laugh. "Then they'll pay for his apartment."

I hate that this is the first I am hearing about this. I hate that all of this has been going on, and I didn't know. Is this the type of person I have become? I've been too wrapped up in Jackson and our own issues that I hadn't lifted my head to see what is right in front of me.

"Marina." I lean forward. "I didn't realize things had gotten so bad."

"Well, it's not like you asked," Lucy mutters under her breath, and I tense at her accusation.

"*Lucy*," Marina warns, shooting her a glare across the table.

"What?" Lucy picks up her wine glass, shrugging before looking right at me. "You haven't been here. Why are you acting like you have?"

"I . . . I'm sorry. My schedule has been crazy, and when I'm not working, I'm—"

"With Jackson," Lucy answers for me, suppressing the urge to roll her eyes. "We know."

"Are . . . are you guys mad at me?" I ask.

Marina and Lucy exchange a look that makes my stomach flip. "It's not that. It's just, we haven't seen you in a while, you know?" Marina offers softly.

I nod, feeling like Lucy's comment was a punch to the gut instead of a simple observation.

"It's not that big of a deal, though." Marina tries to fix the situation, like always. "I'm just worrying about Alex. You know how I am."

Lucy asks another question, one that only Marina can discuss with her, and I fall back in my chair, turning toward the couple on the other side of the restaurant I had been studying earlier. They are leaning back away from the table now, too preoccupied with their phones to notice each other.

We finish paying the check when my phone lights up, Jackson's name appearing across the screen. I look down, flipping it over for now. I'd call him back later, when I was at home and out of the public eye. Halfway to the lobby, my phone chimes again, a text from Jackson.

JACKSON

Call me as soon as you get this.

Before I can answer, I see the flashing of the camera lights beyond the glass. For the past few weeks, paparazzi had been starting to follow me around, but there had only been a few. One or two that would snap a picture of me grocery shopping or running errands. Never this many, not without Jackson.

I scan the restaurant floor. The people who had been staring at me before from behind their menus, openly gawk now that the cameras have decided it was acceptable to crowd my limited form of personal space. Phones lift in the air, pointing in my direction, and then the whispers start between the tables.

Why? Why would the paparazzi be here, now?

"Cassie, what is going on?" Marina panics, her eyes darting between the flashes.

"I don't know," I say, shielding my eyes from the flashes of cameras. "Just walk fast and keep your head down."

Lucy clings to my arm. It's one of the few times I've ever seen her look scared. I inhale a short, sharp breath before stepping outside. Marina and Lucy are on either side of me as we push through the throng of photographers pressing in close.

"Cassie, how do you feel about the split?"

"Was your entire relationship a PR front?"

"Did you really cheat on Jackson with your ex?"

I keep my head down, pushing through the crowds of people until we reach Marina's car. She fumbles with the keys for a few seconds before she unlocks the doors, and we barricade ourselves inside. It's a mess while we try to exit the parking lot. Cameras continue to flash. Muted voices carry through the glass. I keep a hand on my forehead to block the lens of the cameras until we finally pull onto the road.

"What the hell was that?" Lucy spins around to face me.

"Are you okay?" Marina asks, looking into the rearview.

I turn to look out the back window. Thankfully, no one follows. Even still, I instruct Marina to take back roads all the way back home to Santa Monica.

"Cassie?" Lucy asks again.

"I don't know, okay?" I snap at her.

I fumble with my phone, expecting to see a message from Jackson, some sort of explanation, but outside of his request to call him, there is nothing. My hands start to shake when the notifications begin to hit. It starts small, pings against my phone, one after the other, most from numbers I don't have or didn't save, then I get the alert that I had been subconsciously waiting for since I saw the first camera outside the restaurant.

A post from *EDaily*.

I already know it's bad without even clicking into the article.

"Lucy?" I ask in a wavering voice.

Her phone is already in front of her face. Her normally rosy cheeks are stark white. "Cassie." Her voice shakes before she faces me. "I didn't know. I swear."

EVERYTHING YOU NEED TO KNOW ABOUT JACKSON RIDGE'S NEW ROMANCE WITH COSTAR JENN HAMILTON.

Images of Jackson and Jenn appear at the top of the article. There are multiple, taken from a variety of angles. A clip from an interview with Jenn's head resting on Jackson's shoulder. A photo of them leaning close to each other in a dark bar, his lips near her ear. Finally, an image of Jackson and Jenn in front of his condo at three in the morning.

"Jackson Ridge sparks romance rumors with costar Jenn Hamilton. The two star in the new romantic comedy, To Hell and Back *due out at the end of the summer. Sources from* Radium, *a New York City bar, mentioned they couldn't keep their hands off each other. The two were seen leaving together and photographed outside Ridge's condo on the Upper East Side well past midnight. The photograph follows the breaking news that Cassie Taylor has been cheating on Ridge with ex-boyfriend, up-and-coming singer, Noah Vaughn."*

My hands are shaking, but I force myself to keep reading.

"Sources close to the couple report that Cassie Taylor had just been using Ridge as a way to elevate her professional career but had never really broken up with the rocker. When asked about Ridge and Hamilton's budding relationship, a close source reported that there has been 'obvious chemistry' between the two while filming their movie out this later this month."

Underneath the article is a link to a video. Jackson sits next to Jenn, his hand on hers, smiling. Is this what he looks like with *me*? Did I really not notice the difference?

The interviewer's voice fills the car as I click into the video.

"Never have I ever . . . slept with a costar?"

Jenn smiles, throwing Jackson an obvious look, and my whole fucking world stops.

Tears fill my eyes when the camera pans over to Jackson. I watch as he turns his sign around from "No" to "Yes," and I watch when Jenn leans her head on his shoulder, blushing as Jackson rolls his eyes, smiling.

The implication is clear as day, whether it's true or not, and I realize that whatever I had been holding on to was just smashed, in front of the cameras, for the entire world to see.

It's what Jackson warned me about. An article painting me out to be a gold digger, a liar, and a cheater. Maybe I had been prepared for something like this to be released, but I never expected Jackson to be an active participant in the story.

I clear the article from my screen, my hands shaking. The car has stopped moving, and I realize that we are in our parking lot, outside our apartment. My phone rings again, Jackson's name appearing on the screen, but I close it.

Lucy's and Marina's eyes are on me from the front seat.

"There's got to be an explanation," Marina tries. "Cassie, he lov—"

"Don't." I close my eyes.

I know how Marina was going to finish the sentence, but it's a false claim, something she wanted to say to make me feel better.

Jackson doesn't love me. He doesn't even want me. Maybe he never did.

I swing open the back door, slamming it shut and race to my car. I have the keys in the ignition before Marina and Lucy can even follow.

~~~

The gate is closed when I pull into Jackson's driveway. He's supposed to be in New York until Sunday, which is good. I want to get in and get out as soon as possible. I've kept my phone off since the news broke, and I don't plan to turn it back on to hear whatever excuse he wants to peddle this time.

I ignore the emptiness of the house while I make my way into his bedroom, starting to gather my things. My extra phone charger, clothes, whatever I can fit into one of my bags that I've left over.

I am almost through the bedroom when I hear the groan of the gate out front. Headlights appear in the drive, and I pause, looking out the window to watch Jackson run from the car into the house.

"Cassie?" His voice calls from the foyer. I ignore him, tears welling in my eyes when I disappear into his closet. "Cassie?"

I can tell that he is in his bedroom, but I don't answer. I stuff my clothes into the bag, coming to a halt when he appears in the entryway, blocking my way out.
~~~

His eyes go to the bag in my hands. "What are you doing?"

I shove past him toward the bathroom, grabbing my things from the sink. I don't want to look at any of it while I store it away, all reminders of a life that we were trying to build together, a life I wanted to build with him. The one that *he* ruined.

"Cassie!" Jackson appears again, gripping my shoulders, forcing me to stand still. "Just stop for a second. I need to talk to you."

"Oh, *now* you want to talk? Okay, let's talk. I'll ask a question, and you can answer. Did you go home with her?"

"No!" he yells, and then his face twists. "She came home with me."

I let out a bitter laugh. "Much better."

"It wasn't like that, okay? *Nothing* happened."

"You know I'm not just some story to sell airtime. This is my life. *My life*! And you're fucking it up because you can't be honest with yourself."

"I'm not honest?" he yells, matching my anger.

"No, tell me you love it." I stop, waiting for him to contradict me. "This life that you built for yourself, tell me you love it."

Silence.

His eyes go dark, like I just unveiled his deepest secret for the world to see. But it's not the world; it's just me, and he still can't even say it out loud.

"Who leaked the story?" I let out a breath. "The bullshit rumor that I was cheating?" Jackson's eyes flicker, but he doesn't say anything more. "What about the photo of you and Jenn leaving your apartment? Who else knew she was going to be there?"

He turns away, giving me a view of his side profile. His jaw tight, eyes closed, but I don't stop.

"Zana, right? You know she's literally only by your side because you pay her. She gets a cut off everything you do, especially selling fucking airtime. Do you get a commission off every *EDaily* article written about you? You should."

"It's all press! I told you this is what the studio wanted.

Nothing happened between Jenn and me, I swear. It's all bullshit. It's fake."

"Just like us, right? Fake?" Tears fill my eyes, but I blink them away.

His eyebrows tug together. A pained expression flashes across his beautiful face. "Cassie—"

"You know what I don't get? I don't get how you can't see what this does to you. You do this time and time again, and then you wonder why you're so fucking empty. You say you want to change, but I don't think you're actually capable of it, and I'm tired of waiting around for it to happen. I'm done."

My words snap him back, and he looks up at me urgently. "Done?"

"Done." I push past him again, this time heading for the door.

"Cass, come on." He trails behind on my heels. "It's not even fucking real!"

"Stop!" I yell, closing my eyes to steady myself before I reopen them. "Stop pretending like you don't know exactly what to say to hurt me."

He pauses, lowering his head, waiting for me to finish.

"I don't want to do *this*. I don't want to live this double life, never knowing what is real and what is—" I hate the tremble in my voice, so I stop, collecting myself. "You knew what you were doing. You knew it was what the executives wanted to make more money. You knew that this would hurt me, and you didn't *care*."

"Cassie, I can't—"

"You can! You just *won't*. You don't want other people controlling your life, say something. You don't want to act in movies that make you feel like you're just a piece of property, stop. But don't feed me this bullshit excuse that you *have* to. You don't."

I brush past him, my heart pounding with each step I take, Jackson still on my heels.

"Wait!" he says again, his voice more desperate. "Cassie, wait for one fucking second!" I am nearly to the front door when his next words stop me in my tracks. "You're seriously going to give everything up for some stupid story?"

The accusation clangs through me, causing me to shudder. I slowly turn to face him.

"Everything? You've given me everything?" My voice is quiet, but not weak. "I never asked you for *anything*. I only asked for you, and it's pretty clear you can't give that to me."

When I see tears behind his eyes, I know I have to leave. I turn at the same time he reaches for my arm.

"Don't," I say, pulling away, my voice breaking when I release the words that I know will finally make him stop. "Don't touch me."

He freezes, eyes going wide, and I know that my words hurt him more than a slap ever could. I wish I could take them back, but I can't. I can't because if I let him touch me, then I'll forgive him, and I can't keep living my life like this. I won't.

"Cassie." His voice falters, as if he didn't realize that I was actually capable of walking away until I stood at the threshold. He stands there, haunted eyes, soft and pleading. "Don't go."

I force myself to shrug my shoulder. My voice is thick and wobbly when I answer.

"Too late."

CHAPTER 40

Jackson

I can barely stomach the silence, but I make myself tolerate it. After Cassie left, I fell to the floor, head in my hands, and didn't get up for several hours.

That was a week ago.

Now, I feel like I am trapped in a shrine, a living memorial to the life that could have been, passing reminders every time I round the corner. This normal life that gave me so much peace is gone, but its ghosts still wander the halls.

Don't touch me.

I'd rather she had slapped me in the face, punched me in the stomach, any other sort of physical attack that I could heal from, because I don't think I can come back from hearing those words. They follow me into the dark, into the quiet, seeping through every crevice, rotting me from the inside out.

I lean against the wall, flipping on a light switch to avoid the black, and it hits me again, this time harder. Cassie is never coming *home.* I'd never open the front door to find her shoes in the hall, her purse on the floor. I wouldn't round the corner again to find her perched on the bar stool, feet tucked underneath her, hair up, waiting for me.

I pictured it, for a moment, a normal life, away from all the shit that routinely fucks me up, but now it doesn't matter. It was a pipe dream, a senseless wish. It was never going to happen, because if it wasn't with Cassie, what was the point?

I don't sleep. Can't, really. Every time I close my eyes, the intense reminder ripples through me. It's suffocating, and I refuse to use any of my old distractions to wash away all the bad memories, so I toss and turn every night, and when I finally give up, I pace through my empty house.

I always thought I needed everyone's love and attention, needed it to fulfill a void that was created when I was a teenager. I wanted the public to mend the gaping wound in my chest for fear they would recognize my faults and turn their back on me, but I didn't need it. I need *her*.

Sash shows up at my house a few days later. Neither of us say anything when she steps inside. I avoided her because I thought she would yell at me, tell me it's all my fault, further confirming all the worst things I already know about myself. She's quiet as she follows me into the living room, sitting beside me when I collapse on the couch.

"You know I can wait you out," Sash eventually breaks the silence.

"What do you want me to say? I fucked up?" I ask helplessly. "I know. I fucked up."

"I didn't come here to yell at you," Sash says quietly.

"Why not?" I rub my chest, a feeble attempt to ease my aching heart. "I deserve it."

"Jackson." Sash forces me to look at her. "I know how happy Cassie made you. I saw how you were when you were together. So, why? Why did you throw it all away?"

I stay quiet for another moment, picking my next words carefully. "I thought it would hurt less. If I followed through with what everyone wanted, I thought it would hurt less, but . . . I was wrong."

"You can still fix this."

"How?" I ask. "How do I make it right if she won't even fucking talk to me?"

"I'm not sure a verbal apology is what she needs."

Sash's answer is what I was afraid of, what I've always been afraid of, but I know she's right. Nothing I say will actually matter if I don't break the cycle that I hate and step away from it, from all of it.

My phone buzzes again. I turn it off, throwing it against the couch. I don't have to check to see who is on the other line. I've been avoiding Zana all week, something she's let temporarily slide for now. I know next week she won't be as forgiving. There are contracts that need to be signed and the premiere appearance with Jenn that still has to be organized.

"Zana?" Sash guesses.

"She keeps calling."

"Well, at least you are doing something right. Ignore her."

"I have to talk to her eventually."

"No, Jackson. You don't."

I roll my neck. "Look, I know you have an issue with her, but it's not like that. Zana only wants what's best—"

"That's a lie and you know it," Sash cuts me off, releasing a breath after a moment. "God, you really don't know, do you?"

"Know what?" I ask, tone sharpening.

"I've tried to have this conversation with you too many times for you not to listen to me now." I brace myself while Sash leans forward. "Zana leaked the story, Jackson. She leaked the story about you and Victoria."

I flinch, like someone stabbed me or something. I stare at Sash sitting across from me. The color drains from my face as I try to comprehend what she is trying to tell me.

"No." I shake my head. "No," I repeat the word again, refusing to allow it to make sense. It doesn't. It can't.

"Jackson." Sash reaches for me, but I pull away.

"She . . . she wouldn't do that to me."

I look at Sash, sitting across from me, and when I see the tears in her eyes, I push off the couch. I'm on my feet, pacing, hands tearing through my hair.

It can't be true because Zana had been there with me from the beginning. She was all I had. We worked together for ten years. I fucking trusted her. She *made* me trust her. If what Sash is saying is true, then Zana has been lying, to my face, for the past decade.

"She . . ." I trail off, trying to allow a breath, but it gets caught in my throat, and soon I'm gasping for air.

How much of my life had Zana seen? How much had she sold? I think back to every tabloid, every headline that smeared my name through the mud. Every article that called my reputation, everything in my fucking life, into question. She was the source? She did this to me?

I stagger backward into a table, knocking over a lamp that shatters when it hits the floor. Sash jumps to her feet, racing for me while I fall to the ground, head in my hands.

"Hey!" Sash appears in front of me, holding my shoulders. "Look at me." I force my head up and stare at her, trying to find something to center me. "Breathe. You're okay. Just breathe."

Cassie knew.

She fucking knew, and I didn't believe her. *Why*? Why couldn't I have seen this? How could I have been so fucking blind?

"How did you know?" I ask once I've caught my breath.

"I paid attention." She lifts her shoulder. "Zana had access. She knew this would get circulation, knew that she would be attached to your career for the next ten years. She made sure it leaked after you signed your contract."

I sit back, dragging a hand over my face. It makes sense. Zana had access to everything in my personal life. She would have known what it meant, where to sell it to make money off it. Off *me*. How many others did she help publish?

"Why didn't you say anything?" I ask, pleading.

"Jackson." Sash sighs. "Every time I have ever tried to bring it up, you've shut it down or you walked away. You never wanted to talk about it."

I look away, jaw tight. I want to tell her that she's wrong. She should have told me, and if she tried, I would have been able to handle it, but it would be a lie. Ten years later and I'm on the floor. I don't know what sort of damage I would have done then.

"Those first few years, you had blinders on," Sash continues. "You only kept people around back then who fueled whatever narrative you believed in. You didn't want to hear anything else."

I lower my head, recounting decisions made, choices that might not have even existed if I knew. I sit here, letting it all spill over my shoulders, seeping into my head, and I try to see what everyone else may have seen. Zana, operating me like a puppet behind the scenes, making decisions for her over my own well-being. I couldn't bear it, couldn't even think it, because I refused to believe that I was truly and utterly alone, no matter who I surrounded myself with. No one cared.

And I punished the only person who ever did.

Sash sighs, taking a seat on the floor next to me, both our backs resting against the wall while we stare out at the empty house.

"Have you ever heard the saying that you stop aging at the time you become famous?" she asks softly. "Leo mentioned it to me when we first started dating. He thinks fame leaves us mentally stunted, like no matter how we age, we will always revert to behaviors from the time we became famous. Seems pretty dark to be eternally eighteen, never changing, never moving forward."

I chew the inside of my cheek while Sash continues.

"I think it can happen, but it doesn't *have* to happen. I think we have more control than we know. We just have to choose to move away from it, which means making the hard decision, not always the easy one."

Her words hit me in my chest, burrowing deep. How many times had I made the easy choice in my life? Made the decision that benefited me at the expense of others? I've done it countless times before, and I'm still left with nothing.

Cassie chose me, chose to forgive me, time and time again, even when I didn't deserve it, and I took advantage of her kindness. I hurt her for it.

I shake my head, feeling the pressure build, folding me over and then in half. I press a hand over my forehead as my eyes fill with tears.

"I hate it," I say through clenched teeth.

"I know." Sash frowns, wrapping her arms around my shoulders while I lean into her.

"I hate it," I repeat it again, and she just hugs me tighter.

CHAPTER 41

Jackson

I've had time to think about it.

Over a week to turn the decision over in my head, and each time, I arrive at the same conclusion.

It's not one I carelessly made, like so many others. I plotted it out, sat with it long enough to know that although it will be one of the hardest decisions I ever make, it's the right one.

I inhale a breath and step through the hallways. They look the same as they did ten years ago. Before walking through them, I was worried that I would be transported backwards in time, when I had no say, when I had no voice, but each step I take forward, I feel empowered to release the words I've kept buried in my chest.

I round the corner, spotting the large, glass-walled conference room, allowing me to look inside before I walk through the door. The table is full, nearly fifteen people sit around it, all waiting for me.

I roll my shoulders, allowing a short breath, and step inside.

"I'll make this quick." I pull off my sunglasses, taking in the rest of the table. Victoria sits at the other end. Her blue eyes meet mine, and I force myself to hold her gaze, to keep it as long as I can. "I have no interest in pursuing this business relationship any further. I don't plan on signing any documentation today or anytime in the future."

I turn to look directly at Zana. Her eyes are daggers, glaring at me, warning me to keep my fucking mouth shut.

"Whatever was promised to you was a lie. I apologize for wasting anyone's time. Thank you."

Whispers and murmurs break out the moment I turn and walk right back out the door. Victoria knows better than to follow me, but Zana can't stay still. I just publicly embarrassed her, and I know she won't let me walk away without trying to get the last word in.

I walk towards the exit, counting down in my head.

Five, four, three, two—

"Who the hell do you think you are?" Zana stomps toward me in her Louis Vuitton heels.

"Jackson Ridge." I turn and tilt my head, feigning innocence. "You should know me better than anyone. You made me, right?"

She glares, stepping forward. "I don't know what the fuck you think you're doing, but I just laid out a multi-million-dollar deal for you. Go back in there and sign it."

"No."

A single word, but a full sentence.

Zana blinks, pulling back. "No?"

"No," I repeat the word with emphasis, taking a step closer.

I know when I leave this building, I will cease to exist to her, so while I have her full and undivided attention, I need to get everything off my chest, and I need to look at her when I do.

"I don't know why I never put it together. I think I just didn't want to dwell on it. It would have gotten in the way of everything, but I think you knew that, didn't you?"

"What are you talking about?" She nearly spits.

"I'm giving you the chance to tell me yourself. Your last chance to be honest. I don't think that's asking for a lot, considering everything we've been through together. Do you?" She crosses her arms over her chest, and I allow a breath before asking in a low whisper, "Did you leak it?"

"Leak what?" Her voice is pure venom.

"You know what. Did you leak the story about Victoria and me to the press?"

As soon as she rolls her eyes, I have my answer.

I knew it was true from the moment Sash spoke it into existence. Maybe a part of me always knew, deep down. Still, I needed to see her reaction when I said it out loud.

I stare at her, wondering how I could have looked past it all, ignored all the signs when they were in front of me.

"I fucking trusted you," I growl under my breath. "You ruined my life."

"I *gave* you your life." She steps forward, refusing to back down. "I did what we had to do."

"*We*? Since when were you and I a '*we*'?"

"Since you signed your name on that fucking line, ten years ago."

I stand there, letting the words hang there. I wait for the panic to settle in my chest, that strange fizzle that usually goes up my spine when I even think the words, but nothing comes. Something strange happens, an unexpected wave of calm washes over me. The boulder that had been resting on my shoulders for as long as I can remember rolls away, a sudden and intense weight lifted.

"We're done," I tell her.

Her face twists into a grimace. "You can't just—"

"Yeah, I can. We're done." I turn, leaving her behind.

"You walk out that door, your career is over."

I don't turn. The only sound between us is my footsteps on the tile. I know she won't follow, and I know she won't beg. It's just idle threats that she feeds me to keep me in line. It's what she used to keep me in check.

"I gave you everything you wanted!"

I stop at the door, hesitating before I glance over my shoulder.

"I know," I say softly, looking right at her before I kick her out of my life, for good this time. "I just don't want it anymore."

~~~

Climbing the stairs, I realize that I should have come here a long time ago. It should have been the first stop on my list, but I had a lot of shit to clean up. Besides, I know if Cassie had been here when I arrived, the door would have remained shut. Paris Fashion Week started yesterday, and I know she's already landed. I'm hoping that while she is gone, I will have a chance to fix the things that I broke. In fact, I'm counting on it.

I lift my fist to the door, pausing when I catch the end of a muted conversation on the other side.

"I don't care what they say." I recognize Marina's voice. "You *absolutely* have to shave your legs before you go on a date."

I suppress a smile and then collect a breath, knocking twice. I wait, noticing the music softening, and then hear footsteps approaching.

The door swings open to reveal a very short blonde standing before me. I am guessing this is Cassie's second roommate, the one I never officially met, Lucy. Her eyes snap up to mine and widen when she realizes who I am. It doesn't take long for the look of wonder to be replaced with a glare so lethal, it's a miracle I don't fall over.

"What do *you* want?" she asks.

"I was hoping—"

"Cassie isn't here," she cuts me off, crossing her arms over her chest, lifting her chin in the air.

"I know. I'm here to see you and Marina."

Her glare slips for a fraction of a second.

"Who is it, Luce?" A soft voice carries behind her. "Oh."

Marina comes to a halt in the doorway. Her curly, dark hair is pulled away from her face. She looks just as shocked as Lucy standing in the doorway, though more approachable.
~~~

"Can I come in?" I ask.

"No," the blonde snaps.

"*Lucy.*" Marina rolls her eyes, stepping forward to pull the door open, taking me in. "Does Cassie know you're here?"

"No. We haven't spoken since . . ." I trail off, inhaling a breath because I can't say the words out loud. I shake my head. "She doesn't know I'm here."

"Why should we let you in? You hurt her," Lucy says it in a way that implies I hurt *her* as well. "You hurt, Cassie."

"I know." I nod. "But I'm trying to fix it, and I need your help."

Lucy's eyes widen, exchanging a glance with Marina, who nods gently.

"Okay," Marina says, her eyes watching me closely, like I passed whatever lie-detector test she had been operating.

I allow a short breath before I step inside, determined to fix what I broke.

CHAPTER 42

Cassie

I used to have this dream, this recurring nightmare that started when I was a kid. It's not something I've ever grown out of. Even after all these years, it's still the same.

I'm driving on the highway when the brakes give out. No matter how hard I press my foot on the pedal, I can't slow down. The cars ahead of me approach faster and faster, and just before I am about to hit, I wake up. I never experience the crash, but my eyes always fly open, my heart racing, and I have to spend the next few seconds reminding myself that it's not real.

The difference now is that I can't jolt myself awake. My entire life is in the car, and no matter how hard I try to slam the brakes, it doesn't stop the inertia of anything. I keep hurtling forward.

I didn't have the luxury of a partial breakdown over the inevitable fallout between Jackson and me. In a way, it's what I should have expected. What we had was an illusion of perfection, a fantasy that I should have known could never last. Whatever we attempted to build was bound to fall apart at the first sign of trouble. I just wish I could walk away from it as easily as I walked into it.

The first few days, my phone rang nonstop. Messages and voicemails from Jackson appeared every few hours. Outside outlets that had somehow managed to get my number from a variety of my so-called "friends," were looking for comments. I flipped my phone off, deciding to only go through emails to coordinate events, but Jackson was just as inescapable as the press, who seemed content to follow me wherever I went.

The Paris trip approached suddenly and had me scrambling. A once-exciting milestone turned into a media circus. I wore a baseball cap and sunglasses while I walked through the airport, and it still didn't prevent the hundreds of paparazzi from swarming, trying to get a picture before I was safely through security.

The second we touched down, I felt like I was running a marathon. There wasn't a single moment, over the grueling five days, when I had time to myself. I was poked and prodded backstage, practically pushed toward the runway, and then repeated the process all over again.

The entire experience was a beautiful, chaotic blur. Beautiful, in the way I always dreamed it would be. Chaotic, in the way I made it.

As I navigated the publicity and the press, I kept thinking about *him.* I needed a way to rationalize what he did and how he could think that it didn't matter. Unfortunately, I kept arriving at the same conclusion; he felt like he had no other choice.

Every interviewer asked questions about Jackson, how I felt about the break up, if we would ever get back together. The topic was unavoidable, and each question was baited, meant to hook, line, and sink me. I knew that every word I spoke had the capacity to be a headline at this point, and I could understand why people acted the way they did to make it more bearable. Smile even when you didn't feel like it to make the asshole interviewing you feel more comfortable. Laugh off the embarrassing headline so it makes it seem like you didn't care, rather than letting them know it ruined your life. I imagine it's how Jackson feels all the time.

I can see how going along with it would make things easier.

It was a way to appear to be in control. It's why Jackson does the things that he does. It's why he is the way that he is.

While in Paris, I made myself available, but the work felt heavier, in a way. The parties and events scheduled prior to the runway allowed me time to network, meet my agent in person, and create the connections I had always dreamed of, but the second they were over, I felt an incredible weight lift off my shoulders. I was eager to shed the person I had been playing, barricading my true self behind closed doors where I felt like I could actually breathe.

Every day I tried to wear myself out until the last possible moment when I could return to my room, pass out, and just try not to think. It never worked. I ran myself ragged, but every night when my head hit the pillow, my mind kept racing, memories going back to Jackson even without trying.

I hate you. I hate you. I hate you.

I'd turn over on my side, remembering the way Jackson held me while I slept. I closed my eyes and if I concentrated, I could still hear the subtle thump, thump, thump of his heart.

I miss you. I miss you. I miss you.

As the week started winding down, the hole that had been growing in my chest seemed to be getting wider. I knew that the lights and all the distractions would go away, and I'd have to go back to the reality I made for myself. This time, alone.

I've been off the runway for the past thirty minutes, more than half the room has cleared out. The bustling sounds from designers eventually become quiet background noise, and I sit in the chair alone, staring at my reflection. I've never looked more beautiful, but when I look into my mirror, my eyes appear empty, like all the light has been swallowed. I stare at myself a little longer, waiting to see something looking back at me, but I see nothing. Pieces of myself chip away the longer I look.

It's late, well past midnight, when I finally barricade myself behind the locked door of my hotel room. The city of Paris sparkles beyond the glass, but I haven't had it in me to appreciate the view. I drop my bag at the foot of the bed before helping myself to the mini bar. I fall back onto the comforter, swallowing a healthy gulp of the vodka shooter, and I open my phone.

Despite the press' baited questions about my failed relationship following me everywhere I go, I haven't tuned in to what they have actually been publishing about me. Now, with the end of my trip in sight and the real world waiting for me upon my return, I decide to take it all in, bracing myself for the worst.

I swallow a gulp of bitter vodka and open my social media app. There are a few photos of me, but not as many as I had been expecting. Instead, Jackson's face covers nearly every top story from all the major outlets. I had been expecting coverage from his side as well, but the fact that I was made out to be a cheater led me to believe there would be more rumors and attacks on my character.

I click on the first image and scan the caption.

Jackson Ridge Announces Break from Acting. News Comes Just After Zana Hill, Jackson Ridge's Long-Time Agent, Let Go.

Written by Lucy Collins, published by *EDaily*.

I grip the phone in my hand.

"Details regarding the end of the long-time collaboration have been kept quiet, but news broke this morning when Ridge announced that he was stepping away from the career that earned him his millions. Ridge released a statement on his own via his social media page. EDaily *posted below."*

My eyes scan the page, absorbing as much information as quickly as possible.

"Cassie Taylor and Jackson Ridge made their red-carpet debut earlier this summer, but break up rumors surrounded their relationship shortly after Ridge's press tour with Jenn Hamilton for their upcoming rom-com To Hell and Back. *Jackson Ridge denied the accusations that he cheated on Taylor with Hamilton in a recent*

statement but did take responsibility for the manufactured affection generated for the press.

Allegations had also surrounded Taylor cheating with former flame, Noah Vaughn, but the rumors have been proven false. Sources close to Taylor confirm that Vaughn broke off the relationship a month prior to Taylor and Ridge meeting. Vaughn has since been seen stalking Taylor in various areas of the city since their split. The photograph from the grocery store that made headlines a few months ago was a coordinated publicity stunt organized by Vaughn, further proof of his obsession with the spotlight.

Despite Ridge's public declaration clearing Taylor's name in the press, the couple has yet to be photographed together since."

Jackson walked away. Left. Said goodbye to a piece of his life that I never imagined he would part with. The concept is almost too shocking to believe.

The end of the article includes a link to Jackson's social media account. I stare at the statement pinned to the top of his profile.

I have spent the last decade of my life dedicated to my work. I am grateful for every opportunity, but the time has come for me to step away. I intend to focus on my personal life for the time being, prioritizing the people who are most important to me. I appreciate everyone's support at this time and wish for privacy.

I read it once, then again.

Does it change anything?

Does it change *everything*?

I drop my phone, the words ringing in my head. Sleep for the next hour is now completely out of the question, so I reach for the vodka shooter, ready to swallow another gulp of it back when whispers sound from the hallway.

I freeze, panic rising in my throat and quickly jump to the worst conclusion: paparazzi have found a way past the lobby, discovered what floor I am on, what room I am in. I jump from the bed, stepping forward to listen closely.

"You're being too loud." A familiar hushed whisper sounds from the hall.

"She's not gonna open the door if she doesn't know who is knocking!"

"It's supposed to be a surprise!"

I run to the door, unbolt the lock, and throw it open to find Marina and Lucy arguing with each other in the hallway, luggage in hand.

"Surprise!" Marina lifts her shoulder with a wide smile.

I blink once, then again, trying to process what the hell my two best friends would be doing in Paris in the middle of the night. It takes two seconds for me to catch up and then I launch myself at them, barreling into their open arms. My cheeks are wet with tears before I even realize that I am crying. I hug them tightly, a reminder that they are real and not a dream.

"Okay, death grip," Lucy chokes, and I finally release them.

"What are you doing here?" I ask, wiping my eyes.

"We thought you could use some support," Marina says, squeezing my arm. "Sorry we couldn't make it sooner."

"How did you get off work?" I ask Marina before turning to Lucy. "And how did *you* make it all the way across the Atlantic sitting still for ten hours?"

"Sacrifices were made." Lucy tosses her hair over her shoulder. "But it was worth it."

"You're worth it," Marina reminds me.

"You're not mad at me?" I ask.

Lucy frowns. "We were wrong."

"No, you weren't." I shake my head. "You were right. I wasn't around, and it was my fault."

"It's no one's fault. We should have been there for you too." Marina tugs my shoulder, shutting the door behind us. "Come on. Inside."

As soon as they are inside, Lucy's jaw drops to the floor, taking in the suite. I know it's outrageously extravagant, but I hadn't really been paying attention. The entire room is crisp and clean. The only spots of color come from the bouquet of fresh flowers that arrives every day, and a sparkling chandelier hangs from the ceiling.

"I can't believe this is your hotel room." Lucy flings back the curtains, throwing open the doors to the balcony that I haven't bothered to use. The sounds of the city filter through the hotel room, the window blowing the sheer curtains open. "I've never seen anything like it."

"I know." I sigh, leaning heavily into Marina's side. Lucy turns away from the view and reaches for her bag, pulling out a bottle of champagne before presenting it to me. "What's that for?"

"Are you kidding? We're celebrating!" Lucy exclaims.

"Don't think we forgot that we have not all properly celebrated your inevitable rise to fame." Marina says, grabbing glasses from the bar. "You're in Paris. *We're* in Paris, together!"

Lucy pops the bottle out the window, letting the champagne sputter from the top before she pours three glasses.

I take it, holding it in my lap. "I don't really feel like celebrating."

"Which is stupid—" Lucy stops herself after Marina nudges her to soften the blow.

"Cassie." Marina sighs. "It's okay to be hurt about Jackson, but that doesn't mean you can't celebrate anything else in your life."

"Yeah, it does. I would have none of this without him." I let out a shaky breath, my hands tremble lightly, and when I look up at my two best friends who literally traveled across an ocean for me, I realize that I owe them the truth, the whole truth. "I have to tell you something."

"What is it?" Marina kneels on the bed beside me as Lucy shuffles closer.

I allow a deep breath before I let it out. I let everything out.

Every secret that I had kept between Jackson and me, the staged relationship for a leg up in my career. The feeling that everything I had worked for up to this moment seems forced and cheap because it doesn't feel real. It doesn't feel like it's mine.

The way that Jackson's betrayal didn't just feel like a blow to my career, but a loss of a friend, someone who would understand exactly what I am going through in the way that I need.

They listen carefully, reaching for my hand when I need the extra support, but otherwise, they remain quiet. When I finish, I let out a deep breath and look up.

"You—" I stop myself, pulling back. "I mean, you don't seem that surprised."

"Well, I mean, it is shocking, Cassie," Lucy says. "First, that you even thought you needed someone like Jackson to help you get ahead. You have so much talent without—"

Marina clears her throat, a warning to Lucy to keep on track. "What Lucy is trying to say is that . . . well, we sort of already knew."

"What?" The color drains from my face when I look between the two of them. "*How?*"

"You tell her." Lucy nudges Marina's elbow.

Marina inhales a breath. "Jackson showed up at the apartment, just after you left."

"*What?*"

"*I* wanted to kick his ass to the curb," Lucy reassures me.

"*We* figured since he made it all the way, we would hear him out," Marina cuts Lucy off. "He knew you were in Paris, but he said that he wanted to talk to us and sort of explained everything. It filled the gaps that you were never able to fill, but that doesn't mean that we weren't shocked."

I shake my head, trying to sort out a reason why Jackson would tell them. He values his privacy over everything. He doesn't let others *in* for fear of his secrets getting *out*.

"You saw him?" They both nod, eyes heavy. I lift my sleeve, wiping my cheek. "How was he?"

"Shit," Lucy answers quickly.

"He was in rough shape," Marina offers. "He sent us here, paid for our flights, upgraded us to first class. He knew that you didn't want to see him, but he also thought that you might need us."

My chest grows tight. "He sent you here?"

"Yeah." Marina smiles warmly.

Jackson knew, without even being able to communicate with me. He knew what I needed, more than anything in the world. I needed the two people in my life who could pull me out of my own head, bring me back to center. He knew I didn't want to see him, but he also knew what I needed, before I even knew myself.

"And I know you might be mad about the article, but I only wrote about you in a positive light," Lucy says urgently. "I denied every false rumor even thought about you and threw Noah under the bus, like he deserves. I know you never wanted me to write about you, but when Jackson asked me to publish, I figured it would be a good way—"

"Wait, wait." I hold up my hands to stop her. "Jackson did *what*?"

"He asked me to write it," Lucy explains. "He told me he was going to release a statement announcing his retirement and gave me the information I needed. My boss approved it and ran it immediately. *EDaily* broke the story with my name on it. They are processing the paperwork for my promotion as we speak."

Jackson doesn't know Lucy. She could have sold the entire story to the public, written whatever she wanted, but he trusted her because I trust her. It was a leap of faith I would have never thought possible from him, but he did it.

I chew on my lip, mulling over the new information being thrown my way, trying to make sense of it. Is Jackson capable of changing? Do I even want him to be? He's giving me what I needed, honesty and action, but is it too late? Does it even matter?

Marina reaches for my hand. "Jackson sent us here with no agenda. He knew it was what you needed, and he didn't think twice."

"I don't know what to do with that," I confess. "I mean, I'm here, on the other side of the world, in the city of dreams, achieving the career that I always wanted, and I just feel . . . empty."

Marina frowns, squeezing my hand. "You miss him?"

Tears fill my eyes, but I force myself to shrug, not wanting to admit the words out loud. I don't want to admit that I dream about him every time I close my eyes.

I hate what he did, but I don't hate *him*. I can't. I've tried and I've failed. Since I left, I've had time to process that while what Jackson did hurt me, I don't believe it was intentional. It wasn't his idea, and he only went through with it because he felt like he didn't have a choice.

"We love you, Cassie." Marina smiles, bringing me back. "And maybe we weren't here for you before, but we're here for you now. Right?" She turns to Lucy.

"Right." Lucy smiles. "And if you don't want to think about Jackson right now, you don't have to. That's not what this is about. It's not why we're here."

"What do you mean?"

"We're in Paris, together!" Marina gestures at the room, and I smile. "There may come a time when you can stop and process everything with Jackson, but we don't have to right now. We're here for you, to celebrate *you*. Okay?"

"Okay." I force a smile and pull Marina to my chest while Lucy squeezes me from behind.

We drain the entire bottle of champagne, stay up until the early hours of the morning, catching up on everything that we missed in the time apart. Not just the past week, but the months that I neglected their friendship.

When it comes time to fall asleep, we all cram into the bed, snuggled up against one another. I cuddle under the covers, and just before I close my eyes, I look out the open terrace, the lights from the Eiffel Tower sparkling beyond the window.

I eventually fall asleep, holding my two best friends close.

CHAPTER 43

Cassie

"We're going to die."

Marina squeezes her eyes shut, gripping the side of the passenger door while we fly through another yellow light. Our car practically bounces when we land on the other side of the intersection.

It was probably a mistake to let Lucy drive, but Lucy is the only one who will ignore all traffic violations to get us there on time, just not necessarily in one piece.

"Oh, stop being so dramatic." Lucy rolls her eyes, passing another car while we race up the hill.

"It doesn't matter if we get there on time if we are dead!" Marina yells, clutching the armrest.

Lucy turns to Marina, the car starting to drift across the center line. "If you were driving, we would still be in Santa Monica—"

"Eyes on the road!" Marina yells while Lucy jerks the wheel back to center. "You were saying?"

I landed in Los Angeles this morning with Marina and Lucy by my side. I spent the last three days in Paris, recounting every decision I made, trying to compartmentalize what happened and how I feel about it, about all of it. I came to the grand conclusion this afternoon. A conclusion that had Marina and Lucy grabbing their keys and racing in the car to get me to Malibu by sunset. I am now strapped in the back seat, gripping the leather, trying to focus on actually making it there alive instead of worrying about what it will be like when and if I do.

Lucy jerks the car across the lane of traffic and quickly finds a spot in the parking lot, throwing the car into park before she turns around to face me in the back seat, smiling widely.

"Okay, go!"

I stay seated.

"What are you waiting for?" Marina turns.

"I just . . . I don't know if I can do it," I admit.

"Are you kidding me? We drove all this way—" Lucy starts, but Marina cuts her off.

"Cassie." Marina's tone is careful. "We fought life and death to be here. Now's your chance."

"You can do it," Lucy encourages.

I shake out my hands, force in a quick breath, steadying myself.

"Okay . . . okay." I turn to face my two best friends, who I know would do anything for me, if I only asked. "Thank you."

"We love you, now go!" Marina urges.

"Okay." I nod, reaching for the door.

My heart is pounding every step I take. I slide on the uneven path down the trail, trying to spot him without falling off the cliff. Sasha told me he was in Malibu but didn't know where. I was betting everything I had that I would know where to find him.

I lift myself up on my tiptoes, searching for the exact spot that we had sat together when we escaped the world and our lives for a few hours that day, scanning the brush of the hillside. I am about to move on when I catch movement further ahead.

I lower myself, collect one last deep breath, and step off the path toward the lookout to my left. He doesn't see me yet. His eyes are straight ahead, scanning the horizon, watching the sun sink beneath the waves.

"Is this spot taken?"

Jackson's head snaps up, eyes finding mine. His face bathed in the soft, warm glow of the setting sun.

"Cassie?" His voice is breathless as he stands, reaching for me, like he needs physical proof that I am here, but before he touches me, his arms drop, like he remembers who we are to each other now.

Don't touch me.

The last words I spoke to him. I swallow, heavy and regretful.

I haven't seen him in over four weeks, yet the memories all come rushing back to the surface. He looks . . . cautious, careful. The cool, arrogant demeanor of the man I met all those months ago at the restaurant isn't standing before me; it's someone else, someone new.

"Hi," I offer, squinting up at him.

"What are you doing here?"

I lift a shoulder, choosing to stick with honesty. "I don't know."

"How did you find me?"

"I called Sasha after I landed. She said you skipped the premiere and were somewhere in Malibu. I filled in the rest."

He shakes his head. "How?"

"It's where I would have come." I shrug. "How are you?"

He tenses, eyes widening. "Forget about me. How are *you*?"

I let out a breath to give myself more time to think. I've had days to plan out what I was going to say, and I still worry it won't be enough. "Sit?"

He nods, and I take the spot next to him. We are both quiet until Jackson breaks the silence, easing in with an objective question. "How was Paris?"

"It was . . . good. Stressful, chaotic, beautiful." I stop myself, turning to look at him. "Lucy and Marina made it better." I bump his shoulder lightly with my own. "Thank you."

He nods, jaw tight. "Was it what you wanted it to be? Paris?"

"In some ways," I admit. "In theory, I had everything that I wanted." He tenses, but I change the subject, needing answers from him first. "I read your statement. Why did you release it?"

"It's the only way I could get the control back," he says quietly. "Things spiraled. I'm spiraling. It's like I can't fucking breathe without you—"

He stops himself. His left hand tightens into a fist as he rolls his shoulders. I wait for him to regain his composure. He takes a breath before he starts again.

"I ran into her," he says painfully, and once he says her name, I know why. "Victoria. I ran into her a few weeks back and . . . it all hit me again, just as hard as it had the first time. I saw it, what other people see when they look at me, and I hated it. All I could think about was that if I wasn't good enough for this life I made, that I was gonna lose it. Every decision I made was wrapped up in that idea. It felt inescapable. It's why, when the deal to partner with her studio came around, I couldn't say no."

"You signed with her?" I ask, bracing myself.

"No." He looks at me quickly. "I didn't." And then he lets out a deep breath. "I was close. I almost put my name on the line, but . . . I couldn't. I can tell myself that I would have come to the realization eventually, but I don't think it's true. I would have said yes if it wasn't for you."

I swallow, holding his eye, letting the information settle before he begins again.

"I don't think it was conscious. Maybe it was, and that's just an excuse, but I wanted the control back. I needed it, and I thought that if I followed through with what everyone else wanted from me, it would hurt less because it would be my decision. But when I hurt you . . ." He looks up, and a tear escapes my eye, falling down my cheek before I wipe it away. "I didn't want to do it anymore."

I reach for Jackson's hand, taking it in mine. I didn't realize how nervous he was, until I touched him. I hadn't realized his hand had been shaking, until I held it.

"What happened to Zana?"

He tenses, arms going tight. "I don't know. Knowing Zana, she'll find someone else to replace me. Maybe she already has." He allows a breath. "She leaked it. The story . . . about Victoria and me. She was the one who took it to the press. I would guess she was also the source behind the article about your job at *Avenue*." He ducks down to meet my eyes, to make sure I am okay. "I am sorry, Cassie."

I look down at our hands, intertwined, holding each other, memorizing the feeling of his warmth, his palm in mine.

"I worked with her. I brought her into your life and then . . . ruined it." He trails off, looking away.

"You didn't ruin my life, Jackson," I say carefully. "You hurt me. There is a difference." He shakes his head, like he doesn't believe me. I squeeze his hand tighter. "I'm sorry that you saw Victoria again, and I'm sorry you felt like you couldn't talk to me about it."

"It's not your fault." He shakes his head once.

"Would you believe me if I told you what happened to you wasn't yours either?" I ask. He looks away, his jaw tight. "She took advantage of you, Jackson. That wasn't your fault."

He swings his head back around to face me. "And I turned around and did the same to you."

"So did I." I lift my shoulder. "It might have been your idea initially, but I went along with it. I used you to get the things that I thought I wanted."

"Thought?" His voice catches.

I inhale a breath, looking away again as a silence drifts between us, nothing but the sound of waves crashing in the background. I squint into the horizon.

"The fame that you have isn't the kind I have been chasing. I wanted to feel successful, empowered, but I didn't want it to come at the cost of everything else. I'll never want that. I had a lot of time to think in Paris, imagine a future in this industry without losing everything, and I don't think it's all or nothing."

I carefully lock eyes with him.

"I thought about you every day. How you were doing, where you were going. I missed you, and I know that I shouldn't because you hurt me, but it wasn't really your fault, but then it was and mostly now . . ." I let out a sigh. "I don't know what to feel anymore."

I reach out carefully, pressing my hand lightly against his cheek. He sighs deeply, eyes closing, leaning into my touch, like he hadn't really been restful without it. When his green eyes open, finding mine, I see the threat of tears there.

"I am sorry, Cassie. So sorry."

"I know you are," I say, chin wobbling.

I let him adjust to the feeling, communicating that it's okay for him to touch me again. He lifts his hand to mine, resting against his cheek, and when I feel the warmth of his palm, I let out a soft breath.

"I don't want you to give up your life, Jackson. That was never what this was about."

He shakes his head, pulling my hand away from his face, but not letting go. "I didn't do it for you. I mean, I did, but I also did it for me. I don't want to live my life like this anymore, and I couldn't see a way to stop it without a clean break. I want my life to be different. *I* want to be different." He swallows, looking up, and I stare into the soft, green color of his eyes. "Do you think I can be different?"

I nod, tears filling my eyes.

"Do you think you can forgive me?" Jackson asks, his voice wavering.

I lift my shoulder, tears filling my eyes. "Already forgiven."

He closes his eyes for a moment and then turns, squaring his shoulders so that he is facing me.

"I thought I had what I wanted in my life, but I didn't. I

wasn't even close. I'm sorry for hurting you and I understand if you think it's too late, but you deserve to know how I feel. You've always deserved that." He reaches out to touch me. Everything about it is familiar and comforting. His hand cups my jaw, and his thumb swirls gently against my cheek. "I want you, Cassie. I want a normal life with *you*."

I let out a laugh as tears fill my eyes. "Even if it's boring?"

"Life with you could never be boring," he says, his lips twitching into a half smile and then turns to face me. "I assumed that I knew everything you wanted, from the moment I met you, but I never asked. So, I'm asking now. What do you want, Cassie?"

I wait for the things that I've wanted my whole life to come to the forefront of my mind, but it remains blank. All the work, all the fame, I would give up all of it in a second if it meant that this moment in time could exist forever.

What do I want?

"You," I breathe.

His lips meet mine, and I kiss him, memorizing the feel of his mouth against mine, relaxing into his chest, like I just arrived home after an impossibly long journey. Jackson holds me like something valuable, something he is determined to never break again. With his lips against mine and his arms around my waist, it feels like a silent vow between just the two of us, something we are promising to keep whole.

When we finally pull apart, he doesn't move very far. He leans back against the rock face, tugging me to his chest while we watch the sunset catch fire beyond the ocean.

"So, where do we go from here?"

"That's the best part." I look up at him and smile. "We get to make our own rules."

"How about no rules?"

"Just us?" I ask.

"You and me," he says, reaching for my hand.

The gesture reminds me of that moment all those weeks ago

when we stepped out of the car together, hand in hand as the paparazzi swarmed. I lean back into his arms, watching the sun disappear beyond the waves as we settle into our own piece of perfect.

EPILOGUE – ONE MONTH LATER

Cassie

"This weighs a hundred pounds," Lucy complains, hauling another box into my new apartment.

I hired movers to sort and carry up the big stuff, but Marina and Lucy insisted that they were here to help. I'm not sure if it makes it easier or harder. It's not Lucy's complaining; I'm used to that. It's that every time I look at them for too long, I almost break down crying.

When I climbed the stairs to our old apartment this morning, I clung to the railing and tried to remember the first moment I scaled the steps to my home for the last three years. It had seen us through birthdays and break ups. Wine nights and parties. Heartbreaks and wishes. In reality, it's just a pile of bricks and insulation complete with standard appliances and a few walls, but it had been a safe haven through countless pivotal moments in our lives. I'm excited to say hello to the new chapter of my life that I had been working toward, but I am still not over the fact that after today, I will have to leave my old one behind.

Leave *them* behind.

"Is that it?" Marina asks, hands on her hips. Her hair is pulled up into a messy bun, strands spilling over her forehead.

"I think so," I say with a heavy sigh.

My eyes find Jackson when he steps through the doorway. He's wearing a white t-shirt, one sleeve rolled up on his shoulder in the unrelenting September heat. His hair messy, in the most perfect way.

"I'll settle up with the movers," Jackson offers, glancing between us.

I give him a small smile, knowing that we need a few more minutes to ourselves, and then turn to Lucy and Marina after he slips out the door.

"I can't believe you're leaving." Lucy lets out a breath when we are alone. I note the tremor in her voice. Despite Lucy keeping a vice like grip on her emotions most of the time, I know that she hates change.

This day, we knew, was going to be hard for all of us.

"I'm gonna miss you guys," I say, looking between them both. "So much."

"Us too." Marina smiles softly, wrapping me in a tight hug that I hold onto.

Lucy hovers on the outside for a few more seconds before she sighs dramatically and throws her arms around us both. We stand there, in the middle of my new apartment, holding each other, not ready to let go just yet, knowing what it will mean when we do.

Life is changing. Everything is going to change, and whether or not I am ready for it, I can still look back on the old life that I built for myself and smile and hold it close for just another minute longer. I know that this isn't the end of us, but it's the end of our chapter with us existing like this together.

"Got everything?" Marina asks, wiping her eyes when she steps away.

"I think so." I nod, letting out a breath. "So, what's next for you two? New roommate?"

"Like we could ever replace you," Lucy says with an eye roll.

"We'll be okay for a while and will start looking in a few months," Marina says.

"Anything you need from me to help cover rent—"

"Stop," Marina cuts me off. "Not an option."

"It is if you need it."

"We won't," Marina assures me. "This is your new life. Start living it. Okay?"

I nod and look between Marina and Lucy, my two best friends. The sisters that I never had but will always hold close. "I love you guys."

"Me too," Marina says with a smile, nudging Lucy with her elbow when she hesitates to reciprocate, not because she doesn't mean it, but because she doesn't offer the sentiment often.

"Me too," Lucy finally agrees.

I know we could probably stay together all day, Marina and Lucy helping me organize, laughing while we reminisce over the past three years of memories, but Marina is right. I built a life for myself, and I need to find a way to start living it.

After another long and tearful goodbye, on everyone's end but Lucy's, they leave, shutting the door behind them. The finality of the moment now cemented in time. No going backward, just looking forward.

My new apartment couldn't be different from my former in Santa Monica. It's close to Beverly Hills, nestled in a quiet neighborhood, but it came with everything I needed. Two bedrooms, parking, a backyard, and most of all, it's located in a private, gated community. No one in or out without my approval.

I stare out at the cluttered and chaotic space. It's going to take me a few weeks to sort through all the boxes, unpack, and organize, but despite the mess in my living room, I smile.

I made it. This space, this life, it's mine.

I'm distracted, imagining all the possibilities, when Jackson steps back through the door. He appears behind me, wrapping his arms around my waist, bending forward to rest his chin on my shoulder.

"You okay?" he asks quietly.

"Yeah," I say with a sigh.

"How does it feel?"

I twist around to look up at him with a smile. "It feels like it's mine."

He smiles, squeezing my waist.

When Jackson and I walked away from the cliff together in Malibu nearly a month ago, we decided that the only rule that should exist between us is that there are no rules. We aren't governed by expectations or guidelines besides the ones that we set for each other. It's been a rocky few weeks while we have tried to find our footing again, but the difference now is that his hand is there to hold whenever I get unstable.

Jackson stayed true to his word, taking a break from the career that made him his millions, and in truth, I've never seen him happier. The break has allowed him what he always needed, perspective and control. I don't believe that he will step away from the industry forever, but I am hopeful that he will find his own path forward, in his own time and, for once, on his own terms.

For me? Some days still feel like a balancing act, teetering on a tightrope, fearing that one wrong move could send me falling again. I found a way to navigate my career and my life, understanding that some sacrifices need to be made, but nothing that I value most. My friendships, my relationships, and most of all, my privacy, will always be protected. It's not easy, but I've been able to juggle. I'm able to focus on my work now that my personal life is no longer in constant jeopardy.

Jackson and I spend the next few hours attempting to organize the living room. It's late when we finally give up on the project for the day. I am sweaty and exhausted when I collapse onto the patio couch, melting into Jackson's open arms, eyes closing while he strokes his thumb along my ribs.

The small piece of quiet is interrupted a moment later. Our eyes both fall to my phone on the table when it buzzes, a new alert filling my home screen. I reach for it, reading the headline.

CASSIE TAYLOR AND JACKSON RIDGE: TROUBLE IN PARADISE?

I peer up at Jackson, who is already looking down at me, his eyes on my face, not on the article on my screen. I suppress a smile, reaching up to touch the side of his cheek.

"Do you trust me?" I ask.

He leans further into my palm and smiles. "I trust you."

I flip my phone to selfie mode and then I kiss Jackson. The moment our mouths meet, he leans forward, kissing me fully while I raise my middle finger to the camera, snapping the candid photo.

I pull away, studying the slightly blurry photo and open my social media feed, posting it front and center on my story. I wait for the photo to be uploaded before I turn my phone off, tossing it aside and then lean into Jackson.

"Now," I sigh, resting my chin on his chest, fighting a smile. "Where were we?"

ACKNOWLEDGEMENTS

Wow! Thank you to everyone who bought, read and invested the time to read my book, it truly means the world to me!

I started writing this book in the middle of the pandemic and had no idea it would become the finished copy you see today. This book has been through many different stages and formats. I've added, cut and edited many times to finally be in this finished form. In all honesty, I never really truly believed it would be published. It felt like a pipedream, a good idea, but not something actually achievable.

My first attempt at writing a book happened my freshman year of high school. I was fifteen, just me, my laptop, and a head full of far away places and imaginary characters. I'd stay up way past my bedtime, trying to see if I could create on paper, the worlds I was imagining in my head. A much deserved shoutout to Miss Julia Canty, who not only read my first "book" back in 2008, but passed it around her neighborhood like it was the hottest read of the year. Without her relentless enthusiasm, I'm not sure I ever would have ever thought that being a published author was an achievable goal.

To anyone who read unfinished chapters, scribbled-in margins, or listened to me ramble plot summaries during our girl's nights, your encouragement made all the difference. You all helped make this dream feel *possible*, and I hope you know how much you mean to me.

A huge thank you to all my teachers, elementary school through to college, who cheered on my creative chaos and encouraged me to dream bigger than a textbook. You helped shape the storyteller in me.

Vanessa Menodzzi, my brilliant book cover designer. The first time I saw your artwork, I cried. You made my dream come to life.

To The Krew, I adore you. You read my many and very messy drafts, demanded sequels, and were always in my corner. Thank you for being the best sounding board I could ever ask for! You've changed my life for the better and I love you all so much.

And because she *will* come for me if I don't mention her, Sarah McEvoy, my oldest, wisest, most wonderful friend. You are the cool big sister, the secret-keeper, the ear-piercer (in your bathroom at sixteen, no less), and the forever lifeline. Thanks for always being there for me in every stage of my life.

To the Nard Krew, thanks for all the adventures I look forward to every year. Thanks for always being there to discuss pop culture crises and obsess over celebrities. Girl squad for life.

To my high school friends and fellow SUA survivors, please know I miss you lots and think of you often.

To Chris, thank you for proving that love can be just like the movies. Every day with you is cinematic. I love you.

Thank you to my incredible, chaotic and beautiful family who always allowed me to be myself, no matter what. You gave me the best childhood a girl could ask for and shaped my entire life for the better.

To my extraordinary Mom who always encouraged us to use our imagination. Thank you for letting me rewrite book endings I didn't like as a kid, for editing chapters in fourth grade and for always cheering me on in everything I do.

To my amazing Dad, thank you for teaching me how to chase big dreams and build the roadmap to get there. You always taught me to live life like every day is an adventure.

And finally, to the best big brother and sister a girl could ask for.

Shannon, you are the steady hand I always need when I'm overwhelmed. Thank you for talking me off the ledge any time I panicked over other people reading my words and judging me for them. Thank you for always reading *everything* I've ever written and for providing thoughtful and considerate feedback. Without you, this would be a one book series that ended with a break-up. Thanks for allowing me to see the other side and for being one of the kindest and greatest people I know.

Matt, this book would never be published without you. When I told you I wrote a book in 2021, you not only supported me, but helped me make a plan to publish. Weekly calls, monthly check ins, you made the idea of publishing my book actually seem feasible. You championed the story even when it was all over the place and helped me craft it into the final form readers can pick up today. I would still be talking about maybe publishing one day if it wasn't for you.

And finally, to Cassie, Jackson, Marina, and Lucy, the most wonderful imaginary friends, thank you for letting me live out loud on the page. You gave me the freedom to be vulnerable, bold, and honest. I hope my readers enjoyed hanging out with you as much as I did.

Thank you! Love you muchly.

ABOUT THE AUTHOR

Laura Devine lives in Chicago, Illinois and has been dreaming up stories since she was in middle school. She's beyond excited (and slightly in disbelief) that her first novel is officially out in the world. When she's not writing, you'll likely find her watching movies, curled up with a good book, or listening to Ed Sheeran. She drew on her love for romantic comedies to help her write this book and can often be found quoting her favorite movies out loud. She loves her family, her friends, her dog and her boyfriend very much and hopes that they all know so.

All I Ever Wanted is her debut novel.

www.ingramcontent.com/pod-product-compliance
Lightning Source LLC
Chambersburg PA
CBHW031437240626
47154CB00001B/299

* 9 7 9 8 9 9 3 0 4 9 6 1 8 *